PENGUIN MODERN

OUT OF A[
AND
SHADOWS ON THE GRASS

D0174054

Isak Dinesen was the pen-name of Karen Blixen, who was born in Rungsted, Denmark, in 1885. After studying art at Copenhagen, Paris and Rome, she married her cousin, Baron Bror Blixen-Finecke, in 1914. Together they went to Kenya to manage a coffee plantation. After their divorce in 1921, she continued to run the plantation until a collapse in the coffee market forced her back to Denmark in 1931.

Although she had written occasional contributions to Danish periodicals since 1905 (under the *nom de plume* of Osceola), her real debut took place in 1934 with the publication of *Seven Gothic Tales*, written in English under her pen-name. *Out of Africa* (1937) is an autobiographical account of the years she spent in Kenya, while *Shadows on the Grass* (1960) is a collection of writings which take up the Kenyan theme. Many of her other books, including *The Angelic Avengers* (1947), were published in English and Danish simultaneously under the name Pierre Andrezel. Her other collections of stories include *Last Tales* (1957), *Anecdotes of Destiny* (1958) and *Ehrengard* (1963).

Baroness Blixen died in Rungsted in 1962.

OUT
OF AFRICA
AND
SHADOWS
ON THE
GRASS

KAREN BLIXEN

PENGUIN BOOKS

Penguin Books Ltd, 27 Wrights Lane, London W8 5TZ (Publishing and Editorial)
and Harmondsworth, Middlesex, England (Distribution and Warehouse)
Viking Penguin Inc., 40 West 23rd Street, New York, New York 10010, U.S.A.
Penguin Books Australia Ltd, Ringwood, Victoria, Australia
Penguin Books Canada Ltd, 2801 John Street, Markham, Ontario, Canada L3R 1B4
Penguin Books (N.Z.) Ltd, 182–190 Wairau Road, Auckland 10, New Zealand

Out of Africa first published 1937
Published in Penguin Books 1954
Reprinted 1979, 1980, 1981, 1982, 1983, 1984, 1985, 1986 (seventeen times), 1987 (twice)

Copyright 1937 by Karen Blixen
All rights reserved

Shadows on the Grass first published by Michael Joseph 1960
Published in Penguin Books 1984
Copyright © Isak Dinesen, 1960
All rights reserved

This collection published in one edition 1985

Made and printed in Great Britain by
Richard Clay Ltd, Bungay, Suffolk
Filmset in 9/11 Monophoto Times

OUT
OF AFRICA

'EQUITARE, ARCUM TENDERE,
VERITATEM DICERE'

CONTENTS

4. FROM AN IMMIGRANT'S NOTEBOOK

5. FAREWELL TO THE FARM

I
KAMANTE
AND
LULU

'From the forests and highlands
We come, we come.'

The Ngong Farm

I had a farm in Africa, at the foot of the Ngong Hills. The Equator runs across these highlands, a hundred miles to the north, and the farm lay at an altitude of over six thousand feet. In the day-time you felt that you had got high up, near to the sun, but the early mornings and evenings were limpid and restful, and the nights were cold.

The geographical position and the height of the land combined to create a landscape that had not its like in all the world. There was no fat on it and no luxuriance anywhere; it was Africa distilled up through six thousand feet, like the strong and refined essence of a continent. The colours were dry and burnt, like the colours in pottery. The trees had a light delicate foliage, the structure of which was different from that of the trees in Europe; it did not grow in bows or cupolas, but in horizontal layers, and the formation gave to the tall solitary trees a likeness to the palms, or a heroic and romantic air like full-rigged ships with their sails furled, and to the edge of a wood a strange appearance as if the whole wood were faintly vibrating. Upon the grass of the great plains the crooked bare old thorn-trees were scattered, and the grass was spiced like thyme and bog-myrtles; in some places the scent was so strong that it smarted in the nostrils. All the flowers that you found on the plains, or upon the creepers and liana in the native forest, were diminutive like flowers of the downs – only just in the beginning of the long rains a number of big, massive heavy-scented lilies sprang out on the plains. The views were immensely wide. Everything that you saw made for greatness and freedom, and unequalled nobility.

The chief feature of the landscape, and of your life in it, was the air. Looking back on a sojourn in the African highlands, you are struck by your feeling of having lived for a time up in the air. The sky was rarely more than pale blue or violet, with a profusion of mighty, weightless, ever-changing clouds towering up and sailing on it, but it has a blue vigour in it, and at a short distance it painted the ranges of hills and the woods a fresh deep blue. In the middle of the day the air was alive over the land, like a flame burning; it scintillated, waved and shone like running water, mirrored and doubled all objects, and created great Fata Morgana. Up in this high air you breathed easily, drawing in a vital assurance and lightness of heart. In the highlands you woke up in the morning and thought: Here I am, where I ought to be.

The Mountain of Ngong stretches in a long ridge from north to south, and is crowned with four noble peaks like immovable darker blue waves against the sky. It rises eight thousand feet above the sea, and to the east two thousand feet above the surrounding country; but to the west the drop is deeper and more precipitous – the hills fall vertically down towards the Great Rift Valley.

The wind in the highlands blows steadily from the north-north-east. It is the same wind that, down at the coasts of Africa and Arabia, they name the Monsoon, the East Wind, which was King Solomon's favourite horse. Up here it is felt as just the resistance of the air, as the earth throws herself forward into space. The wind runs straight against the Ngong Hills, and the slopes of the hills would be the ideal place for setting up a glider, that would be lifted upwards by the currents, over the mountain top. The clouds, which were travelling with the wind, struck the side of the hill and hung round it, or were caught on the summit and broke into rain. But those that took a higher course and sailed clear of the reef, dissolved to the west of it, over the burning desert of the Rift Valley. Many times I have from my house followed these mighty processions advancing, and have wondered to see their proud floating masses, as soon as they had got over the hills, vanish in the blue air and be gone.

The hills from the farm changed their character many times in the course of the day, and sometimes looked quite close, and at other times very far away. In the evening, when it was getting dark, it would first look, as you gazed at them, as if in the sky a thin silver line was drawn all along the silhouette of the dark mountain; then, as night fell, the four peaks seemed to be flattened and smoothened out, as if the mountain was stretching and spreading itself.

From the Ngong Hills you have a unique view, you see to the south the vast plains of the great game-country that stretches all the way to Kilimanjaro; to the east and north the park-like country of the foot-hills with the forest behind them, and the undulating land of the Kikuyu Reserve, which extends to Mount Kenya a hundred miles away – a mosaic of little square maize-fields, banana-groves and grassland, with here and there the blue smoke from a native village, a small cluster of peaked mole-casts. But towards the west, deep down, lies the dry, moon-like landscape of the African low country. The brown desert is irregularly dotted with the little marks of the thornbushes, the winding river-beds are drawn up with crooked dark-green trails; those are the woods of the mighty, wide-branching mimosa trees, with thorns like spikes; the cactus grows here, and here is the home of the giraffe and the rhino.

The hill-country itself, when you get into it, is tremendously big, picturesque and mysterious; varied with long valleys, thickets, green slopes, and rocky crags. High up, under one of the peaks, there is even a bamboo-grove. There are springs and wells in the hills; I have camped up here by them.

In my day, the buffalo, the eland and the rhino lived in the Ngong Hills; the very old Natives remembered a time when there were elephants there, and I was sorry that the whole Ngong Mountain was not enclosed in the Game Reserve. Only a small part of it was Game Reserve, and the beacon on the southern peak marked the boundary of it. When the colony prospers and Nairobi, the capital, grows into a big city, the Ngong Hills might have made a matchless game park for it. But during my last years in Africa many young Nairobi shop-people ran out into the hills on Sundays, on their motor-cycles, and shot at anything they saw, and I believe that the big game will have wandered away from the hills, through the thorn-thickets and the stony ground farther south.

Up on the very ridge of the hills and on the four peaks themselves it was easy to walk; the grass was short as on a lawn, with the grey stone in places breaking through the sward. Along the ridge, up and down the peaks, like a gentle switchback, there ran a narrow game-path. One morning, at the time that I was camped in the hills, I came up here and walked along the path, and I found on it fresh tracks and dung of a herd of eland. The big peaceful animals must have been up on the ridge at sunrise, walking in a long row, and you cannot imagine that they had come for any other reason than just to look, deep down on both sides, at the land below.

We grew coffee on my farm. The land was in itself a little too high for coffee, and it was hard work to keep it going; we were never rich on the farm. But a coffee-plantation is a thing that gets hold of you and does not let you go, and there is always something to do on it: you are generally just a little behind with your work.

In the wildness and irregularity of the country, a piece of land laid out and planted according to rule looked very well. Later on, when I flew in Africa, and became familiar with the appearance of my farm from the air, I was filled with admiration for my coffee-plantation, that lay quite bright green in the grey-green land, and I realized how keenly the human mind

yearns for geometrical figures. All the country round Nairobi, particularly to the north of the town, is laid out in a similar way, and here live
a people who are constantly thinking and talking of planting, pruning,
or picking coffee, and who lie at night and meditate upon improvements
to their coffee-factories.

  Coffee-growing is a long job. It does not all come out as you imagine,
when, yourself young and hopeful, in the streaming rain, you carry the
boxes of your shining young coffee-plants from the nurseries, and, with
the whole number of farm-hands in the field, watch the plants set in the
regular rows of holes in the wet ground where they are to grow, and then
have them thickly shaded against the sun, with branches broken from the
bush, since obscurity is the privilege of young things. It is four or five years
till the trees come into bearing, and in the meantime you will get drought
on the land, or diseases, and the bold native weeds will grow up thick in
the fields – the black-jack, which has long scabrous seed-vessels that hang
on to your clothes and stockings. Some of the trees have been badly
planted with their tap-roots bent; they will die just as they begin to flower.
You plant a little over six hundred trees to the acre, and I had six hundred
acres of land with coffee; my oxen dragged the cultivators up and down
the fields, between the rows of trees, many thousand miles, patiently,
awaiting coming bounties.

  There are times of great beauty on a coffee-farm. When the plantation
flowered in the beginning of the rains, it was a radiant sight, like a cloud
of chalk, in the mist and the drizzling rain, over six hundred acres of land.
The coffee-blossom has a delicate slightly bitter scent, like the blackthorn
blossom. When the field reddened with the ripe berries, all the women and
the children, whom they call the Totos, were called out to pick the coffee
off the trees, together with the men; then the wagons and carts brought
it down to the factory near the river. Our machinery was never quite what
it should have been, but we had planned and built the factory ourselves
and thought highly of it. Once the whole factory burned down and had
to be built up again. The big coffee-dryer turned and turned, rumbling
the coffee in its iron belly with a sound like pebbles that are washed about
on the sea-shore. Sometimes the coffee would be dry, and ready to take
out of the dryer, in the middle of the night. That was a picturesque
moment, with many hurricane lamps in the huge dark room of the factory,
that was hung everywhere with cobwebs and coffee-husks, and with eager
glowing dark faces, in the light of the lamps, round the dryer; the factory,
you felt, hung in the great African night like a bright jewel in an Ethiop's
ear. Later on the coffee was hulled, graded, and sorted by hand, and
packed in sacks sewn up with a saddler's needle.

Then, in the end, in the early morning, while it was still dark and I was lying in bed, I heard the wagons, loaded high up with coffee-sacks, twelve to a ton, with sixteen oxen to each wagon, starting on their way into Nairobi railway station up the long factory hill, with much shouting and rattling, the drivers running beside the wagons. I was pleased to think that this was the only hill up, on their way, for the farm was a thousand feet higher than the town of Nairobi. In the evening I walked out to meet the procession that came back, the tired oxen hanging their heads in front of the empty wagons, with a tired little Toto leading them, and the weary drivers trailing their whips in the dust of the road. Now we had done what we could do. The coffee would be on the sea in a day or two, and we could only hope for good luck at the big auction-sales in London.

I had six thousand acres of land, and had thus got much spare land besides the coffee-plantation. Part of the farm was native forest, and about one thousand acres were squatters' land, what they called their *shambas*. The squatters are Natives, who with their families hold a few acres on a white man's farm, and in return have to work for him a certain number of days in the year. My squatters, I think, saw the relationship in a different light, for many of them were born on the farm, and their fathers before them, and they very likely regarded me as a sort of superior squatter on their estates. The squatters' land was more intensely alive than the rest of the farm, and was changing with the seasons the year round. The maize grew up higher than your head as you walked on the narrow hard-trampled footpaths in between the tall green rustling regiments, and then again it was harvested. The beans ripened in the fields, were gathered and thrashed by the women, and the stalks and pods were collected and burned, so that in certain seasons thin columns of smoke rose here and there all over the farm. The Kikuyu also grew the sweet potatoes, that have a vine-like leaf and spread over the ground like a dense entangled mat, and many varieties of big yellow and green speckled pumpkins.

Whenever you walk amidst the Kikuyu shambas, the first thing that will catch your eye is the hind part of a little old woman raking in her soil, like a picture of an ostrich which buries her head in the sand. Each Kikuyu family had a number of small round peaked huts and store-huts; the space between the huts was a lively place, the earth hard as concrete; here the maize was ground and the goats milked, and children and chickens were running. I used to shoot spurfowl in the sweet-potato fields round the squatters' houses in the blue late afternoons, and the stock-pigeons cooed out a loud song in the high-stemmed, fringy trees, which were left over, here and there in the shambas, from the forest that had once covered all the farm.

I had moreover a couple of thousand acres of grassland on the farm. Here the long grass ran and fled like sea-waves before the strong wind, and the little Kikuyu herdboys herded their fathers' cows. In the cold season they carried live coals in small wicker baskets with them from the huts, and sometimes caused big grass-fires, which were disastrous to the grazing on the farm. In the years of drought the zebra and the eland came down to the farm's grass-plains.

Nairobi was our town, twelve miles away, down on a flat bit of land amongst hills. Here was the Government House and the big central offices; from here the country was ruled.

It is impossible that a town will not play a part in your life; it does not even make much difference whether you have more good or bad things to say of it, it draws your mind to it, by a mental law of gravitation. The luminous haze on the sky above the town at night, which I could see from some places on my farm, set my thoughts going, and recalled the big cities of Europe.

When I first came to Africa, there were no cars in the country, and we rode in to Nairobi, or drove in a cart with six mules to it, and stabled our animals in the stables of *The Highland Transport*. During all my time, Nairobi was a medley place, with some fine new stone buildings, and whole quarters of old corrugated iron shops, offices, and bungalows, laid out with long rows of eucalyptus trees along the bare dusty streets. The offices of the High Court, The Native Affairs Department, and the Veterinary Department were lousily housed, and I had a great respect for those government officials who could get any work at all done in the little burning hot, inky rooms in which they were set.

All the same Nairobi was a town; here you could buy things, hear news, lunch or dine at the hotels and dance at the Club. And it was a live place, in movement like running water, and in growth like a young thing, it changed from year to year, and while you were away on a shooting safari. The new Government House was built, a stately cool house with a fine ballroom and a pretty garden, big hotels grew up, great impressive agricultural shows and fine flower shows were held, our Quasi Smart Set of the Colony from time to time enlivened the town with rows of quick melodrama. Nairobi said to you: 'Make the most of me and of time. *Wir kommen nie wieder so jung* – so undisciplined and rapacious – *zusammen*.' Generally I and Nairobi were in very good understanding, and at one time I drove through the town and thought: There is no world without Nairobi's streets.

The quarters of the Natives and of the coloured immigrants were very extensive compared to the European town.

The Swaheli town, on the road to the Muthaiga Club, had not a good name in any way, but was a lively, dirty and gaudy place, with, at any hour, a number of things going on in it. It was built mostly out of old paraffin tins hammered flat, in various states of rust, like the coral rock, the fossilized structure, from which the spirit of the advancing civilization was steadily fleeing.

The Somali town was farther away from Nairobi, on account, I think, of the Somalis' system of seclusion of their women. There were in my day a few beautiful young Somali women, of whom all the town knew the names, who went and lived in the Bazaar and led the Nairobi police a great dance; they were intelligent and bewitching people. But the honest Somali women were not seen in the town. The Somali town lay exposed to all winds and was shadeless and dusty, it must have recalled to the Somali their native deserts. Europeans, who live for a long time, even for several generations, in the same place, cannot reconcile themselves to the complete indifference to the surroundings of their homes, of the nomadic races. The Somalis' houses were irregularly strewn on the bare ground, and looked as if they had been nailed together with a bushel of four-inch nails, to last for a week. It was a surprising thing, when you entered one of them, to find it inside so neat and fresh, scented with Arab incenses, with fine carpets and hangings, vessels of brass and silver, and swords with ivory hilts and noble blades. The Somali women themselves had dignified, gentle ways, and were hospitable and gay, with a laughter like silver bells. I was much at home in the Somali village through my Somali servant Farah Aden, who was with me all the time that I was in Africa, and I went to many of their feasts. A big Somali wedding is a magnificent, traditional festivity. As a guest of honour I was taken into the bridal chamber, where the walls and the bridal bed were hung with old, gently glowing weavings and embroideries, and the dark-eyed young bride herself was stiff, like a marshal's baton, with heavy silks, gold, and amber.

The Somali were cattle-dealers and traders all over the country. For the transport of their goods they kept a number of little grey donkeys in the village, and I have seen camels there as well: haughty, hardened products of the desert, beyond all earthly sufferings, like cactus, and like the Somali.

The Somali bring much trouble upon themselves by their terrible tribal quarrels. In this matter they feel and reason differently from other people. Farah belonged to the tribe of Habr Yunis, so that personally in a quarrel I sided with them. At one time there was a great real fight in the Somali town, between the two tribes of Dulba Hantis and Habr Chaolo, with rifle-shooting and fires, and ten or twelve people killed, until the Government interfered. Farah then had a young friend of his own tribe, by name of Sayid, who used to come out to see him at the farm, and who was a graceful boy, so that I was sorry when I was told by my houseboys that Sayid had gone round to visit a Habr Chaolo family in their house, when an angry member of the Dulba Hantis tribe had passed and fired two shots at haphazard through the wall of the house and broken Sayid's leg. I condoled with Farah on his friend's misfortune – 'What? Sayid?' Farah cried out with vehemence. 'That was good enough for Sayid. Why must he go and drink tea in the house of a Habr Chaolo?'

The Indians of Nairobi dominated the big native business quarter of the Bazaar, and the great Indian merchants had their little Villas just outside the town: Jevanjee, Suleiman Virjee, Allidina Visram. They all had a taste for stonework stairs, balusters, and vases, rather badly cut out of the soft stone of the country – like the structures which children build of pink ornamental bricks. They gave tea-parties in their gardens, with Indian pastry in the style of the Villas, and were clever, travelled, highly polite people. But the Indians in Africa are such grasping tradesmen that with them you would never know if you were face to face with a human individual or with the head of a firm. I had been to Suleiman Virjee's house, and when one day I saw the flag at half mast above his big compound of warehouse, I asked Farah: 'Is Suleiman Virjee dead?' 'Half dead,' said Farah. 'Do they put the flag at half mast when he is half dead?' I asked. 'Suleiman is dead,' said Farah. 'Virjee is alive.'

Before I took over the management of the farm, I had been keen on shooting and had been out on many safaris. But when I became a farmer I put away my rifles.

The Masai, the nomadic, cattle-owning nation, were neighbours of the farm and lived on the other side of the river; from time to time some of them would come to my house to complain about a lion that was taking their cows, and to ask me to go out and shoot it for them, and I did so if I could. Sometimes, on Saturday, I also walked out on the Orungi plains to shoot a zebra or two as meat for my farm labourers, with a long tail of optimistic young Kikuyu after me. I shot birds on the farm, spurfowl and guineafowl, that are very good to eat. But for many years I was not out on any shooting expedition.

Still, we often talked on the farm of the safaris that we had been on. Camping places fix themselves in your mind as if you had spent long periods of your life in them. You will remember a curve of your wagon track in the grass of the plain, like the features of a friend.

Out on the safaris, I had seen a herd of buffalo, one hundred and twenty-nine of them, come out of the morning mist under a copper sky, one by one, as if the dark and massive, iron-like animals with the mighty horizontally swung horns were not approaching, but were being created before my eyes and sent out as they were finished. I had seen a herd of elephant travelling through the dense native forest, where the sunlight is strewn down between the thick creepers in small spots and patches, pacing along as if they had an appointment at the end of the world. It was, in giant size, the border of a very old, infinitely precious Persian carpet, in the dyes of green, yellow, and black-brown. I had time after time watched the progression across the plain of the giraffe, in their queer, inimitable, vegetative gracefulness, as if it were not a herd of animals but a family of rare, long-stemmed, speckled gigantic flowers slowly advancing. I had followed two rhinos on their morning promenade, when they were sniffing and snorting in the air of the dawn – which is so cold that it hurts in the nose – and looked like two very big angular stones rollicking in the long valley and enjoying life together. I had seen the royal lion, before sunrise, below a waning moon, crossing the grey plain on his way home from the kill, drawing a dark wake in the silvery grass, his face still red up to the ears, or during the midday siesta, when he reposed contentedly in the midst of his family on the short grass and in the delicate, spring-like shade of the broad acacia trees of his park of Africa.

All these things were pleasant to think of when times were dull on the farm. And the big game was out there still, in their own country; I could go and look them up once more if I liked. Their nearness gave a shine and play to the atmosphere of the farm. Farah – although with time he came to take a vivid interest in farm affairs – and my old native safari-servants, lived in hope of other safaris.

Out in the wilds I had learned to beware of abrupt movements. The creatures with which you are dealing there are shy and watchful, they have a talent for evading you when you least expect it. No domestic animal can be as still as a wild animal. The civilized people have lost the aptitude of stillness, and must take lessons in silence from the wild before they are accepted by it. The art of moving gently, without suddenness, is the first to be studied by the hunter, and more so by the hunter with the camera. Hunters cannot have their own way, they must fall in with the wind, and the colours and smells of the landscape, and they must make the tempo of the ensemble their own. Sometimes it repeats a movement over and over again, and they must follow up with it.

When you have caught the rhythm of Africa, you find that it is the same in all her music. What I learned from the game of the country was useful to me in my dealings with the native people.

The love of woman and womanliness is a masculine characteristic, and the love of man and manliness a feminine characteristic, and there is a susceptibility to the southern countries and races that is a Nordic quality. The Normans must have fallen in love with the foreign countries, first with France and then with England. Those old milords who figure in the history and fiction of the eighteenth century, as constantly travelling in Italy, Greece, and Spain, had not a single southern trait in their nature, but were drawn and held by the fascination of things wholly different from themselves. The old German and Scandinavian painters, philosophers, and poets, when they first came to Florence and Rome, went down on their knees to adore the South.

A queer illogical patience towards an alien world came out in these impatient people. As it is almost impossible for a woman to irritate a real man, and as to the women, a man is never quite contemptible, never altogether rejectable, as long as he remains a man, so were the hasty red-haired northern people infinitely long-suffering with the tropical countries and races. They would stand no nonsense from their own country or their own relations, but they took the drought of the African highlands, and a case of sun-stroke, the rinderpest on their cattle, and the incompetency of their native servants, with humility and resignation. Their sense of individuality itself was lost in the sense of the possibilities that lie in interaction between those who can be made one by reason of their incongruity. The people of southern Europe and the people of mixed blood have not got this quality; they blame it, or scorn it. So the men's men scorn the sighing lover, and the rational women who have no patience with their men are in the same way indignant with Griselda.

As for me, from my first weeks in Africa, I had felt a great affection for the Natives. It was a strong feeling that embraced all ages and both sexes. The discovery of the dark races was to me a magnificent enlargement of all my world. If a person with an inborn sympathy for animals had grown up in a milieu where there were no animals, and had come into contact with animals late in life; or if a person with an instinctive taste for woods and forest had entered a forest for the first time at the age of twenty; or if someone with an ear for music had happened to hear music for the first time when he was already grown up; their cases might have been similar to mine. After I had met with the Natives, I set out the routine of my daily life to the orchestra.

My father was an officer in the Danish and French army, and as a very young lieutenant at Düppel he wrote home: 'Back in Düppel I was officer to a long column. It was hard work, but it was splendid. The love of war is a passion like another, you love soldiers as you love young womenfolk – to madness, and the one love does not exclude the other, as the girls know. But the love of women can include only one at a time, and the love for your soldiers comprehends the whole regiment, which you would like enlarged if it were possible.' It was the same thing with the Natives and me.

It was not easy to get to know the Natives. They were quick of hearing, and evanescent; if you frightened them they could withdraw into a world of their own, in a second, like the wild animals which at an abrupt movement from you are gone – simply are not there. Until you knew a Native well, it was almost impossible to get a straight answer from him. To a direct question as to how many cows he had, he had an eluding reply – 'As many as I told you yesterday.' It goes against the feelings of Europeans to be answered in such a manner, it very likely goes against the feelings of the Natives to be questioned in this way. If we pressed or pursued them, to get an explanation of their behaviour out of them, they receded as long as they possibly could, and then they used a grotesque humorous fantasy to lead us on the wrong track. Even small children in this situation had all the quality of old poker-players, who do not mind if you overvalue or undervalue their hand, so long as you do not know its real nature. When we really did break into the Natives' existence, they behaved like ants, when you poke a stick into their ant-hill; they wiped out the damage with unwearied energy, swiftly and silently – as if obliterating an unseemly action.

We could not know, and could not imagine, what the dangers were that they feared from our hands. I myself think that they were afraid of us more in the manner in which you are afraid of a sudden terrific noise, than as you are afraid of suffering and death. And yet it was difficult to tell, for the Natives were great at the art of mimicry. In the shambas you would sometimes in the early morning come upon a spurfowl which would run in front of your horse as if her wing was broken, and she was terrified of being caught by the dogs. But her wing was not broken, and she was not afraid of the dogs – she could whir up before them the moment she chose – only she had got her brood of young chickens somewhere near by, and she was drawing our attention away from them. Like the spurfowl, the Natives might be mimicking a fear of us because of some other deeper dread the nature of which we could not guess. Or in the end their behaviour to us might be some sort of strange joke, and the shy people were not afraid of us at all. The Natives have, far less than the white people, the sense of risks in life. Sometimes on a safari, or on the farm, in a moment of extreme tension, I have met the eyes of my Native companions, and have felt that we were at a great distance from one another, and that they were wondering at my apprehension of our risk. It made me reflect that perhaps they were, in life itself, within their own element, such as we can never be, like fishes in deep water which for the life of them cannot understand our fear of drowning. This assurance, this art of swimming, they had, I thought, because they had preserved a knowledge that was lost to us by our first parents; Africa, amongst the continents, will teach it to you: that God and the Devil are one, the majesty coeternal, not two uncreated but one uncreated, and the Natives neither confounded the persons nor divided the substance.

On our safaris, and on the farm, my acquaintance with the Natives developed into a settled and personal relationship. We were good friends. I reconciled myself to the fact that while I should never quite know or understand them, they knew me through and through, and were conscious of the decisions that I was going to take, before I was certain about them myself. For some time I had a small farm up at Gil-Gil, where I lived in a tent, and I travelled by the railway to and fro between Gil-Gil and Ngong. At Gil-Gil, I might make up my mind very suddenly, when it began to rain, to go back to my house. But when I came to Kikuyu, which was our station on the railway line, and from where it was ten miles to the farm, one of my people would be there with a mule for me to ride home on. When I asked them how they had known that I was coming down, they looked away, and seemed uneasy, as if frightened or bored, such as we should be if a deaf person insisted on getting an explanation of a symphony from us.

When the Natives felt safe with us from abrupt movements and sudden noises, they would speak to us a great deal more openly than one European speaks to another. They were never reliable, but in a grand manner sincere. A good name – what is called prestige – meant much in the Native world. They seemed to have made up, at some time, a joint appraisement of you, against which no one would afterwards ever go.

At times, life on the farm was very lonely, and in the stillness of the evenings when the minutes dripped from the clock, life seemed to be dripping out of you with them, just for want of white people to talk to. But all the time I felt the silent overshadowed existence of the Natives running parallel with my own, on a different plane. Echoes went from the one to the other.

The Natives were Africa in flesh and blood. The tall extinct volcano of Longonot that rises above the Rift Valley, the broad mimosa trees along the rivers, the elephant and the giraffe, were not more truly Africa than the Natives were – small figures in an immense scenery. All were different expressions of one idea, variations upon the same theme. It was not a congenial upheaping of heterogeneous atoms, but a heterogeneous up-heaping of congenial atoms, as in the case of the oak leaf and the acorn and the object made from oak. We ourselves, in boots, and in our constant great hurry, often jar with the landscape. The Natives are in accordance with it, and when the tall, slim, dark, and dark-eyed people travel – always one by one, so that even the great Native veins of traffic are narrow footpaths – or work the soil, or herd their cattle, or hold their big dances, or tell you a tale, it is Africa wandering, dancing, and entertaining you. In the highlands you remember the poet's words:

> Noble found I
> ever the Native,
> and insipid the Immigrant.

The colony is changing and has already changed since I lived there. When I write down as accurately as possible my experiences on the farm, with the country and with some of the inhabitants of the plains and woods, it may have a sort of historical interest.

A Native Child

Kamante was a small Kikuyu boy, the son of one of my squatters. I used to know my squatter children well, for they both worked for me on the farm, and used to be up round my house herding their goats on the lawns, in the faith that here something of interest might occur. But Kamante must have lived on the farm for some years before I ever met him; I suppose that he had been leading a seclusive existence like a sick animal.

I came upon him for the first time one day when I was riding across the plain of the farm, and he was herding his people's goats there. He was the most pitiful object that you could set eyes on. His head was big and his body terribly small and thin, the elbows and knees stood out like knots on a stick and both his legs were covered with deep running sores from the thigh to the heel. Here on the plain he looked extraordinarily small, so that it struck you as a strange thing that so much suffering could be condensed into a single point. When I stopped and spoke to him, he did not answer, and hardly appeared to see me. In his flat, angular, harassed, and infinitely patient face, the eyes were without glance, dim like the eyes of a dead person. He looked as if he could not have more than a few weeks to live in, and you expected to see the vultures, which are never far away from death on the plain, high up in the pale burning air over his head. I told him to come round to my house the next morning, so that I could try to cure him.

I was a doctor to the people on the farm most mornings from nine to ten, and like all great quacks I had a large circle of patients, and generally between two and a dozen sick people up by my house then.

The Kikuyu are adjusted for the unforeseen and accustomed to the unexpected. Here they differ from the white men, of whom the majority strive to insure themselves against the unknown and the assaults of fate. The Negro is on friendly terms with destiny, having been in her hands all his time; she is to him, in a way, his home, the familiar darkness of the hut, deep mould for his roots. He faces any change in life with great calm. Amongst the qualities that he will be looking for in a master or a doctor or in God, imagination, I believe, comes high up in the list. It may be on the strength of such a taste that the Caliph Haroun al Raschid maintains, to the hearts of Africa and Arabia, his position as an ideal ruler; with him nobody knew what to expect next, and you did not know where you had him. When the Africans speak of the personality of God they speak like the Arabian Nights or like the last chapters of the book of Job; it is the same quality, the infinite power of imagination, with which they are impressed.

To this characteristic in my people I myself owed my popularity, or my fame, as a doctor. When I first came out to Africa I travelled on the boat with a great German scientist, who was going out, for the twenty-third time, to experiment with cures for sleeping-sickness, and who had over a hundred rats and guinea-pigs on the boat with him. He told me that his difficulty with the Native patients had never been any lack of courage in them – in the face of pain or of a great operation they generally showed little fear – but it was their deep dislike of regularity, of any repeated treatment or the systematization of the whole; and this the great German doctor could not understand. But when I myself got to know the Natives, this quality in them was one of the things that I liked best. They had real courage: the unadulterated liking of danger – the true answer of creation to the announcement of their lot – the echo from the earth when heaven had spoken. I sometimes thought that what, at the bottom of their hearts, they feared from us was pedantry. In the hands of a pedant they die of grief.

My patients waited on a paved terrace outside my house. Here they squatted – the old skeletons of men with tearing coughs and running eyes, the young slim smooth brawlers with black eyes and bruised mouths, and the mothers with their feverish children, like little dry flowers, hanging upon their necks. I often had bad burns to treat, for the Kikuyu at night sleep round the fires in their huts, and the piles of burning wood or charcoal may collapse and slide down on them – when at times I had run out of my store of medicine, I found that honey was not a bad ointment for burns. The atmosphere of the terrace was animated, electric, like the atmosphere of the casinos in Europe. The low lively flow of talk would stop when I came out, but the silence was pregnant with possibilities, now the moment had come when anything might happen. They did, however, always wait for me myself to choose my first patient.

I knew very little of doctoring, just what you learn at a first-aid course. But my renown as a doctor had been spread by a few chance lucky cures, and had not been decreased by the catastrophic mistakes that I had made.

If now I had been able to guarantee my patients a recovery in each single case, who knows but that their circle might have thinned out? I should then have attained a professional prestige – here evidently was a highly efficient doctor from *Volaia* – but would they still have been sure that the Lord was with me? For of the Lord they knew from the great years of drought, from the lions on the plains at night, and the leopards near the houses when the children were alone there, and from the swarms of grasshoppers that would come on to the land, nobody knew where from, and leave not a leaf of grass where they had passed. They knew him, too, from the unbelievable hours of happiness when the swarm passed over the maizefield and did not settle, or when in spring the rains would come early and plentiful, and make all the fields and plains flower and give rich crops. So that this highly capable doctor from Volaia might be after all a sort of outsider where the real great things in life were concerned.

Kamante to my surprise turned up at my house the morning after our first meeting. He stood there, a little away from the three or four other sick people present, erect, with his half-dead face, as if after all he had some feeling of attachment to life, and had now made up his mind to try this last chance of holding on to it.

He showed himself with time to be an excellent patient. He came when he was ordered to come, without fault, and he could keep account of time when he was told to come back every third or fourth day, which is an unusual thing with the Natives. He bore the hard treatment of his sores with a stoicism that I have not known the like of. In all these respects I might have held him up as a model to the others, but I did not do so, for at the same time he caused me much uneasiness of mind.

Rarely, rarely, have I met such a wild creature, a human being who was so utterly isolated from the world, and, by a sort of firm, deadly resignation, completely closed to all surrounding life. I could make him answer when I questioned him, but he never volunteered a word and never looked at me. He had no pity whatever in him, and kept a little scornful laughter of contempt, and of knowing better, for the tears of the other sick children, when they were washed and bandaged, but he never looked at them either. He had no wish for any sort of contact with the world round him, the contacts that he had known of had been too cruel for that. His fortitude of soul in the face of pain was the fortitude of an old warrior. A thing could never be so bad as to surprise him: he was, by his career and his philosophy, prepared for the worst.

All this was in the grand manner, and recalled the declaration of faith of Prometheus: 'Pain is my element as hate is thine. Ye rend me now: I care not.' And, 'Ay, do thy worst. Thou art omnipotent.' But in a person of his size it was uncomfortable, a thing to make you lose heart. And what will God think – I thought – confronted with this attitude in a small human being?

I remember well the first time that he ever looked at me and spoke to me of his own accord. This must have been some time along in our acquaintance, for I had given up my first mode of treatment, and was trying a new thing, a hot poultice that I had looked up in my books. In my eagerness to do the thing thoroughly, I made it too hot, and as I put it on his leg and clapped the dressing on top of it Kamante spoke: 'Msabu,' he said, and gave me a great glance. The Natives use this Indian word when they address white women, but they pronounce it a little differently, and change it into an African word, with a diverging ring to it. In Kamante's mouth now it was a cry for help, but also a word of warning, such as a loyal friend might give you, to stop you in a proceeding unworthy of you. I thought of it with hope afterwards. I had ambition as a doctor, and I was sorry to have put on the poultice too hot, but I was glad all the same, for this was the first glimpse of an understanding between the wild child and myself. The stark sufferer, who expected nothing but suffering, did not expect it from me.

As far as my doctoring of him went, things did not, however, look hopeful. For a long time I kept on washing and bandaging his leg, but the disease was beyond me. From time to time he would grow a little better, and then the sores would break out in new places. In the end I made up my mind to take him to the hospital of the Scotch Mission.

This decision of mine for once was sufficiently fatal, and had in it enough possibilities, to make an impression on Kamante – he did not want to go. He was prevented by his career and his philosophy from protesting much against anything, but when I drove him to the mission, and delivered him there in the long hospital building, in surroundings entirely foreign and mysterious to him, he trembled.

I had the Church of Scotland Mission as a neighbour twelve miles to the north-west, five hundred feet higher than the farm; and the French Roman Catholic Mission ten miles to the east, on the flatter land, and five hundred feet lower. I did not sympathize with the missions, but personally I was on friendly terms with them both, and regretted that between themselves they should live in a state of hostility.

The French Fathers were my best friends. I used to ride over with Farah, to hear Mass with them on Sunday morning, partly in order to speak French again, and partly because it was a lovely ride to the mission. For a long way the road ran through the Forest Department's old wattle plantation, and the virile, fresh pinaceous scent of the wattle trees was sweet and cheering in the mornings.

It was an extraordinary thing to see how the Church of Rome was carrying her atmosphere with her wherever she went. The Fathers had planned and built their church themselves, with the assistance of their Native congregation, and they were with reason very proud of it. There was here a fine big grey church with a bell-tower on it; it was laid out on a broad courtyard, above terraces and stairs, in the midst of their coffee-plantation, which was the oldest in the colony and very skilfully run. On the two other sides of the court were the arcaded refectory and the convent buildings, with the school and the mill down by the river, and to get into the drive up to the church you had to ride over an arched bridge. It was all built in grey stone, and as you came riding down upon it, it looked neat and impressive in the landscape, and might have been lying in a southern canton of Switzerland, or in the north of Italy.

The friendly fathers lay in wait for me at the church door, when Mass was over, to invite me to *un petit verre de vin*, across the courtyard in the roomy and cool refectory; there it was wonderful to hear how they knew of everything that was going on in the colony, even to the remotest corners of it. They would also, under the disguise of a sweet and benevolent conversation, draw from you any sort of news that you might possibly have in you, like a small lively group of brown, furry bees – for they all grew long, thick beards – hanging on to a flower for its store of honey. But while they were so interested in the life of the colony, they were all the time in their own French way exiles, patient and cheerful obeisants to some higher orders of a mysterious nature. If it had not been for the unknown authority that kept them in the place, you felt they would not be there, neither would the church of grey stone with the tall bell-tower, nor the arcades, the school, or any other part of their neat plantation and mission station. For when the word of relief had been given, all of these would leave the affairs of the colony to themselves and take a beeline back to Paris.

Farah, who had been holding the two ponies while I had been to church, and to the refectory, on the way back to the farm would notice my cheerful spirits – he was himself a pious Mohammedan and did not touch alcohol, but he took the Mass and the wine as co-ordinant rites of my religion.

The French Fathers sometimes rode on their motor-bicycles to the farm and lunched there; they quoted the fables of Lafontaine to me and gave me good advice on my coffee-plantation.

The Scotch Mission I did not know so well. There was a splendid view, from up there, over all the surrounding Kikuyu country, but all the same the mission station gave me an impression of blindness, as if it could see nothing itself. The Church of Scotland was working hard to put the Natives into European clothes, which, I thought, did them no good from any point of view. But they had a very good hospital at the mission, and at the time when I was there, it was in the charge of a philanthropic, clever head-doctor, Dr Arthur. They saved the life of many of the people from the farm.

At the Scotch Mission they kept Kamante for three months. During that time I saw him once. I came riding past the mission on my way to the Kikuyu railway station, and the road here for a while runs along the hospital grounds. I caught sight of Kamante in the grounds; he was standing by himself at a little distance from the groups of other convalescents. By this time he was already so much better that he could run. When he saw me he came up to the fence and ran with me as long as it was following the road. He trotted along, on his side of the fence, like a foal in a paddock when you pass it on horseback, and kept his eyes on my pony, but he did not say a word. At the corner of the hospital grounds he had to stop, and when, as I rode on, I looked back, I saw him standing stock still, with his head up in the air and staring after me, in the exact manner of a foal when you ride away from it. I waved my hand to him a couple of times; the first time he did not react at all, then suddenly his arm went straight up like a pump-spear, but he did not do it more than once.

*

Kamante came back to my house on the morning of Easter Sunday, and handed me a letter from the hospital people who declared that he was much better and that they thought him cured for good. He must have known something of its contents, for he watched my face attentively while I was reading it, but he did not want to discuss it, he had greater things in his mind. Kamante always carried himself with much collected or restrained dignity, but this time he shone with repressed triumph as well.

All Natives have a strong sense for dramatic effects. Kamante had carefully tied old bandages round his legs all the way up to the knee, to arrange a surprise for me. It was clear that he saw the vital importance of the moment, not in his own good luck, but, unselfishly, in the pleasure that he was to give me. He probably remembered the times when he had seen me all upset by the continual failure of my cures with him, and he knew that the result of the hospital's treatment was an astounding thing. As slowly, slowly, he unwound the bandages from his knee to his heel there appeared, underneath them, a pair of whole smooth legs, only slightly marked by grey scars.

When Kamante had thoroughly, and in his calm grand manner, enjoyed my astonishment and pleasure, he again renewed the impression by stating that he was now a Christian. 'I am like you,' he said. He added that he thought that I might give him a rupee because Christ had risen on this same day.

He went away to call on his own people. His mother was a widow, and lived a long way away on the farm. From what I heard from her later I believe that he did this day make a digression from his habit and unloaded his heart to her of the impressions of strange people and ways that he had received at the hospital. But after his visit to his mother's hut, he came back to my house as if he took it for granted that now he belonged there. He was then in my service from this time till the time that I left the country – for about twelve years.

Kamante when I first met him looked as if he were six years old, but he had a brother who looked about eight, and both brothers agreed that Kamante was the eldest of them, so I suppose he must have been set back in growth by his long illness; he was probably then nine years old. He grew up now, but he always made the impression of being a dwarf, or in some way deformed, although you could not put your finger on the precise spot that made him look so. His angular face was rounded with time, he walked and moved easily, and I myself did not think him bad-looking, but I may have looked upon him with something of a creator's eyes. His legs remained forever as thin as sticks. A fantastic figure he always was, half of fun and half of diabolism; with a very slight alteration, he might have sat and stared down, on the top of the cathedral of Notre Dame in Paris. He had in him something bright and live; in a painting he would have made a spot of unusually intense colouring; with this he gave a stroke of picturesqueness to my household. He was never quite right in the head, or at least he was always what, in a white person, you would have called highly eccentric.

He was a thoughtful person. Perhaps the long years of suffering that he had lived through had developed in him a tendency to reflect upon things, and to draw his own conclusions from everything he saw. He was all his life, in his own way, an isolated figure. Even when he did the same things as other people he would do them in a different way.

I had an evening school for the people of the farm, with a Native schoolmaster to teach them. I got my schoolmasters from one of the missions, and in my time I have had all three – Roman Catholic, Church of England, and Church of Scotland schoolmasters. For the Native education of the country is run rigorously on religious lines; so far as I know, there are no other books translated into Swaheli than the Bible and the hymn-books. I myself, during all my time in Africa, was planning to translate Aesop's fables, for the benefit of the Natives, but I never found time to carry my plan through. Still, such as it was, my school was to me a favourite place on the farm, the centre of our spiritual life, and I spent many pleasant evening hours in the long old store-house of corrugated iron in which it was kept.

Kamante would then come with me, but he would not join the children on the school-benches, he would stand a little away from them, as if consciously closing his ears to the learning, and exulting in the simplicity of those who consented to be taken in, and to listen. But in the privacy of my kitchen, I have seen him copying from memory, very slowly and preposterously, those same letters and figures that he had observed on the blackboard in the school. I do not think that he could have come in with other people if he had wanted to; early in his life something in him had been twisted or locked, and now it was, so to say, to him the normal thing to be out of the normal. He was aware of this separateness of his, himself, with the arrogant greatness of soul of the real dwarf, who, when he finds himself at a difference with the whole world, holds the world to be crooked.

Kamante was shrewd in money matters; he spent little, and did a number of wise deals with the other Kikuyu in goats. He married at an early age, and marriage in the Kikuyu world is an expensive undertaking. At the same time I have heard him philosophizing, soundly and originally, upon the worthlessness of money. He stood in a peculiar relation to existence on the whole; he mastered it, but he had no high opinion of it.

He had no gift whatever for admiration. He might acknowledge, and think well of the wisdom of animals, but there was, during all the time that I knew him, only one human being of whose good sense I heard him speak approvingly; it was a young Somali woman who some years later came to live on the farm. He had a little mocking laughter, of which he made use in all circumstances, but chiefly towards any self-confidence or grandiloquence in other people. All Natives have in them a strong strain of malice, a shrill delight in things going wrong, which in itself is hurting and revolting to Europeans. Kamante brought this characteristic to a rare perfection, even to a special self-irony, that made him take pleasure in his own disappointments and disasters, nearly exactly as in those of other people.

I have met with the same kind of mentality in the old Native women who have been roasted over many fires, who have mixed blood with Fate, and recognize her irony, wherever they meet it, with sympathy, as if it were that of a sister. On the farm I used to let my houseboys deal out snuff – *tombacco* the Natives say – to the old women on Sunday mornings, while I myself was still in bed. On this account I had a queer lot of customers round my house on Sundays, like a very old, rumpled, bald and bony poultry yard; and their low cackling – for the Natives will very rarely speak up loudly – made its way through the open windows of my bedroom. On one particular Sunday morning, the gentle lively flow of Kikuyu communications suddenly rose to ripples and cascades of mirth; some highly humorous incident was taking place out there, and I called in Farah to tell me about it. Farah did not like to tell me, for the matter was that he had forgotten to buy snuff, so that to-day the old women had come a long way, as they say themselves, *boori* – for nothing. This happening was later on a source of amusement to the old Kikuyu women. Sometimes, when I met one of them on a path in the maizefield, she would stand still in front of me, poke a crooked bony finger at me, and, with her old dark face dissolving into laughter, so that all the wrinkles of it were drawn and folded together as by one single secret string being pulled, she would remind me of the Sunday when she and her sisters in the snuff had walked and walked up to my house, only to find that I had forgotten to get it, and that there was not a grain there – Ha ha Msabu!

The white people often say of the Kikuyu that they know nothing of gratitude. Kamante in any case was not ungrateful, he even gave words to his feeling of an obligation. A number of times, many years after our first meeting, he went out of his way to do me a service for which I had not asked him, and when I asked him why he had done it, he said that if it had not been for me he would have been dead a long time ago. He showed his gratitude in another manner as well, in a particular kind of benevolent, helpful, or perhaps the right word is forebearing, attitude towards me. It may be that he kept in mind that he and I were of the same religion. In a world of fools, I was, I think, to him one of the greater fools. From the day when he came into my service and attached his fate to mine, I felt his watchful penetrating eyes on me, and my whole *modus vivendi* subject to a clear unbiased criticism; I believe that, from the beginning, he looked upon the trouble that I had taken to get him cured as upon a piece of hopeless eccentricity. But he showed me all the time great interest and sympathy, and he laid himself out to guide my great ignorance. On some occasions I found that he had given time and thought to the problem, and that he meant to prepare and illustrate his instructions, in order that they should be easier for me to understand.

Kamante began his life in my house as a dog-toto; later he became a medical assistant to me. There I found out what good hands he had, although you would not have thought so from the look of them, and I sent him into the kitchen to be a cook's boy, a marmiton, under my old cook Esa, who was murdered. After Esa's death he succeeded to him, and he was now my chef all the time that he was with me.

Natives have usually very little feeling for animals, but Kamante differed from type here, as in other things. He was an authoritative dog-boy, and he identified himself with the dogs, and would come and communicate to me what they wished, or missed, or generally thought of things. He kept the dogs free of fleas, which are a pest in Africa, and many times in the middle of the night, he and I, called by the howls of the dogs, have, by the light of a hurricane-lamp, picked off them, one by one, the murderous big ants, the *Siafu*, which march alone and eat up everything on their way.

He must also have used his eyes at the time when he had been in the mission hospital – even if it had been, as was ever the case with him, without the slightest reverence or prepossession – for he was a thoughtful, inventive doctor's assistant. After he had left this office, he would at times appear from the kitchen to interfere in a case of sickness, and give me very sound advice.

But as a chef he was a different thing, and precluded classification. Nature had here taken a leap and cut away from the order of precedence of faculties and talents; the thing now became mystic and inexplicable, as ever where you are dealing with genius. In the kitchen, in the culinary world, Kamante had all the attributes of genius, even to that doom of genius – the individual's powerlessness in the face of his own powers. If Kamante had been born in Europe, and had fallen into the hands of a clever teacher, he might have become famous, and would have cut a droll figure in history. And out here in Africa he made himself a name, his attitude to his art was that of a master.

I was much interested in cookery myself, and on my first visit back to Europe, I took lessons from a French chef at a celebrated restaurant, because I thought it would be an amusing thing to be able to make good food in Africa. The chef, Monsieur Perrochet, at that time made me an offer to come in with him in his business of the restaurant, for the sake of my devotion to the art. Now when I found Kamante at hand, as a familiar spirit to cook with, this devotion again took hold of me. There was to me a great perspective in our working together. Nothing, I thought, could be more mysterious than this natural instinct in a savage for our culinary art. It made me take another view of our civilization; after all it might be in some way divine and predestined. I felt like the man who regained his faith in God because a phrenologist showed him the seat in the human brain of theological eloquence: if the existence of theological eloquence could be proved, the existence of theology itself was proved with it, and, in the end, God's existence.

Kamante, in all cooking matters, had a surprising manual adroitness. The great tricks and *tours-de-force* of the kitchen were child's play to his dark crooked hands; they knew on their own everything about omelettes, vol-au-vents, sauces, and mayonnaises. He had a special gift for making things light, as in the legend the infant Christ forms birds out of clay and tells them to fly. He scorned all complicated tools, as if impatient of too much independence in them, and when I gave him a machine for beating eggs he set it aside to rust, and beat whites of egg with a weeding knife that I had had to weed the lawn with, and his whites of eggs towered up like light clouds. As a cook he had a penetrating, inspired eye, and would pick the fattest chicken out of a whole poultry-yard, and he gravely weighed an egg in his hand, and knew when it had been laid. He thought out schemes for improvement of my table, and by some means of communication, from a friend who was working for a doctor far away in the country, he got me seed of a really excellent sort of lettuce, such as I had myself for many years looked for in vain.

He had a great memory for recipes. He could not read and he knew no English, so that cookery books were of no use to him, but he must have held all that he was ever taught stored up in his ungraceful head, according to some systematization of his own, which I should never know. He had named the dishes after some event which had taken place on the day they had been shown to him, and he spoke of the sauce of the lightning that struck the tree, and of the sauce of the grey horse that died. But he did not confound any two of these things. There was only one point that I tried to impress upon him without any success: that was the order of the courses within a meal. It became necessary to me, when I had guests for dinner, to draw up for my chef as it were a pictorial menu: first a soup-plate, then a fish, then a partridge, or an artichoke. I did not quite believe this shortcoming in him to be due to a faulty memory, but he did, I think, in his own heart, maintain that there is a limit to everything and that upon anything so completely immaterial, he would not waste his time.

It is a moving thing to work together with a demon. Nominally the kitchen was mine, but in the course of our co-operation, I felt not only the kitchen, but the whole world in which we were co-operating, pass over into Kamante's hands. For here he understood to perfection what I wished of him, and sometimes he carried out my wishes even before I had told him of them; but as to me I could not make clear to myself how or indeed why he worked as he did. It seemed to me a strange thing that anyone could be so great in an art of which he did not understand the real meaning, and for which he felt nothing but contempt.

Kamante could have no idea as to how a dish of ours ought to taste, and he was, in spite of his conversion, and his connection with civilization, at heart an arrant Kikuyu, rooted in the traditions of his tribe and in his faith in them, as in the only way of living worthy of a human being. He did at times taste the food that he cooked, but then with a distrustful face, like a witch who takes a sip out of her cauldron. He stuck to the maize-cobs of his fathers. Here even his intelligence sometimes failed him, and he came and offered me a Kikuyu delicacy – a roasted sweet potato or a lump of sheep's fat – as even a civilized dog, that has lived for a long time with people, will place a bone on the floor before you, as a present. In his heart he did, I feel, all the time, look upon the trouble that we give ourselves about our food, as upon a lunacy. I sometimes tried to extract from him his views upon these things, but although he spoke with great frankness on many subjects, on others he was very close, so that we worked side by side in the kitchen, leaving one another's ideas on the importance of cooking alone.

I sent Kamante into the Muthaiga Club to learn, and to the cooks of my friends in Nairobi, when I had had a new good dish in their house, and by the time that he had served his apprenticeship, my own house became famous in the colony for its table. This was a great pleasure to me. I longed to have an audience for my art, and I was glad when my friends came out to dine with me; but Kamante cared for the praise of no one. All the same he remembered the individual taste of those of my friends who came most often to the farm. 'I shall cook the fish in white wine for Bwana Berkeley Cole,' he said, gravely, as if he were speaking of a demented person. 'He sends you out white wine himself to cook fish in.' To get the opinion of an authority, I asked my old friend, Mr Charles Bulpett of Nairobi, out to dine with me. Mr Bulpett was a great traveller of the former generation, themselves a generation away from Phineas Fogg; he had been all over the world and had tasted everywhere the best it had to offer, and he had not cared to secure his future so long as he could enjoy the present moment. The books about sport and mountaineering, of fifty years ago, tell of his exploits as an athlete, and of his mountain climbings in Switzerland and Mexico, and there is a book of famous bets called *Light Come Light Go*, in which you can read of how for a bet he swam the Thames in evening clothes and a high hat – but later on, and more romantically, he swam the Hellespont like Leander and Lord Byron. I was happy when he came out to the farm for a *tête-à-tête* dinner; there is a particular happiness in giving a man whom you like very much, good food that you have cooked yourself. In return he gave me his ideas on food, and on many other things in the world, and told me that he had nowhere dined better.

The Prince of Wales did me the great honour to come and dine at the farm, and to compliment me on a Cumberland sauce. This is the only time that I have seen Kamante listening with deep interest when I repeated the praise of his cooking to him, for Natives have very great ideas of kings and like to talk about them. Many months after, he felt a longing to hear it once more, and suddenly asked me, like a French reading-book, 'Did the son of the Sultan like the sauce of the pig? Did he eat it all?'

Kamante showed his good will towards me outside of the kitchen as well. He wanted to help me, in accordance with his own ideas of the advantages and dangers in life.

One night, after midnight, he suddenly walked into my bedroom with a hurricane-lamp in his hand, silent, as if on duty. It must have been only a short time after he first came into my house, for he was very small; he stood by my bedside like a dark bat that had strayed into the room, with very big spreading ears, or like a small African Will-o'-the-wisp, with his lamp in his hand. He spoke to me very solemnly. 'Msabu,' he said, 'I think you had better get up.' I sat up in bed bewildered; I thought that if anything serious had happened, it would have been Farah who would have come to fetch me, but when I told Kamante to go away again, he did not move. 'Msabu,' he said again, 'I think that you had better get up. I think that God is coming.' When I heard this, I did get up, and asked him why he thought so. He gravely led me into the dining-room which looked west, towards the hills. From the door-windows I now saw a strange phenomenon. There was a big grass-fire going on, out in the hills, and the grass was burning all the way from the hill top to the plain; when seen from the house it was a nearly vertical line. It did indeed look as if some gigantic figure was moving and coming towards us. I stood for some time and looked at it, with Kamante watching by my side; then I began to explain the thing to him. I meant to quiet him, for I thought that he had been terribly frightened. But the explanation did not seem to make much impression on him one way or the other; he clearly took his mission to have been fulfilled when he had called me. 'Well, yes,' he said, 'it may be so. But I thought that you had better get up in case it was God coming.'

The Savage in the
Immigrant's House

One year the long rains failed.

That is a terrible, tremendous experience, and the farmer who has lived through it will never forget it. Years afterwards, away from Africa, in the wet climate of a northern country, he will start up at night, at the sound of a sudden shower of rain, and cry, 'At last, at last.'

In normal years the long rains began in the last week of March and went on into the middle of June. Up to the time of the rains, the world grew hotter and drier every day, feverish, as in Europe before a great thunderstorm, only more so.

The Masai, who were my neighbours on the other side of the river, at that time set fire to the bast-dry plains to get new green grass for their cattle with the first rain, and the air over the plains danced with the mighty conflagration; the long grey and rainbow-tinted layers of smoke rolled along over the grass, and the heat and the smell of burning were drifted in over the cultivated land as from a furnace.

Gigantic clouds gathered, and dissolved again, over the landscape; a light distant shower of rain painted a blue slanting streak across the horizon. All the world had only one thought.

On an evening just before sunset, the scenery drew close round you, the hills came near and were vigorous, meaningful, in their clear, deep blue

and green colouring. A couple of hours later you went out and saw that
the stars had gone, and you felt the night air soft and deep and pregnant
with benefaction.

When the quickly growing rushing sound wandered over your head it
was the wind in the tall forest trees – and not the rain. When it ran along
the ground it was the wind in the shrubs and the long grass – and not the
rain. When it rustled and rattled just above the ground it was the wind
in the maize fields – where it sounded so much like rain that you were
taken in, time after time, and even got a certain content from it, as if you
were at least shown the thing you longed for acted on a stage – and not
the rain.

But when the earth answered like a sounding-board in a deep fertile
roar, and the world sang round you in all dimensions, all above and below
– that was the rain. It was like coming back to the sea, when you have
been a long time away from it, like a lover's embrace.

But one year the long rains failed. It was, then, as if the Universe were
turning away from you. It grew cooler, on some days it would be cold,
but there was no sign of moisture in the atmosphere. Everything became
drier and harder, and it was as if all force and gracefulness had withdrawn
from the world. It was not bad weather or good weather, but a negation
of all weather, as if it had been deferred *sine die*. A bleak wind, like a
draught, ran over your head, all colour faded from all things; the smells
went away from the fields and forests. The feeling of being in disgrace with
the Great Powers pressed on you. To the south, the burnt plains lay black
and waste, striped with grey and white ashes.

With every day, in which we now waited for the rain in vain, prospects
and hopes of the farm grew dim, and disappeared. The ploughing,
pruning, and planting of the last months turned out to be a labour of
fools. The farm work slowed off, and stood still.

On the plains and in the hills, the waterholes dried up, and many new
kinds of ducks and geese came to my pond. To the pond on the boundary
of the farm, the zebra came wandering in the early mornings and at sunset
to drink, in long rows, two or three hundred of them, the foals walking
with the mares, and they were not afraid of me when I rode out amongst
them. But we tried to keep them off the land for the sake of our cattle,
for the water was sinking in the ponds. Still it was a pleasure to go down
there, where the rushes growing in the mud made a green patch in the
brown landscape.

The Natives became silent under the drought. I could not get a word
on the prospects out of them, although you would have thought that they
should have known more about the signs of the weather than we did. It

was their existence which was at stake; it was not an unheard-of thing to them – and had not been to their fathers – to lose nine-tenths of their stock in the great years of drought. Their shambas were dry, with a few drooping and withering sweet-potato and maize plants.

After a time I learned their manner from them, and gave up talking of the hard times or complaining about them, like a person in disgrace. But I was European, and I had not lived long enough in the country to acquire the absolute passivity of the Native, as some Europeans will do, who live for many decennaries in Africa. I was young, and by instinct of self-preservation I had to collect my energy on something, if I were not to be whirled away with the dust on the farm-roads, or the smoke on the plain. I began in the evenings to write stories, fairy-tales, and romances, that would take my mind a long way off, to other countries and times.

I had been telling some of the stories to a friend when he came to stay on the farm.

When I got up and went outside, there was a cruel wind blowing, the sky was clear and set with millions of hard stars, everything was dry.

At first I wrote in the evenings only, but later on I often sat down to write in the mornings as well, when I ought to have been out on the farm. It was difficult, out there, to decide whether we ought to plough the maize field up again and plant it a second time, and whether we ought to strip the withering coffee berries off the trees to save the trees, or not. I put the decisions off from day to day.

I used to sit and write in the dining-room, with papers spread all over the dinner table, for I had accounts and estimates of the farm to do, in between my stories, and little desolate notes from my farming manager to answer. My houseboys asked me what I was doing; when I told them I was trying to write a book, they looked upon it as a last attempt to save the farm through the hard times, and took an interest in it. Later they asked me how my book was proceeding. They would come in, and stand for a long time watching the progress of it, and in the panelled room their heads were so much the colour of the panels, that at night it looked as if they were white robes only, keeping me company with their backs to the wall.

My dining-room looked west, and had three long windows that opened out to the paved terrace, the lawn, and the forest. The land here sloped down to the river that formed the boundary between me and the Masai. You could not see the river itself from the house, but you could follow its winding course by the design of the dark-green big acacias which grew along it. To the other side of it the wood-clad land rose again, and over the woods were the green plains that reached to the foot of the Ngong Hills.

'And were my faith so strong that it could move mountains, that is the mountain that I would make come to me.'

The wind blew from the east: the doors of my dining-room, to lee, were always open, and for this reason the west side of the house was popular with the Natives; they laid their way round it, to keep in touch with what was going on inside. From the same motive the little Native herdboys brought their goats round and made them graze on the lawn.

These little boys, who wandered about on the farm in the company of their fathers' herds of goats and sheep, looking up grazing for them, did in a way form a link between the life of my civilized house and the life of the wild. My houseboys distrusted them and did not like them to come into the rooms, but the children had a real love and enthusiasm for civilization; to them it held no dangers at all, for they could leave it again whenever they liked. The central symbol of it to them was an old German cuckoo-clock that hung in the dining-room. A clock was entirely an object of luxury in the African highlands. All the year round you could tell, from the position of the sun, what the time was, and as you had no dealings with railways, and could arrange your life on the farm according to your own wishes, it became a matter of no importance. But this was a very fine clock. In the midst of a cluster of pink roses, at every full hour, a cuckoo here flung up its little door and threw itself forward to announce the hour in a clear insolent voice. Its apparition was every time a fresh delight to the young people of the farm. From the position of the sun, they judged accurately when the moment for the midday call was due, and by a quarter to twelve I could see them approaching the house from all sides, at the tail of their goats, which they dared not leave behind. The heads of the children and of the goats swam through the bush and long grass of the forest like heads of frogs in a pond.

They left their flocks on the lawn and came in noiselessly on their bare feet; the bigger ones were about ten years and the youngest two years. They behaved very well, and kept up a sort of self-made ceremonial for their visits, which came to this: that they could move about freely in the house so long as they did not touch anything, nor sit down, nor speak unless spoken to. As the cuckoo rushed out on them, a great movement of ecstasy and suppressed laughter ran through the group. It also some-times happened that a very small herdboy, who did not feel any respon-sibility about the goats, would come back in the early morning all by himself, stand for a long time in front of the clock, now shut up and silent, and address it in Kikuyu in a slow sing-song declaration of love, then gravely walk out again. My houseboys laughed at the herdboys, and confided to me that the children were so ignorant that they believed the cuckoo to be alive.

Now my houseboys came in themselves to watch the work of the typewriter. Kamante sometimes stood by the wall for an hour in the evening, his eyes ran to and fro like dark drops under the eyelashes, as if he meant to learn enough about the machine to take it to pieces and put it together again.

One night as I looked up I met these profound attentive eyes and after a moment he spoke. 'Msabu,' he said, 'do you believe yourself that you can write a book?'

I answered that I did not know.

To figure to oneself a conversation with Kamante one must imagine a long, pregnant, as if deeply responsible, pause before each phrase. All Natives are masters in the art of the pause and thereby give perspective to a discussion.

Kamante now made such a long pause, and then said, 'I do not believe it.'

I had nobody else to discuss my book with; I laid down my paper and asked him why not. I now found that he had been thinking the conversation over before, and prepared himself for it; he stood with the Odyssey itself behind his back, and here he laid it on the table.

'Look, Msabu,' he said, 'this is a good book. It hangs together from the one end to the other. Even if you hold it up and shake it strongly, it does not come to pieces. The man who has written it is very clever. But what you write,' he went on, both with scorn and with a sort of friendly compassion, 'is some here and some there. When the people forget to close the door it blows about, even down on the floor and you are angry. It will not be a good book.'

I explained to him that in Europe the people would be able to fix it all up together.

'Will your book then be as heavy as this?' Kamante asked, weighing the Odyssey.

When he saw that I hesitated he handed it to me in order that I might judge for myself.

'No,' I said, 'it will not, but there are other books in the library, as you know, that are lighter.'

'And as hard?' he asked.

I said it was expensive to make a book so hard.

He stood for some time in silence and then expressed his greater hopes of my book, and perhaps also repentance of his doubts, by picking up the scattered pages from the floor and laying them on the table. Still he did not go away, but stood by the table and waited, and then asked me gravely: 'Msabu, what is there in books?'

As an illustration, I told him the story from the Odyssey of the hero and Polyphemus, and of how Odysseus had called himself Noman, had put out Polyphemus' eye, and had escaped tied up under the belly of a ram.

Kamante listened with interest and expressed as his opinion, that the ram must have been of the same race as the sheep of Mr Long, of Elmentaita, which he had seen at the cattle-show in Nairobi. He came back to Polyphemus, and asked me if he had been black, like the Kikuyu. When I said no, he wanted to know if Odysseus had been of my own tribe or family.

'How did he,' he asked, 'say the word, *Noman*, in his own language? Say it.'

'He said *Outis*,' I told him. 'He called himself Outis, which in his language means Noman.'

'Must you write about the same thing?' he asked me.

'No,' I said, 'people can write of anything they like. I might write of you.'

Kamante, who had opened up in the course of the talk, here suddenly closed again; he looked down himself and asked me in a low voice, what part of him I would write about.

'I might write about the time when you were ill and were out with the sheep on the plain,' I said, 'what did you think of then?'

His eyes wandered over the room, up and down; in the end he said vaguely: '*Sejui*' – I know not.

'Were you afraid?' I asked him.

After a pause, 'Yes,' he said firmly, 'all the boys on the plain are afraid sometimes.'

'Of what were you afraid?' I said.

Kamante stood silent for a little while, then he looked at me; his face became collected and deep, his eyes gazed inward:

'Of Outis,' he said. 'The boys on the plain are afraid of Outis.'

A few days later, I heard Kamante explain to the other houseboys that in Europe the book which I was writing could be made to stick together, and that with terrible expense it could even be made as hard as the Odyssey, which was again displayed. He himself, however, did not believe that it could be made blue.

Kamante had a talent of his own that became of use to him in my house. He could, I believe, cry when he wanted to.

If ever I scolded him in earnest, he stood up straight before me and looked me in the face, with the watchful, deep sadness which the faces of the Natives take on in a single moment; then his eyes swelled, and filled with heavy tears that slowly, one by one, rolled out and down over his cheeks. I knew them to be pure crocodile's tears, and in other people they would not have affected me. But with Kamante it was a different thing. His flat wooden face, on these occasions, sank back into the world of darkness and infinite loneliness, in which he had dwelt for many years. Such heavy, dumb tears he might have wept as a little boy on the plain with the sheep round him. They made me uneasy, and gave to the sins for which I scolded him a different aspect, a smaller look, so that I did not want to go on talking about them. In a way it was a demoralizing thing. Still I believe that by strength of the true human understanding which existed between us, Kamante knew in his heart that I looked through his tears of contrition and did not take them for more than they were – indeed that he himself looked upon them more as a ceremony due to the higher powers, than as any attempt to deceive.

He often referred to himself as a Christian. I did not know what idea he attached to the name, and once or twice I tried to catechize him, but he then explained to me that he believed what I believed, and that, since I myself must know what I believed, there was no sense in me questioning him. I found that this was more than an evasion, it was in a way his positive programme, or confession of faith. He had given himself under the God of the white people. In his service he was prepared to carry out any order, but he would not take upon himself to give reasons for a working system which might prove to be as unreasonable as the working systems of the white people themselves.

It sometimes happened that my behaviour clashed with the teachings of the Scotch Mission, where he had been converted; then he would ask me who was right.

The lack of prejudice in the Natives is a striking thing, for you expect to find dark taboos in the primitive people. It is due, I believe, to their acquaintance with a variety of races and tribes, and to the lively human intercourse that was brought upon East Africa, first by the old traders of ivory and slaves, and in our days by the settlers and big-game hunters. Nearly every Native, down to the little herdboys of the plains, has in his day stood face to face with a whole range of nations as different from one another, and to him, as a Sicilian to an Eskimo: Englishmen, Jews, Boers, Arabs, Somali, Indians, Swaheli, Masai and Kavirondo. As far as receptivity of ideas goes the Native is more of a man of the world than the

suburban or provincial settler or missionary, who has grown up in a
uniform community and with a set of stable ideas. Much of the misunderstanding between the white people and the Natives arises from this fact.

It is an alarming experience to be, in your person, representing
Christianity to the Natives.

There was a young Kikuyu by the name of Kitau, who came in from
the Kikuyu Reserve and took service with me. He was a meditative boy,
an observant, attentive servant, and I liked him well. After three months
he one day asked me to give him a letter of recommendation to my old
friend Sheik Ali bin Salim, the *Lewali* of the Coast, at Mombasa, for he
had seen him in my house and now, he said, he wished to go and work
for him. I did not want Kitau to leave just when he had learned the routine
of the house, and I said to him that I would rather raise his pay. No, he
said, he was not leaving to get any higher pay, but he could not stay. He
told me that he had made up his mind, up in the Reserve, that he would
become either a Christian or a Mohammedan, only he did not yet know
which. For this reason he had come and worked for me, since I was a
Christian, and he had stayed for three months in my house to see the
testurde – the ways and habits – of the Christians. From me he would go
for three months to Sheik Ali in Mombasa and study the *testurde* of the
Mohammedans; then he would decide. I believe that even an archbishop,
when he had had these facts laid before him, would have said, or at least
have thought, as I said: 'Good God, Kitau, you might have told me that
when you came here.'

The Mohammedans will not eat meat of any animal that has not had
its throat cut by a Mohammedan in the orthodox manner. This is often
a difficulty on a safari, where you carry few provisions with you, and are
dependent for your servants' food on the game you shoot. When you
shoot a kongoni and it falls, your Mohammedans rush at it, as upon
wings, to be in time to cut the throat of it before it dies, and you yourself
watch them in suspense, with burning eyes, for if they are seen standing
over it with hanging arms and head, it means that the kongoni has died
before they got up to it, and you will have to stalk another kongoni, or
your gunbearers will go starving.

When in the beginning of the war I was going out with my ox-wagons,
the night before I started I happened to meet the Mohammedan Shereef
up at Kijabe; I asked him if he could not give my people dispensation from
the law for as long as our safari lasted.

The Shereef was a young man, but wise, and he talked with Farah and
Ismail and pronounced: 'This lady is a disciple of Jesus Christ. When she
fires off her rifle, she will say, or at least in her heart say: *In the name of*

God, which will make her bullets equivalent to the knife of the orthodox Mohammedan. For the length of time of this journey, you can eat the meat of the animals that she shoots.'

The prestige of the Christian religion in Africa was weakened by the intolerance that the one Christian church showed towards the other.

On Christmas nights while I was in Africa I used to drive over to the French Mission to hear the Midnight Mass. It was generally hot at this time of the year; as you drove through the wattle plantation, you heard the chiming of the mission bell a long way in the clear warm air. A crowd of happy, lively people were at the place round the church when you arrived, the French and Italian shopkeepers of Nairobi with their families had come out, the nuns from the convent school were present, and the Native congregation swarmed in gay clothes. The big fine church was lighted with many hundred candles and with great transparencies which the Fathers had themselves made.

When Christmas came, in the first year after Kamante had come into my house, I told him that I was going to take him with me to the Mass, as a fellow Christian, and described to him the beautiful things that he was going to see there, in the manner of the Fathers themselves. Kamante listened to it all, moved in his soul, and put on the best clothes he had. But when the car was at the door, he came back in great agitation of mind and said that he could not possibly come with me. He did not want to give me his reasons, and flinched from my questions; in the end it came out. No, he could not go, he had by now realized that it was to the French Mission that I meant to take him, and he had been so strongly warned against that mission when he had been in hospital. I explained to him that this was all a misunderstanding, and that he must come now. But at that he began to turn to stone before my eyes; he died, he turned up his eyes so that only the white showed in them and sweated in the face.

'No, no, Msabu,' he whispered, 'I am not coming with you. There inside that big church, I know it well, there is a Msabu who is *mbaia sana*' – terribly bad.

When I heard this I became very sad, but I thought that now I would indeed have to take him with me so that the Virgin herself could enlighten him. The Fathers had a life-size pasteboard statue of the Virgin in their church, all blue and white, and the Natives are generally impressed by statues, while it is difficult for them to conceive the idea of a picture. So I promised Kamante my protection and took him with me, and when he walked into the church, very close at my heels, he forgot all his scruples. It happened to be the finest Christmas Mass that they had ever had at the mission. There was in the church a very big Nativity – a grotto with the Holy Family, just out from Paris, which was illuminated by radiant stars in a blue sky, and it had round it a hundred toy animals, wooden cows and pure white cotton-wool lambs, without any petty consideration as to their size, that must have raised ecstasy in the hearts of the Kikuyus.

After Kamante had become a Christian he was no longer afraid to touch a dead body.

Earlier in his life he had been afraid of it, and when a man, who had been carried on a stretcher up to the terrace by my house, died there, he would no more than the others lend a hand to carry him back; he did not recede, like the other people, on to the lawn, but he stood immovable upon the pavement, a little dark monument. Why the Kikuyu, who personally have so little fear of death, should be so terrified to touch a corpse, while the white people, who are afraid to die, handle the dead easily, I do not know. Here once more you feel their reality to be different from our realities. But all farmers know that here is a domain on which you cannot control the Native, and that you will save yourself trouble if you give up the idea at once, for he will really rather die than change his ways.

Now the terror had disappeared out of Kamante's heart; he scorned it in his kinsmen. He did even show off a little here, as if to boast of the power of his God. It happened that I had opportunities to test his faith, and that Kamante and I came to carry three dead people between us, in the course of our life on the farm. One was a young Kikuyu girl who was run over by an ox-cart outside my house. The second was a young Kikuyu who was killed while he was felling trees in the forest. The third was an old white man who came to live on the farm, played a part in the life of it, and died there.

He was a countryman of mine, an old blind Dane by the name of Knudsen. One day when I was in Nairobi he fumbled his way up to my car, presented himself, and asked me to give him a house on my land, as he had no place in the world to stay in. I had at that time been reducing my staff of white people on the plantation, and had an empty bungalow that I could lend him, and he came out and lived on the farm for six months.

He was a singular figure to have on a highland farm: so much a creature of the sea that it was as if we had had an old clipped albatross with us. He was all broken by the hardships of life, and by disease and drink, bent and crooked, with the curious colouring of red-haired people gone white, as if he had in reality strewn ashes upon his head, or as if he was marked by his own element and had been salted. But there was an unquenchable flame in him which no ashes could cover. He came of Danish fisherman stock and had been a sailor, and later one of the very early pioneers of Africa – whatever wind it was that blew him there.

Old Knudsen had tried a great many things in his life, preferably such as have to do with water or fish or birds, and had done well on none of them. At one time, he told me, he had owned a very fine fishing concern on Lake Victoria, with many miles of the best fishing nets in the world, and with a motorboat. But during the war he had lost it all. In his recounting of this tragedy of his, there was a dark moment of fatal misunderstanding, or of the treason of a friend. I do not know which, for the tale was never quite the same at the various times when it was told to me, and it brought Old Knudsen into a terrible state of mind when he came to this point of his recital. There was, all the same, some real fact in the story, for in compensation of his losses, the Government, while he was staying with me, paid him a sort of pension of a shilling a day.

All this he told me on the occasions when he came up on a visit to my house. He often took refuge with me, for he was uncomfortable in his own bungalow. The small Native boys, whom I gave him as servants, ran away from him again and again, because he frightened them by rushing at them blindly, head foremost, and fumbling with his stick. But when he was in high spirits he would sit on my verandah over a cup of coffee and sing Danish patriotic songs to me, all by himself, with great energy. It was a pleasure to both him and me to speak Danish, so we exchanged many remarks over insignificant happenings on the farm, just for the joy of talking. But I did not always have patience with him, for when he had once arrived it was difficult to make him stop talking and go away; in our daily intercourse he had, as was to be expected, much of the Ancient Mariner, or of the Old Man of the Sea.

He had been a great artist at the making of fishing nets – the best fishing nets in the world, he told me – and here, in the bungalow of the farm, he made *kibokos* – the Native whips which are cut out of hippo hide. He would buy a hippo hide from the Natives or the farmers up at Lake Naivasha, and if he was lucky he could make fifty kibokos out of one hide. I have still a riding-whip which he gave me; it is a very fine whip. This work spread a terrible stench round his house, like the stench round the nest of some old carrion-bird. Later on, when I made a pond on the farm, he was nearly always to be found by the pond, in deep thought, with his reflection vertically under him, like a sea-bird in a zoo.

Old Knudsen had in his frail sunken breast the simple, fierce, irascible, wild heart of a small boy, who burns with the unadulterated love of

fighting; he was a great romantic bully and combatant. He was a singularly good hater, always afire with indignation and rage against nearly all
the people and institutions with which he came in touch; he called heaven
to let fire and brimstone rain down on them, and 'painted the devil on
the wall', as we say in Denmark, in a Michaelangelesque manner. He was
highly delighted whenever he could set other people by the ears, like a
small boy who sets two dogs fighting, or a dog at a cat. It was an
impressive and formidable thing that Old Knudsen's soul should still –
after his long hard life, and when he had at last, so to say, been washed
into a quiet creek where he might have lain with his sails slackened – cry
out for opposition and adversity, like the soul of a boy. It made me respect
it, as the soul of a Berserk.

He never spoke of himself except in the third person, as 'Old Knudsen',
and never without boasting and bragging to the last degree. There was
not a thing in the world that Old Knudsen would not undertake and carry
through, and not a champion fighter whom Old Knudsen could not knock
down. Wherever other people were concerned, he was a black pessimist,
and he foresaw a near, catastrophic, and well-deserved end to all their
activities. But on his own behalf he was a furious optimist. A short time
before he died he confided to me, under the promise of secrecy, a
tremendous plan. It would make Old Knudsen, at last, a millionaire and
put all his enemies to shame. He was, he told me, going to lift, from the
bottom of Lake Naivasha, the hundred thousand tons of guano dropped
there, from the time of the creation of the world, by the swimming-birds.
In a last colossal effort he made a journey from the farm to Lake
Naivasha, to study and work out the details of his plan. He died in the
lustre of it. The scheme had in it all the elements dear to his heart: deep
water, birds, hidden treasures; it had even a flavour of the things that one
ought not to talk to ladies about. At the top of it he saw, with the eyes
of his mind, triumphant Old Knudsen himself, with a trident, controlling
the waves. I do not remember if he ever explained to me how the guano
was to be brought up from the bottom of the lake.

The great exploits and achievements of Old Knudsen and his eminence
in everything, as he reported these things to me, were clearly at variance
with the weakness and impotence of the old man who reported them; in
the end you felt that you were dealing with two separate and essentially
different individualities. The mighty figure of Old Knudsen rose in the
background, unbeaten and triumphant, the hero of all the adventures,
and it was his old, bent and worn servant whom I knew, and who never
tired of telling me about him. This little, humble man had made it his
mission in life to uphold and extol the name of Old Knudsen, even to

death. For he had really seen Old Knudsen, which nobody else except God ever had, and after that he would stand no heresy in anyone.

One single time have I heard him make use of the first personal pronoun. This was a couple of months before he died. He had had a bad heart-attack, the same thing that killed him in the end, and when I had not seen him on the farm for a week I went down to his bungalow to get news of him, and I found him, in the middle of the stench from the hippo hide, in bed in a very bare and untidy room. He was ashen grey in the face, his dim eyes were sunk deep back. He did not answer me or speak a word when I spoke to him. Only after a long time, and when I had already got up to go away, he suddenly said in a small hoarse voice, 'I am very sick.' At that time there was no talk of Old Knudsen, who surely was never ill or overcome; it was the servant, who just for once allowed himself to express his individual misery and anguish.

Old Knudsen was dull on the farm, so from time to time he locked the door of his house, made off and disappeared from our horizon. It was most often, I think, when he had had news that an old friend, some other pioneer of the glorious past, had arrived in Nairobi. He would stay away, for a week or a fortnight, until we had half forgotten his existence, and he always came back so terribly ill and worn out that he could hardly drag himself along, or unlock his door. He then kept to himself for a couple of days. I believe that on these occasions he was afraid of me, for he thought that I would be sure to have disapproved of his escapades, and that I would now profit by his weakness to triumph over him. Old Knudsen, although he would sometimes sing of the sailor's bride who loves the waves, in his heart had a deep mistrust of woman, and saw her as the enemy of man, by instinct, and on principle, out to stop his fun.

On the day of his death he had in this way been absent for a fortnight, and nobody on the farm was aware that he had come back. But he himself must this time have meant to make an exception from his rule, for he had been on the way from his own house to mine, by a path which ran through the plantation, when he fell down and died. Kamante and I found him lying on the path as, late in the afternoon, we were going out to look for mushrooms on the plain, in the new short grass, for it was April, in the beginning of the long rains.

It was befitting that it should be Kamante who found him, for, alone of all the Natives of the farm, he had shown Old Knudsen sympathy. He had even taken an interest in him, as one deviation from the normal in another, and from time to time of his own accord had brought him eggs, and kept an eye on his Totos, which had prevented them from running away altogether.

The old man lay on his back, his hat had rolled a little away when he fell, his eyes were not quite closed. In death he looked essentially collected. There you are at last, Old Knudsen – I thought.

I wanted to carry him to his house, but I knew that it would be of no use to call in any of the Kikuyus who might be about or working in their own shambas close by, to help me; they would only run away immediately when they saw why I had called them. I ordered Kamante to run back to the house and fetch down Farah to assist me. But Kamante did not move.

'Why do you want me to run?'

'Well you see yourself,' I said, 'that I cannot carry the old Bwana alone, and you Kikuyus are fools, you are afraid to carry a dead man.'

Kamante set up his little mocking noiseless laughter. 'You again forget, Msabu,' he said, 'that I am a Christian.'

He lifted the old man's feet while I bore his head, and between us we carried him to his bungalow. From time to time we had to stop, lay him down, and rest; then Kamante stood up erect and looked straight down at Old Knudsen's feet, with what I think will have been the Scotch Mission manner in the presence of death.

As we had laid him on his bed, Kamante went about the room, and into the kitchen, in search of a towel to cover his face with – he only found an old newspaper. 'The Christians did that at the hospital,' he explained to me.

A long time afterwards Kamante had great satisfaction out of the thought of this instance of my ignorance. He would work with me in the kitchen, filled with secret pleasure, and suddenly break out laughing. 'Do you remember, Msabu,' he said, 'the time when you had forgotten that I was a Christian, and thought that I should be afraid to help you to carry the *Msungu Mse*?' – the old white man.

Kamante as a Christian was no longer afraid of snakes. I heard him state to the other boys that a Christian might at any moment put his heel upon the head of the largest snake and crush it. I have not seen him try to do so, but I saw him standing very still, with a set face and his hands behind his back, within a short distance of the cook's hut when a puff-adder had appeared on its roof. All the children of my household spread in large circles around it, like chaff before the wind, with wild wails, while Farah went into the house to fetch my gun, and shot the puff-adder.

When it was all over, and the waves had settled down again, Nyore, the Sice's son, said to Kamante, 'Why, you Kamante, did you not set your heel upon the head of the big bad snake and crush it?'

'Because it was up on the roof,' said Kamante.

At one time, I tried to shoot with a bow and arrow. I was strong, but it was difficult for me to bend the Wanderobo bow which Farah had got for me; still in the end, and after long practice, I became skilful as an archer.

Kamante was very small then: he used to watch me when I was shooting on the lawn, and seemed doubtful about the undertaking, and one day said to me: 'Are you a Christian still when you are shooting with a bow? I thought that the Christian way was with a rifle?'

I showed him in my pictorial Bible an illustration to the tale of Hagar's son: 'And God was with the lad; and he grew, and dwelt in the wilderness, and became an archer.'

'Well,' said Kamante, 'he was like you.'

Kamante had a good hand with sick animals, as with my Native patients. He took out splinters from the dogs' feet, and once cured one of them when it had been bitten by a snake.

For some time I had in the house a stork with a broken wing. He was a decided character: he walked through the rooms and when he came into my bedroom he fought tremendous duels, as with the rapier, with swaggering and flapping of wings, with his image in my looking-glass. He followed Kamante about between the houses, and it was impossible not to believe that he was deliberately imitating Kamante's stiff measured walk. Their legs were about the same thickness. The little Native boys had an eye for caricature and shouted with joy when they saw the pair pass. Kamante understood the joke, but he never paid much attention to what other people thought of him. He sent off the little boys to collect frogs for the stork in the bogs.

It was also Kamante who had charge of Lulu.

A Gazelle

Lulu came to my house from the woods as Kamante had come to it from the plains.

To the east of my farm lay the Ngong Forest Reserve, which then was nearly all virgin forest. To my mind it was a sad thing when the old forest was cut down, and eucalyptus and grevillea planted in its place; it might have made a unique pleasure ground and park for Nairobi.

An African native forest is a mysterious region. You ride into the depths of an old tapestry, in places faded and in others darkened with age, but marvellously rich in green shades. You cannot see the sky at all in there, but the sunlight plays in many strange ways, falling through the foliage. The grey fungus, like long drooping beards, on the trees, and the creepers hanging down everywhere, give a secretive, recondite air to the native forest. I used to ride here with Farah on Sundays, when there was nothing to do on the farm, up and down the slopes, and across the little winding forest streams. The air in the forest was cool like water, and filled with the scent of plants, and in the beginning of the long rains when the creepers flowered, you rode through sphere after sphere of fragrance. One kind of African Daphne of the woods, which flowers with a small cream-coloured sticky blossom, had an overwhelming sweet perfume, like lilac, and wild lily of the valley. Here and there, hollow tree-stems were hung up in ropes of hide on a branch; the Kikuyu hung them there to make the bees build in them, and to get honey. Once as we turned a corner in the forest, we saw a leopard sitting on the road, a tapestry animal.

Here, high above the ground, lived a garrulous restless nation, the little grey monkeys. Where a pack of monkeys had travelled over the road, the smell of them lingered for a long time in the air, a dry and stale, mousy smell. As you rode on you would suddenly hear the rush and whizz over your head, as the colony passed along on its own ways. If you kept still in the same place for some time you might catch sight of one of the monkeys sitting immovable in a tree, and, a little after, discover that the whole forest round you was alive with his family, placed like fruits on the branches, grey or dark figures according to how the sunlight fell on them, all with their long tails hanging down behind them. They gave out a peculiar sound, like a smacking kiss with a little cough to follow it; if from the ground you imitated it, you saw the monkeys turn their heads from one side to the other in an affected manner, but if you made a sudden movement they were all off in a second, and you could follow the decreasing swash as they cleaved the tree-tops, and disappeared in the wood like a shoal of fishes in the waves.

In the Ngong Forest I have also seen, on a narrow path through thick growth, in the middle of a very hot day, the giant forest hog, a rare person to meet. He came suddenly past me, with his wife and three young pigs, at a great speed, the whole family looking like uniform, bigger and smaller figures cut out in dark paper, against the sunlit green behind them. It was a glorious sight, like a reflection in a forest pool, like a thing that had happened a thousand years ago.

Lulu was a young antelope of the bushbuck tribe, which is perhaps the prettiest of all the African antelopes. They are a little bigger than the fallow-deer; they live in the woods, or in the bush, and are shy and fugitive, so that they are not seen as often as the antelopes of the plains. But the Ngong Hills, and the surrounding country, were good places for bushbuck, and if you had your camp in the hills, and were out hunting in the early morning, or at sunset, you would see them come out of the bush into the glades, and as the rays of the sun fell upon them their coat shone red as copper. The male has a pair of delicately turned horns.

Lulu became a member of my household in this way:

I drove one morning from the farm to Nairobi. My mill on the farm had burnt down a short time before, and I had had to drive into town many times to get the insurance settled and paid out; in this early morning I had my head filled with figures and estimates. As I came driving along the Ngong road a little group of Kikuyu children shouted to me from the roadside, and I saw that they were holding a very small bushbuck up for me to see. I knew that they would have found the fawn in the bush, and that now they wanted to sell it to me, but I was late for an appointment in Nairobi, and I had no thought for this sort of thing, so I drove on.

When I was coming back in the evening and was driving past the same place, there was again a great shout from the side of the road and the small party was still there, a little tired and disappointed, for they may have tried to sell the fawn to other people passing by in the course of the day, but keen now to get the deal through before the sun was down, and they held up the fawn high to tempt me. But I had had a long day in town, and some adversity about the insurance, so that I did not care to stop or talk, and I just drove on past them. I did not even think of them when I was back in my house, and dined and went to bed.

The moment that I had fallen asleep I was woken up again by a great feeling of terror. The picture of the boys and the small buck, which had now collected and taken shape, stood out before me, clearly, as if it had been painted, and I sat up in bed as appalled as if someone had been trying to choke me. What, I thought, would become of the fawn in the hands of the capturers who had stood with it in the heat of the long day, and had held it up by its joined legs? It was surely too young to eat on its own. I myself had driven past it twice on the same day, like the priest and the Levite in one, and had given no thought to it, and now, at this moment, where was it? I got up in a real panic and woke up all my houseboys. I told them that the fawn must be found and brought me in the morning, or they would all of them get their dismissal from my service. They were immediately up to the idea. Two of my boys had been in the car with me the same day, and had not shown the slightest interest in the children or the fawn; now they came forward, and gave the others a long list of details of the place and the hour and of the family of the boys. It was a moonlight night; my people all took off and spread in the landscape in a lively discussion of the situation; I heard them expatiating on the fact that they were all to be dismissed in case the bushbuck were not found.

Early next morning when Farah brought me in my tea, Juma came in with him and carried the fawn in his arms. It was a female, and we named her Lulu, which I was told was the Swaheli word for a pearl.

Lulu by that time was only as big as a cat, with large quiet purple eyes. She had such delicate legs that you feared they would not bear being folded up and unfolded again, as she lay down and rose up. Her ears were smooth as silk and exceedingly expressive. Her nose was as black as a truffle. Her diminutive hoofs gave her all the air of a young Chinese lady of the old school, with laced feet. It was a rare experience to hold such a perfect thing in your hands.

Lulu soon adapted herself to the house and its inhabitants and behaved as if she were at home. During the first weeks the polished floors in the rooms were a problem in her life, and when she got outside the carpets her legs went away from her to all four sides; it looked catastrophic but she did not let it worry her much and in the end she learnt to walk on the bare floors with a sound like a succession of little angry finger-taps. She was extraordinarily neat in all her habits. She was headstrong already as a child, but when I stopped her from doing the things she wanted to do, she behaved as if she said: Anything rather than a scene.

Kamante brought her up on a sucking-bottle, and he also shut her up at night, for we had to be careful of her as the leopards were up round the house after nightfall. So she held to him and followed him about. From time to time when he did not do what she wanted, she gave his thin legs a hard butt with her young head, and she was so pretty that you could not help, when you looked upon the two together, seeing them as a new paradoxical illustration to the tale of the Beauty and the Beast. On the strength of this great beauty and gracefulness, Lulu obtained for herself a commanding position in the house, and was treated with respect by all.

In Africa I never had dogs of any other breed than the Scotch deer-hound. There is no more noble or gracious kind of dog. They must have lived for many centuries with men to understand and fall in with our life and its conditions the way they do. You will also find them in old paintings and tapestries, and they have in themselves a tendency to change, by their looks and manners, their surroundings into tapestry; they bring with them a feudal atmosphere.

The first of my tribe of deerhounds, who was named Dusk, had been given to me as a wedding present, and had come out with me when I began my life in Africa, on *The Mayflower*, so to say. He was a gallant, generous character. He accompanied me when during the first months of the war I did transport for the government, with ox-wagons in the Masai Reserve. But a couple of years later he was killed by zebra. By the time that Lulu came to live in my house I had two of his sons there.

The Scotch deerhound went well with African scenery and the African Native. It may be due to the altitude – the highland melody in all three – for he did not look so harmonious at sea-level in Mombasa. It was as if the great, spare landscape, with the plains, hills, and rivers, was not complete until the deerhounds were also in it. All the deerhounds were great hunters and had more nose than the greyhounds, but they hunted by sight and it was a highly wonderful thing to see two of them working together. I took them with me when I was out riding in the Game Reserve, which I was not allowed to do, and there they would spread the herds of zebra and wildebeest over the plain, as if it were all the stars of heaven running wild over the sky. But when I was out in the Masai Reserve shooting I never lost a wounded head of game if I had the deerhounds with me.

They looked well in the native forests too, dark grey in the sombre green shades. One of them, in here, all by himself, killed a big old male baboon, and in the fight had his nose bitten straight through, which spoilt his noble profile but by everyone on the farm was considered an honourable scar, for the baboons are destructive beasts and the Natives detest them.

The deerhounds were very wise, and knew who amongst my houseboys were Mohammedans, and not allowed to touch dogs.

During my first years in Africa I had a Somali gunbearer named Ismail, who died while I was still out there. He was one of the old-time gun-bearers, and there are no such people now. He had been brought up by the great old big-game hunters of the beginning of the century, when all Africa was a real deer-park. His acquaintance with civilization was entirely of the hunting fields, and he spoke an English of the hunting world, so that he would talk of my big and my young rifle. After Ismail had gone back to Somaliland, I had a letter from him which was addressed to *Lioness Blixen*, and opened: *Honourable Lioness*. Ismail was a strict Mohammedan, and would not for the life of him touch a dog, which caused him much worry in his profession. But he made an exception with

Dusk and never minded my taking him with us in a mule-trap, he would even let Dusk sleep in his tent. For Dusk, he said, would know a Mohammedan when he saw him, and would never touch him. Indeed, Ismail assured me, Dusk could see at once who was a sincere Mohammedan at heart. He once said to me: 'I know now that the Dusk is of the same tribe as you yourself. He laughs at the people.'

Now my dogs understood Lulu's power and position in the house. The arrogance of the great hunters was like water with her. She pushed them away from the milk-bowl and from their favourite places in front of the fire. I had tied a small bell on a rein round Lulu's neck, and there came a time when the dogs, when they heard the jingle of it approaching through the rooms, would get up resignedly from their warm beds by the fireplace, and go and lie down in some other part of the room. Still, nobody could be of a gentler demeanour than Lulu was when she came and lay down, in the manner of a perfect lady who demurely gathers her skirts about her and will be in no one's way. She drank the milk with a polite, pernickety mien, as if she had been pressed by an overkind hostess. She insisted on being scratched behind the ears, in a pretty forbearing way, like a young wife who pertly permits her husband a caress.

When Lulu grew up and stood in the flower of her young loveliness she was a slim delicately rounded doe, from her nose to her toes unbelievably beautiful. She looked like a minutely painted illustration to Heine's song of the wise and gentle gazelles by the flow of the river Ganges.

But Lulu was not really gentle, she had the so-called devil in her. She had, to the highest degree, the feminine trait of appearing to be exclusively on the defensive, concentrated on guarding the integrity of her being, when she was really, with every force in her, bent upon the offensive. Against whom? Against the whole world. Her moods grew beyond control or computation, and she would go for my horse, if he displeased her. I remembered old Hagenbeck in Hamburg, who had said that of all animal races, the carnivora included, the deer are the least to be relied on, and that you may trust a leopard, but if you trust a young stag, sooner or later he falls upon you in the rear.

Lulu was the pride of the house even when she behaved like a real shameless young coquette; but we did not make her happy. Sometimes she walked away from the house for hours, or for a whole afternoon. Sometimes when the spirit came upon her and her discontent with her surroundings reached a climax, she would perform, for the satisfaction of her own heart, on the lawn in front of the house, a war-dance, which looked like a brief zigzagged prayer to Satan.

'Oh Lulu,' I thought, 'I know that you are marvellously strong and that you can leap higher than your own height. You are furious with us now, you wish that we were all dead, and indeed we should be so if you could be bothered to kill us. But the trouble is not as you think now, that we have put up obstacles too high for you to jump, and how could we possibly do that, you great leaper? It is that we have put up no obstacles at all. The great strength is in you, Lulu, and the obstacles are within you as well, and the thing is, that the fullness of time has not yet come.'

One evening Lulu did not come home and we looked out for her in vain for a week. This was a hard blow to us all. A clear note had gone out of the house and it seemed no better than other houses. I thought of the leopards by the river and one evening I talked about them to Kamante.

As usual he waited some time before he answered, to digest my lack of insight. It was not till a few days later that he approached me upon the matter. 'You believe that Lulu is dead, Msabu,' he said.

I did not like to say so straight out, but I told him I was wondering why she did not come back.

'Lulu,' said Kamante, 'is not dead. But she is married.'

This was pleasant, surprising news, and I asked him how he knew of it.

'Oh yes,' he said, 'she is married. She lives in the forest with her *bwana*' – her husband, or master. 'But she has not forgotten the people; most mornings she is coming back to the house. I lay out crushed maize to her at the back of the kitchen, then just before the sun comes up, she walks round there from the woods and eats it. Her husband is with her, but he is afraid of the people because he has never known them. He stands below the big white tree by the other side of the lawn. But up to the house he dares not come.'

I told Kamante to come and fetch me when he next saw Lulu. A few days later before sunrise he came and called me out.

It was a lovely morning. The last stars withdrew while we were waiting, the sky was clear and serene but the world in which we walked was sombre still, and profoundly silent. The grass was wet; down by the trees where the ground sloped it gleamed with the dew like dim silver. The air of the morning was cold, it had that twinge in it which in northern countries means that the frost is not far away. However often you make the experience – I thought – it is still impossible to believe, in this coolness and shade, that the heat of the sun and the glare of the sky, in a few hours' time, will be hard to bear. The grey mist lay upon the hills, strangely taking shape from them; it would be bitterly cold on the buffalo if they were about there now, grazing on the hillside, as in a cloud.

The great vault over our heads was gradually filled with clarity like a glass with wine. Suddenly, gently, the summits of the hill caught the first sunlight and blushed. And slowly, as the earth leaned towards the sun, the grassy slopes at the foot of the mountain turned a delicate gold, and the Masai woods lower down. And now the tops of the tall trees in the forest, on our side of the river, blushed like copper. This was the hour for the flight of the big, purple wood-pigeons which roosted by the other side of the river and came over to feed on the Cape-chestnuts in my forest. They were here only for a short season in the year. The birds came surprisingly fast, like a cavalry attack of the air. For this reason the morning pigeon-shooting on the farm was popular with my friends in Nairobi; to be out by the house in time, just as the sun rose, they used to come out so early that they rounded my drive with the lamps of their cars still lighted.

Standing like this in the limpid shadow, looking up towards the golden heights and the clear sky, you would get the feeling that you were in reality walking along the bottom of the sea, with the currents running by you, and were gazing up towards the surface of the ocean.

A bird began to sing, and then I heard, a little way off in the forest, the tinkling of a bell. Yes, it was a joy, Lulu was back, and about in her old places! It came nearer, I could follow her movements by its rhythm; she was walking, stopping, walking on again. A turning round one of the boys' huts brought her upon us. It suddenly became an unusual and amusing thing to see a bushbuck so close to the house. She stood immovable now, she seemed to be prepared for the sight of Kamante, but not for that of me. But she did not make off, she looked at me without fear and without any remembrance of our skirmishes of the past or of her own ingratitude in running away without warning.

Lulu of the woods was a superior, independent being, a change of heart had come upon her, she was in possession. If I had happened to have known a young princess in exile, and while she was still a pretender to the throne, and had met her again in her full queenly estate after she had come into her rights, our meeting would have had the same character. Lulu showed no more meanness of heart than King Louis Philippe did, when he declared that the King of France did not remember the grudges of the Duke of Orleans. She was now the complete Lulu. The spirit of offensive had gone from her; for whom, and why, should she attack? She was standing quietly on her divine rights. She remembered me enough to feel that I was nothing to be afraid of. For a minute she gazed at me; her purple smoky eyes were absolutely without expression and did not wink, and I remembered that the Gods or Goddesses never wink, and felt that I was face to face with the ox-eyed Hera. She lightly nipped a leaf of grass as she passed me, made one pretty little leap, and walked on to the back of the kitchen, where Kamante had spread maize on the ground.

Kamante touched my arm with one finger and then pointed it towards the woods. As I followed the direction, I saw, under a tall Cape chestnut tree, a male bushbuck, a small tawny silhouette at the outskirts of the forest, with a fine pair of horns, immovable like a tree stem. Kamante observed him for some time, and then laughed.

'Look here now,' he said, 'Lulu has explained to her husband that there is nothing up by the houses to be afraid of, but all the same he dares not come. Every morning he thinks that to-day he will come all the way, but, when he sees the house and the people, he gets a cold stone in the stomach' – this is a common thing in the Native world, and often gets in the way of the work on the farm – 'and then he stops by the tree.'

For a long time Lulu came to the house in the early mornings. Her clear bell announced that the sun was upon the hills; I used to lie in bed, and wait for it. Sometimes she stayed away for a week or two, and we missed her and began to talk of the people who went to shoot in the hills. But then again my houseboys announced: 'Lulu is here,' as if it had been the married daughter of the house on a visit. A few times more I also saw the bushbuck's silhouette amongst the trees, but Kamante had been right, and he never collected enough courage to come all the way to the house.

One day, as I came back from Nairobi, Kamante was keeping watch for me outside the kitchen door, and stepped forward, much excited, to tell me that Lulu had been to the farm the same day and had had her Toto – her baby – with her. Some days after, I myself had the honour to meet her amongst the boys' huts, much on the alert and not to be trifled with, with a very small fawn at her heels, as delicately tardive in his movements as Lulu herself had been when we first knew her. This was just after the long rains, and, during those summer months, Lulu was to be found near the houses, in the afternoon, as well as at daybreak. She would even be round there at midday, keeping in the shadow of the huts.

Lulu's fawn was not afraid of the dogs, and would let them sniff him all over, but he could not get used to the Natives or to me, and if we ever tried to get hold of him, the mother and the child were off.

Lulu herself would never, after her first long absence from the house, come so near to any of us that we could touch her. In other ways she was friendly; she understood that we wanted to look at her fawn, and she would take a piece of sugar-cane from an outstretched hand. She walked up to the open dining-room door, and gazed thoughtfully into the twilight of the rooms, but she never again crossed the threshold. She had by this time lost her bell, and came and went away in silence.

My houseboys suggested that I should let them catch Lulu's fawn, and keep him as we had once kept Lulu. But I thought it would make a boorish return for Lulu's elegant confidence in us.

It also seemed to me that the free union between my house and the antelope was a rare, honourable thing. Lulu came in from the wild world to show that we were on goods terms with it, and she made my house one with the African landscape, so that nobody could tell where the one stopped and the other began. Lulu knew the place of the giant forest-hog's lair and had seen the rhino copulate. In Africa there is a cuckoo which sings in the middle of the hot days in the midst of the forest, like the sonorous heartbeat of the world. I had never had the luck to see her, neither had anyone that I knew, for nobody could tell me how she looked. But Lulu had perhaps walked on a narrow green deerpath just under the branch on which the cuckoo was sitting. I was then reading a book about the old great Empress of China, and of how after the birth of her son, young Yahanola came on a visit to her old home; she set forth from the Forbidden City in her golden, green-hung palanquin. My house, I thought, was now like the house of the young Empress's father and mother.

The two antelopes, the big and the small, were round by my house all that summer; sometimes there was an interval of a fortnight, or three weeks, between their visits, but at other times we saw them every day. In the beginning of the next rainy season my houseboys told me that Lulu had come back with a new fawn. I did not see the fawn myself, for by this time they did not come up quite close to the house, but later I saw three bushbucks together in the forest.

The league between Lulu and her family and my house lasted for many years. The bushbucks were often in the neighbourhood of the house, they came out of the woods and went back again as if my grounds were a province of the wild country. They came mostly just before sunset, and first moved in amongst the trees like delicate dark silhouettes on the dark green, but when they stepped out to graze on the lawn in the light of the afternoon sun their coats shone like copper. One of them was Lulu, for she came up near to the house, and walked about sedately, pricking her ears when a car arrived, or when we opened a window; and the dogs would know her. She became darker in colour with age. Once I came driving up in front of my house with a friend and found three bushbucks on the terrace there, round the salt that was laid out for my cows.

It was a curious thing that apart from the first big bushbuck, Lulu's bwana, who had stood under the Cape chestnut with his head up, no male bushbuck was amongst the antelopes that came to my house. It seemed that we had to do with a forest matriachy.

The hunters and naturalists of the colony took an interest in my bushbucks, and the game warden drove out to the farm to see them, and did see them here. A correspondent wrote about them in the *East African Standard*.

The years in which Lulu and her people came round to my house were the happiest of my life in Africa. For that reason, I came to look upon my acquaintance with the forest antelopes as upon a great boon, and a token of friendship from Africa. All the country was in it, good omens, old convenants, a song:

'Make haste, my beloved, and be thou like to a roe or to a young hart upon the mountain of spices.'

During my last years in Africa I saw less and less of Lulu and her family. Within the year before I went away I do not think that they ever came. Things had changed; south of my farm land had been given out to farmers and the forest had been cleared here, and houses built. Tractors were heaving up and down where the glades had been. Many of the new settlers were keen sportsmen and the rifles sang in the landscape. I believe that the game withdrew to the west and went into the woods of the Masai Reserve.

I do not know how long an antelope lives; probably Lulu has died a long time ago.

Often, very often, in the quiet hours of daybreak, I have dreamed that I have heard Lulu's clear bell, and in my sleep my heart has run full of joy. I have woken up expecting something very strange and sweet to happen, just now, in a moment.

When I have then lain and thought of Lulu, I have wondered if in her life in the woods she ever dreamed of the bell. Would there pass in her mind, like shadows upon water, pictures of people and dogs?

If I know a song of Africa – I thought – of the giraffe, and the African new moon lying on her back, of the ploughs in the fields, and the sweaty faces of the coffee-pickers, does Africa know a song of me? Would the air over the plain quiver with a colour that I had had on, or the children invent a game in which my name was, or the full moon throw a shadow over the gravel of the drive that was like me, or would the eagles of Ngong look out for me?

I have not heard from Lulu, since I went away, but from Kamante I have heard, and from my other houseboys in Africa. It is not more than a month since I had the last letter from him. But these communications from Africa come to me in a strange, unreal way, and are more like shadows, or mirages, than like news of a reality.

For Kamante cannot write, and he does not know English. When he, or my other people, take it into their heads to send me their tidings, they go to one of the professional Indian or Native letter-writers who are sitting with their writing desk, paper, pen, and ink, outside the post offices, and explain to them what shall be in the letter. The professional writers do not know much English either, and can hardly be said to know how to write, but they themselves believe that they can. To show off their skill they enrich the letters with a number of flourishes, which makes them difficult to decipher. They have also a habit of writing the letters in three or four different kinds of ink, and, whatever their motive for this is, it gives the impression that they are short of ink and are squeezing the last drop out of a number of ink-bottles. From all these efforts come the sort of messages that people got from the Oracle of Delphi. There is a depth in the letters that I get; you feel that there is some vital communication which has been heavy on the heart of the sender, which has made him walk in a long way from the Kikuyu Reserve to the post office. But it is wrapped up in darkness. The cheap and dirty little sheet of paper that, when it comes to you, has travelled many thousand miles, seems to speak and speak, even to scream to you, but it tells you nothing at all.

Kamante, however, in this as in most other ways, is different from other people. As a correspondent he has a manner of his own. He puts three or four letters into the same envelope, and has them marked: *1st Letter, 2nd Letter*, and so on. They all contain the same things, repeated over and over. Perhaps he wants to make a deeper impression upon me by repetition, he had that way in talking when there was anything that he particularly wanted me to understand or remember. Perhaps it is difficult for him to break off when he feels that he has got into contact with a friend at such a great distance.

Kamante writes that he has been out of work for a long time. I was not surprised to hear of it, for he was really caviare to the general. I had educated a royal cook and left him in a new colony. It was with him a case of 'open sesame'. Now the word has been lost, and the stone has closed for good round the mystic treasures that it had in it. Where the great chef walked in deep thought, full of knowledge, nobody sees anything but a little bandy-legged Kikuyu, a dwarf with a flat, still face.

What has Kamante got to say when he walks in to Nairobi, takes up his stand before the greedy supercilious Indian letter-writer, and expounds to him a message that is to go round half the world? The lines are crooked and there is no order in the phrases of the letter. But Kamante has in him a greatness of soul of which the people who knew him will still hear the note in the cracked disordered music; even as an echo of the harp of the herdboy David.

This is a '2nd letter':

'I was not forget you Memsahib. Honoured Memsahib. Now all your servants they never glad because you was from the country. If we was bird we fly and see you. Then we turn. Then your old farm it was good place for cow small calf black people. Now they had no anything cows goat sheep they has no anything. Now all bad people they enjoy in their heart because your old servant they come poor people now. Now God know in his heart all this to help sometime your servant.'

And in a '3rd letter' Kamante gives an example of the way in which the Native can say a handsome thing to you, he writes:

'Write and tell us if you turn. We think you turn. Because why? We think that you shall never can forget us. Because why? We think that you remembered still all our face and our mother names.'

A white man who wanted to say a pretty thing to you would write: 'I can never forget you.' The African says: 'We do not think of you, that you can ever forget us.'

2

A
SHOOTING
ACCIDENT ON
THE FARM

The Shooting Accident

On the evening of the nineteenth of December I walked out of my house before going to bed, to see if there was any rain coming. Many farmers in the highlands were, I believe, doing the same thing at that hour. Sometimes, in a lucky year, we would get a few heavy showers just round Christmas, and it was a great thing for the young coffee, which has set on the trees after the flowering in the short rains of October. This night there was no sign of rain. The sky was serene and silently triumphant, resplendent with stars.

The stellar heaven of the equator is richer than that of the north, and you see it more because you are out more at night. In northern Europe, winter nights are too cold to allow one much pleasure in the contemplation of the stars, and in summer one hardly distinguishes them within the clear night sky, that is as pale as a dog-violet.

The tropical night has the companionability of a Roman Catholic cathedral compared to the Protestant churches of the north, which let you in on business only. Here in the great room everybody comes and goes, this is the place where things are going on. To Arabia and Africa, where the sun of the midday kills you, night is the time for travelling and enterprise. The stars have been named here, they have been guides to human beings for many centuries, drawing them in long lines across the desert sands and the sea, one towards the east, and another to the west, or the north and south. Cars run well at night, and it is pleasant to motor under the stars; you get into the habit of fixing visits to friends up-country by the time of the next full moon. You start safaris by the new moon, to have the benefit of the whole row of moonlight nights. It is then strange, when back on a visit to Europe, to find your friends of the towns living out of touch with the moves of the moon and almost in ignorance of them. The young moon was the sign of action to Khadija's camel man, whose caravan was to start off when she appeared in the sky. With his face towards her he was one of the 'philosophers who spin out of moonlight systems of the universe'. He must have looked at her much, that he made her his sign in which to conquer.

I had got a name amongst the Natives, because a number of times I had happened to be, on the farm, the first to see the new moon, like a thin silver bow in the sunset; particularly because, two or three years running, I had been the first to catch sight of the new moon of the month of Ramadan, the Mohammedan's holy month.

The farmer slowly turns his eyes all round the horizon. First to the east, for from the east, if it comes, comes the rain, and there stands clear Spica in the Virgin. Then south, to greet the Southern Cross, doorkeeper of the great world, faithful to travellers and beloved by them, and higher up, under the luminous streak of the Milky Way, Alpha and Beta in the Centaur. To the south-west sparkles Sirius, great in heaven, and the thoughtful Canopus, and to the west above the faint outline of the Ngong Hills, now nearly unbroken, the radiant diamond ornament, Rigel, Betelgeuse and Bellatrix. He turns to the north last, for to the north we go back in the end, and there he runs upon the Great Bear himself, only he is now calmly standing on his head on account of the heavenly perspective, and that has all the air of a bearish joke, that cheers the heart of the Nordic emigrant.

People who dream when they sleep at night know of a special kind of happiness which the world of the day holds not, a placid ecstasy, and ease of heart, that are like honey on the tongue. They also know that the real glory of dreams lies in their atmosphere of unlimited freedom. It is not the freedom of the dictator, who enforces his own will on the world, but the freedom of the artist, who has no will, who is free of will. The pleasure of the true dreamer does not lie in the substance of the dream, but in this: that there things happen without any interference from his side, and altogether outside his control. Great landscapes create themselves, long splendid views, rich and delicate colours, roads, houses, which he has never seen or heard of. Strangers appear and are friends or enemies, although the person who dreams has never done anything about them. The ideas of flights and pursuit are recurrent in dreams and are equally enrapturing. Excellent witty things are said by everybody. It is true that if remembered in the day-time they will fade and lose their sense, because they belong to a different plane, but as soon as the one who dreams lies down at night, the current is again closed and he remembers their excellence. All the time the feeling of immense freedom is surrounding him and running through him like air and light, an unearthly bliss. He is a privileged person, the one who has got nothing to do, but for whose enrichment and pleasure all things are brought together; the Kings of Tarshish shall bring gifts. He takes part in a great battle or ball, and wonders the while that he should be, in the midst of those events, so far privileged as to be lying down. It is when one begins to lose the consciousness of freedom, and when the idea of necessity enters the world at all, when there is any hurry or strain anywhere, a letter to be written or a train to catch, when you have got to work, to make the horses of the dream gallop, or to make the rifles go off, that the dream is declining, and turning into the nightmare, which belongs to the poorest and most vulgar class of dreams.

The thing which in the waking world comes nearest to a dream is night in a big town, where nobody knows one or the African night. There too is infinite freedom: it is there that things are going on, destinies are made round you, there is activity on all sides, and it is none of your concern.

Here now, as soon as the sun was down, the air was full of bats, cruising as noiselessly as cars upon asphalt; the nighthawk swept past too: the bird that sits on the road and in the eyes of which the lights of your car gleam red a moment before he flutters up vertically in front of your wheels. The little spring-hares were out on the roads, moving in their own way, sitting down suddenly and jumping along to a rhythm, like miniature kangaroos. The cicadas sing an endless song in the long grass, smells run along the earth and falling stars run over the sky, like tears over a cheek. You are the privileged person to whom everything is taken. The Kings of Tarshish shall bring gifts.

A few miles out, in the Masai Reserve, the zebra are now changing their pasture, the flocks wander over the grey plain like lighter stripes upon it, the buffalo are out grazing on the long slopes of the hills. My young men of the farm would come by, two or three together, walking one after the other like narrow dark shadows on the lawn; they were afoot and aiming straight at their own object, they were not working for me, and it was none of my concern. They themselves accentuated the position by just slackening their pace as they caught sight of my burning cigarette-end outside the house, and saluting without stopping.

'Jambo Msabu.'

'Jambo Morani' – young warriors – 'where are you going?'

'We are going to Kathegu's manyatta. Kathegu has a big Ngoma on to-night. Good-bye, Msabu.'

If they walk together in bigger parties they will bring their own drum to the dance, and you hear it a long way away, like the throbbing of a small pulse in the finger of the night. And suddenly, to the ear that has not been listening for it, comes what is not so much a sound as a deep vibration of the air, the distant short roar of the lion. He is afoot, he is hunting, things are going on, out there where he is. It is not repeated, but it has widened the horizon; the long dungas and the waterhole are brought to you.

As I was standing before my house a shot fell, not far off. One shot. Then again the stillness of the night closed on all sides. After a while, as if they had been pausing to listen and were now taking it up once more, I heard the cicadas chiming their monotonous little song in the grass.

There is something strangely determinate and fatal about a single shot in the night. It is as if someone had cried a message to you in one word, and would not repeat it. I stood for some time wondering what it had meant. Nobody could aim at anything at this hour, and, to scare away something, a person would fire two shots or more.

It might have been my old Indian carpenter Pooran Singh down at the mill, firing at a couple of hyena that had slunk into the millyard and were eating the straps of oxhide hung up there, with stones as weights to them, to be made into reins for our wagons. Pooran Singh was no hero, but he might have put the door of his hut ajar for the sake of his reins and blown off his old shotgun. Still he would have let off both barrels, and would probably have loaded and shot again, once he had tasted the sweetness of heroism. But one shot – and then silence?

I waited for some time for the second shot; nothing came, and as I looked again at the sky there was no rain coming either. So I went to bed, taking a book with me, and leaving the lamp to burn. In Africa, when you pick up a book worth reading, out of the deadly consignments which good ships are being made to carry out all the way from Europe, you read it as an author would like his book to be read, praying to God that he may have it in him to go on as beautifully as he has begun. Your mind runs, transported, upon a fresh deep green track.

Two minutes later a motor-cycle rounded the drive at a terrific speed and stopped in front of the house, and someone knocked hard upon the long window of my sitting-room. I put on a skirt and a coat and a pair of shoes, took the lamp and went out. Outside was my mill-manager, wild-eyed and sweating in the lamplight. His name was Belknap, he was an American and an exceptionally capable, inspired mechanic, but of an uneven mind. With him things were either nearing the Millennium, or dark without a glimpse of hope. When he first came into my employ he had upset me by his varying views of life, and of prospects and conditions of the farm, as if he had had me up in an enormous mental swing; later I had got used to them. These ups and downs were no more than a kind of emotional daily gymnastics to a lively temperament, much in need of exercise, and to which too little was happening; it is a common phenomenon with energetic young white men in Africa, particularly with those who have spent their early life in towns. But here he came out of the hands of a tragedy, and was as yet undecided as to whether he should satiate his hungry soul by making the most of it, or escape from its grimness by making as little of it as possible, and in this dilemma he looked like a very young boy running for his life to announce a catastrophe; he stuttered as he spoke. In the end he made very little of it, for it held no part in it for him to play, and fate had let him down once more.

By this time, Farah had come from his house, and listened to his narrative with me.

Belknap told me how peacefully and pleasantly the tragedy had started. His cook had had a day off, and in his absence a party had been given in the kitchen by the seven-year-old kitchen-toto, Kabero, a son of my old squatter and nearest neighbour on the farm, the old fox Kaninu. As, late in the evening, the company became very gay, Kabero had brought in his master's gun and, to his wild friends of the plains and shambas, had acted the part of a white man. Belknap was a keen poultry farmer: he made capons and poulardes and bought up pure-bred chicken at the Nairobi sales, and he kept a shotgun on his verandah to frighten away hawks and cerval-cats. When later we talked the case over, Belknap held that the gun had not been loaded, but that the children had looked up the cartridges and loaded it themselves, but here I think that his memory failed him, they could hardly have done it if they had wanted to, and it was more likely that the gun had for once been left loaded on the verandah. However it got there, the cartridge was in the barrel when Kabero, in the greatness of youth and popularity, aimed straight in amongst his guests and pulled the trigger. The shot had boomed through the house. Three of the children had been slightly wounded, and had fled from the kitchen in terror. Two were there now, badly hurt or dead. Belknap finished his tale by a long anathema of the continent of Africa and of the things that happen there.

While he talked, my houseboys had come out, very silent; they went in again, and brought out a hurricane-lamp. We got out dressing and disinfectant. It would be a waste of time to try to start the car, and we ran as quickly as we could through the forest down to Belknap's house. The swinging hurricane-lamp threw our shadows from the one side of the narrow road to the other. As we ran on, we were met by a succession of short raw cracked shrieks – death squeals of a child.

The kitchen door was flung back, as if Death, after having rushed in, had rushed out again, and left the place in dire devastation, a chicken-house that the badger has been in. There was a kitchen lamp burning on the table and smoking sky-high, and in the small room the smell of gunpowder still hung. The gun was on the table beside the lamp. There was blood all over the kitchen: I slipped in it on the floor. Hurricane-lamps are difficult to direct on to any particular spot, but they give a very striking illumination of a whole room of situation; I remember the things I have seen by the light of a hurricane-lamp better than others.

I knew the children who had been shot, from the plains of the farm, where they had herded their fathers' sheep. Wamai, Jogona's son, a lively little boy who had for some time been a pupil at the school, was lying on the floor between the door and the table. He was not dead, but not far from death, and unconscious even though he groaned a little. We lifted him aside, to be able to move. The child that shrieked was Wanyangerri, who had been the youngest of the party in the kitchen. He was sitting up, leaning forwards, towards the lamp; the blood spouted, like water from a post, from his face – if one could still say that, for he must have stood straight in front of the barrel when it was fired and it had taken his lower jaw clean off. He held his arms out from his sides and moved them up and down like pump-spears, as the wings of a chicken go, after it has had its head cut off.

When you are brought suddenly within the presence of such disaster, there seems to be but one advice – it is the remedy of the shooting-field and the farmyard: that you should kill quickly and at any cost. And yet you know that you cannot kill, and your brain turns with fear. I put my hands to the child's head and pressed it in my despair, and, as if I had really killed him, he at the same moment stopped screaming, and sat erect with his arms hanging down, as if he was made of wood. So now I know what it feels like to heal by imposition of hands.

It is a difficult thing to bandage a patient whose face is half shot off, in your endeavour to stop the bleeding you may choke him. I had to lift the little boy on to Farah's knee, and make Farah hold his head in position for me, for if it fell forward I could not get the dressing fastened, and if it fell back the blood ran down and filled his throat. In the end, while he sat so still, I got the bandages placed.

We lifted Wamai on to the table and held the lamp up to look at him. He had received the full charge of the gun into his throat and chest. He did not bleed much, only a thin trail of blood ran down from the corner of his mouth. It was surprising to see this Native child, who had been as full of life as a fawn, so quiet now. While we looked at him his own face changed and took on an expression of deep surprise. I sent Farah to the house to fetch the car, for we had no time to waste in bringing the children into hospital.

While we waited I inquired after Kabero, the boy who had fired the gun and shed all this blood. Belknap then told me a queer story about him. A couple of days earlier Kabero had bought an old pair of shorts from his master, and was to pay him with a rupee from his wages. When the shot fell, and Belknap ran out to the kitchen, Kabero was standing in the middle of the room with the smoking gun in his hand. He stared at Belknap for a second, and then dived into the pocket of the very shorts that he had so newly bought and had put on for the party, drew up a rupee and laid it on the table with his left hand, while with his right he threw the gun also on the table. And in that final settlement with the world he was gone; he actually, although we did not know of it at the moment, in this great gesture, disappeared from the face of the earth. It was an unusual behaviour in a Native, for they generally manage to keep a debt, and in particular a debt to a white man, within the outskirts of their mind. Perhaps the moment to Kabero had looked so much like the day of judgement, that he felt he had got to play up to it; perhaps he was trying, in the hour of need, to secure a friend. Or the shock, the boom, and the death of his friends round him, had knocked in the whole of the boy's small sphere of ideas, so that bits of the periphery had been flung into the very centre of his consciousness.

At that time I had an old Overland car. I shall never write anything against her, for she served me well through many years. But it was rare that she could be induced to run on more than two cylinders. Her lights were out of order too, so that I used to drive in to dances at the Muthaiga Club with a hurricane-lamp swaddled in a red silk handkerchief for a back light. She had to be pushed into starting, and upon this night it took a long time.

Visitors to my house had been complaining of the state of my road, and during the death-drive of that night I realized that they had been right. I first let Farah drive, but I thought that he was deliberately going into all the deep holes and wagon-tracks of the road, and I took the steering-wheel myself. For this I had to get off by the pond to wash my hands in the dark water. The distance to Nairobi seemed infinitely long. I thought that I might have driven home to Denmark in the time that it took us.

The Native hospital of Nairobi lies on the hill just before you drive down into the cup of the town. It was dark now, and seemed peaceful. We had much trouble to wake it up; in the end we got hold of an old Goan doctor or doctor's assistant, who appeared in a queer sort of negligée. He was a big fat man of a very placid manner, and had a strange way of making the same gesture first with one hand and then with the other. As I helped to lift Wamai out of the car I thought that he stirred and stretched himself a little, but when we brought him into the brightly lighted room in the hospital, he was dead. The old Goan kept waving his hand at him, saying: 'He is dead.' And then again at Wanyangerri, saying: 'He is alive.' I never saw this old man again, for I never came back to the hospital at night, which was probably his hour there. At the time, I thought his manner very annoying, but afterwards I felt as if fate itself in a number of big white cloaks, the one on the top of the other, had met us at the threshold of the house, dealing out life and death impartially.

Wanyangerri woke up from his trance when we took him into the hospital, and at once got into a terrible panic; he would not be left but clung to me and to anybody near him and cried and wept in the greatest anguish. The old Goan in the end calmed him by some injection, looked at me over his spectacles and said: 'He is alive.' I left the children there, the dead and the live, upon two stretchers, for their different fates.

Belknap, who had come in with us on his motor-bicycle, mostly so as to help us to push the car into starting, should she stop on the road, now thought that we ought to report the accident to the police. So we drove down into town to the River Road Police Station, and thereby ran straight into the night-life of Nairobi. There was no white police officer present when we came, and while they sent for him we waited outside in the car. The street had an avenue of tall eucalyptus trees, the tree of all pioneer-towns of the highlands; at night their very long narrow leaves give out a queer pleasant smell, and look strange in the light of the street-lamps. A big buxom young Swaheli woman was carried into the police station by a group of Native policemen; she resisted with all her might, scratched their faces, and screamed like a pig. A party of brawlers were brought in, still eager, upon the steps of the station, to go for one another; and a thief, I believe, who had just been caught, came down the street with a whole tail of night-revellers after him, who were taking his part, or the part of the police, and were loudly debating the case. In the end a young police officer arrived, straight, I believe, from a gay party. He was a disappoint-ment to Belknap, for he began to take down his report with the keenest interest and at a terrific speed, but then fell into deep thoughts, dragged his pencil slowly over the page and finally gave up writing and put his pencil back into his pocket. I was cold in the night air. At last we could drive home.

While I was still in bed the next morning, I felt, by the concentrated stillness outside the house, that there were many people about it. I knew who they were: the old men of the farm, squatting upon the stones, munching, sniffing their *tombacco*, spitting, and whispering. I also knew what they wanted: they had come to inform me that they wished to set a Kyama on the case of the shot of last night, and of the death of the children.

A Kyama is an assembly of the Elders of a farm, which is authorized by the Government to settle the local differences amongst the squatters. The members of the Kyama gather round a crime, or an accident, and will sit over it for many weeks, battening upon mutton, talk, and disaster. I knew that now the old men would want to talk the whole matter over with me, and also that they would, if they could, in the end make me come into their court to give the final judgement in the case. I did not want to take up an endless discussion of the tragedy of the night, at this moment, and sent for my horse to get out and away from them.

As I came out from the house I found, as I expected, the whole circle of the Ancients to the left of it, near the boys' huts. For the sake of their own dignity as an assembly they pretended not to see me, until they realized that I was going away. They then stumbled on to their old legs in great haste, and began to flap their arms at me. I waved my hand to them in return, and rode off.

Riding in the Reserve

I rode into the Masai Reserve. I had to cross the river to get there; riding on, I got into the Game Reserve in a quarter of an hour. It had taken me some time, while I had lived on the farm, to find a place where I could get over the river on horseback: the descent was stony, and the slope up the other side very steep, but 'once in – how the delighted spirit pants for joy'.

Here lay before you a hundred miles' gallop over grass and open undulating land; there was not a fence nor a ditch, and no road. There was no human habitation except the Masai villages, and those were deserted half the year, when the great wanderers took themselves and their herds off to other pastures. There were low thorn trees regularly spread over the plain, and long deep valleys with dry river-beds of big flat stones, where you had to find a deerpath here and there to take you across. After a little while you became aware of how still it was out here. I made a verse about it:

Across the plain the long grass runs, before the blowing weather,
In loneliness the plain, the wind, the heart, play together.

Now, looking back on my life in Africa, I feel that it might altogether be described as the existence of a person who had come from a rushed and noisy world, into a still country.

A little before the rains, the Masai burn off the old dry grass, and while the plains are thus lying black and waste they are unpleasant to travel on: you will get the black charred dust, which the hoofs of your horse raise, all over you and into your eyes, and the burnt grass-stalks are sharp as glass; your dogs get their feet cut on them. But when the rains come, and the young green grass is fresh on the plains, you feel as if riding upon springs, and the horse gets a little mad with the pleasantness. The various kinds of gazelles come to the green places to graze, and there look like toy animals stood upon a billiard table. You may ride into a herd of eland; the mighty peaceful beasts will let you get close to them before they start trotting off, their long horns streaming backwards over their raised necks, the large loose flaps of breastskin, that make them look square, swaying as they jog. They seem to have come out of an old Egyptian epitaph, but there they have been ploughing the fields, which gives them a familiar and domesticated air. The giraffe keep farther away in the Reserve.

At times, in the first month of the rains, a sort of wild white fragrant pink flowers so richly all over the Reserve that at a distance the plains look patched with snow.

I turned to the animal world from the world of men; my heart was heavy with the tragedy of the night. The old men sitting at my house made me uneasy; in old times people must have had that feeling when they thought it likely that a witch of the neighbourhood had fixed her mind upon them, or was at the very moment carrying a wax-child under her clothes, to be baptized with their own name.

My relations with the Natives in the legal affairs of the farm were altogether of a queer nature. Since, before anything, I wanted peace on the land, I could not keep out of them, for a dispute between the squatters, which has not been solemnly settled, was like those sores that you get in Africa, and which they there call veldt-sores: they heal on the surface if you let them, and go on festering and running underneath until you dig them up to the bottom and have them cleaned all through. The Natives themselves were aware of this, and if they really wanted a matter settled they would ask me to give judgement.

As I knew nothing of their laws the figure that I cut at these great courts of justice would often be that of a prima donna who does not remember a word of her part and has to be prompted through it by the rest of the cast. This task my old men took upon themselves with tact and patience. It would also at times be the figure of an affronted prima donna who is shocked by her rôle and, refusing to go on with it, walks off the stage. When this happened, my audience took it as a hard blow from the hand of destiny, an act of God outside their understanding; they looked on it in silence and spat.

The ideas of justice of Europe and Africa are not the same and those of the one world are unbearable to the other. To the African there is but one way of counter-balancing the catastrophes of existence, it shall be done by replacement; he does not look for the motive of an action. Whether you lie in wait for your enemy and cut his throat in the dark; or you fell a tree, and a thoughtless stranger passes by and is killed: so far as punishment goes, to the Native mind, it is the same thing. A loss has been brought upon the community and must be made up for, some- where, by somebody. The Native will not give time or thought to the weighing up of guilt or desert: either he fears that this may lead him too far, or he reasons that such things are no concern of his. But he will devote himself, in endless speculations, to the method by which crime or disaster shall be weighed up in sheep and goats – time does not count to him; he leads you solemnly into a sacred maze of sophistry. In those days this went against my ideas of justice.

All Africans are the same in these rites. The Somali have a very different mentality from the Kikuyu and a deep contempt for them, but they will sit down in identical manner to weigh up murder, rape, or fraud against their stock at home in Somaliland – dearly beloved she-camels, and horses, the names and pedigree of which are written in their hearts.

Once the news came to Nairobi of how Farah's little brother, who was ten years old, in a place called Buramur, had taken up a stone and thrown it at a boy of a different tribe, knocking out two of his teeth. Over this matter representatives of the two tribes met at the farm to sit upon the floor of Farah's house and talk, night after night. Old lean men came, who had been to Mecca and wore a green turban, arrogant young Somalis who, when they were not attending to really serious matters, were gun- bearers to the great European travellers and hunters, and dark-eyed, round-faced boys, who were shyly representing their family and who did not say a word, but were devoutly listening and learning. Farah told me that the matter was considered so grave because the boy's looks had been ruined: he might find it difficult, when his time came, to get married, and would have to come down in his pretensions as to birth or beauty in his bride. In the end the penance was fixed at fifty camels, which means half weregild, full weregild being one hundred camels. Fifty camels were then bought, far away in Somaliland, to be, ten years hence, laid on to the price of a Somali maiden, and to turn her eyes off the two missing teeth of her bridegroom; perhaps the foundation of a tragedy was laid. Farah himself considered that he had got off lightly.

The Natives of the farm never realized my views on their legal systems, and they came to me first of all for their indemnification when any ill-luck befell them.

Once, in the coffee-picking season, a young Kikuyu girl named Wamboi was run over by a bullock cart outside my house and killed. The carts were taking coffee from the field to the mill, and I had forbidden anybody to go riding on them. Otherwise I should have had at every trip a party of gay coffee-picking girls and children taking a slow joy-ride – for anybody can walk quicker than a bullock – all across the farm, and it would be too heavy on my bullocks. The young drivers, however, did not have it in them to send away the dreamy-eyed girls who kept running alongside their carts and begging for this great pleasure; all they could do was to tell them to jump off where the road came into sight of my house. But Wamboi fell as she jumped and the wheel of the cart went over her small dark head and broke the skull; a little blood trailed in the cart-track.

I sent for her old father and mother, who came in from the picking-field and wailed over her. I knew that this would also mean a heavy loss to them, for the girl had been of marriage-age, and would have brought them in her price of sheep and goats and a heifer or two. This they had been looking forward to since her birth. I was considering how much I ought to help them, when they forestalled me by turning upon me, with great energy, their claim for a full indemnification.

No, I said, I would not pay. I had told the girls of the farm that I would not have them riding on the carts, all people were aware of that. The old people nodded; there was nothing here with which they did not agree, but they stuck to their claim immovably. Their argument was that somebody must pay. They could get no contradiction to the principle into their heads, no more than they could have got the theory of relativity in there. And it was not greed or spite which, when I broke off the discussion and went back, made them follow at my heels; it was, as if I had been indeed magnetic, a law of nature.

They sat down and waited outside my house. They were poor people, small and underfed; they looked like a pair of little badgers on my lawn. They sat there till the sun was down and I could hardly distinguish them against the grass. They were sunk in deep grief; their bereavement and their economic loss melted into one overwhelming distress. Farah was away for the day; in his absence, at the time when the lamps were lighted in my house, I sent them out money to buy a sheep to eat. It was a bad move; they took it as the first sign of exhaustion in a besieged city and sat down for the night. I do not know if they would have had it in them to go away, if it had not been that, late in the evening, they conceived the idea of running the young cart-driver for their damage. The idea lifted them off the grass and away, suddenly, without a word, and took them early next morning to Dagoretti, where our Assistant District Commissioner lived.

It brought upon the farm a long murder case and many swaggering young Native policemen. But all that the A.D.C. offered to do for them was to have the driver hanged for murder, and even that he gave up when he had got the evidence in the case, and the Ancients would not hold a Kyama upon the matter after both he and I had turned it away. So in the end the old people had to sit down under a law of relativity of which they did not understand a word, as other people have had to do.

At times I grew tired of my Ancients of the Kyama and told them what I thought of them – 'You old men,' I said, 'are fining the young men in order that it shall be impossible for them to collect any money for themselves. The young men cannot move for you, and then you buy up all the girls yourselves.' The old men listened attentively, the small black eyes in their dry and wrinkled faces glittered, their thin lips moved gently as if they were repeating my words: they were pleased to hear, for once, an excellent principle put into speech.

With all our diversities of views, my position as a judge to the Kikuyu held a profusion of potentialities, and was dear to me. I was young then, and had meditated upon the ideas of justice and injustice, but mostly from the angle of the person who is being judged; in a judge's seat I had not been. I took great trouble to judge rightly, and for peace on the farm. At times, when the problems became difficult, I had to retire and take time to think them over, covering my head with a mental cloak so that nobody should come and talk to me about them. This was always an effective move with the people of the farm, and I heard them, a long time afterwards, talk with respect of the case that had been so deep that no one could look through it in less than a week. One can always impress a Native by wasting more time over a matter than he does himself, only it is a difficult thing to accomplish.

But that the Natives should want me for a judge, and that they should consider my verdict of value to them, of this the explanation is found in their mythological or theological mentality. The Europeans have lost the faculty for building up myths or dogma, and for what we want of these we are dependent upon the supplies of our past. But the mind of the African moves naturally and easily upon such deep and shadowy paths. This gift of theirs comes out strongly in their relations with white people.

You find it already in the names which they deal out to the Europeans with whom they come in contact, after a very short acquaintance. You have got to know these names if you are to send a runner with letters to a friend, or find the way in a car to his house, for the Native world knows him by no other name. I have had an unsociable neighbour, who would never entertain a guest in his house, who was named *Sahana Modja* – One Cover. My Swedish friend Eric Otter was *Resase Modja* – One Cartridge – which meant that he did not need more than one single cartridge to kill, and which was a fine name to be known by. There was a keen automobilist of my acquaintance, who was called 'Half man – half car'. When Natives name white men after animals – the fish, the giraffe, the fat bull – their minds run upon the lines of the old fables, and these white men, I believe, in their dark consciousness figure as both men and beasts.

And there is magic in words: a person who has for many years been known to all his surroundings by the name of an animal in the end comes to feel familiar with and related to the animal: he recognizes himself in it. When he is back in Europe it is strange to him to feel that no one ever connects him with it.

Once, in the London Zoo, I saw again an old retired government official, whom in Africa I had known as *Bwana Tembu* – Mr Elephant. He was standing, all by himself, before the elephant-house, sunk in deep contemplation of the elephants. Perhaps he would go there often. His Native servants would have thought it in the order of things that he should be there, but probably no one in all London, except I who was there only for a few days, would have quite understood him.

The Native mind works in strange ways, and is related to the mind of bygone people, who naturally imagined that Odin, so as to see through the whole world, gave away one of his eyes; and who figured the God of love as a child, ignorant of love. It is likely that the Kikuyu of the farm saw my greatness as a judge in the fact that I knew nothing whatever of the laws according to which I judged.

Because of their gift for myths, the Native can also do things to you against which you cannot guard yourself and from which you cannot escape. They can turn you into a symbol. I was well aware of the process, and for my own use I had a word for it – in my mind I called it that they were brazen-serpenting me. Europeans who have lived for a long time with Natives will understand what I mean, even if the word is not quite correctly used according to the Bible. I believe that in spite of all our activities in the land, of the scientific and mechanical progress there, and of Pax Britannica itself, this is the only practical use that the Natives have ever had out of us.

They could not make use of all white men for the purpose, and not of one man and another equally. They gave us, within their world, precedence of rank according to our utility to them as brazen-serpents. Many of my friends – Denys Finch-Hatton, both Galbraith and Berkeley Cole, Sir Northrup MacMillan – ranked highly with the Natives in this capacity.

Lord Delamere was a brazen-serpent of the first magnitude. I remember that I once travelled in the highlands at the time when the great pest of hoppers came on to the land. The grasshoppers had been there the year before, now their small black offspring appeared, to eat what they had left, and to leave not a leaf of grass where they had passed. To the Natives this was a terrible blow; after what they had gone through it was too much for them to bear. Their hearts broke, they panted, or howled like dying dogs, they ran their heads against a wall in the air before them. I then happened to tell them how I had driven through Delamere's farm and had seen the hoppers on it, all over the place, in his paddocks and on his grazing land, and I added that Delamere had been in great rage and despair about them. At that same moment the listeners became quiet and almost at ease. They asked me what Delamere had said of his misfortune, and again asked me to repeat it, and then they said no more.

I did not, as a brazen-serpent, carry the weight of Lord Delamere, still there were occasions when I came in useful to the Natives.

During the war, when the fate of the Carrier Corps lay upon the whole Native world, the squatters of the farm used to come and sit round my house. They did not speak, not even amongst themselves, they turned their eyes upon me and made me their brazen-serpent. I could not very well chase them away, seeing that they did no harm, and besides, if I had done so they would have gone and sat down in some other place. It was a singularly hard thing to bear. I was helped through with it by the fact that my brother's regiment was at that time sent on to the foremost trenches at Vimy Ridge: I could turn my eyes upon him and make him my brazen-serpent.

The Kikuyu made me a chief mourner, or woman of sorrows, when a great distress befell us on the farm. It was what would happen now over the shooting accident. Because I grieved for the children, the people of the farm found it in them to lay the matter aside, and let it rest there for the time being. In regard to our misfortunes they looked upon me as the congregation looks upon the priest who empties the cup alone, but on their behalf.

There is this about witchcraft, that when it has once been practised on you, you will never completely rid yourself of it. I thought it a painful, a very painful process to be hung upon the pole, I wished that I could have escaped it. Still, many years after, there will be occasions when you find yourself thinking: 'Am I to be treated in such a way? – I, who have been a brazen-serpent!'

As I was riding back to the farm, on crossing the river and actually in the water, I met a party of Kaninu's sons, three young men and a boy. They carried spears and came along quickly. When I stopped them and asked for news of their brother Kabero they stood, the water half-way to their knees, with still set faces and downcast eyes; they spoke slowly. Kabero, they said, had not come back, and nothing had been heard of him since he had run away last night. They were now certain that he was dead. He would either have killed himself in his despair – since the idea of suicide comes very naturally to all Natives, and even to Native children – or he had been lost in the bush and the wild animals had eaten him. His brothers had been round looking for him in all directions; they were now on their way out into the Reserve to try to find him there.

When I came up the river-bank on my own land, I turned and looked out over the plain; my land was higher up than the land of the Reserve. There was no sign of life anywhere on the plain, except that a long way out the zebra were grazing and galloping about. As the party of searchers emerged from the bush on the other side of the river, they went on quickly, walking one by one; their small group looked like a short caterpillar rapidly winding its way along on the grass. At times the sun glinted on their weapons. They seemed fairly confident of their direction, but what would it be? In their search for the lost child, their only guide would be the vultures that are always hanging in the sky above a dead body on the plain, and will give you the exact spot of a lion-kill.

But this would be only a very small body, not much of a feast for the gluttons of the air: there would not be many of them to spot it, nor would they be staying on for a very long time.

All this was sad to think of. I rode home.

Wamai

I went to the Kyama followed by Farah. I always had Farah with me in my dealings with the Kikuyu, for while he showed but little sense where his own quarrels were concerned, and like all Somalis would lose his head altogether wherever his tribal feelings and feuds came in, about other people's differences he had wisdom and discretion. He was, besides, my interpreter, for he spoke Swaheli very well.

I knew before I arrived at the assembly that the chief object of the proceeding would now be to shear Kaninu as close as possible. He would see his sheep driven away to all sides, some to indemnify the families of the dead and wounded children, some to maintain the Kyama. From the beginning this went against me. For Kaninu, I thought, had lost his son just as the other fathers, and the fate of his child seemed to me the most tragic of the lot. Wamai was dead and out of it, and Wanyangerri was in hospital, where people were looking after him, but Kabero had been abandoned by all, and nobody knew where his bones lay.

Now Kaninu lent himself exceptionally well to his rôle of the ox, fattened for a feast. He was one of my biggest squatters; on my squatter-list he is down for thirty-five head of cattle, five wives, and sixty goats. His village was close to my wood: I therefore saw much of his children and his goats, and continually had to run in his women for cutting down my big trees. The Kikuyu know nothing of luxury: the richest amongst them live as the poor, and if I went into Kaninu's hut I would find nothing there in the way of furniture except perhaps a small wooden stool to sit on. But there were a number of huts at Kaninu's village, and a lively swarming of old women, young people and children round them. And a long row of cattle, about milking time at sunset, advanced towards the village across the plains, with their blue shadows walking gently on the grass beside them. All this gave to the old lean man in the leather mantle, with the net of fine wrinkles in his dark, shrewd face all filled up with dirt, the orthodox halo of a nabob of the farm.

I and Kaninu had had many heated arguments. I had indeed been threatening to turn him off the farm, all over a particular traffic of his.

Kaninu was on good terms with the neighbouring Masai tribe, and had married four or five of his daughters off to them. The Kikuyu themselves told me how in the old times the Masai had thought it beneath them to intermarry with Kikuyu. But in our days the strange dying nation, to delay its final disappearance, has had to come down in its pride; the Masai women have no children and the prolific young Kikuyu girls are in demand with the tribe. All Kaninu's offspring were good-looking people, and he had brought back a number of sleek romping young heifers across the border of the Reserve in exchange for his young daughters. More than one old Kikuyu paterfamilias in this period became rich in the same way. The big Chief of the Kikuyu, Kinanjui, had sent, I was told, more than twenty of his daughters to the Masai, and had got over a hundred head of cattle back from them.

But a year ago the Masai Reserve had been put into quarantine for foot-and-mouth disease, and no stock could be taken out of it. Here was a grave dilemma in the existence of Kaninu. For the Masai are wanderers, and change their abode according to season, rain, and grazing, and those cows in their herds which lawfully belonged to Kaninu were dragged all over the land and would at times be a hundred miles away, where nobody knew what was happening to them. The Masai are unscrupulous cattle-dealers with anyone, and more so with the Kikuyu whom they despise. They are fine warriors and are said to be great lovers. In their hands the hearts of Kaninu's daughters were turning like the hearts of the Sabine women of old, and he could no longer rely on them. Therefore the resourceful old Kikuyu took to having his cattle shifted at night, when the District Commissioner and the Veterinary Department were supposed to be asleep, over the water to my farm. This was real villainous behaviour on his part, for the quarantine regulations are amongst those which the Natives understand; they think highly of them. Had these cows been found on my land, the farm itself would have been put into quarantine. I therefore set out watchmen down by the river to catch Kaninu's retainers, and on moonlight nights there had been many great dramatic ambuscades, and swift flights along the silver stream, and the heifers, upon which the whole concern turned, stampeded and ran away in all directions.

Jogona, the father of the child Wamai who had been killed, was, on the other hand, a poor man. He had but one old wife, and all he owned in the world were three goats. He was not likely to make more, for he was a very simple person. I knew Jogona well. A year before the accident, and the sitting of the Kyama, a terrible murder had taken place on the farm. Two Indians who were leasing a mill from me a little way higher up the river, and were grinding mealie for the Kikuyu, had been killed in the night, their goods had been stolen, and the murderers were never found. The murder scared off all the Indian traders and storekeepers of the district, as if they had been blown away by a storm; I had had to arm Pooran Singh down at my own mill with an old shotgun to make him stay on, and even at that it had taken much persuasion. I myself had thought, the first nights after the murder, that I heard footsteps round the house, so for a week I had kept a night watchman there, and this man was Jogona. He was very gentle, and would have been of no use against murderers, but he was a friendly old man and pleasant to talk with. He had the manners of a gay child, his broad face wore an inspired and keen expression, and whenever he looked at me he laughed. He now seemed very pleased to see me at the Kyama.

But the Koran itself, which I was studying in those days, says: 'Thou shalt not bend the justice of the law for the benefit of the poor.'

Besides myself, at least one member of the assembly was aware that its purpose was now the flaying of Kaninu: this was Kaninu himself. The other old men sat around, infinitely attentive, and with all their wits collected for the proceedings. Kaninu, on the ground, had drawn his big cloak of goatskin over his head; from time to time he gave out under it a whine or whimper, like that of a dog which is exhausted by howling and is just keeping its misery alive.

The old men wanted to begin with the case of the wounded child Wanyangerri, because it gave them endless opportunity for palaver. What was the indemnification to be if Wanyangerri were dead? If he were disfigured? If he had lost the faculty of speech? Farah, on my behalf, told them that I would not discuss this matter until I had been in Nairobi and had seen the doctor of the hospital. They swallowed their disappointment and got their arguments on the next case ready.

It was up to the Kyama, I told them through Farah, to get this case settled quickly, and they should not sit over it for the rest of their lives. It was clear that it was not a murder case, but a bad accident.

The Kyama honoured my speech with their attention, but as soon as it was finished they opposed it.

'Msabu, we know nothing,' they said. 'But here we see that you do not know enough either, and we understand only a little of what you say to us. It was Kaninu's son who fired the shot. Otherwise how would he be the only one not hurt by it? If you want to hear more about it Mauge here will tell you. His son was there and had one of his ears shot off.'

Mauge was one of the wealthiest squatters, a sort of rival of the farm to Kaninu. He was a very stately man to look at, and his words had weight, although he spoke very slowly and from time to time had to stop and think. 'Msabu,' he said. 'My son told me: the boys all held the gun the one after the other and pointed it at Kabero. But he would not explain to them how to shoot with it, no he would not explain it at all. In the end he took the gun back, and at the same moment it shot, it wounded all the children and killed Wamai, Jogona's son. This is exactly how it happened.'

'I knew all that already,' I said, 'and it is what is called bad luck, and an accident. I might have fired the shot from my house, or you, Mauge, from yours.'

This created a great stir in the Kyama. They all looked at Mauge, who became very uneasy. Then they talked for some time amongst themselves, very lowly, as in a whisper. At last they took up the discussion again. 'Msabu,' they said, 'this time we do not understand one word of what you are saying. We can only believe that you are thinking of a rifle, since you yourself shoot so well with a rifle, but not so well with a shotgun. If it had been a rifle you would have been quite right. But nobody could shoot with a shotgun from your house, or from Mauge's house, down to the house of Bwana Menanya, and kill the people within the house.'

After a short pause I said: 'Everybody now knows that it was Kaninu's son who fired the gun. Kaninu will pay Jogona a number of sheep to make up for the loss. But everybody also knows that Kaninu's son was not a bad child and did not mean to kill Wamai, and the Kaninu will not pay as many sheep as if that had been the case.'

Here an old man by the name of Awaru spoke. He was in closer contact with civilization than the others, for he had been seven years in jail.

'Msabu,' he said, 'you say that Kaninu's son was not bad and that therefore Kaninu will not pay out very many sheep. But if his son had wanted to kill Wamai and had thus been a very bad child, would that have been a good thing to Kaninu? Would he have been so pleased about that, that he would have paid many more sheep?'

'Awaru,' I said, 'you know that Kaninu has lost his son. You go to the school yourself, so you know that this boy was clever at school. If he was as good in all other ways, it is a very bad thing to Kaninu to lose him.'

There was a long pause, not a sound in the ring. At the end of it Kaninu, as if suddenly reminded of a forgotten pain or duty, gave out a long wail.

'Memsahib,' said Farah, 'let these Kikuyu now name the figure that they have in their hearts.' He spoke in Swaheli to me, so that the assembly should understand him, and succeeded in making them ill at ease, for a figure is a concrete thing, which no Native likes to give out. Farah let his eyes run all round the circle and in a haughty way suggested: 'One hundred.' A hundred sheep was a fantastic number, which nobody would seriously have thought of. A silence fell upon the Kyama. The old men felt themselves at the mercy of Somali mockery, and chose to lie low under it. A very old man whispered 'Fifty' but the figure seemed to carry no weight but to be blown aloft in the current of air of Farah's joke.

After a moment Farah himself briskly said 'Forty' in the manner of the experienced cattle-trader, at home with figures and stock. The word set astir the latent ideas of the meeting; they began to talk very lively amongst themselves. They would now need time, and would meditate and cackle much, but all the same a basis for negotiations had been laid. When we were at home again Farah said to me confidently: 'I think that these old men will take forty sheep from Kaninu.'

Kaninu at the Kyama had one more ordeal to go through. For old broad-bellied Kathegu, another big squatter of the farm, father and grandfather to an enormous household, here rose and proposed to go through the sheep and goats which Kaninu was to hand over, indicating them individually one by one. This was all contrary to the custom of any Kyama. Jogona could never have invented the scheme, and I could only believe it to be founded upon an agreement between Kathegu and Jogona, for the benefit of Kathegu. I waited a little to see what would come of it.

Kaninu, to begin with, seemed to give himself up to his martyrdom, he ducked his head and pulled, as if, for each animal named, a tooth was being drawn out of him. But when at last Kathegu, himself hesitating, designated a big yellow goat without horns, Kaninu's heart broke and his strength gave out. He came forward, out of his cloak, in one mighty gesture. For one moment he roared like a bull at me, a bellow for help, an awful *de profundis*, until he saw, in a quick glance, that I was on his side, and that he was not to lose the yellow goat. He then sat down without another sound; only after a while he gave Kathegu a very deep sarcastic glance.

After about a week of sittings and supernumerary sittings of the Kyama, the indemnification was finally fixed at forty sheep, to be paid by Kaninu to Jogona, but no individual sheep were to be indicated in the transfer.

A fortnight later Farah, in the evening while I was dining, gave me fresh news of the case.

Three old Kikuyu from Nyeri, he told me, had arrived at the farm the day before. They had heard of the case in their huts up at Nyeri, and had walked from there to appear on the stage and to plead that Wamai was not the son of Jogona but was their late brother's son, and that therefore the compensation for his death should lawfully fall to them.

I smiled at the impudence, and remarked to Farah that this was just like the Kikuyu of Nyeri. No, said Farah thoughtfully, he believed that they were right. Jogona had indeed come from Nyeri to the farm six years ago, and, from what Farah had gathered, Wamai was not Jogona's son, 'and never had been', Farah said. It was, he went on, a great stroke of luck to Jogona that he had, two days before, been handed over twenty-five of his forty sheep. Otherwise Kaninu would have let them wander off to Nyeri so as to save himself the pain. Farah said, of meeting them on the farm now that they were no longer his. But Jogona would have to look out still, for the Nyeri Kikuyu were not easy to shake off. They had taken up their abode on the farm and were threatening to bring the case before the D.C.

In this way I was prepared for the appearance, a few days later, before my house, of the Nyeri people, who belonged to a low class of Kikuyu, and had all the look of three dirty and shaggy hyenas that had slunk one hundred and fifty miles upon Wamai's blood-track. With them came Jogona, in a state of great agitation and distress. The difference in the attitude of the parties probably arose from that fact that the Nyeri Kikuyu had nothing to lose, while Jogona had twenty-five sheep. The three strangers sat on the stones with no more manifestation of life than three ticks upon a sheep. I had no sympathy with their cause, for, whatever the circumstances were, they had taken no interest in the dead child while he had lived, and I was now sorry for Jogona, who had behaved well at the Kyama, and had, I believed, grieved over Wamai. Jogona, when I questioned him, trembled and sighed so that it was impossible to understand him, and we got no further on this occasion.

But two days later Jogona came back early in the morning, when I was at my typewriter, and asked me to write down for him the account of his relations to the dead child and its family. He wanted to take the report before the D.C. at Dogoretti. Jogona's very simple manner was impressive because he felt so strongly about things and was entirely without self-consciousness. It was evident that he was looking upon his present resolution as upon a great enterprise, which was not without danger; he went to it with awe.

I wrote his statement down for him. It took a long time, for it was a long report of events more than six years old, and in themselves extremely complicated. Jogona, as he was going through it, continually had to break off his tale to think things over or to go back in it and reconstruct it. He was, most of the time, holding his head with both hands, at moments gravely slapping the crown of it as if to shake out the facts. Once he went and leaned his face against the wall, as the Kikuyu women do when they are giving birth to their children.

I took a duplicate of the report; I have still got it.

It was extremely difficult to follow, it gave a lot of complicated circumstances and irrelevant details. It was not surprising to me that Jogona had found it difficult to recollect, it was more surprising that he should be able to recollect the facts at all. It began:

'At the time when Waweru Wamai, of Nyeri, was about to die – *nataka kufa*, wished to die, they have it in Swaheli – he had two wives. The one wife had three daughters; after Waweru's death she married another man. The other wife, Waweru had not yet paid for altogether: he still owed her father two goats for her. This wife had overstrained herself when she lifted a load of firewood and had had a miscarriage and nobody knew if she would bear any more children . . .'

It went on in this way, and dragged the reader into a thick maze of Kikuyu conditions and relations:

'This wife had one small child by the name of Wamai. At that time he was sick, and the people believed that he had got smallpox. Waweru was very fond of his wife and of her child, and when he was dying he was very much worried because he did not know what would become of her when he himself should be dead. He therefore sent for his friend Jogona Kanyagga, who lived not far away. Jogona Kanyagga owed Waweru, at this time, three shillings for a pair of shoes. Waweru now suggested to him that they should make an agreement . . .'

The agreement came to this, that Jogona should take over his dying friend's wife and child, and pay to her father the two goats that were still due to him from the sum of her purchase price. From now the report became a list of expenses, which Jogona had brought upon himself through the adoption of the child Wamai. He had, he stated, purchased an extraordinary good medicine for Wamai just after he had taken him over, when he was sick. At some time he had bought rice from the Indian duca for him, as he did not thrive on maize. Upon one occasion he had had to pay five rupees to a white farmer of the neighbourhood, who said that Wamai had chased one of his turkeys into a pond. This last amount of hard cash, which he had probably had difficulty in raising, had stamped itself upon the mind of Jogona; he came back to it more than once. From Jogona's manner it appeared that he had, by this time, forgotten that the child whom he had now lost had not been his own. He was shaken by the arrival and the claim of the three Nyeri people, in many ways. Very simple people seem to have a talent for adopting children, and feeling towards them as if they were their own; the facile hearts of the European peasants do the same without effort.

When Jogona had at last come to the end of his tale, and I had got it all down, I told him that I was now going to read it to him. He turned away from me while I was reading, as if to avoid all distractions.

But as I read out his own name. 'And he sent for Jogona Kanyagga, who was his friend and who lived not far away,' he swiftly turned his face to me, and gave me a great fierce flaming glance, so exuberant with laughter that it changed the old man into a boy, into the very symbol of youth. Again as I had finished the document and was reading out his name, where it figured as a verification below his thumbmark, the vital direct glance was repeated, this time deepened and calmed, with a new dignity.

Such a glance did Adam give the Lord when he formed him out of the dust, and breathed into his nostrils the breath of life, and man became a living soul. I had created him and shown him himself: Jogona Kanyagga of life everlasting. When I handed him the paper, he took it reverently and greedily, folded it up in a corner of his cloak and kept his hand upon it. He could not afford to lose it, for his soul was in it, and it was the proof of his existence. Here was something which Jogona Kanyagga had performed, and which would preserve his name for ever: the flesh was made word and dwelt among us full of grace and truth.

The world of the written word was opened to the Native of Africa at the time when I lived out there. I had then, if I wanted to, an opportunity of catching the past by its tail and of living through a bit of our own history: the period when the large plain population of Europe had in the same way had the letter revealed to them. In Denmark it happened a good hundred years ago, and from what I have been told by people who were very old when I was a child, I believe that the reaction in both cases has been nearly exactly the same. Human beings can but rarely have shown such a humble and ecstatic devotion to the principle of Art for Art's sake.

These communications from one young Native to another were still generally composed by professional letter-writers, for, although some of the old people were carried away by the spirit of the age, and a few very old Kikuyu attended my school and patiently toiled through the A B C, most of the elder generation withheld themselves distrustfully from the phenomenon. Only a few of the Natives could read, and my houseboys, and the squatters and labourers of the farm, therefore brought their letters to me to have them read out. As I opened and studied one letter after another, I wondered at the insignificance of the contents. It was the common mistake of a prejudiced civilized person. You might as well have set to herborize the little olive branch that Noah's dove brought home. Whatever it looked like, it carried more weight than all the ark with the animals in it; it contained a new green world.

The Natives' letters were all very much alike, they kept close to a sanctioned and sacred formula, and ran more or less as follows: 'My dear friend Kamau Morefu. I will now take the pen in my hand' – in an unliteral sense, for it was the professional scribe who was writing, 'to write you a letter, for I have for a long time wished to write a letter to you. I am very well and it is my hope that you are, by the grace of God, very well. My mother is very well. My wife is not very well, but I still have the hope that your wife will be, by the mercy of God, well.' – Here would follow a long list of names, with a short report attached to each of them, mostly insignificant, although at times very fantastic. Then the letter was closed. 'Now my friend Kamau, I will finish this letter, for I have got too little time to write to you. Your friend Ndwetti Lori.'

To transfer similar messages between young studious Europeans a hundred years ago, postillions vaulted into the saddle, horses galloped, post-horns were blown, and paper with ligulate gilt edges was manufactured. The letters were welcomed, cherished, and preserved; I have seen a few of them myself.

Before I learned to speak Swaheli, my relation to this Native world of letters had a curious feature to it: I could read out what they wrote without understanding a word of it. The Swaheli tongue has had no written language until the white people took upon themselves to make up one; with care it was spelled out as it is pronounced, and it has got no antiquated orthography to entrap a reader. I would then sit and read out their writings orthodoxly, word for word, with the receivers of the letters in breathless suspense all around me, and could follow the effect of my reading without in the least knowing what it was all about. Sometimes they would burst into tears at my words, or wring their hands, at other times they cried out with delight; the most common reaction to the lection was laughter, and they were continually doubled up by convulsions of laughter while I read.

When later on I got so far as to understand what I was reading, I learned that the effect of a piece of news was many times magnified when it was imparted in writing. The messages that would have been received with doubt and scorn if they had been given by word of mouth – for all Natives are great sceptics – were now taken as gospel truth. Natives are, in the same way, extremely quick of hearing towards any confounding of a word in speech; such a mistake gives them a great malicious pleasure, and they will never forget it, and may name a white man for his lifetime after a slip of his tongue; but if a mistake was made in writing, which was often the case, as the Scribes were ignorant people, they would insist on construing it into some sense, they might wonder over it and discuss it, but they would believe the most absurd things rather than find fault with the written word.

In one of the letters that I read out to a boy on the farm, the writer, amongst other news, gave the laconic message: 'I have cooked a baboon.' I explained that he must have meant that he had caught a baboon, since also in Swaheli the two words are somewhat alike. But the receiver of the letter would by no means consent to it.

'No, Msabu, no,' he said, 'what has he written in my letter? What is written down?'

'He has written,' I said, 'that he has cooked a baboon, but how would he cook a baboon? And if he had really done so he would write more to tell you of why and how he did it.'

The young Kikuyu grew very ill at ease at such criticism of the scriptural word; he asked to have his letter back, folded it up carefully and walked away with it.

As to Jogona's statement which I took down, it proved very useful to him, for when the D.C. had read it, he dismissed the appeal of the Nyeri people, who walked scowling back to their own village, without having got anything off the farm.

The document now became Jogona's great treasure. I saw it again more than once. Jogona made a little leather bag for it, embroidered with beads, and hung it on a strap round his neck. From time to time, mostly on Sunday mornings, he would suddenly appear in my door, lift the bag off and take out the paper to have it read to him. Once when I had been ill, and was for the first time again out riding, he caught sight of me at a distance, ran after me a long way, and stood by my horse all out of breath, to hand me his document. At each reading his face took on the same impress of deep religious triumph, and after the reading he solicitously smoothed out his paper, folded it up and put it back in the bag. The importance of the account was not lessened but augmented with time, as if to Jogona the greatest wonder about it was that it did not change. The past, that had been so difficult to bring to memory, and that had probably seemed to be changing every time it was thought of, had here been caught, conquered, and pinned down before his eyes. It had become history; with it there was now no variableness neither shadow of turning.

Wanyangerri

When I was next in Nairobi, I went to see Wanyangerri in the Native Hospital.

As I had so many squatter families on my land, I was hardly ever without a patient in there, I was an *habituée de la maison*, and on friendly terms with the matron and the orderlies. I have never seen a person who put on paint and powder so thick as the matron; within her white coif her broad face looked like the face of those Russian wooden dolls which will unscrew, and have then got another doll inside them, and another inside that, and which are sold under the name of Katinka. She was a kind and capable matron, as you would expect of Katinka. On Thursdays they moved all beds out of the wards to an open square between them, while they cleaned and aired the houses; this was a pleasant day in hospital. There was a great fine view from the court, with the dry Athi plains in the foreground, and far away the blue mountain of Donyo Sabouk and the long Mua Hills. It was a curious thing to see my old Kikuyu women in beds with white sheets to them, like seeing an old worn-out mule, or other patient beast of burden there; they themselves laughed to me at the situation, but sourly, as an old mule might do, for Natives are afraid of hospitals.

The first time that I saw Wanyangerri in hospital, he was so shaken and overcome that I thought the best thing for him would be to die. He was frightened of everything, weeping all the time that I was with him, and begging to be taken back to the farm; he shook and trembled in his bandages.

It was a week till I came in again. I found him then calm and collected, he received me with dignity. He was, however, very pleased to see me, and the orderly told me that he had been waiting impatiently for my arrival. For he could to-day tell me, with much assertiveness, and spitting out the words through a tube in his mouth, that he had been killed the day before, and was going to be killed again in a few days' time.

The doctor who treated Wanyangerri had been to the war in France, and had patched up many people's faces; he took trouble about him and made a success of the work. He put in a metal band for a jawbone and screwed it on to the bones left in the face, and he plucked up the bits of torn flesh and stitched them together to make a sort of chin for him. He even, Wanyangerri told me, had a bit of skin taken from the shoulder to fill up his patchwork. When at the end of the treatment the bandages came off, the face of the child was much changed, and looked queer, like the head of a lizard, because it had got no chin. But he was able to eat in a normal way and to speak, although after the accident he always lisped a little. All this took many months. When I came to see Wanyangerri he asked me for sugar, so I used to bring a few spoonfuls in a bit of paper.

The Natives, if they are not paralysed and benumbed by their terror of the unknown, growl and grumble much in hospital, and invent schemes for getting away. Death is one of these; they do not fear it. The Europeans who have built and equipped the hospitals, and who are working in them, and have with much trouble got the patients dragged there, complain with bitterness that the Natives know nothing of gratitude, and that it is the same whatever you do to them.

To white people there is something vexatious and mortifying in this state of mind in the Natives. It is indeed the same whatever you do to them; you can do but little, and what you do disappears, and will never be heard of again; they do not thank you, and they bear you no malice, and even should you want to, you cannot do anything about it. It is an alarming quality; it seems to annul your existence as an individual human being, and to inflict upon you a rôle not of your own choosing, as if you were a phenomenon in nature, as if you were the weather.

The immigrant Somalis in this respect differ from the Natives of the country. Your behaviour to them affects them strongly; in fact, you can hardly move without affecting the fierce burning prigs of the desert in one way or the other, and, very often, not without deeply hurting them. They have a keen sense of gratitude and will also bear malice for ever. A benefit, like an offence or a slight, is written in stone in their hearts. They are severe Mohammedans and, like all Mohammedans, have a moral code according to which they will judge you. With the Somalis you can make or destroy your prestige within an hour.

The Masai here hold a position peculiar to themselves amongst the Native tribes. They remember, they can thank you, and they will bear you a grudge. They all bear us all a grudge, which will be wiped out only when the tribe is wiped out itself.

But the unprejudiced Kikuyu, Wakambas, or Kavirondos, know of no code. They have it that most people are capable of most things, and you cannot shock them if you want to. It is, it can be said, a poor or perverted Kikuyu, to whom it makes any difference what you do to him. Left to their own nature, and to the tradition of their nation, they will look upon our activities as upon those of nature. They judge you not, but they are keen observers. The sum of their observations is what you pass for with them, your good or bad name.

The very poor people of Europe, in this way, are like the Kikuyus. They judge you not, but sum you up. If they like or esteem you at all, it is in the manner in which people love God; not for what you do to them, not at all for what you do to them, but for what you are.

One day in my wanderings through the hospital I saw three new patients there, a very black man with a thick heavy head, and two boys, who were all three bandaged at the throat. One of the orderlies in the ward was a hunchback and a narrator, who took a pleasure in explaining to me the most intriguing cases in his house. As he saw me stopping before the beds of the newcomers he came up and told me their story.

They were Nubians in the band of the King's African Rifles, the black soldiers of Kenya. The boys were drummers, and the man a horn-player. The horn-player had had serious controversies in his life, and had lost his head over them as it will happen to Natives. First he had fired his rifle right and left over the barracks, and when the magazine was empty he had shut himself up with the two boys, in his hut of corrugated iron there, and had tried to cut their throats and his own. The orderly was sorry that I had not seen them when they had been brought in last week, for then they had all been covered in blood, and I would have believed them to be dead. Now they were out of danger, and the murderer had got his senses back.

As the story-teller went through his tale, the three persons in the bed upon whom it turned were following it with deep attention. They interrupted him to correct the details of his tale, the boys, who had great difficulty in speaking, turning to the man in the bed between them to make him confirm their statement, confident that he would assist them to let me have the story as effectively as possible.

'Did you not foam at the mouth, did you not shriek?' they asked him. 'Did you not say that you would cut us up in bits as big as a grasshopper?'

The manslayer said, 'Yes, yes,' with a mournful mien.

At times I would be kept in Nairobi for half a day, waiting for a business meeting, or for the European mail when the train from the coast was late. On such occasions when I did not know what to do, I used to drive up to the Native Hospital and take a couple of the convalescents there out for a short joy-ride. At the time when Wanyangerri was in hospital, the governor, Sir Edward Northey, kept a couple of young lions, which he was sending on to the London Zoo, caged up in the Government House grounds. They were a great attraction to the people in hospital; they all asked to be taken to see them. I had promised the patients of the K.A.R. band to take them up there when they were well enough for it, but none of them would come until they could all go together. The horn-player was the slowest to recover, one of the boys was even discharged from hospital before he was well enough to go with me. The boy came back to hospital every day to inquire about him, so as to be sure to have his drive. I found him outside there one afternoon, and he told me that the bugler still had a very terrible headache, but that this was only to be expected since his head had been so filled with devils.

In the end they came, all three, and stood before the cage sunk in contemplation. One of the young lions, angry at being stared at for such a long time, suddenly got up, stretched himself and gave a short roar, so that the onlookers got a shock, and the smallest boy took cover behind the bugler. As we were driving back he said to him: 'That lion was as villainous as you were.'

During all this time Wanyangerri's case was lying dormant out on the farm. His people sometimes came and asked me how he was getting on, but, with the exception of his little brother, they seemed scared of going in to see him. Kaninu also came round to my house late in the evening, like an old badger out reconnoitring, to sound me about the child. Farah and I, between ourselves, at times weighed up his sufferings, and computed them in sheep.

Farah also, a couple of months after the accident, informed me of a new feature of the case.

On these occasions he would come in while I was dining, stand erect by the end of the table and take upon himself to enlighten my ignorance. Farah spoke both English and French well, but stuck to certain mistakes peculiar to him. He would say 'exactly' in the place of 'except' – 'all the cows have come home, exactly the grey cow', and instead of correcting him I took to using the same expressions when I talked to him. His face and countenance were assured and dignified, but he would often start in a vague manner: 'Memsahib,' he said, 'the Kabero.' This was the programme then. I waited for what was to follow.

After a pause Farah took up the subject again. 'You think, Memsahib,' he said, 'that Kabero is dead and has been eaten by the hyenas. He is not dead. He is with the Masai.'

In two minds I asked him how he knew of this. 'Oh, I know,' he said, 'Kaninu has got too many girls married to Masai. When Kabero could not think of anybody who would help him exactly the Masai, he ran out to his sister's husband. It is true that he had a bad time, he sat all night in a tree and the hyenas stood around it underneath. Now he is living with the Masai. There is a rich old Masai, who has got many hundred cows, who has no children himself and wants to get Kabero. Kaninu knows of all this very well, and has been out to talk it over with the Masai many times. But he is afraid to tell you, he believes that if the white people know of it, Kabero will be hanged in Nairobi.'

Farah always spoke of the Kikuyu in an arrogant way. 'The Masai wives,' he said, 'bear no children. They are pleased enough to get Kikuyu children. They steal too many. Still, this Kabero,' he went on, 'he will come back to the farm when he grows up, for he will not want to live like the Masai, always going from one place to the other. The Kikuyu are too lazy for that.'

From the farm, the tragic fate of the disappearing Masai tribe the other side of the river could be followed from year to year. They were fighters who had been stopped fighting, a dying lion with his claws clipped, a castrated nation. Their spears had been taken from them, their big dashing shields even, and in the Game Reserve the lions followed their herds of cattle. Once, on the farm, I had three young bulls transmuted into peaceful bullocks for my ploughs and wagons, and afterwards shut up in the factory yard. There in the night the hyenas smelled the blood and came up and killed them. This, I thought, was the fate of the Masai.

'Kaninu's wife,' said Farah, 'is sorry to lose her son for so many years.'

I did not send for Kaninu, for I did not know whether to believe what Farah had told me or not, but when he next came to my house I went out to talk to him. 'Kaninu,' I asked him, 'is Kabero alive? Is he with the Masai?' You will never find a Native unprepared for any action of yours, and Kaninu immediately burst into weeping over his lost child. I listened to him and looked at him for a little while. 'Kaninu,' I said again, 'bring Kabero here. He will not be hanged. His mother shall keep him with her on the farm.' Kaninu had not stopped his laments to listen, but he must have caught my unfortunate word of hanging; his wails were drawn into a deeper note, he dived into descriptions of the promise that Kabero had given, and of his own preference for him above all his other children.

Kaninu had a lot of children and grandchildren who, as his village was so near to my house, were always about it. Amongst them was a very small grandson of his, the son of one of these daughters of Kaninu who had married into the Masai Reserve, but who had come back from it and had brought her child with her. This child's name was Sirunga. The mixture of blood in him had come out in the quaintest vitality, such a wild profusion of inventiveness and whims that he was like nothing quite human: a small flame, a nightbird, a diminutive genie of the farm. But he had epilepsy, and, because of that, the other children were afraid of him, chasing him away from their games and naming him *Sheitani* – the devil – so that I had adopted him into my household. As he was ill he could do no work, but he filled with me exceedingly well the office of a fool or jester and followed me about everywhere like a small fidgety black shadow. Kaninu knew of my affection for the child, and till now had smiled at it in a grandfatherly way; now he seized it, turned it at me and worked it for all it was worth. He declared with great strength that he would rather have Sirunga ten times eaten by leopards than he would lose Kabero, indeed now that Kabero was lost let Sirunga go as well, it would make no difference – for Kabero, Kabero had been the apple of his eye and his heart's blood.

If Kabero were indeed dead, this was David grieving over his son Absalom, a tragedy to be left to itself. But if he were alive and hidden with the Masai it was more than tragic, it was a fight or flight, a struggle for the life of a child.

I have seen, on the plains, the gazelles play this game when I have unknowingly come upon the spot where they were hiding their newborn fawn. They would dance to you, step up before you, jump, caper, or pretend to be lame and unable to run – all to distract your attention from their young. And suddenly, actually under the hoofs of your horse, you saw the fawn, immovable, the small head stretched out flat on the grass, lying low for his life while his mother dances for it. A bird will do the same tricks to protect her young ones, flap and flutter and even cleverly act the rôle of the wounded bird, which trails her broken wing on the ground.

Here was Kaninu performing for me. Was there so much warmth and so many gambols left in the old Kikuyu when he thought his son's life at stake? His bones creaked in the dance, he was even changing his sex in it, and had taken on the appearance of an old woman, a hen, a lioness – the game was so plainly a feminine activity. It was a grotesque performance, but at the same time highly respectable, like the cock ostrich taking turns with the hen in sitting on her eggs. No woman's heart could have remained unmoved by the manoeuvre.

'Kaninu,' I said to him, 'when Kabero wants to return to the farm he can do so and no harm shall come to him. But you must bring him up here to me yourself at that time.' Kaninu became dead silent, he bowed his head and walked away sadly as if he had now lost his last friend in the world.

*

I may as well tell here that Kaninu remembered, and did as he had been told. Five years afterwards, when I had almost forgotten the whole affair, he one day through Farah applied for an interview. I found him standing outside the house, on one leg, very dignified, but at the bottom of his heart uneasy. He addressed me in an amiable way. 'Kabero is back,' he said. By that time I had learned the art of the pause, I did not say a word. The old Kikuyu felt the weight of my silence, he changed feet, and his eyelids quivered. 'My son Kabero has come back to the farm,' he repeated. I asked: 'He is back from Masai?' Immediately, by the fact that he had made me speak, Kaninu took it that our reconciliation was effected; he did not smile yet, but all the cunning little wrinkles in his face were adjusted for a smile. 'Yes, Msabu, yes, he is back from the Masai,' he said, 'he has come back to work for you.' The government in the intermediate time had introduced the *Kipanda*, the registration of each individual Native, in the country, so that we would now have to call a police officer out from Nairobi to make a lawful inhabitant of the farm out of Kabero. Kaninu and I appointed the day.

Upon that day, Kaninu and his son arrived a long time before the police officer. Kaninu presented Kabero to me in a jovial manner, but at heart he was a little frightened of his recovered son. He had reason to be so, for the Masai Reserve had had from the farm a small lamb, and now gave us back a young leopard. Kabero must have had Masai blood in him, the habits and discipline of Masai life could not in themselves have worked the metamorphosis. Here he stood, a Masai from head to foot.

A Masai warrior is a fine sight. Those young men have, to the utmost extent, that particular form of intelligence which we call *chic*; daring, and wildly fantastical as they seem, they are still unswervingly true to their own nature, and to an immanent ideal. Their style is not an assumed manner, nor an imitation of a foreign perfection; it has grown from the inside, and is an expression of the race and its history, and their weapons and finery are as much part of their being as are a stag's antlers.

Kabero had adopted the Masai fashion in hair-dressing, he wore his hair long and braided with string into a thick pigtail and a leather strap round the brow. He had acquired the Masai carriage of the head, with the chin stretched forward, as if he were presenting you his sullen arrogant face upon a tray. He had also the general rigid, passive, and insolent bearing of the Moran, that makes of him an object for contemplation, such as a statue is, a figure which is to be seen, but which itself does not see.

The young Masai Morani live upon milk and blood; it is perhaps this diet that gives them their wonderful smoothness and silkiness of skin.

Their faces, with the high cheek-bones and boldly swung jaw-bones, are sleek, without a line or groove in them, swollen; the dim unseeing eyes lie therein like two dark stones tightly fitted into a mosaic; altogether the young Morani have a likeness to mosaics. The muscles of their necks swell in a particular sinister fashion, like the neck of the angry cobra, the male leopard, or the fighting bull, and the thickness is so plainly an indication of virility that it stands for a declaration of war to all the world with the exception of the woman. The great contrast, or harmony, between these swollen smooth faces, full necks, and broad rounded shoulders, and the surprising narrowness of their waist and hips, the leanness and spareness of the thigh and knee and the long, straight, sinewy leg gives them the look of creatures trained through hard discipline to the height of rapacious-ness, greed, and gluttony.

The Masai walk stiffly, placing one slim foot straight in front of the other, but their movements of arm, wrist, and hand are very supple. When a young Masai shoots with a bow and arrow, and lets go the bow-string, you seem to hear the sinews of his long wrist singing in the air with the arrow.

The police officer from Nairobi was a young man lately out from England and full of zeal. He spoke Swaheli very well, so that I and Kaninu did not understand what he said, and he became absorbed in interest in the old case of the shooting accident, and put Kaninu to a cross-examination under which the Kikuyu turned into wood. When he had finished it, he told me that he thought Kaninu had been monstrously treated, and that the whole case ought to be taken up in Nairobi. 'That will mean years of your life and mine,' I said. He asked me to be allowed to remark that this was no consideration to be taken, where the execution of justice was concerned. Kaninu looked to me; for a moment he believed that he was being trapped. In the end it was found that the case was too old to be taken up, and nothing more was done about it, except that Kabero was regularly registered on the farm.

But all these things were to happen only a long time later. For five years Kabero was dead to the farm, wandering with the Masai, and Kaninu had much to go through still. Before the case had done with him, forces came into play which seized him and ground him very small.

Of those I cannot tell much. First because they were in themselves of a hidden nature, and secondly, because at the time things were happening to me myself, that took my thoughts off Kaninu and his fate, and left, in my mind, the general affairs of the farm in the background like that distant mountain of Kilimanjaro, which sometimes I could see from my land, and sometimes not. The Natives would take such periods of distraction of mine meekly, as if I had been in reality lifted from their existence into another plane; afterwards they referred to them as to times when I had been away. 'That big tree fell down,' they said. 'My child died, while you were with the white people.'

When Wanyangerri was well enough to leave hospital, I fetched him back to the farm, and from that time only saw him at intervals, at a Ngoma or on the plains.

A few days after his return his father, Wainaina, and his grandmother presented themselves at my house. Wainaina was a small rotund man, a rare thing in a Kikuyu, for they are nearly all of them lean people. He grew a spare thin beard, and another peculiarity of his was that he could not look you straight in the face. He made the impression of a mental troglodyte, who wants to be left to himself. With him came his mother, a very old Kikuyu woman.

Native women shave their heads, and it is a curious thing how quickly you yourself will come to feel that these little round neat skulls, which look like some kind of dusky nuts, are the sign of true womanliness, and that a crop of hair on the head of a woman is as unladylike as a beard. Wainaina's old mother had left the little tufts of white hair on her shrivelled scalp to grow, and thereby, as much as an unshaven man, she conveyed the impression of dissoluteness or shamelessness. She leant on her stick and left it to Wainaina to speak, but her silence was striking sparks the while; she seemed to be all loaded with a graceless vitality, of which she had passed none on to her son. The two were in reality Uraka and Laskara, but of that I did not know till later.

They had come shuffling up to my house on a peaceful errand. Wanyangerri, his father told me, could chew no maize, they were poor people and short of flour and they had got no milking cow. Would I not, till Wanyangerri's case was settled, allow him a little milk from my cows? Otherwise they did not see how they were to keep the child alive until the time when his indemnification should come in. Farah was away in Nairobi on one of his private Somali lawsuits, and in his absence I consented to let Wanyangerri have a bottle of milk a day from my herd of Native cows, and instructed my houseboys, who seemed strangely unwilling or uncomfortable about the arrangement, to let him fetch it from us every morning.

A fortnight passed, or three weeks; then one evening Kaninu came to the house. He suddenly stood in the room where I was reading by the fire after dinner. As the Natives generally prefer a discussion to take place outside the house, the manner in which he shut the door behind him prepared me for surprising communications. But the first surprise was that Kaninu was dumb. The subtle and honeyed tongue was as dead as if it had been cut out of him, and the room, with Kaninu in it, remained silent. The big old Kikuyu was looking very ill, he hung upon his stick, there seemed to be no body inside his cloak, his eyes were dim like the eyes of a corpse, and he kept on wetting his dry lips with his tongue.

When at last he began to speak it was only to state, slowly and dismally, that he thought things were bad. A little later he added in a vague manner, as if it were altogether a matter to be ignored that he had now paid over ten sheep to Wainaina. And now Wainaina, he went on, wanted a cow and calf from him as well, and he was going to give them to him. Why had he done that, I asked him, when no judgement had yet been given? Kaninu did not answer, he did not even look at me. He was, this evening, a traveller or pilgrim who had no continuing city. He had come in, as it were on his way, to report to me, and now he was off again. I could not but think that he was ill; after a pause I said that I would take him into hospital the next day. At that he gave me a short, painful glance: the old mocker was being bitterly mocked. But before he went away he did a curious thing, he lifted up a hand to his face as if it were wiping off a tear. It would be a strange thing, like the flowering of the pilgrim's staff, should Kaninu have tears in him to shed, and stranger still that he should put them to no use. I wondered what had been happening on the farm while I had had my thoughts off it. When Kaninu had gone I sent for Farah and asked him.

Farah at times was loth to speak about Native affairs, as if they were beneath him to dwell upon and me to hear of. In the end he consented to tell me, all the time looking past me out of the window, at the stars. At the bottom of Kaninu's loss of heart was Wainaina's mother, who was a witch and had cast a spell upon him.

'But, Farah,' I said, 'Kaninu, surely, is much too old and wise to believe in a spell.'

'No,' said Farah slowly. 'No, Memsahib. For this old Kikuyu wife can really do these things, I think.'

The old woman had told Kaninu that his cows would live to see that it would have been better to them had Kaninu at the beginning given them to Wainaina. Now Kaninu's cows were going blind, one after another. And under the ordeal Kaninu's heart was slowly breaking, like the bones and tissue of those people who, in old times, were put to the torture of ever increased weights laid on to them.

Farah spoke of Kikuyu witchcraft in a dry, concerned manner, as of foot-and-mouth disease on the farm, which we ourselves would not catch, but by which we might lose our cattle.

I sat late in the evening thinking of the witchery on the farm. At first it looked ugly, as if it had come up from an old grave to flatten its nose upon my window-panes. I heard the hyena wailing some way off, down by the river, and remembered that the Kikuyu had their were-wolves, old women who at night take on the shape of hyenas. Perhaps Wainaina's mother was trotting along the river now, baring her teeth in the night air. And I had by now become used to the idea of witchcraft, it seemed a reasonable thing, so many things are about, at night, in Africa.

'This old woman is mean,' I thought in Swaheli, 'she uses her arts in making Kaninu's cows blind, and she leaves it to me to keep her grand-child alive, on a bottle of milk a day, from my own cows.'

I thought: 'This accident and the things which have come from it, are getting into the blood of the farm, and it is my fault. I must call in fresh forces, or the farm will run into a bad dream, a nightmare. I know what I will do, I will send for Kinanjui.'

A Kikuyu Chief

The big Chief Kinanjui lived about nine miles north-east of the farm, in the Kikuyu Reserve near the French Mission, and ruled over more than a hundred thousand Kikuyus. He was a crafty old man, with a fine manner, and much real greatness to him, although he had not been born to be a chief, but had been made so, many years ago, by the English, when they could no longer get on with the legitimate ruler of the Kikuyus of the district.

Kinanjui was a friend of mine, and had been helpful to me on many occasions. His manyatta, to which I had ridden over a few times, was as dirty and as full of flies as those of the other Kikuyus. But it was much bigger than any other I had seen, for in his position of a chief Kinanjui had given himself over fully to the joys of marriage. The village was alive with wives of his of all ages, from skinny toothless old hags on crutches to slim, moon-faced, gazelle-eyed wenches, their arms and long legs wound up in shining copper wire. His children were everywhere, in clusters, like the flies. The young men, his sons, erect, with decorated heads, went to and fro, and caused much trouble. Kinanjui had told me once that he had at the moment fifty-five sons who were Morani.

Sometimes the old chief would come walking over to my farm in a gorgeous fur cloak, accompanied by two or three white-haired senators and a few of his warrior-sons, on a friendly visit, or to take a rest from governmental affairs. He would then pass the afternoon in one of the verandah chairs that had been carried out on the lawn for him, smoking the cigars that I sent him out, with his councillors and his guard squatting on the grass round him. My houseboys and squatters, when they had news of his arrival, came and grouped themselves there, and entertained him with the happenings on the farm, the whole company forming a sort of political club under the tall trees. Kinanjui in these meetings had a manner of his own: when he thought that the discussions were dragging out too long, he leant back in his chair, and, while still keeping the fire in his cigar alive, he closed his eyes and drew his breath deeply and slowly, in a low regular snore, a sort of official, *pro forma* sleep, which he may have cultivated for use in his own council of state. I sometimes had a chair moved out for a talk with him, and on these occasions Kinanjui sent away everybody, to point out that now the world was going to be governed in earnest. He was not, at the time I knew him, the man that he had been, life had taken much out of him. But when he talked freely and openly, for my private ear, he showed much originality of mind, and a rich, daring, imaginative spirit; he had thought the matter of life over and held his own strong views upon it.

A few years earlier a thing had happened which had strengthened the friendship between me and Kinanjui.

He came to my house one day when I was lunching with a friend who was on his way up country; I had no time to give the Kikuyu chief till my friend had gone. Kinanjui would expect to be offered a drink while he was waiting, and after his long walk in the sun, but I did not have enough of one thing to make up a glassful, so my guest and I filled a tumbler with all the different sorts of strong liquor that I had in the house. I thought that the stronger I made it, the longer it would keep Kinanjui occupied, and I took it out to him myself. But Kinanjui, after having with a little gentle smile just wetted his lips, gave me as deep a glance as I have ever had from a man, laid his head back and emptied the glass to the last drop.

Half an hour later, when my friend had just driven off, my houseboys came in and said: 'Kinanjui is dead.' I felt, in one moment, the tragedy and the scandal rise up before me like great grave shadows. I went out to see him.

He was lying on the ground in the shade of the kitchen, with no expression whatever in his face, with blue lips and fingers, dead-cold. It was like having shot an elephant: by an act of yours a mighty and majestic creature, which has walked the earth, and held his own opinions of everything, is walking it no more. He looked degraded as well, for the Kikuyu had poured water over him, and had taken off him his big cloak of monkey-skin. Naked he was like an animal when you have cut from it the trophy, for the sake of which you have killed it.

I meant to send Farah for a doctor, but we could not get the car started, and Kinanjui's people kept on begging us to wait a little before we did anything.

An hour later, as I was going out again, with a heavy heart, to talk to them, my boys came in to me once more and said: 'Kinanjui has gone home.' It seemed that he had suddenly got up, draped his cloak about him, and his retainers round him, and had walked off, the nine miles to his village, without a word.

After this time, I believed, Kinanjui felt that I had run a risk, even braved a danger – for you are not allowed to give Natives alcohol – to make him happy. He had been to the farm since, and had smoked a cigar with us, but he had not mentioned a drink. I would have given it to him had he asked for it, but I knew that he would not ask any more.

I now sent a runner to Kinanjui's village and explained to him the whole affair of the shooting. I asked him to come over to the farm to finish it. I suggested that we should give Wainaina the cow and calf of which Kaninu had talked, and then let the whole matter finish at that. I was looking forward to Kinanjui's arrival, for he had the quality, which everyone values in a friend, of being effective.

By this letter of mine, the case, that had for some time been becalmed, fetched wind and ended up dramatically.

One afternoon, as I was riding back to my house, I just caught sight of a car that came along at a terrible speed, rounding the drive upon two wheels. It was a scarlet car with a lot of nickel on it. I knew it, it belonged to the American Consul of Nairobi, and I wondered what urgent business it was which brought the consul to my house at such a pace. But as I was getting off my horse at the back of the house, Farah came out to tell me that the Chief Kinanjui had arrived. He had come in his own car, which he had the day before bought from the American Consul, and he did not want to get out of it till I had seen him in it.

I found Kinanjui sitting up straight in the car, immovable as an idol. He had on a large cloak of blue monkey-skins, and on his head a skull-cap, of the kind which the Kikuyu make out of sheeps' stomachs. He was always an impressive figure, tall and broad, with no fat on him anywhere;

his face too was proud, long and bony, with a slanting forehead like that of a Red Indian. He had a broad nose, so expressive that it looked like the central point of the man, as if the whole stately figure was there only to carry the broad nose about. Like the trunk of an elephant, it was both boldly inquisitive and extremely sensitive and prudent, intensely on the offensive, and on the defensive as well. And an elephant, finally, like Kinanjui, would have a head of the very greatest nobility if he did not look so clever.

Kinanjui now did not open his mouth or wince while I paid him my compliments on the car, he stared straight in front of him in order that I should see his face in profile like a head struck upon a medal. As I walked round to the front of the car, he turned his head so as to keep his regal profile towards me; perhaps he really had in his mind the King's head on the rupee. One of his young sons was driver to him, and the car was boiling hard. When the ceremony was over, I invited Kinanjui to come out of the car. He collected his big cloak round him in a majestic gesture and descended, and in that one movement he stepped back two thousand years, into Kikuyu justice.

On the western wall of my house there was a stone seat and in front of it a table made out of a mill-stone. This stone had a tragic history : it was the upper mill-stone of the mill of the two murdered Indians. After the murder nobody dared to take over the mill, it was empty and silent for a long time, and I had the stone brought up to my house to form a table top, to remind me of Denmark. The Indian millers had told me that their mill-stone had come over the sea from Bombay, as the stones of Africa are not hard enough for the work of grinding. On the top side a pattern was carved, and it had a few large brown spots on it, which my houseboys held to be the blood of the Indians, that would never come off. The mill-stone table in a way constituted the centre of the farm, for I used to sit behind it in all my dealings with the Natives. From the stone seat behind the mill-stone, I and Denys Finch-Hatton had one New Year seen the new moon and the planets of Venus and Jupiter all close together, in a group on the sky; it was such a radiant sight that you could hardly believe it to be real, and I have never seen it again.

I took my seat there now, with Kinanjui on the bench on my left. Farah took up his stand on my right hand, and therefrom kept a watchful eye on the Kikuyus, who had been gathering round the house, and who kept coming in as the news of Kinanjui's arrival spread on the farm.

Farah's attitude to the Natives of the country was a picturesque thing. No more than the attire and countenance of the Masai warriors, had it been made yesterday, or the day before; it was the product of many centuries. The forces which had built it up had constructed great buildings in stone as well, but they had crumbled into dust a long time ago.

When you first come to the country, landing at Mombasa, you will see, amongst the old light-grey baobab trees – which look not like any earthly kind of vegetation but like porous fossilizations, gigantic belemnites – grey stone ruins of houses, minarets, and wells. The same sort of ruins are to be found all the way up the coast, at Takaunga, Kalifi, and Lamu. They are the remnants of the towns of the ancient Arab traders in ivory and slaves.

The dhows of the traders knew all the African fairways, and trod the blue paths to the central marketplace of Zanzibar. They were familiar with it at the time when Aladdin sent to the sultan four hundred black slaves loaded with jewels, and when the sultana feasted with her Negro lover while her husband was hunting, and was put to death for it.

Probably, as these great merchants grew rich, they brought their harems with them to Mombasa and Kalifi, and themselves remained in their villas, by the long white breakers of the ocean, and the flowering flaming trees, while they sent their expeditions up into the highlands.

For from the wild hard country there, the scorched dry plains, and unknown waterless stretches, from the land of the broad thorn-trees along the rivers, and the diminutive, strong-smelling wild flowers of the black soil, came their wealth. Here, upon the roof of Africa, wandered the heavy, wise, majestic bearer of the ivory. He was deep in his own thoughts and wanted to be left to himself. But he was followed, and shot with poisoned arrows by the little dark Wanderobos, and with long, muzzle-loaded, silver-inlaid guns by the Arabs; he was trapped and thrown into pits all for the sake of his long smooth light-brown tusks, that they sat and waited for at Zanzibar.

Here, also, little bits of forest soil were cleared, burned, and planted with sweet potatoes and maize, by a peace-loving shy nation, which was not much good at fighting, or at inventing anything, but wished to be left to themselves, and which, with the ivory, was in great demand on the market.

The greater and lesser birds of prey gathered up here:

'Tous les tristes oiseaux mangeurs de chair humaine ...
S'assemblent. Et les uns laissant un crâne chauve.
Les autres aux gibets essuyant leur bec fauve,
D'autres, d'un mat rompu quittant les noirs agrès ...

The cold sensual Arabs came, contemptuous of death, with their minds, out of business times, on astronomy, algebra, and their harems. With them came their young illegitimate half-brothers the Somali – impetuous, quarrelsome, abstinent, and greedy, who made up for their lack of birth by being zealous Mohammedans, and more faithful to the commandments of the prophet than the children got in wedlock. The Swaheli went along with them, slaves themselves and slave-hearted, cruel, obscene, thievish, full of good sense and jests, running to fat with age.

Up country they were met by the Native bird of prey of the highlands. The Masai came, silent, like tall narrow black shadows, with spears and heavy shields, distrustful of strangers, red-handed, to sell their brothers.

The different birds must have sat together up here and talked. Farah told me that in the old time, before the Somali brought their own women down from Somaliland, their young men could marry with the daughters of the Masai only, out of all the tribes of the country. This must have been in many ways a strange alliance. For the Somali are a religious people, and the Masai have no religion whatever, nor the slightest interest in anything above this earth. The Somali are clean, and take much trouble over their ablutions and hygiene, while the Masai are a dirty nation. The Somali, too, attach the greatest importance to the virginity of their brides, but the young Masai girls take their morals very lightly. Farah gave me the explanation at once. The Masai, he said, had never been slaves. They cannot be made slaves, they cannot even be put in prison. They die in prison if they are brought there, within three months, so the English law of the country holds with no penalty of imprisonment for the Masai: they are punished by fines. This stark inability to keep alive under the yoke has given the Masai, alone amongst all the Native tribes, rank with the immigrant aristocracy.

All the birds of prey lived with their burning eyes upon the gentle rodents of the land. The Somali here had their own position. Somalis are not good at being all on their own, they are very excitable, and, wherever they go, if they are left to themselves they will waste much time and blood over their tribal moral system. But they are fine seconds in command, and perhaps the Arab capitalists have often given them charge of daring undertakings and difficult transports while they stayed in Mombasa themselves. Therefore their relation to the Natives was nearly exactly that of the sheepdog to the sheep. They watched them untiringly, their sharp teeth bared. Would they die before the coast was reached? Would they escape? The Somali have a keen sense of money and values, they will have given up food and sleep for the sake of their charges, and must have come back from the expeditions worn to skin and bone.

The habit is in their blood still. When we had the Spanish flu on the farm, Farah was very ill with it himself, but he followed me about, all shivering with fever, to bring medicine to the squatters and to force it into them. He had been told that paraffin was very good against the disease, and therefore he bought paraffin for the farm. His little brother Abdullai, who was with us then, was very bad with flu, and Farah was much worried about him. Still, that was only the inclination of the heart, a frivolous matter. Duty, bread, and reputation lay with the farm labour, and the dying sheepdog stuck to his job. Farah also had much insight in what was going on in Native circles, although I do not know from where he had his knowledge, for, with the exception of the biggest amongst them, he kept no company with the Kikuyu.

The sheep themselves, the patient nations, with no teeth or claws to them, no power and no earthly protector, got through their destiny, as they get through it now, on their immense gift for resignation. They did not die under the yoke, like the Masai, or storm against fate, as the Somali do when they believe themselves injured, cheated, or slighted. They were friends with God in foreign countries, and in chains. They also kept up a peculiar self-feeling in their relations to those who persecuted them. They were aware that the profit and prestige of their tormentors lay with them themselves: they were the central figures in the chase and the commerce, they were the goods. Upon the long track of blood and tears, the sheep, deep in their dark dumb hearts, had made for themselves a bobtailed philosophy, and thought not highly of the shepherds or the dogs. 'You have no rest either day or night,' they said, 'you run with your hot tongues out, panting, you are kept awake at night so that your dry eyes smart in the day-time, all on our account. You are here on our account. You exist for our sake, not we for your sake.' The Kikuyu of the farm at times had a flippant manner towards Farah, as a lamb may skip in the face of the sheepdog just to make him get up and run.

Farah and Kinanjui met here, the sheepdog and the old ram. Farah stood up erect in his red and blue turban, black embroidered Arab waistcoat and Arab silk robe, as thoughtful, decorous a figure as you would find anywhere in the world. Kinanjui was spreading himself on the stone seat, naked but for the mantle of monkey furs on his shoulders, an old Native, a clod of the soil of the African highlands. They treated each other with respect, although, when they had no direct dealings, in accordance with some ceremonial they pretended not to see one another.

It was easy to imagine the two, a hundred years earlier or more, holding a converse over a consignment of slaves, undesirable members of the tribe, of whom Kinanjui was ridding himself. Farah would be keeping, all the time, at the back of his mind the idea of swooping upon the old chief himself, a fat morsel, so as to have him included in his parcel. Kinanjui would follow, without fault, every one of Farah's thoughts, and, through the whole sitting, he would be carrying the weight of the situation, the weight, too, of his own scared and heavy heart. For he was the central figure, he was the goods.

The big meeting which was to settle the case of the shooting accident began in a peaceful spirit. The people of the farm were all pleased to see Kinanjui. The oldest squatters got up and came to exchange a few remarks with him, then walked back and took their seats on the grass. A couple of old women from the periphery of the assembly shrieked a greeting to me: 'Jambo Jerie!' Jerie is a Kikuyu name. The old women of the farm addressed me by it, and the very small children made use of it as well, but the young people and the men never called me Jerie. Kaninu was present at the meeting, in the midst of his large family, like a scarecrow somehow called to life, with burning, attentive eyes. Wainaina and his mother came along and sat a little away from the others.

I told the people, slowly and in an effective manner, that the matter between Kaninu and Wainaina had been settled and the settlement put down on paper. Kinanjui had come over to certify it. Kaninu was to give Wainaina a cow with a heifer calf at foot, and by that the affair should be ended, since nobody could stand it any longer.

Kaninu and Wainaina had been informed of the decision beforehand, and Kaninu was instructed to have the cow and calf ready. The activities of Wainaina were of an underground nature, in the daylight he was like a mole above the ground, and looked as soft as a mole does there.

When I had read up the agreement I told Kaninu to bring along the cow. Kaninu got up and waved both arms up and down many times to two of his young sons, who were holding the cow behind the boys' huts. The ring opened while the cow and calf were slowly led into the middle of it.

At the same moment the atmosphere of the meeting changed, as when a thunderstorm comes up in the horizon, and quickly rises to zenith.

There is nothing in the world which to the Kikuyu holds the interest and importance of a cow with a heifer calf at foot. Bloodshed, witchcraft, sexual love, or the wonders of the white men's world, all evaporate and disappear near the great flaming furnace of their passion for livestock, which smells of the stone age, like a fire you strike with a flint.

Wainaina's mother broke into a long wail and shook a dry arm and finger at the cow. Wainaina joined her, all stuttering and breaking in his speech, as if someone else were speaking through him; he raised his voice to heaven. He would not accept the cow; she was the oldest in Kaninu's herd, and the calf that she had now got with her, that surely was the last which she would ever bear.

The clan of Kaninu cried out and cut him short in a furious staccato inventory of the qualities of the cow, behind which you felt a great bitterness, and contempt of death.

The people of the farm did not have it in them to remain silent where a cow and calf were being discussed. Everyone present gave out his opinion. The old men seized one another by the arm and shook out their last asthmatic breath in praise or condemnation of the cow. The shrill voices of their old women fell in and followed them up, as in a canon. The young men spat out short deadly remarks at one another in deep voices. In two or three minutes the open place by my house was boiling over like a witch's cauldron.

I looked towards Farah and he looked back at me, but like a man in a dream. I saw that he was a sword half-way out of the scabbard, which in a moment would be flashing right and left in the strife. For the Somali are themselves stock-owners and cattle-traders. Kaninu threw me a glance like a drowning man, who is finally carried away by the current. I took a look at the cow. She was a grey cow with deeply curved horns, and was standing patiently in the very centre of the cyclone that she had raised. When all fingers were being pointed at her she began to lick her calf. I thought that she did have, somehow, the look of an old cow.

At last I turned my eyes back to Kinanjui. I do not know whether he had been looking at the cow at all. While I looked at him he did not even wince. He sat immovable, like some bulk without either intelligence or sympathies just set down by my house. He turned his side to the screaming crowd, and I realized how much the profile is the true face of a king. It is a Native faculty thus to transform yourself, in a single movement, into lifeless matter. I do not think that Kinanjui could have spoken or moved without fanning the flames of passion; as it was he kept sitting on them to quell them. Not everybody could have done it.

Little by little the fury died down, the people stopped shrieking and began to talk in an everyday manner; in the end they became silent one by one. Wainaina's mother, when she thought that nobody watched her, crawled a few steps on her stick to have a closer look at the cow. Farah turned and came back to civilization, with a little, wry smile.

When everything was quiet we made the parties in the case come round to the mill-stone table, dip their thumb in cart-grease, and press their thumbmark down upon the document of the agreement. Wainaina did it very reluctantly, whimpering a little when he set his thumb to the paper, as if it was burning him. The agreement ran as follows:

The following agreement has been made at Ngong to-day, the 26th of September, between Wainaina wa Bemu and Kaninu wa Muture. The Chief Kinanjui is present here and sees it all.

The agreement states that Kaninu shall pay to Wainaina a cow with a heifer calf. This cow and heifer calf shall be given to Wainaina's son Wanyangerri, who was, on the 19th December last year, shot by a shotgun which was fired by mistake by Kaninu's son Kabero. The cow and calf shall be the property of Wanyangerri.

With the payment of this cow and her heifer calf the Shaurie shall be finally settled. Nobody, after this, must speak of it or mention it at all.

Ngong, 26th September.

Wainaina's mark.
Kaninu's mark.

I was here and heard the document read.

The mark of the Chief Kinanjui.

The cow and her heifer calf were handed over to Wainaina in my presence.

Baroness Blixen.

3

VISITORS
TO THE
FARM

'Post res perditas'

Big Dances

We had many visitors to the farm. In pioneer countries hospitality is a necessity of life not to the travellers alone but to the settlers. A visitor is a friend, he brings news, good or bad, which is bread to the hungry minds in lonely places. A real friend who comes to the house is a heavenly messenger, who brings the *panis angelorum.*

When Denys Finch-Hatton came back after one of his long expeditions, he was starved for talk, and found me on the farm starved for talk, so that we sat over the dinner-table into the small hours of the morning, talking of all the things we could think of, and mastering them all, and laughing at them. White people, who for a long time live alone with Natives, get into the habit of saying what they mean, because they have no reason or opportunity for dissimulation, and when they meet again their conversation keeps the Native tone. We then kept up the theory that the wild Masai tribe, in their Manyatta under the hills, would see the house all afire, like a star in the night, as the peasants of Umbria saw the house wherein Saint Francis and Saint Clare were entertaining one another upon theology.

The greatest social functions of the farm were the *Ngomas* – the big Native dances. At these occasions we entertained up to fifteen hundred or two thousand guests. The entertainment offered by the house was however in itself modest. We would give the old bald mothers of the dancing Morani and the *Nditos* – the maidens – snuff, and the children – at those dances to which children were brought – sugar, distributed by Kamante in wooden spoons, and I sometimes asked the D.C.'s permission for my squatters to make tembu, a deadly drink, fabricated from sugar cane. But the real performers, the indefatigable young dancers, brought the glory and luxury of the festivity with them, they were immune to foreign influence, and concentrated upon the sweetness and fire within themselves. One thing only did they demand from the outside world: a space of level ground to dance on. This was to be found near my house: the big lawn was plain under the trees, and the square in the forest between my boys' huts had been laid out level. For this reason the farm was highly thought of by the young people of the country, and the invitations to my balls much valued.

The Ngomas were held sometimes in the day and sometimes at night. In the day-time the Ngomas needed more room, since they brought with them as many onlookers as dancers; they therefore took place on the lawn. At most Ngomas the dancers stand in a large circle, or in a number of smaller circles, and there keep jumping up and down, the head thrown back, or stamping the ground to a rhythm, throwing themselves forward on one foot, and back on to the other, or again slowly and solemnly walking round sideways with their faces to the centre of the ring, the prominent dancers separating themselves from the ring, to perform, jump, and run in the middle of it. The day-time Ngomas left their mark stamped upon the lawn in larger and smaller dry brown rings, as if the grass had here been burnt away by fire, and these magic rings would only slowly disappear.

The big day-time Ngomas had the character more of a fair than a ball. Crowds of onlookers followed the dancers and grouped themselves under the trees. When the rumour of the Ngoma had spread widely enough we would even see here the flighty ladies of Nairobi – the *Malaya*, a pretty word in Swaheli – arriving in style, in Ali Khan's mule-traps, all wrapped in lengths of gay large-patterned calico, and looking, when seated, like large flowers on the grass. The honest young girls on the farm in their traditional oiled and greased leather skirts and mantles, took up their position close to them, and frankly discussed their clothes and manners, but the beauties of the town, cross-legged, remained as quiet as glass-eyed dolls of dark wood, and smoked their little cigars. Swarms of children, enraptured by the dances, and keen to learn and imitate, stormed from one ring to another, or were carried away to form little dancing-rings of their own on the outskirts of the lawn, and there jumped up and down.

The Kikuyu, when going to a Ngoma, rub themselves all over with a particular kind of pale red chalk, which is much in demand and is bought and sold; it gives them a strangely *blond* look. The colour is neither of the animal nor the vegetable world; in it the young people themselves look fossilized, like statues cut in rock. The girls in their demure, bead-embroidered, tanned leather garments cover these, as well as themselves, with the earth, and look all one with them – clothed statues in which the folds and draperies are daintily carried out by a skilled artist. The young men are naked for a Ngoma, but on such occasions make much out of their coiffures, clapping the chalk on to their manes and pigtails, and carrying their limestone heads high. During my last years in Africa, the Government forbade the people to put chalk on the head. In both sexes the rigout is of the greatest effect: diamonds and high decorations will not impart to their bearers a more decided gala appearance. Whenever at a distance you catch sight, in the landscape, of a group of red-chalked Kikuyu on the march, you feel the atmosphere vibrating with festivity.

An open-air dance in the day suffers from lack of limitation. The stage is far too big for it – where does it begin and where end? The small figures of the individual dancers may be all dyed, with the entire back-part of an ostrich floating behind their heads, and the bold cavalier-like cockspurs made of Colobus-monkey skin at the heels, they cannot help looking spread and scattered under the tall trees. The show – including larger and smaller rings of dancers, spread-out groups of onlookers, and children running to and fro – flings your eyes from one corner of it to the other. The whole scene has some likeness to those old pictures of a battle, observed from an eminence, in which you will see the cavalry advancing at one side, while the artillery takes up its position at the other, and isolated figures of ordnance officers gallop diagonally across the field of view.

The day-time Ngomas were likewise very noisy affairs. The dancing music from flutes and drums was often drowned in the clamour from the audience, the dancing girls themselves gave out a strange, long-drawn and shrill shriek when, in one of the figures executed by male dancers, a Moran made a jump, or swung his spear over his head, in an exceptionally fine manner. An unbroken stream of congenial conversation was kept up amongst the old people on the grass. It was pleasant here to watch a couple of ancient Kikuyu women carousing with a calabash between them, absorbed in gay talk, presumably of the days when they had themselves cut a figure in the dancing ring, their faces more and more radiant with happiness as, in the course of the afternoon, the sun sank lower, and the supply of tembu in the calabash as well. At times, when the group was joined by a couple of old husbands, one of the women would be so carried away by the memories of her young days that she stumbled to her feet and, flapping the arms, took a running step or two in the true Ndito manner. She was ignored by the crowd but enthusiastically applauded by her little circle of contemporaries.

But the Ngomas of the night were set about in earnest.

They were held in the autumn only, after the maize-harvesting, and below the full moon. I do not think that they had any religious significance to them, but they may have done so once; the manner of the performers and onlookers suggested a mysterious and sacred moment. These dances may have been a thousand years old. Some of them – which was highly approved of by the mothers and grandmothers of the dancers – were held by the white settlers to be immoral; they felt that they must have them prohibited by law. One time, when I came back from a holiday in Europe, I found that twenty-five of my young warriors had, in the height of the coffee-picking season, been sent to jail by my manager for having danced a forbidden dance at a night Ngoma on the farm. My manager informed me that his wife could not possibly put up with the dance. I upbraided the elders of the squatters for having held their Ngoma near my manager's house, but they gravely explained to me that they had been dancing at Kathegu's manyatta, four or five miles away from it. I then had to go to Nairobi to talk matters over with our D.C., who let the whole lot of dancers come back to the farm to pick coffee.

The night dances were fine spectacles. Here you were not in doubt as to the theatre of the show; it was formed by the fires and extended as far out as the light spread, indeed fire was the central principle of the Ngoma. It was not really needed for the dancing, for the moonlight of the African highlands is marvellously clear and white; it was brought to create an effect. The fire made of the dancing place a stage of the first order, it collected all the colours and movements within it into a unity.

Natives will rarely overdo an effect. They had no great flaming bonfires lighted. Firewood was carried to the dancing place during the day before the dance by the squatter women of the farm, who will have looked upon themselves as hostesses to the feast, and was here piled up in the centre of the dancing ring. The old women who honoured the ball with their presence at night took their seats round this central pile, and from there a row of small fires, like a circle of stars, were fed through the hours of the night. The dancers again were dancing and running outside the fires with the forest night as a background. The place had to be fairly big or the heat and smoke would get into the eyes of the old onlookers, but it was all the same an enclosed place in the world, as if it had been a large house for the joint use of all within it.

Natives have no sense or taste for contrasts; the umbilical cord of nature has, with them, not been quite cut through. They held their Ngomas only during the time of the full moon. When the moon did her best they did theirs. With the landscape bathing and swimming in gentle powerful light from the sky, to the great illumination over Africa they added their little red-hot glow.

The guests arrived in small parties, sometimes three at a time, sometimes a dozen or fifteen – friends who came together by appointment, or who had joined company on the road. Many of these dancers had walked fifteen miles to get to the Ngoma. When travelling many together they brought flutes or drums with them, so that, on the night of the big dance, all the roads and pathways of the country would resound and ring with music, like jingles shaken at the face of the moon. At the entrance to the dancing ring the wanderers paused and waited for the ring to open to them; sometimes, when they came from very far away, or were sons of the big neighbouring Chiefs, they were received into it by one of the old squatters or prominent dancers of the farm, or by the monitors of the dance.

The monitors of the Ngoma were young men from the farm like the others, but they were there to keep up the ceremonial of the dance, and made the most of their position. Before the dancing began, they strutted up and down in front of the dancers with knitted brows and a grave face; as the dance grew livelier they ran from one side of the ring to another, to watch that everything was going as it should. They were effectively armed, carrying bundles of sticks tied together, the one end of which they kept burning, by dipping them from time to time into the fire. They kept a sharp eye upon the dancers, and wherever they espied anything of an unseemly nature going on, they were at them at once; with a terrible expression and a furious snarl they hurled their whole bunch of sticks, the burning end foremost, straight at the body of the offender. The victim was seen to be bent double at the stroke, but he never gave a sound. Perhaps a burn of this kind was no dishonourable wound to be carrying away from a Ngoma.

In one of the dances the girls would stand demurely upon the feet of the young men and clasp them round the waist, while the young warriors, with an outstretched arm at each side of the girl's head, held on to their spear with both hands, from time to time lifting it and striking it down to the ground with all their might. It made a pretty picture, of the young women of the tribe having taken refuge at the bosom of their men against some great danger, and of the men guarding them, even by letting them stand on their feet, protecting them against snakes or any other dangers from the ground. As the dance went on for hours the faces of the dancers took on an expression of angelic ecstasy, as if they were really all ready to die for one another.

They had other dances in which the dancers ran in and out amongst the fires, where one head-dancer made a number of very high jumps and leaps, and there was much swinging of spears; it was, I believe, built upon a lion-hunt.

They had singers at the Ngoma, as well as flutes and drums. Some of these singers were famous all over the country, and were made to come from far away. Their singing was more a rhythmical recitation than a song. They were improvisers, and made up their ballads off-hand, with the quick, attentive chorus of the dancers joining in. It was pleasant to listen, in the night air, to the one gentle voice being raised, and to the regularly repeated, measured call of young voices. But as it went on all night, with the drums falling in for an effect from time to time, it became both deadly monotonous and strangely excruciating to hear, as if you could not bear either to have it going on for one moment longer, or to have it ever stopped.

The most famous singer of my day came from Dagoretti. He had a clear strong voice and was, besides, himself a great dancer. When singing he would walk or run inside the dancing ring in a long-sliding stride, half-kneeling at every step; he held the one flat hand to the corner of his mouth; it was probably done to concentrate the sound, but it gave the effect of a great dangerous secret being confided to the congregation. He looked like the African echo itself. He used to move his audience to happiness or to a warlike mood as he chose, or to real convulsions of laughter. He sang one formidable song, a war song, in which the singer is, I believe, imagined running from village to village calling the nation to war, and describing to them the massacre and the loot. A hundred years ago it would have made the blood of the white immigrants run cold. But generally he was not so terrifying. One night he sang three songs, which I asked Kamante to translate to me. The first of them was a fantasy: the whole party of the dancers were imagined getting hold of a ship and sailing to Volaia. The second song, Kamante explained to me, was all in praise of the old women, the mothers and grandmothers of the singer and the dancers. This song sounded sweet to me: it was long, and must have described in detail the wisdom and kindness of the toothless bald old Kikuyu wives, who listened at the pile of firewood in the centre of the place, and nodded their heads. The third song was short, but drew great shouts of laughter from everybody; the singer had to raise his shrill voice to be heard through it, and laughed himself as he sang. The old women, who had now been put in good humour by being so strongly flattered, beat their thighs, and threw up big gapes, like crocodiles, at it. Kamante was loth to translate it to me, he said it was nonsense, and gave it me only very much shortened. The theme of it was simple: after a recent epidemic of plague, the Government had set a price upon each dead rat handed in to the D.C.s – the song described how the rats, universally pursued, were taking refuge in the beds of the old and young women of the tribe, and what happened to them there. It must have been amusing in its details, which I did not get; Kamante himself, while translating it to me very much against his wish, at times could not repress a sour smile.

At one of the night Ngomas a dramatic incident took place.

The Ngoma was a farewell feast, given in my honour a short time before I was going to Europe on a visit. We had had a good year: it was held in great style, there may have been fifteen hundred Kikuyu present. The dance had been going on for a few hours; as I came out to have another look at it before going to bed, a chair was placed for me with its back to one of the boys' huts, and I was entertained by a couple of the old squatters.

All at once a great stir ran through the ring of dancers, a deep movement of surprise or fear, a curious sound, as when the wind blows through a bed of rushes. The dance slowed up, slowed up, but it did not stop yet. I asked one of the old men what was the matter. He answered quickly, in a low voice: 'Masai na-kudja' – the Masai are coming.

The news must have been brought by a runner, for it lasted some time before anything more happened; probably the Kikuyu were sending back to say that their guests would be received. It was against the law for the Masai to come to a Kikuyu Ngoma, too much trouble had arisen from this kind of thing in the past. My houseboys came up and stood by my chair; everybody looked towards the entrance of the dancing ground. When the Masai came in, the dance stopped altogether.

There were twelve young Masai warriors walking in, and when they had taken a few steps they stopped, waited, and looked neither right nor left; they blinked a little towards the fire. They were naked except for their weapons and their magnificent head-dresses. One of them had on the lion-skin head-dress of the Moran at war. A broad stripe of scarlet was painted vertically from the knee to the foot, as if the blood was running down the leg. They stood erect, stiff-legged, their heads thrown back, silent and deadly grave; their attitude was at the same time that of the conqueror and the prisoner. It was felt that they had come to the Ngoma against their own will. The dull beating of the drum had run across the river into the Reserve, had gone on, and gone on, and troubled the hearts of the young warriors there; twelve of them had not had it in them to resist the call.

The Kikuyu were deeply agitated, too, but they behaved well to their guests. The chief dancer of the farm welcomed them into the dancing ring, where in deep silence they took their place, and the dance was begun once more. It was, however, different from what it had been before, the air was loaded now. The drums began to beat in a louder voice, and a more rapid rhythm. Had the Ngoma gone on, we should have seen some striking feats, when Kikuyu and Masai would have taken upon themselves to show one another their vigour and skill as dancers. But it did not come to that: there are things which cannot be carried through even with the goodwill of everybody concerned.

What happened I do not know. All of a sudden the ring swayed, and was broken, someone shrieked aloud: in some seconds the whole place before me was a mass of running, thronging people, there was the sound of blows and of bodies falling to the ground, and over our heads the night air was undulating with spears. We all got up, even the wise old women of the centre, who crawled on to the stacks of firewood to see what was going on.

When the emotion had calmed down, and the storming crowd had dissolved again, I found myself in the centre of the swarm, with a little cleared space round me. Two of the old squatters came up to me, and reluctantly explained what had happened: the violation of law and order committed by the Masai, and the present state of things: a Masai and three Kikuyu were badly wounded, 'cut to pieces', their expression was. Would I now, they went on gravely, consent to sew them up again? – otherwise everybody was likely to get much trouble from the *Selikali* – the Government. I asked the old man what the fighters had had cut off. 'The head,' he answered proudly, with the Native instinct to make the most of a catastrophe. At that moment Kamante was seen to advance across the place, carrying a long-threaded darning needle, and my thimble. I still hesitated, and at that moment old Awaru came forward. He had learned tailoring during the seven years that he had been in prison. He must have been looking for an opportunity for practising, and showing off his craft, for he volunteered to take charge of the case, and at once the interest concentrated upon him. He did indeed sew up the wounded, they got well under his hands, and he himself in after times made much of the achievement, but Kamante told me in confidence that the heads had not been off.

As the presence of the Masai at the dance had been illegal, we for a long time had to conceal the wounded Masai in the hut reserved for white visitors' servants. Here he recovered, and from here in the end he disappeared without a word of thanks to Awaru. It comes hard, I believe, to the heart of a Masai to be wounded – and healed – by Kikuyu.

When towards the end of the night of the Ngoma, I walked out to ask for news of the wounded people, I found, in the grey morning air, the fires still smouldering. A number of young Kikuyu were in action round them, leaping and poking long sticks into the embers, under the direction of a very old squatter wife, Wainaina's mother. They were making a spell to prevent the Masai from having any success in love with the Kikuyu girls.

A Visitor from Asia

The Ngomas were neighbourly and traditionally social functions. In the course of time, it was the younger brothers and sisters and, later on, the sons and daughters of the first dancers known to me, who came to the dancing ground.

But we had visitors from distant countries as well. The monsoon blows from Bombay: wise and experienced old people travelled in ships, all the way from India, and came to the farm.

There was in Nairobi a big Indian timber merchant by the name of Choleim Hussein, with whom I had done many deals when I was first clearing my land and who was a zealous Mohammedan and a friend of Farah's. One day he arrived at the house and asked for permission to bring a High Priest from India on a visit. He was coming all over the sea, Choleim Hussein told me, to inspect his congregations of Mombasa and Nairobi: the congregations on their side were eager to entertain him well, and, working their brains, they could think of nothing better than this visit to the farm. Would I let him come? When I said that he would be welcome, Choleim Hussein went on to explain that the rank and holiness of the old man were such that he could eat nothing which had been cooked in pots ever used by infidels. But I need not bother about that, he quickly added, the Mohammedan congregation of Nairobi would prepare the meal and send it out in good time; would I only let the High Priest partake of it in my house? As I agreed, Choleim Hussein after a little while took up the matter again, with difficulty. There was one more point, only one. Wherever the High Priest went, etiquette demanded that he should receive a present, in a house like mine it could be no less than one hundred rupees. But I need not let that worry me, he hurried to explain, the money had been collected amongst the Mohammedans of Nairobi, who only asked me to hand it over to the Priest. But would the Priest, I asked, believe it to be a present from me? Of this I could extract no explanation from Choleim Hussein; there are times when coloured people cannot make themselves clear to save their lives. At first I declined the rôle intended for me, but looking at the disappointed faces of Choleim Hussein and

Farah, which had a moment before been radiant with hope, I gave up my pride and thought that I would let the High Priest think what he liked.

On the day of the visit I had forgotten about it and gone out in the field to try my new tractor. Titi, Kamante's little brother, was sent out to me there. The tractor made such a noise that I could not hear what he had got to say, and it was so difficult to start that I dared not stop it; Titi ran alongside of it all through the field like a small mad dog, panting and snapping in the deep ground and the long thick tail of dust, until at the end of the field we came to a pause. 'The Priests have come,' he roared to me. 'What Priests?' I asked back. 'All the Priests,' he proudly explained; they had arrived in four carts, six in each. I went with him back to the house, and as I got near I caught sight of a swarm of white-robed figures spread on the lawn, as if a flight of big white birds had settled round my house, or a company of angels swooped on to the farm. It will have been a whole Spiritual Court sent from India to keep up the flame of orthodoxy in Africa. There was, however, no mistaking the dignified figure of the High Priest as he advanced towards me, escorted by two subordinates, and, at a respectful distance, by Choleim Hussein. He was a very short old man with a delicate, refined face, as if carved in very old ivory. The retinue drew near, to stand guard upon our meeting, and then withdrew; I was expected to entertain my guest alone.

We could not speak a word to one another, for he understood neither English nor Swaheli, and I did not know his language. We had to express our great mutual respect by pantomime. He had already, I saw, been shown the house. All the plate that it possessed was set out on the table, and flowers arranged according to Indian and Somali taste. I went and sat down with him on the stone seat to the west. There, under the breathless attention of the onlookers, I handed him over the hundred rupees which were wrapped up in a green handkerchief belonging to Choleim Hussein.

I had somehow been prejudiced against the old Priest on account of his preciseness – on seeing him so very old and small I, for a moment, thought that the situation might be awkward to him. But as we sat together in the afternoon sun, in no way pretending to keep up any conversation, but keeping one another company in a friendly spirit, I felt that to him nothing at all could be awkward. He conveyed a strange impression of being in safety, and completely secure. He had a courteous little manner with him, and smiled and nodded, as I pointed out the hills and the tall trees to him, as if he were interested in everything, and incapable of surprise at anything. I wondered if this consistency was produced by an entire ignorance of the evil of the world, or by a deep knowledge and acceptance of it. For whether there be no venomous snakes in the world, or whether you shall have arrived, by injecting ever-stronger doses of venom into your blood, at a stage of perfect immunity to it, in the end it must come to the same thing. The look of the old man's calm face was that of a very young infant, which has not yet learnt to speak, and which is interested in everything, and by the nature of things incapable of surprise. I might have sat, on the stone seat, through an hour of the afternoon, in the company of a very small child, a noble infant, some old Master's child Jesus – from time to time touching the rocker of the cradle with a spiritual foot. The faces of very old women of the world, who have seen all of it, and through it, will have that same look. It is not a masculine expression – it goes with the swaddling-clothes and the woman's frock, and went well with the beautiful white cashmere robes of my old guest. In a person in male clothes I have seen it only in a clever clown in a circus.

The old man was tired, and would not get up, while the other Priests were taken by Choleim Hussein down to the river to see the mill. As he was like a bird himself he seemed to take an interest in birds. I had at that time a tame stork by the house, and I kept a flock of geese which were never killed, but were there to make the place look like Denmark. The old Priest showed much interest in them; by pointing to the corners of the world he tried to find out from where they came. My dogs were on the lawn, to make the millennium character of the afternoon perfect. I had thought that Farah and Choleim Hussein would have had them shut up in the kennel, for Choleim Hussein, as a true Mohammedan, was all in a panic about them whenever he came to the farm to do business. But here they were walking about, amongst the white-robed clergy, indeed the lion by the lamb. Those were the dogs supposed by Ismail to know a Mohammedan by sight.

Before he went away the High Priest gave me, in memory of his visit, a ring with a pearl. I felt then that I, too, wanted to give him something, in addition to the sham gift of the rupees, and I sent Farah to the store to fetch the skin of a lion which had a short time ago been shot on the farm. The old man took hold of one of the big claws, and with a clear attentive eye tried the sharpness of it on his cheek.

After he had gone away, I wondered whether he had taken into his lean, noble head every single thing within the horizon of the farm, or nothing whatever. Something he had noticed, for three months later I had a letter from India, very wrongly addressed and delayed in the post. In it an Indian prince asked me to sell to him one of my 'grey dogs', of which a High Priest had made mention to him, and to fix my own price.

The Somali Women

Of one group of visitors, who played a great part on the farm, I cannot write much, for they would not have liked it. Those were Farah's women.

When Farah married, and brought his wife from Somaliland to the farm, with her came a lively and gentle little flight of dusky doves: her mother, her younger sister, and a young cousin who had been brought up with the family. Farah told me that such was the custom of his country. The marriages of Somaliland are arranged by the elders of the families with consideration as to the birth, wealth, and reputation of the young people; in the best families the bride and bridegroom have not seen one another till the wedding-day. But the Somali are a chivalrous nation, and do not leave their maidens unprotected. It is good manners in a new-married husband to take up his abode in his wife's village for six months after the wedding; during this time she may still hold her own as a hostess and a person of local knowledge and influence. Sometimes he cannot do so; then the bride's female relations do not hesitate to keep her company a bit into married life, even when this to them means lifting, and wandering into distant countries.

The circle of Somali women in my household was later completed by a little motherless girl of the tribe whom Farah took on, not, I think, without an eye to a likely profit when her time to marry should come, after the pattern of Mordecai and Esther. This little girl was an exceedingly bright and vivacious child, and it was a curious thing to see how, as she grew up, the maidens took her in hand, and scrupulously formed her into a young virgin *comme il faut*. When she first came to live with us she was eleven years old, and was ever breaking away from the domain of the family to follow me about. She rode my pony and carried my gun, or she would run with the Kikuyu Totos to the fishing pond, tucking up her skirts and galloping bare-footed round the rushy bank with a landing-net. The little Somali girls have their hair all shaven off, leaving only a ring of dark curls round the head and one long lock at the top of it; it is a pretty fashion, and it gave the child the air of a very gay and malicious young monk. But with time, and under the influence of the grown-up girls, she was transformed, and was herself fascinated and possessed by the process of her transformation. Exactly as if a heavy weight had been tied on to her legs, she took to walking slowly, slowly; she held her eyes cast down after the best pattern, and made it a point of honour to disappear at the arrival of a stranger. Her hair was cut no more, and when the day came that it was long enough, it was, by the other girls, parted and plaited into a number of little pigtails. The novice gave herself up gravely and proudly to all the hardships of the rite; it was felt that she would rather die than fall short in her duties towards it.

The old woman, Farah's mother-in-law, was, Farah told me, in her own country held in high esteem on account of the excellent education which she had given her daughters. They were there the glass of fashion and the mould of maidenly form. Indeed here were three young women of the most exquisite dignity and demureness. I have never known ladies more ladylike. Their maiden modesty was accentuated by the style of their clothes. They wore skirts of imposing amplitude; it took, I know – for I have often bought silk or calico for them – ten yards of material to make one of them. Inside these masses of stuff their slim knees moved in an insinuating and mysterious rhythm:

> Tes nobles jambes, sous les volants qu'elles chassent,
> Tourmentent les désirs obscurs et les agacent,
> Comme deux sorcières qui font
> Tourner un philtre noir dans un vase profond.

The mother herself was an impressive figure, very stout, with the powerful and benevolent placidity of a female elephant, contented in her strength. I have never seen her angry. Teachers and pedagogues ought to have envied her that great inspiring quality which she had in her; in her hands education was no compulsion and no drudgery, but a great noble conspiracy into which her pupils were by privilege admitted. The little house that I had built for them in the woods was a small High-school of White Magic, and the three young girls, who walked so gently upon the forest paths round it, were like three young witches who were studying at it as hard as they could, for at the end of their apprenticeship great mightiness would be theirs. They were competing in excellence in a congenial spirit; probably where you are in reality upon the market, and have your price openly discussed, rivalry takes on a frank and honest character. Farah's wife, who was no longer in suspense as to her price, was holding a special position, like that of the good pupil who has already obtained a scholarship in witchcraft; she might be observed in confidential talks with the old head magician, and such an honour never fell to the maidens.

All the young women had a high idea of their own value. A Moham-medan virgin cannot marry beneath her, such a thing would call down the gravest blame upon her family. A man may marry beneath him – that is good enough for him – and young Somalis have been known to take Masai wives. But while a Somali girl may marry into Arabia, an Arab girl cannot marry into Somaliland, for the Arabs are the superior race on account of their nearer relationship with the Prophet, and, amongst the Arabs themselves, a maiden belonging to the Prophet's family cannot marry a husband outside it. By virtue of their sex, the young females of the race have a claim to an upward social career. They themselves inno-cently compared the principle to that of a stud-farm of purebreds, for the Somali think very highly of mares.

By the time that we had become well acquainted, the girls asked me if it could be true what they had heard, that some nations in Europe gave away their maidens to their husbands for nothing. They had even been told, but they could not possibly realize the idea, that there was one tribe so depraved as to pay the bridegroom to marry the bride. Fie and shame on such parents, and on girls who gave themselves up to such treatment. Where was their self-respect, where their respect for woman, or for virginity? If they themselves had had the misfortune to be born into that tribe, the girls told me, they would have vowed to go into their grave unmarried.

In our days we have in Europe no opportunity to study the technique of maidenly prudery, and from the old books I had failed to catch the charm of it. Now I understood how my grandfather and great-grandfather were forced to their knees. The Somali system was at once a natural necessity and a fine art, it was both religion, strategy, and ballet, and was practised in all respects with due devotion, discipline, and dexterity. The great sweetness of it lay in the play of opposite forces within it. Behind the eternal principle of refutation, there was much generosity; behind the pedantry what risibility, and contempt of death. These daughters of a fighting race went through their ceremonial of primness as through a great graceful war-dance; butter would not melt in their mouth, neither would they rest till they had drunk the heart's blood of their adversary; they figured like three ferocious young she-wolves in seemly sheep's clothing. The Somali are wiry people, hardened in deserts and on the sea. Heavy weights of life, strenuous pressure, high waves, and long ages, must have gone to turn their women into such hard, shining amber.

The women made Farah's house home-like in the manner of a nomadic people, who may have to break their tents at any time, with many rugs and embroidered covers hung on the walls. Incense to them was an important component to a home; many of the Somali incenses are very sweet. In my life at the farm I saw few women, and I got into the habit of sitting, at the end of the day, for a quiet hour with the old woman and the girls in Farah's house.

They took an interest in everything, and little things pleased them. Small mishaps on the farm, and jokes on our local affairs, set them laughing like a whole chime of jingles in the house. When I was to teach them to knit they laughed over it as over a comical puppet-show.

There was no ignorance in their innocence. They had all assisted at childbirths and death-beds, and discussed the particulars of them coldly with the old mother. Sometimes, to entertain me, they would relate fairy tales in the style of the Arabian Nights, mostly in the comical genre, which treated love with much frankness. It was a trait common to all these tales that the heroine, chaste or not, would get the better of the male characters and come out of the tale triumphant. The mother sat and listened with a little smile on her face.

Within this enclosed women's world, so to say, behind the walls and fortifications of it, I felt the presence of a great ideal, without which the garrison would not have carried on so gallantly; the idea of a Millennium when women were to reign supreme in the world. The old mother at such times would take on a new shape, and sit enthroned as a massive dark symbol of that mighty female deity who had existed in old ages, before the time of the prophet's God. Of her they never lost sight, but they were, before all, practical people with an eye on the needs of the moment and with infinite readiness of resource.

The young women were very inquisitive as to European customs, and listened attentively to descriptions of the manners, education, and clothes of white ladies, as if out to complete their strategic education with the knowledge of how the males of an alien race were conquered and subdued.

Their own clothes played a tremendous part in their lives, which was no wonder, since to them they were all at once material of war, booty of war, and symbols of victory, like conquered banners. Their husband, the Somali, is abstinent by nature, indifferent to food and drink and to personal comfort, hard and spare as the country he comes from: woman is his luxury. For her he is insatiably covetous, she is to him the supreme good of life: horses, camels, and stock may come in and be desirable, too, but they can never outweigh the wives. The Somali women encourage their men in both inclinations of their nature. They scorn any softness in a man with much cruelty; and with great personal sacrifices they hold up their own price. These women cannot acquire a pair of slippers in any possible way except through a man, they cannot own themselves but must needs belong to some male, to a father, a brother or a husband, but they are still the one supreme prize of life. It is a surprising thing, and to the honour of both parties, what amounts of silks, gold, amber, and coral the Somali women get out of their men. At the end of the long, strenuous trading-safaris, the hardships, risks, stratagems, and endurances were all turned into female apparel. The young girls who had no men to squeeze, in their little tent-like house were making the most of their pretty hair and looking forward to the time when they should be conquering the conqueror, and extorting from the extortioner. They were all very good at lending one another their finery, and took pleasure in dressing up the young sister, who was the beauty of the lot, in her married sister's best clothes; even, with laughter, in her cloth-of-gold head-dress, which the virgin could not lawfully wear.

The Somali are given to law-suits and long feuds, and we were hardly ever without a case that needed Farah's frequent presence in Nairobi, or meetings of the tribe at the farm. At such times the old woman, when I came to the house, would pump me on the cases in a gentle and intelligent manner. She might have questioned Farah, who would have told her all she wanted to know, for he had a great respect for her. But she took the other course, I believe, from diplomacy. In this way she could still maintain, should it suit her, a woman's ignorance of men's affairs, and a womanly incapability to understand a single word of them. If she gave advice it should be uttered in Sibylline fashion, divinely inspired, and nobody should ever hold her to account.

At these big meetings of the Somali at the farm or at the great religious celebrations, the women had much to do with the arrangement and the food. They were not themselves present at the banquet, and they could not go into the Mosque, but they were ambitious as to the success and splendour of the party, and did not even amongst themselves let out what in their hearts they thought of it all. On these occasions they so strongly reminded me of the ladies of a former generation in my own country, that in my mind I saw them in bustles and long narrow trains. Not otherwise did the Scandinavian women of the days of my mother and grandmothers – the civilized slaves of good-natured barbarians – do the honours at those tremendous sacred masculine festivals: the pheasant-shoots and great *battues* of the autumn season.

The Somali have been slave-owners for innumerable generations, and their women got on well with the Natives and with them had an unconcerned placid way. To the Native, service with the Somali and the Arab is less difficult than with the white people, for the tempo of life of the coloured races is everywhere the same. Farah's wife was popular with the Kikuyu of the farm, and Kamante many times told me that she was very clever.

With those of my white friends who frequently came to stay at the farm, like Berkeley Cole and Denys Finch-Hatton, the young Somali women were friendly; they frequently talked of them and knew a surprising lot about them. They conversed with them, when they met, in a sisterly manner, their hands in the folds of their skirts. But the relations were complicated because both Berkeley and Denys had Somali servants, and those the girls could not, for the life of them, meet. No sooner had Jama or Bilea, turbaned, lean and dark-eyed, shown themselves on the farm, than my young Somali women were gone from the face of it, not a bubble showing where they had sunk. If during these times they wanted to see me, they came sneaking round the corners of the house, drawing one of their skirts together over their faces. The Englishmen said that they were pleased by the confidence shown them, but in their hearts, I believe, a little cold wind blew at the consciousness of being thought so harmless.

I sometimes took the girls out for a drive or a visit; I was careful then to question the mother as to the correctness of it, for I would not begrime names that were as fresh as Dian's visage. To the one side of the farm lived a young Australian married woman who was for a few years a charming neighbour to me; she would ask the Somali girls over for tea. Those were great occasions. They then dressed up as pretty as a bouquet of flowers, and as we were driving along, the car behind me twittered like an aviary. They took the greatest interest in the house, the clothes, even – as he was seen riding or ploughing in the distance – in the husband of my friend. As tea was served, it came out that it was only the married sister and the children who could partake of it, to the young girls it was forbidden as too exciting. They had to content themselves with cakes and did so demurely, with a good grace. There was some discussion about the little girl, who was with us – could she still drink tea, or had she reached an age to which it would prove too dangerous? The married sister held that she might have it, but the child gave us a deep, dark, proud glance, and rejected the cup.

The cousin was a pensive girl with red-brown eyes, she could read Arabic and knew passages of the Koran by heart. She was of a theological turn of mind, and we had many religious discussions and talks about the wonders of the world. From her I learned the true paraphrase of the story of Joseph and Potiphar's wife. She would admit Jesus Christ to have been born of a virgin, but not as the son of God, for God could have no sons in the flesh. Mariammo, who was the loveliest of maidens, had been walking in the garden, and a great angel, sent by the Lord, with his wingfeather had touched her shoulder: from this she conceived. In the course of our debates I one day showed her a picture postcard of Thorvaldsen's statue of Christ, in the Cathedral of Copenhagen. Upon that she fell in love, in a gentle and ecstatic way, with the Saviour. She could never hear enough about him, she sighed and changed colour as I narrated. About Judas she was much concerned – what sort of man was he, how could there be people like that – she herself would be only too happy to scratch out his eyes. It was a great passion, in the nature of the incense which they burned in their houses, and which, made from dark wood grown upon distant mountains, is sweet and strange to our senses.

I asked the French Fathers if I might bring my party of young Mohammedan women to the mission, and when they agreed in their friendly lively manner – pleased that something was going to happen – we one afternoon drove over to them, and one by one solemnly entered the cool church. The young women had never been in such a lofty building. As they looked up they held their hands over their heads to protect themselves should it fall down upon them. There were statues in the church, and, with the exception of the picture postcard, they had never in their lives seen anything like them. At the French Mission there is a life-size statue of the Virgin, all in white and light blue, with a lily in her hand, and beside her another of St Joseph with the infant on his arm. The girls were struck dumb in front of them, the beauty of the Virgin made them sigh. Of St Joseph they knew already, and they thought highly of him, for being such a loyal husband and protector to the Virgin; now they gave him deep thankful glances because he carried the child for his wife as well. Farah's wife, who was then expecting her child, kept near the Holy Family all the time she stayed in the church. The Fathers prided themselves much on their church windows, which were done up in a paper imitation of stained glass, and represented the passion of Christ. The young cousin became all lost and absorbed in these windows, she walked round the church with her eyes on them, wringing her hands, her own knees bending as under the weight of the cross. On the way home they said very little; they were afraid, I believe, to betray their ignorance by any questions they might make. Only a couple of days later did they ask me if the Fathers could make the Virgin or St Joseph come down from their plinths.

The young cousin was married from the farm, in a pretty bungalow which was then empty, and which I lent to the Somalis for the occasion. The wedding was a splendid affair and lasted for seven days. I was present at the head ceremony, when a procession of women, all singing, led the bride to meet the singing procession of men who brought the bridegroom to her. She had never seen him till then, and I wondered if she had imagined him in the likeness of Thorvaldsen's Christ, or if she would have had two ideals, a heavenly and an earthly love, on the model of the romances of chivalry. In the course of the week I drove over there more than once. At whatever hour I arrived I found the house ringing with festive life and fumigated with wedding incense. Sword-dances, and great dances of the women, went with a swing; big deals in cattle were done amongst the old men, guns were fired, and mule-traps from town were arriving or leaving. At night, in the light of hurricane-lamps on the verandah, the loveliest dyes of Arabia and Somaliland were going in and out of the carts and the house: carmoisin, prune pure, Sudan brown, rose bengale, and saffranine.

Farah's son was born on the farm, Ahamed, whom they called Saufe, which means, I believe, a saw. In his heart there was none of the timidity of the Kikuyu children. When he was a tiny infant, swaddled like an acorn, with hardly any body to his dark round head, he sat up erect, and looked you straight in the face: it was like holding a small falcon on your hand, a lion-cub on the knee. He had inherited his mother's gaiety of heart, and, when he could run about, became a big joyful adventurer who held much influence in the young Native world of the farm.

Old Knudsen

Sometimes visitors from Europe drifted into the farm like wrecked timber into still waters, turned and rotated, till in the end they were washed out again, or dissolved and sank.

Old Knudsen, the Dane, had come to the farm, sick and blind, and stayed there for the time it took him to die, a lonely animal. He walked along the roads all bent over his misery; for long periods he was without speech, for he had no strength left over from the hard task of carrying it, or, when he spoke, his voice, like the voice of the wolf or hyena, was in itself a wail.

But when he recovered breath, and for a little while was without pain, then sparks flew from the dying fire once more. He would then come to me and explain how he had got to fight with a morbid melancholic disposition in himself, an absurd tendency to see things black. It must be outreasoned, for the outward circumstances they were not amiss, they were, the devil take him, not to be despised. Only pessimism, pessimism – that was a bad vice!

It was Knudsen who advised me to burn charcoal and sell it to the Indians of Nairobi, at a time when we were, on the farm, more than usually hard up. There were thousands of rupees in it, he assured me. And it could not fail under the aegis of Old Knudsen, for he had, at one time of his tumultuous career, been to the utmost north of Sweden, and there had learned the craft at his finger's end. He took upon himself to instruct the Natives in the art. While we were thus working together in the wood I talked much with Knudsen.

Charcoal-burning is a pleasant job. There is undoubtedly something intoxicating about it, and it is known that charcoal-burners see things in a different light from other people; they are given to poetry and taradiddle, and wood-demons come and keep them company. Charcoal is a beautiful thing to turn out, when your kiln is burnt and opened up, and the contents spread on the ground. Smooth as silk, matter defecated, freed of weight, and made imperishable, the dark experienced little mummy of the wood.

The *mise en scène* of the art of charcoal-burning is in itself as lovely as possible. As we were cutting down the undergrowth only – for charcoal cannot be made from thick timber – we were still working under the crowns of the tall trees. In this stillness and shade of the African forest, the cut wood smelt like gooseberries; and the piercing, fresh, rank, sour smell of the burning kiln was as bracing as a sea breeze. The whole place had a theatrical atmosphere which, under the equator, where there are no theatres, was of infinite charm. The thin blue whorls of smoke from the kilns arose at regular distances, and the dark kilns themselves looked like tents on the stage; the place was a smugglers' or soldiers' camp in a romantic opera. The dark figures of the Natives moved noiselessly amongst them. Where the underwoods have been cleared away in an African forest you will always get a great number of butterflies, which seem to like to cluster on the stubs. It was all mysterious and innocent. In the surroundings, the small crooked form of Old Knudsen fitted in wonderfully well, flickering about, red-topped, agile, now that he had got a favourite job to attend to, sneering and encouraging, like a Puck grown old and blind and very malicious. He was conscientious about his work and surprisingly patient with his Native pupils. We did not always agree. In Paris, where as a girl I went to a painting school, I had learnt that olive-wood will make the best charcoal, but Knudsen explained that olive had no knots in it, and, seven thousand devils in hell, everyone knew that the heart of things was in their knots.

A particular circumstance here in the wood soothed Knudsen's hot temper. The African trees have a delicate foliage, mostly digitate, so that when you have cleared away the dense undergrowth, so to say hollowing out the forest, the light is like the light in a beechwood in May at home, when the leaves are just unfolded, or hardly unfolded yet. I drew Knudsen's attention to the likeness, and the idea pleased him, for all the time of the charcoal-burning he kept up and developed a fantasy: we were on a Whit Sunday picnic in Denmark. An old hollow tree he christened Lottenburg, after a place of amusement near Copenhagen. When I had a few bottles of Danish beer hidden in the depths of Lottenburg, and invited him to a drink there, he condescended to think it a good joke.

When we had all our kilns lighted we sat down and talked of life. I learned much about Knudsen's past life, and the strange adventures that had fallen to him wherever he had wandered. You had, in these conversations, to talk of Old Knudsen himself, the one righteous man – or you would sink into that black pessimism against which he was warning you. He had experienced many things: shipwrecks, plague, fishes of unknown colouring, drinking-spouts, water-spouts, three contemporaneous suns in the sky, false friends, black villainy, short successes, and showers of gold that instantly dried up again. One strong feeling ran through his Odyssey: the abomination of the law, and all its works, and all its doings. He was a born rebel, he saw a comrade in every outlaw. A heroic deed meant to him in itself an act of defiance against the law. He liked to talk of kings and royal families, jugglers, dwarfs, and lunatics, for them he took to be outside the law – and also of any crime, revolution, trick, and prank, that flew in the face of the law. But for the good citizen he had a deep contempt, and law-abidingness in any man was to him the sign of a slavish mind. He did not even respect, or believe in, the law of gravitation, which I learnt while we were felling trees together: he saw no reason why it should not be – by unprejudiced, enterprising people – changed into the exact reverse.

Knudsen was eager to imprint on my mind the names of people he had known, preferably of swindlers and scoundrels. But he never in his narrations mentioned the name of a woman. It was as if time had swept his mind both of Elsinore's sweet girls, and of the merciless women of the harbour towns of the world. All the same, when I was talking with him I felt in his life the constant presence of an unknown woman. I cannot say who she may have been: wife, mother, school-dame or wife of his first employer – in my thoughts I called her Madame Knudsen. I imagined her short because he was so short himself. She was the woman who ruins the pleasure of man, and therein is always right. She was the wife of the curtain-lectures, and the housewife of the big cleaning-days, she stopped all enterprises, she washed the faces of boys, and snatched away the man's glass of gin from the table before him; she was law and order embodied. In her claim of absolute power she had some likeness to the female deity of the Somali women, but Madame Knudsen did not dream of enslaving by love, she ruled by reasoning and righteousness. Knudsen must have met her at a young age, when his mind was soft enough to receive an ineffaceable impression. He had fled from her to the sea, for the sea she loathes, and there she does not come, but ashore again in Africa he had not escaped her, she was still with him. In his wild heart, under his white-red hair, he feared her more than he feared any man, and suspected all women of being in reality Madame Knudsen in disguise.

Our charcoal-burning in the end was no financial success. From time to time it would happen that one of our kilns caught fire, and there was our profit gone up in smoke. Knudsen himself was much concerned about our failure, and speculated hard upon it: at last he declared that nobody in the world could burn charcoal if they did not have a fair supply of snow at hand.

Knudsen also helped me to make a pond on the farm. The farm road in one place ran through a wide cup of grassy ground; there was a spring here, and I thought out the plan of building a dam below it and turning the place into a lake. You are always short of water in Africa. It would be a great gain to the cattle to be able to drink in the field, and save themselves the long journey down to the river. This idea of a dam occupied all the farm day and night, and was much discussed; in the end, when it was finished, it was to all of us a majestic achievement. It was two hundred feet long. Old Knudsen took a great interest in it, and taught Pooran Singh to fabricate a dam-scoop. We had trouble with the dam when it was built, because it would not hold water when, after a long dry period, the big rains began; it gave way in a number of places and was half washed away more than once. It was Knudsen who struck upon the scheme of strengthening the earthwork by driving the farm oxen and the squatters' stock across the dam whenever they came to the pond to drink. Every goat and sheep had to contribute to the great work and stamp the structure. He had some big bloody fights with the little herdboys down here, for Knudsen insisted that the cattle should walk over slowly, but the wild young Totos wanted them galloping across, tails in the air. In the end, when I had sided with Knudsen and he had got the better of the Totos, the long file of cattle, sedately marching along the narrow bank, looked against the sky like Noah's procession of animals going into the ark; and Old Knudsen himself, counting them, his stick under his arm, looked like the boatbuilder Noah, content in the thought that everybody but himself was soon to drown.

In the course of time, I got a vast expanse of water here, seven feet deep in places; the road went through the pond, it was very pretty. Later on we even built two more dams lower down and in this way obtained a row of ponds, like pearls upon a string. The pond now became the heart of the farm. It was always much alive, with a ring of cattle and children round it, and in the hot season, when water-holes dried up in the plains and the hills, the birds came to the farm: herons, ibis, kingfishers, quails, and a dozen varieties of geese and duck. In the evening, when the first stars sprang out in the sky, I used to go and sit by the pond, and then the birds came home. Swimming birds have purposeful flight, unlike that of other birds: they are on a journey, going from one place to another – and what perspective is there not in the roading wild swimmers! The duck concluded their orbit over the glass-clear sky, to swoop noiselessly into the dark water like so many arrow-heads let off backwards by a heavenly archer. I once shot a crocodile in the pond; it was a strange thing, for he must have wandered twelve miles from the Athi river to get there. How did he know that there would be water now, where it had never been before?

When the first pond was finished, Knudsen communicated to me the plan of putting fish into it. We had in Africa a kind of perch, which was good to eat, and we dwelt much upon the idea of rich fishing on the farm. It was not, however, an easy thing to get them: the Game Department had set out perch in ponds but would let nobody fish there yet. But Knudsen confided to me his knowledge of a pond of which no one else in the world knew, where we could get as many fish as we wanted. We would drive there, he explained, draw a net through the pond, and take the fish back in the car in tins and vats in which they would keep alive on the way if we remembered to put water-weeds in with the water. He was so keen on his scheme that he trembled while developing it to me; with his own hands he made one of his inimitable fishing-nets for it. But as the time for the expedition drew near it took on a more and more mysterious aspect. It should be undertaken, he held, on a full moon night, about midnight. At first we had meant to take three boys with us, then he reduced the number to two and to one, and kept asking whether he was absolutely trustworthy. In the end he declared that it would be better that he and I should go by ourselves. I thought this a bad plan, for we would not be able to carry the tins into the car, but Knudsen insisted that it would be by far the best, and added that we ought to tell no one of it.

I had friends in the Game Department, and I could not help it, I had to ask him: 'Knudsen, to whom do these fish that we are going to catch,

really belong?' Not a word answered Knudsen. He spat, a regular old
sailor's spit – stretched out his foot in the old patched shoe and rubbed
out the spittle on the ground, turned on his heel and walked off dead
slowly. He drew his head down between his shoulders as he went; now
he could not longer see at all, but was fumbling before him with his stick;
he was once more a beaten man, a homeless fugitive in a low, cold world.
And as if in his gesture he had pronounced a spell I stood upon the spot
where he had left me, victorious, in Madame Knudsen's slippers.

The fishing project was never again approached between Knudsen and
me. Only some time after his death did I, with the assistance of the Game
Department, set perch into the pond. They thrived there, and added their
silent, cool, mute, restive life to the other life of the pond. In the middle
of the day one could, on passing the pond, see them standing near the
surface, like fish made out of dark glass in the dim sunny water. My Toto
Tumbo was sent to the pond with a primitive fishing-rod and drew up a
perch of two pounds whenever an unexpected guest arrived at the house.

When I had found old Knudsen dead on the farm road, I sent in a
runner to the police of Nairobi and reported his death. I had meant to
bury him on the farm, but late at night two police officers came out in
a car to fetch him, and brought a coffin with them. In the meantime a
thunderstorm had broken out, and we had had three inches of rain, for
this was just at the beginning of the long rainy season. We drove down
to his house through torrents and sheets of water; as we carried Knudsen
out to the car the thunder rolled over our heads like cannons, and the
flashes of lightning stood on all sides thick as ears in a cornfield. The car
had no chains to it and could hardly keep on the road, it swung from one
side of it to another. Old Knudsen would have liked it; he would have been
satisfied with his exit from the farm.

Afterwards I had a disagreement with the Nairobi municipality over his
funeral arrangements; it developed into a heated argument and I had to
go into town about it more than once. It was a legacy left to me by
Knudsen: a last tilt, by proxy, at the face of the law. Thus I was no longer
Madame Knudsen, but a brother.

A Fugitive Rests on the Farm

There was one traveller who came to the farm, slept there for one night, and walked off not to come back, of whom I have since thought from time to time. His name was Emmanuelson; he was a Swede and when I first knew him he held the position of *maître d'hôtel* at one of the hotels of Nairobi. He was a fattish young man with a red puffed face, and he was in the habit of standing by my chair when I was lunching at the hotel, to entertain me in a very oily voice of the old country, and of mutual acquaintances there; he was so persistently conversational that after a while I changed over to the only other hotel which in those days we had in the town. I then only vaguely heard of Emmanuelson; he seemed to have a gift for bringing himself into trouble, and also to differ, in his tastes and ideas of the pleasures of life, from the customary. So he had become unpopular with the other Scandinavians of the country. Upon one afternoon he suddenly appeared at the farm, much upset and frightened, and asked me for a loan so as to get off to Tanganyika at once, as otherwise he believed he would be sent to jail. Either my help came too late or Emmanuelson spent it on other things, for a short time after I heard that he had been arrested in Nairobi, he did not go to prison but for some time he disappeared from my horizon.

One evening I came riding home so late that the stars were already out, and caught sight of a man waiting outside my house on the stones. It was Emmanuelson, and he announced himself to me in a cordial voice: 'Here comes a vagabond, Baroness.' I asked him how it was that I should find him there, and he told me that he had lost his way and so been landed at my house. His way to where? To Tanganyika.

That could hardly be true – the Tanganyika road was the great highway and easy to find, my own farm road took off from it. How was he going to get to Tanganyika? I asked him. He was going to walk, he informed me. That, I answered, was not a possible thing to do for anyone: it would mean three days through the Masai Reserve without water, and the lions were bad there just now. The Masai had been in the same day to complain about them and had asked me to come out and shoot one for them.

Yes, yes, Emmanuelson knew of all that, but he was going to walk to Tanganyika all the same. For he did not know what else to do. He was wondering now whether, having lost his way, he could bear me company for dinner and sleep at the farm to start early in the morning. If that was not convenient to me he would set out straight away while the stars were out so bright.

I had remained sitting on my horse while I talked to him, to accentuate that he was not a guest in the house, for I did not want him to dine with me. But as he spoke, I saw that he did not expect to be invited either. He had no faith in my hospitality or in his own power of persuasion, and he made a lonely figure in the dark outside my house, a man without a friend. His hearty manner was adapted to save not his own face, which was past it, but mine; if now I sent him away it would be no unkindness, but quite all right. This was courtesy in a hunted animal – I called for my *sice* to take the pony, and got off – 'Come in, Emmanuelson,' I said, 'you can dine here and stay over the night.'

In the light of the lamp Emmanuelson was a sad sight. He had on a long black overcoat such as nobody wears in Africa, he was unshaven and his hair was not cut, his old shoes were split at the toe. He was bringing no belongings with him to Tanganyika, his hands were empty. It seemed that I was to take the part of the high priest who presents the goat alive to the Lord, and sends it into the wilderness. I thought that here we needed wine. Berkeley Cole, who generally kept the house in wine, some time ago had sent me a case of a very rare burgundy, and I now told Juma to open a bottle from it. When we sat down for dinner and Emmanuelson's glass was filled he drank half of it, held it towards the lamp, and looked at it for a long time like a person attentively listening to music. '*Fameux*,' he said, '*fameux*; this is a Chambertin 1906.' It was, and that gave me respect for Emmanuelson.

Otherwise he did not say much to begin with, and I did not know what to say to him. I asked him how it was that he had not been able to find any work at all. He answered that it was because he knew nothing of the things with which people out here occupied themselves. He had been dismissed at the hotel; besides he was not really a *maître d'hôtel* by profession.

'Do you know anything of book-keeping?' I asked him.

'No. Nothing at all,' he said. 'I have always found it very difficult to add two figures together.'

'Do you know about cattle at all?' I went on. 'Cows?' he asked. 'No, no. I am afraid of cows.'

'Can you drive a tractor, then?' I asked. Here a faint ray of hope appeared on his face. 'No,' he said, 'but I think that I could learn that.'

'Not on my tractor though,' I said, 'but tell me, Emmanuelson, what have you ever been doing? What are you in life?'

Emmanuelson drew himself up straight. 'What am I?' he exclaimed. 'Why, I am an actor.'

I thought: Thank God, it is altogether outside my capacity to assist this lost man in any practical way; the time has come for general human conversation. 'You are an actor?' I said. 'That is a fine thing to be. And which were your favourite parts when you were on the stage?'

'Oh I am a tragic actor,' said Emmanuelson. 'My favourite parts were that of Armand in *La Dame aux Camélias* and of Oswald in *Ghosts*.'

We talked for some time of these plays, of the various actors whom we had seen in them and of the way in which we thought that they should be acted. Emmanuelson looked round the room. 'You have not,' he asked, 'by any chance got the plays of Henrik Ibsen here? Then we might do the last scene of *Ghosts* together, if you would not mind taking the part of Mrs Alving.'

I had not got Ibsen's plays.

'But perhaps you will remember it?' said Emmanuelson warming to his plan. 'I myself know Oswald by heart from beginning to end. That last scene is the best. For a real tragic effect, you know, that is impossible to beat.'

The stars were out and it was a very fine warm night; there was not long, now, to the big rains. I asked Emmanuelson if he did really mean to walk to Tanganyika.

'Yes,' he said, 'I am going, now, to be my own prompter.'

'It is a good thing for you,' I said, 'that you are not married.'

'Yes,' said he, 'yes.' After a little while he added modestly: 'I am married though.'

In the course of our talk, Emmanuelson complained of the fact that out here a white man could not hold his own against the competition from the Natives, who worked so much cheaper. 'Now in Paris,' he said, 'I could always, for a short time, get a job as a waiter in some café or other.'

'Why did you not stay in Paris, Emmanuelson?' I asked him.

He gave me a swift clear glance. 'Paris?' he said, 'no, no, indeed. I got out of Paris just in the nick of time.'

Emmanuelson had one friend in the world to whom in the course of the evening he came back many times. If he could only get in touch with him again, everything would be different, for he was prosperous and very generous. This man was a conjuror and was travelling all over the world. When Emmanuelson had last heard of him he had been in San Francisco.

From time to time we talked of literature and the theatre and then again we would come back to Emmanuelson's future. He told me how his countrymen out here in Africa had one after another turned him out.

'You are in a hard position, Emmanuelson,' I said, 'I do not know that I can think of anyone who is, in a way, harder up against things than you are.'

'No, I think so myself,' he said. 'But then there is one thing of which I have thought lately and of which perhaps you have not thought: some person or other will have to be in the worst position of all people.'

He had finished his bottle and pushed his glass a little away from him. 'This journey,' he said, 'is a sort of gamble to me, *le rouge et noir*. I have a chance to get out of things, I may even be getting out of everything. On the other hand if I get to Tanganyika I may get into things.'

'I think you will get to Tanganyika,' I said, 'you may get a lift from one of the Indian lorries travelling on that road.'

'Yes, but there are lions,' said Emmanuelson, 'and the Masai.'

'Do you believe in God, Emmanuelson?' I asked him.

'Yes, yes, yes,' said Emmanuelson. He sat in silence for a time. 'Perhaps you will think me a terrible sceptic,' he said, 'if I now say what I am going to say. But with the exception of God I believe in absolutely nothing whatever.'

'Look here, Emmanuelson,' I said, 'have you got any money?'

'Yes, I have,' he said, 'eighty cents.'

'That is not enough,' I said, 'and I myself have got no money in the house. But perhaps Farah will have some.' Farah had got four rupees.

Next morning, some time before sunrise, I told my boys to wake up Emmanuelson and to make breakfast for us. I had thought, in the course of the night, that I should like to take him in my car for the first ten miles of his way. It was no advantage to Emmanuelson, who would still have another eighty miles to walk, but I did not like to see him step straight from the threshold of my house into his uncertain fate, and besides I wished to be, myself, somewhere within this comedy or tragedy of his. I made him up a parcel of sandwiches and hard-boiled eggs, and gave him with it a bottle of the Chambertin 1906 since he appreciated it. I thought that it might well be his last drink in life.

Emmanuelson in the dawn looked like one of those legendary corpses whose beards grow quickly in the earth, but he came forth from his grave with a good grace and was very placid and well-balanced as we drove on. When we had come to the other side of the Mbagathi river, I let him down from the car. The morning air was clear and there was not a cloud in the sky. He was going towards the south-west. As I looked round to the opposite horizon, the sun just came up, dull and red: like the yoke of a hard-boiled egg, I thought. In three or four hours she would be white-hot, and fierce upon the head of the wanderer.

Emmanuelson said good-bye to me; he started to walk, and then came back and said good-bye once more. I sat in the car and watched him, and I think that as he went he was pleased to have a spectator. I believe that the dramatic instinct within him was so strong that he was at this moment vividly aware of leaving the stage, of disappearing, as if he had, with the eyes of his audience, seen himself go. Exit Emmanuelson. Should not the hills, the thorn trees, and the dusty road take pity and for a second put on the aspect of cardboard?

In the morning breeze his long black overcoat fluttered round his legs, the neck of the bottle stuck up from one of its pockets. I felt my heart filling with the love and gratitude which the people who stay at home are feeling for the wayfarers and wanderers of the world, the sailors, explorers, and vagabonds. As he came to the top of the hill he turned, took off his hat and waved it to me; his long hair was blown up from his forehead.

Farah, who was with me in the car, asked me: 'Where is that Bwana going?' Farah called Emmanuelson a Bwana for the sake of his own dignity, since he had slept in the house.

'To Tanganyika,' I said.

'On foot?' asked he.

'Yes,' I said.

'Allah be with him,' said Farah.

In the course of the day I thought much of Emmanuelson, and went out of the house to look towards the Tanganyika road. In the night, about ten o'clock, I heard the roar of a lion far away to the south-east; half an hour later I heard him again. I wondered if he was sitting upon an old black overcoat. During the following week I tried to get news of Emmanuelson, and told Farah to ask his Indian acquaintances who were running lorries to Tanganyika whether any lorry had passed or met him on the road. But nobody knew anything of him.

Half a year later I was surprised to receive a registered letter from Dodoma, where I knew no one. The letter was from Emmanuelson. It contained the fifty rupees that I had first lent him when he had been trying to get out of the country, and Farah's four rupees. Apart from this sum – the last money in all the world that I had expected to see again – Emmanuelson sent me a long, sensible, and charming letter. He had got a job as a bartender in Dodoma, whatever kind of bar they may have there, and was getting on well. He seemed to have in him a talent for gratitude; he remembered everything of his evening on the farm, and came back many times to the fact that there he had felt amongst friends. He told me in detail about his journey to Tanganyika. He had much good to say of the Masai. They had found him on the road and had taken him in, had shown him great kindness and hospitality, and had let him travel with them most of the way, by many circuits. He had, he wrote, entertained them so well, with recounts of his adventures in many countries, that they had not wanted to let him go. Emmanuelson did not know any Masai language, and for his Odyssey he must have fallen back upon pantomime.

It was fit and becoming, I thought, that Emmanuelson should have sought refuge with the Masai, and that they should have received him. The true aristocracy and the true proletariat of the world are both in understanding with tragedy. To them it is the fundamental principle of God, and the key – the minor key – to existence. They differ in this way from the bourgeoisie of all classes, who deny tragedy, who will not tolerate it, and to whom the word tragedy means in itself unpleasantness. Many misunderstandings between the white middle-class immigrant settlers and the Natives arise from this fact. The sulky Masai are both aristocracy and proletariat, they would have recognized at once in the lonely wanderer in black, a figure of tragedy; and the tragic actor had come, with them, into his own.

Visits of Friends

The visits of my friends to the farm were happy events in my life, and the farm knew it.

When one of Denys Finch-Hatton's long safaris was drawing to its end, it happened that I would find, on a morning, a young Masai standing upon one long slim leg outside my house. 'Bedâr is on his way back,' he announced. 'He will be here in two or three days.'

In the afternoon, a squatter Toto from the outskirts of the farm sat and waited on the lawn, to tell me, when I came out: 'There is a flight of guinea-fowl down by the bend of the river. If you want to shoot them for Bedâr when he comes I will come out with you at sunset to show you where to find them.'

To the great wanderers amongst my friends, the farm owed its charm,

I believe, to the fact that it was stationary and remained the same whenever they came to it. They had been over vast countries and had raised and broken their tents in many places, now they were pleased to round my drive that was steadfast as the orbit of a star. They liked to be met by familiar faces, and I had the same servants all the time that I was in Africa. I had been on the farm longing to get away, and they came back to it longing for books and linen sheets and the cool atmosphere in a big shuttered room; by their camp-fires they had been meditating upon the joys of farm life, and as they arrived they asked me eagerly: 'Have you taught your cook to make an *omelette à la chasseur*? – and have the gramophone records from *Petrouchka* arrived by the last mail?' They came and stayed in the house also when I was away, and Denys had the use of it, when I was on a visit in Europe. 'My sylvan retreat,' Berkeley Cole called it.

In return for the goods of civilization, the wayfarers brought me trophies from their hunts: leopard and cheetah skins, to be made into fur coats in Paris, snake and lizard skins for shoes, and marabout feathers.

To please them I experimented, while they were away, with many curious recipes out of old cookery books, and worked to make European flowers grow in my garden.

Once, when I was at home, an old lady in Denmark gave me twelve fine peony-bulbs which I brought into the country with me at some trouble, as the import regulations about plants were strict. When I had them planted, they sent up, almost immediately, a great number of dark carmoisin curvilinear shoots, and later a lot of delicate leaves and rounded buds. The first flower which unfolded was called *Duchesse de Nemours*: it was a large single white peony, very noble and rich, it gave out a profusion of fresh sweet scent. When I cut it and put it in water in my sitting-room, every single white person entering the room stopped and remarked upon it. Why, it was a peony! But soon after this, all the other buds of my plants withered and fell off, and I never got more than that one flower.

Some years later I talked with the English gardener of Lady McMillan, of Chiromo, about the peonies. 'We have not succeeded in growing peonies in Africa,' he said, 'and shall not do so till we manage to make an imported bulb flower here, and can take the seed from that flower. This is how we got delphinium into the colony.' In that way I might have introduced peonies into the country and made my name immortal like the Duchesse de Nemours herself; and I had ruined the glory of the future by picking my unique flower and putting it in water. I have very often dreamed that I have seen the white peony growing, and I have rejoiced because after all I had not cut it off.

Friends from farms up country, and from the town, arrived at the house. Hugh Martin, of the Land Office, came out from Nairobi to entertain me; a brilliant person, versed in the rare literature of the world, who had passed his life peacefully in the civil service of the East, and there, amongst other things, had developed an innate talent for looking like an immensely fat Chinese idol. He called me Candide, and was himself a curious Doctor Pangloss of the farm, firmly and placidly rooted in his conviction of the meanness and contemptibleness of human nature and of the universe, and content in his faith, for why should it not be so? He hardly ever moved out of the large chair in which he had once placed himself. With his bottle and glass before him, and a sedately beaming face, he there spread and expanded upon his theories of life, luminating with ideas, like some fantastical quick phosphoric growth of matter and thought, a fat man at peace with the world and resting in the Devil, with the stamp of cleanliness upon him that the Devil's disciples bear, in preference to many of those of the Lord.

Young, big-nosed Gustav Mohr from Norway, of an evening suddenly swooped on the house from the farm he managed, on the other side of Nairobi. He was a rousing farmer and helped me in the work of the farm in word and deed, more than any other man in the country – with a simple vigorous readiness as if it were standing to reason that farms, or Scandinavians, were to slave for one another.

Here he was now flung on to the farm by his own burning mind, like a stone out of a volcano. He was going mad, he said, in a country which expected a man to keep alive on talk of oxen and sisal; his soul was starving and he could stand it no longer. He began the moment he came into the room and went on till after midnight, holding forth on love, communism, prostitution, Hamsun, the Bible, and poisoning himself with very bad tobacco all the time. He would hardly eat, he would not listen, if I tried to get a word in he shrieked, glowing with the fire within him, and butting the air with his wild light head. He had much in him to rid himself of, and was generating more as he spoke. Suddenly, at two o'clock at night, he had no more to say. He would then sit peacefully for a little while, a humble look on his face, like a convalescent in a hospital garden, get up, and drive away at a terrible speed, prepared to keep alive, once more, for a while, on sisal and oxen.

Ingrid Linstrom came to stay on the farm when she could get away for a day or two from her own farm, her turkeys, and market gardening at

VISITORS TO THE FARM

Njoro. Ingrid was as fair of skin as of mind, and the daughter and wife of Swedish officers. She and her husband had come out with their children to Africa on a joyous adventure, a picnic, to make a fortune quickly, and had bought up flax-land because at that time flax was £500 a ton, and when, just after that, flax fell to £40, and flax-land and flax-machinery were worth nothing, she put in all her strength to save the farm for her family, planning her poultry farm and her market garden, and working like a slave. In the course of that strife she fell deeply in love with the farm, with her cows and pigs, Natives and vegetables, with the very soil of her bit of Africa, in such a great desperate passion that she would have sold both husband and children to keep it. She and I, during the bad years, had wept in one another's arms at the thought of losing our land. It was a joyful time when Ingrid came to stay with me, for she had all the broad bold insinuating joviality of an old Swedish peasant woman, and in her weather-beaten face the strong white teeth of a laughing Valkyrie. Therefore does the world love the Swedes, because in the midst of their woes they can draw it all to their bosom and be so gallant that they shine a long way away.

Ingrid had an old Kikuyu cook and houseboy named Kemosa, who filled a number of offices with her, and looked upon all her activities as his own. He slaved for her in the market garden and poultry yard, and also acted as a duenna to her three small daughters, travelling with them to and from their boarding school. When I came up to visit her on her farm at Njoro, Ingrid told me, Kemosa lost all his balance of mind, let go his hold of everything else, and made the grandest possible preparations for my reception, killing off her turkeys, so much was he impressed with Farah's greatness. Ingrid said he looked upon his acquaintance with Farah as upon the greatest honour of his existence.

Mrs Darrell Thompson of Njoro, whom I hardly knew, came out to see me when the doctors had informed her that she had only got a few more months to live. She told me that she had just been buying a pony in Ireland, a prize-jumper – for horses were to her, in death as in life, the height and glory of existence – and that now, after she had talked with the doctors, she had at first meant to cable home to stop him coming out, but then she had made up her mind to leave him to me when she herself should die. I did not think much about it until, after her death half a year later, the pony, Poor-box, made his appearance at Ngong. Poor-box, when he came to live with us, proved himself the most intelligent being on the farm. He was not much to look at, stumpy and long past his youth. Denys Finch-Hatton used to ride him, but I never cared much to do so. But by pure politics and circumspection, by knowing exactly what he wanted to do, amongst the young shining fiery horses brought out for the occasion by our wealthiest people of the colony, he won the jumping competition of Kabete, which was held in honour of the Prince of Wales. With his usual collected unassuming mien and countenance he brought home a big silver medal and, after a week of extreme anxiety, raised great radiant waves of rapture and triumph in my household and on all the farm. He died from horse-sickness, six months later, and was buried outside his stable under the lemon trees, and much lamented; his name lived a long time after him.

Old Mr Bulpett, whom the Club called Uncle Charles, used to come out to dine with me. He was a great friend of mine, and a kind of ideal to me, the English gentleman of the Victorian age, and quite at home in our own. He had swum the Hellespont, and had been one of the first to climb the Matterhorn, and he had been, in his early youth, in the eighties perhaps, La Belle Otéro's lover. I was told that she had ruined him altogether and let him go. It was to me as if I were sitting down to dinner with Armand Duval or the Chevalier des Grieux themselves. He had many lovely pictures of Otéro, and liked to talk about her.

Once, at dinner in Ngong, I said to him: 'I see that La Belle Otéro's memoirs have been published. Are you in them?'

'Yes,' he said, 'I am in them. Under another name, but still there.'

'What does she write about you?' I asked.

'She writes,' he said, 'that I was a young man who went through a hundred thousand for her sake within six months, but that I had full value for my money.'

'And do you consider,' I said and laughed, 'that you did have full value?'

He thought my question over for a very short moment. 'Yes,' he said. 'Yes, I had.'

Denys Finch-Hatton and I went with Mr Bulpett for a picnic to the top of the Ngong Hills on his seventy-seventh birthday. As we sat up there we came to discuss the question of whether, if we were offered a pair of real wings, which could never be laid off, we would accept or decline the offer.

Old Mr Bulpett sat and looked out over the tremendous big country below us, the green land of Ngong, and the Rift Valley to the west, as if ready to fly off over it at any moment. 'I would accept,' he said, 'I would certainly accept. There is nothing I should like better.' After a little time of thought he added: 'I suppose that I should think it over, though, if I were a lady.'

The Noble Pioneer

As far as Berkeley Cole and Denys Finch-Hatton were concerned, my house was a communist establishment. Everything in it was theirs, and they took a pride in it, and brought home the things they felt to be lacking. They kept the house up to a high standard in wine and tobacco, and got books and gramophone records out from Europe for me. Berkeley arrived with his car loaded up with turkeys' eggs, and oranges from his own farm on Mount Kenya. They both had the ambition to make me a judge of wine, as they were, and spent much time and thought on the task. They took the greatest pleasure in my Danish table glass and china, and used to build up on the dinner table a tall shining pyramid of all my glass, the one piece on top of the other; they enjoyed the sight of it.

Berkeley, when he stayed on the farm, had a bottle of champagne out in the forest every morning at eleven o'clock. Once, as he was taking leave of me, and thanking me for his time on the farm, he added that there had been one shadow in the picture, for we had been given coarse and vulgar glasses for our wine under the trees. 'I know, Berkeley,' I said, 'but I have so few of my good glasses left, and the boys will break them when they have to carry them such a long way.' He looked at me gravely, my hand in his. 'But, my dear,' he said, 'it has been so sad.' So afterwards he had my best glasses brought out in the wood.

It was a curious thing about Berkeley and Denys – who were so deeply regretted by their friends in England when they emigrated, and so much beloved and admired in the colony – that they should be, all the same, outcasts. It was not a society that had thrown them out, and not any place in the whole world either, but time had done it, they did not belong to their century. No other nation than the English could have produced them, but they were examples of atavism, and theirs was an earlier England, a world which no longer existed. In the present epoch they had no home, but had got to wander here and there, and in the course of time they also came to the farm. Of this they were not themselves aware. They had, on the contrary, a feeling of guilt towards their existence in England which they had left, as if, just because they were bored with it, they had been running away from a duty with which their friends had put up. Denys, when he came to talk of his young days – although he was so young still – and of his prospects, and the advice that his friends in England sent him, quoted Shakespeare's Jacques:

> 'If it do come to pass
> That any man turn ass,
> Leaving his wealth and ease,
> A stubborn will to please ...'

But he was wrong in his view of himself, so was Berkeley, and so perhaps was Jacques. They believed that they were deserters, who sometimes had to pay for their wilfulness, but they were in reality exiles, who bore their exile with a good grace.

Berkeley, if he had had his small head enriched with a wig of long silky curls, could have walked in and out of the court of King Charles II. He might have sat, a nimble youth from England, at the feet of the aged d'Artagnan, the d'Artagnan of *Vingt ans après*, have listened to his wisdom, and kept the sayings in his heart. I felt that the law of gravitation did not apply to Berkeley, but that he might, as we sat talking at night by the fire, at any moment go straight up through the chimney. He was a very good judge of men, with no illusions about them and no spite. Out of a kind of devilry, he was most charming to the people of whom he had the poorest opinion. When he really chalked his soles for the job he was an inimitable buffoon. But to be a wit in the manner of Congreve and Wycherley *en plein vingtième siècle* takes a few more qualities than Congreve or Wycherley themselves had got in them: a glow, grandezza, the wild hope. Where the jest was carried far in its daring and arrogance, sometimes it became pathetic. When Berkeley, a little heated, and as if translucent with wine, really got on his high horse, on the wall behind him the shadow of it began to grow and move, falling into a haughty and fantastical canter, as if it came of a noble breed and its sire's name had been Rozinante. But Berkeley himself, the invincible jester, lonely in his African life, half an invalid – for his heart always gave him trouble – with his beloved farm on Mount Kenya every day more in the hands of the banks, would have been the last to recognize or fear the shadow.

Small, very slight, red-haired, with narrow hands and feet, Berkeley carried himself extremely erect, with a little Artagnanesque turn of the head to right and left, the gentle motion of the unbeaten duellist. He walked as noiselessly as a cat. And, like a cat, he made every room that he sat in a place of comfort, as if he had had in him a source of heat and fun. If Berkeley had come and sat with you upon the smoking ruin of your house, he would, like a cat, have made you feel that you were in a picked snug corner. When he was at his ease you expected to hear him purr, like a big cat, and when he was sick, it was more than sad and distressing, it was formidable as is the sickness of a cat. He had no principles, but a surprising stock of prejudices, as you would expect in a cat.

If Berkeley were a cavalier of the Stuarts' day, Denys should be set in an earlier English landscape, in the days of Queen Elizabeth. He could have walked arm in arm, there, with Sir Philip, or Francis Drake. And the people of Elizabeth's time might have held him dear because to them he would have suggested that antiquity, the Athens, of which they dreamed and wrote. Denys could indeed have been placed harmoniously in any period of our civilization, *tout comme chez soi*, all up till the opening of the nineteenth century. He would have cut a figure in any age, for he was an athlete, a musician, a lover of art, and a fine sportsman. He did cut a figure in his own age but it did not quite fit in anywhere. His friends in England always wanted him to come back, they wrote out plans and schemes for a career for him there, but Africa was keeping him.

The particular, instinctive attachment which all Natives of Africa felt towards Berkeley and Denys, and towards a few other people of their kind, made me reflect that perhaps the white men of the past, indeed of any past, would have been in better understanding and sympathy with the coloured races than we, of our industrial age, shall ever be. When the first steam engine was constructed, the roads of the races of the world parted, and we have never found one another since.

There was a shadow cast over my friendship with Berkeley by the circumstance that Jama, his young Somali servant, was of a tribe at war with Farah's tribe. To people familiar with the clannish feelings of the Somali, those dark deep desert glances that were exchanged over our dinner table, when the two were waiting on Berkeley and me, bode as ill as possible. Late in the evening we fell to talking of what we were to do when we should be coming out in the morning to find both Farah and Jama cold, with daggers in their hearts. In these matters the enemies knew neither fear nor sense, they were held back from bloodshed and ruin solely by their feelings of attachment, such as they were, for Berkeley and me.

'I dare not,' said Berkeley, 'tell Jama tonight that I have changed my mind, and that I shall not this time be going to Eldoret, where lives the young woman that he is in love with. For then his heart will turn to stone against me, it will be a matter of no importance to him if my clothes are brushed, and he will go out and kill Farah.'

Jama's heart, however, never did turn to stone towards Berkeley. He had been with him a long time, and Berkeley often talked about him. He told me how once, over a matter in which Jama held himself to be right, Berkeley had lost his temper and had hit the Somali. 'But then, my dear, you know,' said Berkeley, 'at the very same moment I had one straight back in my face.'

'And how did it go then?' I asked him.

'Oh it went all right,' Berkeley said, modestly. After a little while he added: 'It was not so bad. He is twenty years younger than me.'

This incident had left no trace in the attitude of either the master or the servant. Jama had a quiet, slightly patronizing manner towards Berkeley, such as most Somali servants have towards their employers. After Berkeley's death, Jama did not want to stay in the country, but went back to Somaliland.

Berkeley had a great, ever unsatisfied, love of the sea. It was a favourite dream of his that he and I should – when we had made money – buy a dhow and go trading to Lamu, Mombasa, and Zanzibar. We had our plans all worked out and our crew ready, but we never did make money.

Whenever Berkeley was tired or unwell he fell back on his thoughts of the sea. He then grieved over his own foolishness in having spent a lifetime anywhere but on salt water, and used strong language about it. Once when I was going to Europe and he was in this mood, to please him I conceived the plan of bringing out two ship's lanterns, starboard and port, to hang by the entrance door of my house, and told him of it.

'Yes, it would be nice,' he said, 'the house would be in that way like a ship. But they must have sailed.'

So in Copenhagen in a sailors' shop by one of the old canals, I bought a pair of big old heavy ship's lanterns, which had for many years sailed in the Baltic. We had them up on each side of the door, it faced east and we were pleased to think that the lamps were correctly placed; as the earth, on her course through the ether, throws herself forward, there would be no collision. These lamps gave Berkeley much content of heart. He often used to come to the house quite late, and ordinarily at a great speed, but when the lamps were lighted he drove slowly, slowly, up the drive, to let the little red and green stars in the night sink into his soul and bring back old pictures, reminiscences of shipfaring, to feel as if he were indeed approaching a silent ship on dark water. We developed a signalling system in regard to the lamps, changing their place or taking down the one, so that he should know, already while in the forest, in what mood he would find his hostess and what sort of dinner was awaiting him.

Berkeley, like his brother Galbraith Cole and his brother-in-law Lord Delamere, was an early settler, a pioneer of the colony, and intimate with the Masai, who in those days were the domineering nation of the land. He had known them before the European civilization – which in the depths of their hearts they loathed more than anything else in the world – cut through their roots; before they were moved from their fair north country. He could speak with them of the old days in their own tongue. Whenever Berkeley was staying on the farm, the Masai came over the river to see him. The old chiefs sat and discussed their troubles of the present time with him, his jokes would make them laugh, and it was as if a hard stone had laughed.

Because of Berkeley's knowledge of, and friendship with, the Masai, a most imposing ceremony came to take place on the farm.

When the Great War first broke out, and the Masai had news of it, the blood of the old fighting tribe was all up. They had visions of splendid battles and massacres, and they saw the glory of the past returning once more. I happened to be out, during the first months of the war, alone with Natives and Somali, with three ox-wagons, doing transport for the English Government, and trekking through the Masai Reserve. Whenever the people of a new district heard of my arrival they came round to my camp, with shining eyes, to ask me a hundred questions of the war and the Germans – was it true that they were coming from the air? In their minds they were running breathless, to meet danger and death. At night the young warriors swarmed round my tent, in full war paint, with spears and swords; sometimes, in order to show me what they were really like, they would give out a short roar, an imitation of the lion's roar. They did not doubt then that they would be allowed to fight.

But the English Government did not think it wise to organize the Masai to make war on white men, be they even Germans, and it forbade the Masai to fight, and put an end to all their hopes. The Kikuyu were to take part in the war as carriers, but the Masai were to keep their hands off their weapons. But in 1918, when conscription had been introduced in regard to all the other Natives of the colony, the Government thought it necessary to call out the Masai as well. An officer of the K.A.R., with his regiment, was sent to Narok to procure three hundred Morani as soldiers. By this time the Masai had lost their sympathy with the war and refused to come. The Morani of the district disappeared into the woods and the bush. In the pursuit of them the K.A.R. Troops by mistake fired on a manyatta, and two old women were killed. Two days after, the Masai Reserve was in open revolt, swarms of Morani swept through the country, killed a number of Indian traders, and burned down more than fifty dukhas. The situation was serious, and the Government did not want to force it. Lord Delamere was sent down to negotiate with the Masai and in the end a compromise was set up. The Masai were allowed to take out the three hundred Morani themselves, and they were let off with a joint fine in punishment of their devastation in the Reserve. No Morani appeared, but by that time the Armistice put an end to the whole matter.

During the time of all these events, some of the old big Masai chiefs had made themselves useful to the English military, by sending out their young men to scout on the movements of the Germans in the Reserve and on the border. Now that the war was over, the government wanted to show their recognition of their services. A number of medals were sent out from home to be distributed amongst the Masai, and as far as twelve of the medals were concerned Berkeley, who knew the Masai so well and could speak Masai, was asked to deal them out.

My farm bordered on the Masai Reserve and Berkeley came to ask me if he might stay with me and give out the medals from my house. He was a little nervous about the enterprise, and told me that he had no clear idea what was expected from him. On a Sunday we drove together a long way down into the Reserve, and talked with the people in the manyattas, in order to summon the chiefs in question to the farm on such and such a day. Berkeley in his very young days had been an officer in the 9th Lancers, and he was then, I have been told, the smartest young officer in his regiment. Still, as, towards sunset, we were driving home again, he began to speak to me of the military calling and mentality, and to develop his ideas upon them, in the manner of a civilian.

The distribution of the medals, although in itself of no special consequence, was an event of great dimensions and weight. So much wisdom, sagacity, and tact were displayed in it, on both sides, as to make it stand for an act in the history of the world, or a symbol:

> '... His Darkness and his Brightness
>   exchanged a greeting of extreme politeness.'

The old Masai had arrived, followed by retainers of sons of theirs. They sat and waited on the lawn, from time to time discussing my cows grazing there; perhaps they had a faint hope that, in reward of their services, they were to be made a present of a cow. Berkeley kept them waiting a long time, which was, I believe, to them in the order of things; in the meantime he had an armchair carried out on the lawn in front of the house, in which to sit while he gave out the medals. When in the end he came forth from the house he looked, in this dark company, very fair, red-haired and light-eyed. He had now the complete brisk cheerful carriage and expression of an efficient young officer, so that I learned that Berkeley, who could let his face express so many things, could also in the hour of need make it an absolute blank. He was followed by Jama, who had on a very fine Arabian waistcoat all embroidered in gold and silver, which Berkeley had let him buy for the occasion, and who carried the box with the medals.

Berkeley stood up in front of his chair to speak, and so active was the uprightness of his slight small figure that the old people got on to their feet, one by one, and stood facing him, their eyes in his, gravely. What the speech was about I cannot say, as it was in Masai. It sounded as if he were briefly informing the Masai that an unbelievable benefit was to be bestowed upon them, and that the explanation of the happenings was their own incredibly praiseworthy behaviour. But seeing that it was Berkeley who spoke, and that from the faces of the Masai you would never learn anything, it may have contained something quite different, of which I should never have thought. When he had spoken, without a moment's pause he let Jama bring up the box, and took out the medals, solemnly reading out, one after another, the names of the Masai chiefs, and handing them their medals with a generously outstretched arm. The Masai took them from him very silently, in an outstretched hand. The ceremony could only have been carried through so well by two parties of noble blood and great family traditions; may democracy take no offence.

A medal is an inconvenient thing to give to a naked man, because he has got no place to fix it on to, and the old Masai chiefs kept standing with theirs in their hand. After a time a very old man came up to me, held out his hand with a medal in it, and asked me to tell him what it had got on it. I explained it to him as well as I could. The silver coin had on the one side a head of Britannia, and upon the other side the words: '*The Great War for Civilization*'.

I have later told some English friends of the incident of the medals, and they have asked: 'Why was not the king's head on the medals? It was a great mistake.' I myself do not think so: it seems to me that the medals should not be made too attractive, and that the whole matter was well arranged. It may still be that it is this sort of thing which we shall be given at the time when our reward is great in heaven.

When Berkeley was taken ill, I was about to go to Europe on a holiday. He was then a member of the Legislative Council of the colony, and I telegraphed to him: 'Will you not come and stay at Ngong for the sitting of the council bring bottles.' He wired back: 'Your telegram straight from heaven arriving with bottles.' But when he came to the farm, his car all filled up with wine, he did not care to drink it. He was very pale, and even sometimes quite silent. His heart was bad, and he could not do without Jama, who had been taught to give him the injections for it, and he had many worries that lay on it heavily; he lived in great fear of losing his farm. Still, by his presence, he turned my house into a chosen, comfortable corner of the world.

'I have come to the stage, Tania,' he said to me gravely, 'when I can only drive in the very best of cars, only smoke the finest cigars, and only drink the most exquisite vintages of wine.' While he was staying with me then, he told me one evening that the doctor had ordered him to go to bed and stay in bed for a month. I said to him that if he would follow the order, and stay in bed for a month at Ngong, I would give up my journey to remain there and look after him, and go to Europe next year. He thought my offer over for a little while. 'My dear,' he said, 'I could not do it. If I did it to please you, what should I be afterwards?'

I said good-bye to him then with a heavy heart. While I was sailing home, past Lamu and Takaunga, where our dhow was to have found her way, I thought of him. But in Paris I heard that he had died. He had dropped down dead before his house, as he was stepping out of the car. He was buried on his farm, where he wished to be.

When Berkeley died, the country changed. His friends felt it at the time, with great sadness, and many people came to feel it later. An epoch in the history of the colony came to an end with him. In the course of the years many things were reckoned from this turning point, and people said: 'When Berkeley Cole lived' or 'Since Berkeley died'. Up till his death the country had been the Happy Hunting Grounds, now it was slowly changing and turning into a business proposition. Some standards were lowered when he went: a standard of wit, as it was soon felt – and such a thing is sad in a colony; a standard of gallantry – soon after his death people began to talk of their troubles; a standard of humanity.

As Berkeley went away, a grim figure made her entrance upon the stage from the opposite wing – *la dure nécessité maîtresse des hommes et des dieux*. It was a strange thing that a small slight man should have been able to keep her from the door, for so long a time as he drew breath. The yeast was out of the bread of the land. A presence of gracefulness, gaiety, and freedom, an electric power-factor was out. A cat had got up and left the room.

Wings

Denys Finch-Hatton had no other home in Africa than the farm. He lived in my house between his safaris, and kept his books and his gramophone there. When he came back to the farm, it gave out what was in it; it spoke – as the coffee-plantations speak, when with the first showers of the rainy season they flower, dripping wet, a cloud of chalk. When I was expecting Denys back, and heard his car coming up the drive, I heard, at the same time, the things of the farm all telling what they really were. He was happy on the farm; he came there only when he wanted to come, and it knew, in him, a quality of which the world besides was not aware, a humility. He never did but what he wanted to do, neither was guile found in his mouth.

Denys had a trait of character which to me was very precious, he liked to hear a story told. For I have always thought that I might have cut a figure at the time of the plague of Florence. Fashions have changed, and the art of listening to a narrative has been lost in Europe. The Natives of Africa, who cannot read, have still got it; if you begin to them: 'There was a man who walked out on the plain, and there he met another man,' you have them all with you, their minds running upon the unknown track of the men on the plain. But white people, even if they feel that they ought to, cannot listen to a recital. If they do not become fidgety, and remember things that should be done at once, they fall asleep. The same people will ask you for something to read, and may then sit all through an evening absorbed in any kind of print handed them, they will even then read a speech. They have been accustomed to take in their impressions by the eye.

Denys, who lived much by the ear, preferred hearing a tale told to reading it; when he came to the farm he would ask: 'Have you got a story?' I had been making up many while he had been away. In the evenings he made himself comfortable, spreading cushions like a couch in front of the fire, and with me sitting on the floor, cross-legged like Scheherazade herself, he would listen, clear-eyed, to a long tale, from when it began until it ended. He kept better account of it than I did myself, and at the dramatic appearance of one of the characters, would stop me to say: 'That man died in the beginning of the story, but never mind.'

Denys taught me Latin, and to read the Bible, and the Greek poets. He himself knew great parts of the Old Testament by heart, and carried the Bible with him on all his journeys, which gained him the high esteem of the Mohammedans.

He also gave me my gramophone. It was a delight to my heart, it brought a new life to the farm, it became the voice of the farm – 'The soul within a glade the nightingale is'. Sometimes Denys would arrive unexpectedly at the house, while I was out in the coffee-field or the maize-field, bringing new records with him; he would set the gramophone going, and as I came riding back at sunset, the melody streaming towards me in the clear cool air of the evening would announce his presence to me, as if he had been laughing at me, as he often did. The Natives liked the gramophone, and used to stand round the house to listen to it; some of my houseboys picked out a favourite tune and asked me for it, when I was alone with them in the house. It was a curious thing that Kamante should stick, in his preference, with much devotion to the Adagio of Beethoven's Piano Concerto in C Major; the first time that he asked me for it he had some difficulty in describing it, so as to make clear to me which tune it was that he wanted.

Denys and I, however, did not agree in our tastes. For I wanted the old composers, and Denys, as if courteously making up to the age for his lack of harmony with it, was as modern as possible in his taste in all arts. He liked to hear the most advanced music. 'I would like Beethoven all right,' he said, 'if he were not vulgar.'

Denys and I, whenever we were together, had great luck with lions. Sometimes he came back from a shooting safari of two or three months, vexed that he had been unable to get a good lion for the people from Europe whom he had taken out. In the meantime the Masai had been to my house and had asked me to come out and shoot a certain lion or lioness which was killing off their cattle, and Farah and I had been out, camping in their manyatta, sitting up over a kill, or walking out in the early morning, without as much as finding the track of a lion. But when Denys and I went for a ride, the lions of the plains would be about, as in attendance, we would come upon them then and there at a meal, or see them crossing the dry river-beds.

On a New Year's morning, before sunrise, Denys and I found ourselves on the new Narok road, driving along as fast as we could go on a rough road.

Denys, the day before, had lent a heavy rifle to a friend of his who was going south with a shooting party, and late in the night he remembered that he had neglected to explain to him a certain trick in the rifle, by which the hair-trigger might be put out of action. He was worried about it and afraid that the hunter would come to some sort of harm by his ignorance. We could then think of no better remedy than that we should start as early as possible, take the new road and try to overtake the shooting party at Narok. It was sixty miles, through some rough country; the safari was travelling by the old road and would be going slowly as it had heavy loaded lorries with it. Our only trouble was that we did not know if the new road would have been brought through all the way to Narok.

The early morning air of the African highlands is of such a tangible coldness and freshness that time after time the same fancy there comes back to you: you are not on earth but in dark deep waters, going ahead along the bottom of the sea. It is not even certain that you are moving at all: the flows of chilliness against your face may be the deep-sea currents, and your car, like some sluggish electric fish, may be sitting steadily upon the bottom of the sea, staring in front of her with the glaring eyes of her lamps, and letting the submarine life pass by her. The stars are so large because they are not real stars but reflections, shimmering upon the surface of the water. Alongside your path on the sea-bottom, live things, darker than their surroundings, keep on appearing, jumping up and sweeping into the long grass, as crabs and beach-fleas will make their way into the sand. The light gets clearer, and about sunrise, the sea-bottom lifts itself towards the surface, a new created island. Whirls of smells drift quickly past you, fresh rank smells of the olive-bushes, the brine scent of burnt grass, a sudden quelling smell of decay.

Kanuthia, Denys's boy, who sat in the back of the box-body car, gently touched my shoulder and pointed to the right. To the side of the road, twelve or fifteen yards away from it, was a dark bulk, a manatee taking a rest on the sands, and on the top of it something was stirring in the dark water. It was, I saw later, a big dead giraffe bull, that had been shot two or three days before. You are not allowed to shoot the giraffe, and Denys and I later had to defend ourselves against the charge of having killed this one, but we could prove that it had been dead some time when we came upon it, though it was never found by whom or why it had been killed. Upon the huge carcass of the giraffe a lioness had been feeding, and now raised her head and shoulder above it to watch the passing car.

Denys stopped the car, and Kanuthia lifted the rifle that he carried off his shoulder. Denys asked me in a low voice: 'Shall I shoot her?' – for he very courteously looked on the Ngong Hill as my private hunting-ground.

We were going across the land of the same Masai who had been to my house to bewail the loss of their cattle; if this was the animal which had killed one after the other of their cows and calves, the time had come to put an end to her. I nodded.

He jumped from the car and slid back a few steps; at the same moment the lioness dived down behind the body of the giraffe, he ran round the giraffe to get within shot of her, and fired. I did not see her fall: when I got out and up to her she was lying dead in a big black pool.

There was no time to skin her, we must drive on if we were to cut off the safari at Narok. We gazed round and took note of the place; the smell of the dead giraffe was so strong that we could not very well pass it unknowingly.

But when we had driven a further two miles there was no more road. The tools of the road-labourers lay here; on the other side of them was the wide stony land, just grey in the dawn, all unbroken by any touch of man. We looked at the tools and at the country, we would have to leave Denys's friend to take his chance with the rifle. Afterwards, when he came back, he told us that he had never had an opportunity to use it. So we turned back, and as we turned we got our faces to the eastern sky, reddening over the plains and the hills. We drove towards it and talked all the time of the lioness.

The giraffe came within view, and by this time we could see him clearly and distinguish – where the light fell on to his side – the darker square spots on his skin. And as we came near to him we saw that there was a lion standing on him. In approaching we were a little lower than the carcass; the lion stood straight up over it, dark, and behind him the sky was now all aflame. *Lion Passant Or*. A bit of his mane was lifted by the wind. I rose up in the car, so strong was the impression that he made, and Denys at that said: 'You shoot this time.' I was never keen to shoot with his rifle, which was too long and heavy for me, and gave me a bad shock; still, here the shot was a declaration of love, should the rifle not then be of the biggest calibre? As I shot it seemed to me that the lion jumped straight up in the air, and came down with his legs gathered under him. I stood, panting, in the grass, aglow with the plenipotence that a shot gives you, because you take effect at a distance. I walked round the carcass of the giraffe. There it was – the fifth act of a classic tragedy. They were all dead now. The giraffe was looking terribly big, austere, with his four stiff legs and long stiff neck, his belly torn open by the lions. The lioness, lying on her back, had a great haughty snarl on her face, she was the *femme fatale* of the tragedy. The lion was lying far from her, and how was it that he had learned nothing by her fate? His head was laid on his two front paws, his mighty mane covered him as a royal mantle, he too was resting in a big pool, and by now the morning air was so light that it showed scarlet.

Denys and Kanuthia pulled up their sleeves and while the sun rose they skinned the lions. When they took a rest we had a bottle of claret, and raisins and almonds, from the car; I had brought them with us to eat on the road, because it was New Year's Day. We sat on the short grass and ate and drank. The dead lions, close by, looked magnificent in their nakedness: there was not a particle of superfluous fat on them, each muscle was a bold controlled curve, they needed no cloak, they were, all through, what they ought to be.

As we sat there, a shadow hastened over the grass and over my feet, and looking up I could distinguish, high in the light-blue sky, the circling of the vultures. My heart was as light as if I had been flying it, up there, on a string, as you fly a kite. I made a poem:

> The eagle's shadow runs across the plain,
> Towards the distant, nameless, air-blue mountains.
> But the shadows of the round young zebra
> Sit close between their delicate hoofs all day,
>   where they stand immovable.
> And wait for the evening, wait to stretch out, blue,
> Upon a plain, painted brick-red by the sunset,
> And to wander to the water-hole.

Denys and I had another dramatic adventure with lions. It happened, in reality, before the other, in the early days of our friendship.

One morning, during the spring rains, Mr Nichols, a South African, who was then my manager, came to my house all aflame, to tell me that in the night two lions had been to the farm and had killed two of our oxen. They had broken through the fence of the oxen's fold, and they had dragged the dead oxen into the coffee-plantation; one of them they had eaten up there, but the other was lying amongst the coffee-trees. Would I now write him a letter to go and get strychnine in Nairobi? He would have it laid out in the carcass at once, for he thought that the lions would be sure to come back in the night.

I thought it over; it went against me to lay out strychnine for lions, and I told him that I could not see my way to do it. At that his excitement changed over into exasperation. The lions, he said, if they were left in peace over this crime, would come back another time. The bullocks they had killed were our best working bullocks, and we could not afford to lose any more. The stable of my ponies, he reminded me, was not far from the oxen's enclosure: had I thought of that? I explained that I did not mean to keep the lions on the farm, only I thought that they should be shot and not poisoned.

'And who is going to shoot them?' asked Nichols. 'I am no coward, but I am a married man and I have no wish to risk my life unnecessarily.' It was true that he was no coward, he was a plucky little man. 'There would be no sense in it,' he said. No, I said, I did not mean to make him shoot the lions. But Mr Finch-Hatton had arrived the night before and was in the house, he and I would go. 'Oh, that is O.K.,' said Nichols.

I then went in to find Denys. 'Come now,' I said to him, 'and let us go and risk our lives unnecessarily. For if they have got any value at all it is this that they have got none. *Frei lebt wer sterben kann.*'

We went down and found the dead bullock in the coffee-plantation, as Nichols had told me; it had hardly been touched by the lions. Their spoor was deep and clear in the soft ground, two big lions had been here in the night. It was easy to follow through the plantation and up to the wood round Belknap's house, but by the time that we came there it had rained so heavily that it was difficult to see anything, and in the grass and the bush at the edge of the wood we lost the track.

'What do you think, Denys,' I asked him. 'Will they come back to-night?'

Denys had great experience with lions. He said that they would come back early in the night to finish the meat, and that we ought to give them time to settle down on it, and go down to the field ourselves at nine o'clock. We would have to use an electric torch from his safari outfit, to shoot by, and he gave me the choice of the rôles, but I would rather let him shoot and myself hold the torch for him.

In order that we might find our way up to the dead ox in the dark, we cut up strips of paper and fastened them on the rows of coffee-trees between which we meant to walk, marking our way in the manner of Hanzl and Gretl with their little white stones. It would take us straight to the kill, and at the end of it, twenty yards from the carcass, we tied a larger piece of paper to the tree, for here we would stop, sweep the light on and shoot. Late in the afternoon, when we took out the torch to try it, we found that the batteries of it had been running down and that the light it gave was only faint. There was not time to go into Nairobi with it now, so that we should have to make the best of it as it was.

It was the day before Denys's birthday, and while we dined, he was in a melancholic mood, reflecting that he had not had enough out of life till now. But something, I consoled him, might still happen to him before his birthday morning. I told Juma to get out a bottle of wine to be ready for us when we should come back. I kept on thinking of the lions; where would they be now, at this moment? Were they crossing the river, slowly, silently, the one in front of the other, the gentle cold flow of the river turning round their chests and flanks?

At nine o'clock we went out.

It rained a little, but there was a moon; from time to time she put out her dim white face high up in the sky, behind layers and layers of thin clouds, and was then dimly mirrored in the white-flowering coffee-field. We passed the school at a distance; it was all lighted up.

At this sight a great wave of triumph and of pride in my people swept through me. I thought of King Solomon, who says: 'The slothful man saith, There is a lion in the way; a lion is in the streets.' Here were two lions just outside their door, but my school children were not slothful and had not let the lions keep them from school.

We found our marked two rows of coffee-trees, paused a moment, and proceeded up between them, one in front of the other. We had moccasins on, and walked silently. I began to shake and tremble with excitement, I dared not come too near to Denys for fear that he might feel it and send me back, but I dared not keep too far away from him either, for he might need my torchlight any moment.

The lions, we found afterwards, had been on the kill. When they heard us, or smelt us, they had walked off it a little way into the coffee-field to let us pass. Probably because they thought that we were passing too slowly, the one of them gave a very low hoarse growl, in front and to the right of us. It was so low that we were not even sure that we had heard it. Denys stopped a second; without turning he asked me: 'Did you hear?' 'Yes,' I said.

We walked a little again and the deep growling was repeated, this time straight to the right. 'Put on the light,' Denys said. It was not altogether an easy job, for he was much taller than I, and I had to get the light over his shoulder on to his rifle and farther on. As I lighted the torch the whole world changed into a brilliantly lighted stage, the wet leaves of the coffee-trees shone, the clods of the ground showed up quite clearly.

First the circle of light struck a little wide-eyed jackal, like a small fox; I moved it on, and there was the lion. He stood facing us straight, and he looked very light, with all the black African night behind him. When the shot fell, close to me, I was unprepared for it, even without comprehension of what it meant, as if it had been thunder, as if I had been myself shifted into the place of the lion. He went down like a stone. 'Move on, move on,' Denys cried to me. I turned the torch farther on, but my hand shook so badly that the circle of light, which held all the world, and which

I commanded, danced a dance. I heard Denys's laugh beside me in the dark – 'The torch-work on the second lion,' he said to me later, 'was a little shaky.' – But in the centre of the dance was the second lion, going away from us and half hidden by a coffee-tree. As the light reached him he turned his head and Denys shot. He fell out of the circle, but got up and into it again, he swung round towards us, and just as the second shot fell, he gave one long irascible groan.

Africa, in a second, grew endlessly big, and Denys and I, standing upon it, infinitely small. Outside our torchlight there was nothing but darkness, in the darkness in two directions there were lions, and from the sky rain. But when the deep roar died out, there was no movement anywhere, and the lion lay still, his head turned away on to his side, as in a gesture of disgust. There were two big dead animals in the coffee-field, and the silence of night all around.

We walked up to the lions and paced out the distance. From where we had stood the first lion was thirty yards away and the other twenty-five. They were both full-grown, young, strong, fat lions. The two close friends, out in the hills or on the plains, yesterday had taken the same great adventure into their heads, and in it they had died together.

By now all the school children were coming out of the school, pouring down the road to stop in sight of us and there to cry out in a low soft voice: 'Msabu. Are you there? Are you there? Msabu, Msabu.'

I sat on a lion and cried back to them: 'Yes I am.'

Then they went on, louder and more boldly: 'Has Bedâr shot the lions? Both two?' When they found that it was so, they were at once all over the place, like a swarm of small spring-hares of the night, jumping up and down. They, then and there, made a song upon the event; it ran as follows: 'Three shots. Two lions. Three shots. Two lions.' They embroidered and embellished it as they sang it, one clear voice falling in after the other: 'Three good shots, two big strong bad kali lions.' And then they all joined into an intoxicated refrain: 'A.B.C.D.' – because they came straight from the school, and had their heads filled with wisdom.

In a short time a great number of people came to the spot, the labourers from the mill, the squatters of the near manyattas, and my houseboys, carrying hurricane-lamps. They stood round the lions and talked about them, then Kanuthia and the sice, who had brought knives, set to skin them. It was the skin of one of these lions that, later, I gave to the Indian High Priest. Pooran Singh himself appeared on the stage, in a negligée which made him look unbelievably slight, his melliferous Indian smile shone in the midst of his thick black beard, he stuttered with delight when he spoke. He was anxious to procure for himself the fat of the lions, that with his people is held in high esteem as a medicine – from the pantomime by which he expressed himself to me, I believe against rheumatism and impotence. With all this the coffee-field became very lively, the rain stopped, the moon shone down on them all.

We went back to the house and Juma brought and opened our bottle. We were too wet, and too dirty with mud and blood to sit down to it, but stood up before a flaming fire in the dining-room and drank our live, singing wine up quickly. We did not speak one word. In our hunt we had been a unity and we had nothing to say to one another.

Our friends got a good deal of entertainment out of our adventure. Old Mr Bulpett when next we came in to a dance at the Club would not speak to us the whole evening.

To Denys Finch-Hatton I owe what was, I think, the greatest, the most transporting pleasure of my life on the farm: I flew with him over Africa. There, where there are few or no roads and where you can land on the plains, flying becomes a thing of real and vital importance in your life, it opens up a world. Denys had brought out his Moth machine; it could land on my plain on the farm only a few minutes from the house, and we were up nearly every day.

You have tremendous views as you get up above the African highlands, surprising combinations and changes of light and colouring, the rainbow on the green sunlit land, the gigantic upright clouds and big wild black storms, all swing round you in a race and a dance. The lashing hard showers of rain whiten the air askance. The language is short of words for the experiences of flying, and will have to invent new words with time. When you have flown over the Rift Valley and the volcanoes of Suswa and Longonot, you have travelled far and have been to the lands on the other side of the moon. You may at other times fly low enough to see the animals on the plains and to feel towards them as God did when he had just created them, and before he commissioned Adam to give them names.

But it is not the visions but the activity which makes you happy, and the joy and glory of the flyer is the flight itself. It is a sad hardship and slavery to people who live in towns, that in all their movements they know of one dimension only; they walk along the line as if they were led on a string. The transition from the line to the plane into the two dimensions, when you wander across a field or through a wood, is a splendid liberation to the slaves, like the French Revolution. But in the air you are taken into the full freedom of the three dimensions; after long ages of exile and dreams the homesick heart throws itself into the arms of space. The laws of gravitation and time,

> '... in life's green grove,
> Sport like tame beasts, none knew how
> gentle they could be!'

Every time that I have gone up in an aeroplane and looking down have realized that I was free of the ground, I have had the consciousness of a great new discovery. 'I see,' I have thought. 'This was the idea. And now I understand everything.'

One day Denys and I flew to Lake Natron, ninety miles south-east of the farm, and more than four thousand feet lower, two thousand feet above sea level. Lake Natron is the place from where they take soda. The bottom of the lake and the shores are like some sort of whitish concrete, with a strong, sour and salt smell.

The sky was blue, but as we flew from the plains in over the stony and bare lower country, all colour seemed to be scorched out of it. The whole landscape below us looked like delicately marked tortoise-shell. Suddenly, in the midst of it was the lake. The white bottom, shining through the water, gives it, when seen from the air, a striking, an unbelievable azure colour so clear that for a moment you shut your eyes at it; the expanse of water lies in the bleak tawny land like a big bright aquamarine. We had been flying high, now we went down, and as we sank our own shade, dark blue, floated under us upon the light blue lake. Here live thousands of flamingos, although I do not know how they exist in the brackish water – surely there are no fish here. At our approach they spread out in large circles and fans, like the rays of a setting sun, like an artful Chinese pattern on silk or porcelain, forming itself and changing, as we looked at it.

We landed on the white shore, that was white-hot as an oven, and lunched there, taking shelter against the sun under the wing of the aeroplane. If you stretched out your hand from the shade, the sun was so hot that it hurt you. Our bottles of beer when they first arrived with us, straight out of the ether, were pleasantly cold, but before we had finished them, in a quarter of an hour, they became as hot as a cup of tea.

While we were lunching, a party of Masai warriors appeared on the horizon, and approached quickly. They must have spied the aeroplane landing from a distance, and resolved to have a close look at it, and a walk of any length, even in a country like this, means nothing to a Masai. They came along, the one in front of the other, naked, tall and narrow, their weapons glinting; dark like peat on the yellow-grey sand. At the feet of each of them lay and marched a small pool of shadow: these were, besides our own, the only shadows in the country as far as the eye reached. When they came up to us they fell in line, there were five of them. They stuck their heads together and began to talk to one another about the aeroplane and us. A generation ago they would have been fatal to us to meet. After a time one of them advanced and spoke to us. As they could only speak Masai and we understood but little of the language, the conversation soon slackened, he stepped back to his fellows and a few minutes later they all turned their backs upon us, and walked away, in single file, with the wide white burning salt-plain before them.

'Would you care,' said Denys, 'to fly to Naivasha? But the country lying between is very rough, we could not possibly land anywhere on the way. So we shall have to go up high and keep up at twelve thousand feet.'

The flight from Lake Natron to Naivasha was *das Ding an sich*. We took a bee-line, and kept at twelve thousand feet all the way, which is so high that there is nothing to look down for. At Lake Natron I had taken off my lambskin-lined cap, now up here the air squeezed my forehead, as cold as iced water; all my hair flew backwards as if my head was being pulled off. This path, in fact, was the same as was, in the opposite direction, every evening taken by the Roc, when, with an elephant for her young in each talon, she swished from Uganda home to Arabia. Where you are sitting in front of your pilot, with nothing but space before you, you feel that he is carrying you upon the outstretched palms of his hands, as the Djinn carried Prince Ali through the air, and that the wings that bear you onward are his. We land at the farm of our friends at Naivasha; the mad diminutive houses, and the very small trees surrounding them, all threw themselves flat upon their backs as they saw us descending.

When Denys and I had not time for long journeys we went out for a short flight over the Ngong Hills, generally about sunset. These hills, which are amongst the most beautiful in the world, are perhaps at their loveliest seen from the air, when the ridges, bare towards the four peaks, mount, and run side by side with the aeroplane, or suddenly sink down and flatten out into a small lawn.

Here in the hills were buffaloes. I had even, in my very young days – when I could not live till I had killed a specimen of each kind of African game – shot a bull out here. Later on, when I was not so keen to shoot as to watch the wild animals, I had been out to see them again. I had camped in the hills by a spring half way to the top, bringing my servants, tents, and provisions with me, and Farah and I had been up in the dark, ice cold mornings to creep and crawl through bush and long grass, in the hope of catching a glimpse of the herd; but twice I had had to go back without success. That the herd lived there, neighbours of mine to the west, was still a value in the life on the farm, but they were serious-minded, self-sufficient neighbours, the old nobility of the hills, now somehow reduced; they did not receive much.

But one afternoon as I was having tea with some friends of mine from up-country, outside the house, Denys came flying from Nairobi and went over our heads out westwards; a little while after he turned and came back and landed on the farm. Lady Delamere and I drove down to the plain to fetch him up, but he would not get out of his aeroplane.

'The buffalo are out feeding in the hills,' he said, 'come out and have a look at them.'

'I cannot come,' I said. 'I have got a tea-party up at the house.'

'But we will go and see them and be back in a quarter of an hour,' said he.

This sounded to me like the propositions which people make to you in a dream. Lady Delamere would not fly, so I went up with him. We flew in the sun, but the hillside lay in a transparent brown shade, which soon we got into. It did not take us long to spy the buffalo from the air. Upon one of the long rounded green ridges which run, like folds of a cloth gathered together at each peak, down the side of the Ngong mountain, a herd of twenty-seven buffalo were grazing. First we saw them a long way below us, like mice moving gently on a floor, but we dived down, circling over and along their ridge, a hundred and fifty feet above them and well within shooting distance; we counted them as they peacefully blended and separated. There was one very old big black bull in the herd, one or two younger bulls, and a number of calves. The open stretch of sward upon which they walked was closed in by bush; had a stranger approached on the ground they would have heard or scented him at once, but they were not prepared for advance from the air. We had to keep moving above them all the time. They heard the noise of our machine and stopped grazing, but they did not seem to have it in them to look up. In the end they realized that something very strange was about; the old bull first walked out in front of the herd, raising his hundredweight horns, braving the unseen enemy, his four feet planted on the ground – suddenly he began to trot down the ridge and after a moment he broke into a canter. The whole clan now followed him, stampeding headlong down, and as they switched and plunged into the bush, dust and loose stones rose in their wake. In the thicket they stopped and kept close together: it looked as if a small glade in the hill had been paved with dark grey stones. Here they believed themselves to be covered to the view, and so they were to anything moving along the ground, but they could not hide themselves from the eyes of the bird of the air. We flew up and away. It was like having been taken into the heart of the Ngong Hills by a secret unknown road.

When I came back to my tea-party, the teapot on the stone table was still so hot that I burned my fingers on it. The prophet had the same experience when he upset a jug of water, and the Archangel Gabriel took him, and flew with him through the seven heavens, and when he returned, the water had not yet run out of the jug.

In the Ngong Hills there also lived a pair of eagles. Denys in the afternoons used to say: 'Let us go and visit the eagles.' I have once seen one of them sitting on a stone near the top of the mountain, and getting up from it, but otherwise they spent their life up in the air. Many times we have chased one of these eagles, careening and throwing ourselves on to one wing and then to the other, and I believe that the sharp-sighted bird played with us. Once, when we were running side by side, Denys stopped his engine in mid-air, and as he did so I heard the eagle screech.

The Natives liked the aeroplane, and for a time it was the fashion on the farm to portray her, so that I would find sheets of paper in the kitchen, or the kitchen wall itself covered with drawings of her, with the letters A B A K carefully copied out. But they did not really take any interest in her or in our flying.

Natives dislike speed, as we dislike noise; it is to them, at the best, hard to bear. They are also on friendly terms with time, and the plan of beguiling or killing it does not come into their heads. In fact the more time you can give them, the happier they are, and if you commission a Kikuyu to hold your horse while you make a visit, you can see by his face that he hopes you will be a long, long time about it. He does not try to pass the time then, but sits down and lives.

Neither do the Natives have much sympathy with any kind of machinery or mechanics. A group of the young generation have been carried away by the enthusiasm of the European for the motor-car, but an old Kikuyu said to me of them that they would die young, and it is likely that he was right, for renegades come of a weak line of the nation. Amongst the inventions of civilization which the Natives admire and appreciate are matches, a bicycle, and a rifle; still they will drop these the moment there is any talk of a cow.

Frank Greswolde-Williams, of the Kedong Valley, took a Masai with him to England as a sice, and told me that a week after his arrival he rode his horses in Hyde Park as if he had been born in London. I asked this man when he came back to Africa what he found very good in England. He thought my question over with a grave face and after a long time courteously said that the white men had got very fine bridges.

I have never seen an old Native who, for things which moved by themselves without apparent interference by man or by the forces of Nature, expressed anything but distrust and a certain feeling of shame. The human mind turns away its eye from witchcraft as from something unseemly. It may be forced to take an interest in the effects of it, but it will have nothing to do with the inside working, and no one has ever tried to squeeze out of a witch the exact recipe for her brew.

Once, when Denys and I had been up, and were landing on the plain of the farm, a very old Kikuyu came up and talked to us:

'You were up very high today,' he said, 'we could not see you, only hear the aeroplane sing like a bee.'

I agreed that we had been up high.

'Did you see God?' he asked.

'No, Ndwetti,' I said, 'we did not see God.'

'Aha, then you were not up high enough,' he said, 'but now tell me: do you think that you will be able to get up high enough to see him?'

'I do not know, Ndwetti,' I said.

'And you, Bedâr,' he said, turning to Denys, 'what do you think? Will you get up high enough in your aeroplane to see God?'

'Really I do not know,' said Denys.

'Then,' said Ndwetti, 'I do not know at all why you two go on flying.'

4

FROM
AN IMMIGRANT'S
NOTEBOOK

The Fireflies

Here in the highlands, when the long rains are over, and in the first week of June nights begin to be cold, we get the fireflies in the woods.

On an evening you will see two or three of them, adventurous lonely stars floating in the clear air, rising and lowering, as if upon waves, or as if curtseying. To that rhythm of their flight they lighten and put out their diminutive lamps. You may catch the insect and make it shine upon the palm of your hand, giving out a strange light, a mysterious message; it turns the flesh pale green in a small circle round it. The next night there are hundreds and hundreds in the woods.

For some reason they keep within a certain height, four or five feet, above the ground. It is impossible then not to imagine that a whole crowd of children of six or seven years are running through the dark forest carrying candles, little sticks dipped in a magic fire, joyously jumping up and down, and gambolling as they run, and swinging their small pale torches merrily. The woods are filled with a wild frolicsome life, and it is all perfectly silent.

The Roads of Life

When I was a child I was shown a picture – a kind of moving picture inasmuch as it was created before your eyes and while the artist was telling the story of it. This story was told, every time, in the same words.

In a little round house with a round window and a little triangular garden in front there lived a man.

Not far from the house there was a pond with a lot of fish in it.

One night the man was woken up by a terrible noise, and set out in the dark to find the cause of it. He took the road to the pond.

One night the man was woken up by a terrible noise, and set out in the dark to find the cause of it. He took the road to the pond.

Here the story-teller began to draw, as upon a map of the movements of an army, a plan of the roads taken by the man.

He first ran to the South. Here he stumbled over a big stone in the middle of the road and a little farther he fell into a ditch, got up, fell into a ditch, got up, fell into a third ditch, and got out of that.

Then he saw that he had been mistaken, and ran back to the North. But here again the noise seemed to him to come from the South, and he again ran back there. He first stumbled over a big stone in the middle of the road, then a little later he fell into a ditch, got up, fell into another ditch, got up, fell into a third ditch, and got out of that.

He now distinctly heard that the noise came from the end of the pond. He rushed to the place, and saw that a big leakage had been made in the dam, and the water was running out with all the fishes in it. He set to work and stopped the hole and only when this had been done did he go back to bed.

When now the next morning the man looked out of his little round window – thus the tale was finished, and dramatically as possible – what did he see? – A stork!

I am glad that I have been told this story and I will remember it in the hour of need. The man in the story was cruelly deceived, and had obstacles put in his way. He must have thought: 'What ups and downs! What a run of bad luck!' He must have wondered what was the idea of all his trials: he could not know that it was a stork. But through them all he kept his purpose in view; nothing made him turn around and go home; he finished his course, he kept his faith. That man had his reward. In the morning he saw the stork. He must have laughed out loud then.

The tight place, the dark pit in which I am now lying, of what bird is it the talon? When the design of my life is completed, shall I, shall other people see a stork?

Infandum, regina, jubes renovare dolorem. Troy in flames, seven years of exile, thirteen good ships lost. What is to come out of it? 'Unsurpassed elegance, majestic stateliness, and sweet tenderness.'

You are bewildered when you read the second article of faith of the Christian Church: That he was crucified, dead and buried, that he went down into Hell, and also did rise again the third day, that he ascended into Heaven, and from thence shall come again.

What ups and downs, as terrible as those of the man in the story. What is to come out of all this? – The second article of the Creed of half the world.

The Wild Came to the Aid of the Wild

My manager during the war had been buying up oxen for the army. He told me that he had then, down in the Masai Reserve, bought from the Masai a number of young oxen, which were offspring of Masai cattle and buffalo. It is a much debated question whether it is possible to cross domestic animals with the game; many people have tried to create a type of small horse fitted to the country, by breeding from zebra and horses, though I myself have never seen such cross-breeds. But my manager assured me that these oxen were really half-buffalo. They had been, the Masai told him, a much longer time growing up than the ordinary cattle, and the Masai, who were proud of them, were by this time pleased to get rid of them, as they were very wild.

It was found to be hard work to train these oxen for the wagon or plough. One strong young animal amongst them gave my manager and his Native ox-drivers endless trouble. He stormed against the men, he broke their yokes, he foamed and bellowed; when tied up he shovelled up earth in thick black clouds, he turned up the bloodshot white of his eyes, and blood, the men said, was running from his nose. The man, like the beast, towards the end of their struggle, was dead beat, the sweat streaming down his aching body.

'To break the heart of this ox,' my manager narrated, 'I had him thrown in the bullocks' paddock, with his four legs tied hard together, and a rein round his muzzle, and even then, as he was lying dumb on the ground, long scalding jets of steam stood out from his nose and terrible snorts and sighs came from his throat. I was looking forward to seeing him under the yoke for many years to come. I went to bed in my tent and I kept on dreaming of this black ox. I was woken up by a big row, the dogs barking and the Natives shouting and yelling down by the paddock. Two herd-boys came into my tent all trembling and told me that they believed a lion had got in amongst the oxen. We ran down to the place and took lamps with us, and I myself brought my rifle. As we came near to the paddock the noise died down a little. In the light of the lamps I saw a speckled thing making off. A leopard had been at the tied-up ox, and had eaten the right hind-leg off him. We would never come to see him in the yoke now.

'Then,' said my manager, 'I took my rifle and shot the ox.'

Esa's Story

At the time of the war I had a cook named Esa, an old man of much sense and a gentle disposition. One day when I was in Mackinnon's grocery shop in Nairobi, buying tea and spices, a small lady with a sharp face came up to me and remarked that she knew Esa was in my service; I said that it was so. 'But he has been with me before,' said the lady, 'and I want him back.' I said that I was sorry about that, as she would not get him. 'Oh, I do not know about that,' she said. 'My husband is a government official. Will you please tell Esa when you go home, that I want him back, and that if he does not come he will be taken for the Carrier Corps? I understand,' she added, 'that you have got enough servants without Esa.'

I did not tell Esa of these happenings straight away; only the next evening did I remember about them, and told him that I had met his old mistress, and of what she had said to me. To my surprise Esa was immediately beside himself with fear and despair. 'Oh, why did you not tell me at once, Memsahib?' said he. 'The lady will do what she has told you, and I must leave you tonight.' 'That is all nonsense,' I said. 'I do not think that they can take you like that.' 'God help me,' said Esa, 'I am afraid it may be too late already.' 'But what am I to do for a cook, Esa?' I asked him. 'Well,' said Esa, 'you will not have me for a cook either when I am with the Carrier Corps, or when I am lying dead, as I shall surely then be very soon.'

So deep was the fear of the Carrier Corps in the people in those days that Esa would not listen to anything I had to say. He asked me for the loan of a hurricane-lamp, and set off in the night to Nairobi, with what belongings he had in the world tied up in a cloth.

Esa was away from the farm for nearly a year. During that time I saw him a couple of times in Nairobi and once I passed him on the Nairobi road. He was growing old and thin, and drawn in the face, in the course of this year; his dark round head was going grey on the top. In the town he would not stop to speak to me, but when we met on the flat road and I pulled up my car, he put down the chicken-coop which he was carrying on his head, and settled down to a talk.

He had, as before, a gentle manner, but all the same he was changed, and it was now difficult to get into contact with him; he remained, all through our conversation, absent-minded, as if at a distance. He had been ill-used by fate, and deadly frightened, and had had to draw upon resources unknown to me, and through these experiences he had become chastened or clarified. It was like talking with an old acquaintance who had entered upon his novitiate in a monastery.

He asked me about things on the farm, taking it, as Native servants usually do, that his fellow-servants in his absence were behaving as badly as possible to the white master. 'When will the war be over?' he asked me. I said that I had been told that now it would not last much longer. 'If it lasts ten years longer,' he said, 'you must know that I shall have forgotten to make the dishes you have taught me.'

The mind of the little old Kikuyu, upon the road across the plains, was running upon the same line as that of Brillat-Savarin, who said that if the Revolution had lasted five years longer, the art of making a chicken ragout would have been lost.

It was obvious that Esa's regrets were mainly on my behalf, and to put an end to his commiserations I asked him how he was himself. He thought my question over for a minute; there were thoughts which had to be collected from far away before he could answer. 'Do you remember, Memsahib,' he said in the end, 'that you said it was hard on the oxen of the Indian firewood-contractors to be inspanned every day, and never to have a whole day's rest, as the farm oxen have got? Now, with the lady, I am like an Indian firewood-contractor's ox.' Esa looked away when he had spoken, apologetically. Natives have in themselves very little feeling for animals; my saying about the Indian's oxen probably had struck him as very far-fetched. That now he should, on his own, come back to it for himself, was to him an unaccountable thing.

During the war it was to me a cause of much annoyance that all letters which I wrote or received were opened by a little sleepy Swedish censor in Nairobi. He can never have found anything the least suspicious in them, but he came, I believe, within a monotonous life, to take an interest in the people on whom they turned, and to read my letters as you read a serial in a magazine. I used to add in my own letters a few threats against our censor, to be carried out after the end of the war, for him to read. When the end of the war came he may have remembered these threats, or he may on his own have woken up and repented; in any case he sent a runner to the farm with news of the Armistice. I was alone in the house when the runner arrived; I walked out in the woods. It was very silent there, and it was strange to think that it was silent on the fronts of France and Flanders as well – all the guns had been stilled. In this stillness Europe and Africa seemed near to one another, as if you could have walked by the forest-path on to Vimy Ridge. When I came back to the house I saw a figure standing outside. It was Esa with his bundle. He at once told me that he had come back and that he had brought me a present.

Esa's present was a picture, framed and under glass, of a tree, very carefully penned down in ink, every one of its hundred leaves painted a clear green. Upon each leaf, in diminutive Arabic letters, a word was written in red ink. I take it that the writings came out of the Koran, but Esa was incapable of explaining what they meant; he kept on wiping off the glass with his sleeve and assuring me that it was a very good present. He told me that he had had the picture made, during his year of trial, by the old Mohammedan priest of Nairobi. It must have taken the old man hours and hours to print it down.

Esa now stayed with me till he died.

The Iguana

In the Reserve I have sometimes come upon the iguanas, the big lizards, as they were sunning themselves upon a flat stone in a river-bed. They are not pretty in shape, but nothing can be imagined more beautiful than their colouring. They shine like a heap of precious stones or like a pane cut out of an old church window. When, as you approach, they swish away, there is a flash of azure, green, and purple over the stones; the colour seems to be standing behind them in the air, like a comet's luminous tail.

Once I shot an iguana. I thought that I should be able to make some pretty things from his skin. A strange thing happened then, that I have never afterwards forgotten. As I went up to him, where he was lying dead upon his stone, and actually while I was walking the few steps, he faded and grew pale; all colour died out of him as in one long sigh, and by the time that I touched him he was grey and dull like a lump of concrete. It was the live impetuous blood pulsating within the animal which had radiated out all that glow and splendour. Now that the flame was put out, and the soul had flown, the iguana was as dead as a sandbag.

Often since I have, in some sort, shot an iguana, and I have remembered the one of the Reserve. Up at Meru I saw a young Native girl with a bracelet on, a leather strap two inches wide, and embroidered all over with very small turquoise-coloured beads which varied a little in colour and played in green, light blue, and ultramarine. It was an extraordinarily live thing; it seemed to draw breath on her arm, so that I wanted it for myself, and made Farah buy it from her. No sooner had it come upon my own arm than it gave up the ghost. It was nothing now, a small, cheap, purchased article of finery. It had been the play of colours, the duet between the turquoise and the 'nègre' – that quick, sweet, brownish black, like peat and black pottery, of the Native's skin – that had created the life of the bracelet.

In the Zoological Museum of Pietermaritzburg, I have seen, in a stuffed deep-water fish in a showcase, the same combination of colouring, which there had survived death; it made me wonder what life can well be like, on the bottom of the sea, to send up something so live and airy. I stood in Meru and looked at my pale hand and at the dead bracelet. It was as if an injustice had been done to a noble thing, as if truth had been suppressed. So sad did it seem that I remembered the saying of the hero in a book that I had read as a child: 'I have conquered them all, but I am standing amongst graves.'

In a foreign country and with foreign species of life one should take measures to find out whether things will be keeping their value when dead. To the settlers of East Africa I give the advice: 'For the sake of your own eyes and heart, shoot not the iguana.'

Farah and the Merchant of Venice

Once a friend at home wrote out to me and described a new staging of *The Merchant of Venice*. In the evening as I was reading the letter over again, the play became vivid to me, and seemed to fill the house, so much that I called in Farah to talk with him about it, and explained the plot of the comedy to him.

Farah, like all people of African blood, liked to hear a story told, but only when he was sure that he and I were alone in the house did he consent to listen to one. It was therefore when the houseboys were back in their own huts, and any passer-by from the farm, looking in through the windows, would have believed him and me to be discussing household matters, that I narrated, and he listened, standing up immovable at the end of the table, his serious eyes on my face.

Farah gave his full attention to the affairs of Antonio, Bassanio, and Shylock. Here was a big, complicated business deal, somewhat on the verge of the law, the real thing to the heart of a Somali. He asked me a question or two as to the clause of the pound of flesh: it obviously seemed to him an eccentric, but not impossible agreement; men might go in for that sort of thing. And here the story began to smell of blood – his interest in it rose. When Portia came upon the stage, he pricked up his ears; I imagined that he saw her as a woman of his own tribe, Fatima with all sails set, crafty and insinuating, out to outman man. Coloured people do not take sides in a tale, the interest to them lies in the ingeniousness of the plot itself; and the Somali, who in real life have a strong sense of values, and a gift for moral indignation, give these a rest in their fiction. Still, here Farah's sympathy was with Shylock, who had come down with the cash; he repugned his defeat.

'What?' said he. 'Did the Jew give up his claim? He should not have done that. The flesh was due to him, it was little enough for him to get for all that money.'

'But what else could he do,' I asked, 'when he must not take one drop of blood?'

'Memsahib,' said Farah, 'he could have used a redhot knife. That brings out no blood.'

'But,' I said, 'he was not allowed to take either more or less than one pound of flesh.'

'And who,' said Farah, 'would have been frightened by that, exactly a Jew? He might have taken little bits at a time, with a small scale at hand to weigh it on, till he had got just one pound. Had the Jew no friends to give him advice?'

All Somalis have in their countenance something exceedingly dramatic. Farah, with the slightest change of mien and carriage, now took on a dangerous aspect, as if he were really in the Court of Venice, putting heart into his friend or partner Shylock, in the face of the crowd of Antonio's friends, and of the Doge of Venice himself. His eyes flickered up and down the figure of the merchant before him, with the breast bared to the knife.

'Look, Memsahib,' he said, 'he could have taken small bits, very small.

He could have done that man a lot of harm, even a long time before he had got that one pound of his flesh.'

I said: 'But in the story the Jew gave it up.'

'Yes, that was a great pity, Memsahib,' said Farah.

The Elite of Bournemouth

I had as neighbour a settler who had been a doctor at home. Once, when the wife of one of my houseboys was about to die in childbirth, and I could not get into Nairobi, because the long rains had ruined the roads, I wrote to my neighbour and asked him to do me the great service of coming over and helping her. He very kindly came, in the midst of a terrible thunder-storm and torrents of tropical rain, and, at the last moment, by his skill, he saved the life of the woman and the child.

Afterwards he wrote me a letter to say that although he had for once, on my appeal, treated a Native, I must understand that he could not let that sort of thing occur again. I myself would fully realize the fact, he felt convinced, when he informed me that he had before now practised to the élite of Bournemouth.

Of Pride

The neighbourhood of the Game Reserve and the presence, outside our boundary, of the big game, gave a particular character to the farm, as if we had been the neighbours of a great king. Very proud things were about, and made their nearness felt.

The barbarian loves his own pride, and hates, or disbelieves in, the pride of others. I will be a civilized being. I will love the pride of my adversaries, of my servants, and my lover; and my house shall be, in all humility, in the wilderness a civilized place.

Pride is faith in the idea that God had, when he made us. A proud man is conscious of the idea, and aspires to realize it. He does not strive towards a happiness, or comfort, which may be irrelevant to God's idea of him. His success is the idea of God, successfully carried through, and he is in love with his destiny. As the good citizen finds his happiness in the fulfilment of his duty to the community, so does the proud man find his happiness in the fulfilment of his fate.

People who have no pride are not aware of any idea of God in the making of them, and sometimes they make you doubt that there has ever been much of an idea, or else it has been lost, and who shall find it again? They have got to accept as success what others warrant to be so, and to take their happiness, and even their own selves, at the quotation of the day. They tremble, with reason, before their fate.

Love the pride of God beyond all things, and the pride of your neighbour as your own. The pride of lions: do not shut them up in zoos. The pride of your dogs: let them not grow fat. Love the pride of your fellow-partisans, and allow them no self-pity.

Love the pride of the conquered nations, and leave them to honour their father and their mother.

The Oxen

Saturday afternoon was a blessed time on the farm. First of all, there would now be no mail in till Monday afternoon, so that no distressing business letters could reach us till then, and this fact in itself seemed to close the whole place in, as within an enceinte. Secondly, everybody was looking forward to the day of Sunday, when they would rest or play all the day, and the squatters could work on their own land. The thought of the oxen on Saturday pleased me more than all other things. I used to walk down to their paddock at six o'clock, when they were coming in after the day's work and a few hours' grazing. Tomorrow, I thought, they would do nothing but graze all day.

We had one hundred and thirty-two oxen on the farm, which meant eight working teams and a few spare oxen. Now in the golden dust of the sunset they came wandering home across the plain in a long row, walking sedately, as they did all things; while I sat sedately on the fence of the paddock, smoking a cigarette of peace, and watching them. Here came Nyose, Ngufu and Faru, with Msungu – which means a white man. The drivers also often give to their teams the proper names of white men, and Delamere is a common name in an ox. Here came old Malinda, the big yellow ox that I liked best of the lot; his skin was strangely marked with shadowy figures, like starfishes, from which pattern perhaps he had his name, for Malinda means a skirt.

As in civilized countries all people have a chronic bad conscience towards the slums, and feel uncomfortable when they think of them, so in Africa you have got a bad conscience, and feel a pang, when you think of the oxen. But towards the oxen on the farm, I felt as, I suppose, a king will be feeling towards his slums: 'You are I, and I am you.'

The oxen in Africa have carried the heavy load of the advance of European civilization. Wherever new land has been broken they have broken it, panting and pulling knee-deep in the soil before the ploughs, the long whips in the air over them. Where a road has been made they have made it; and they have trudged the iron and tools through the land, to the yelling and shouting of the drivers, by tracks in the dust and the long grass of the plains, before there ever were any roads. They have been inspanned before daybreak, and have sweated up and down the long hills, and across dungas and river-beds, through the burning hours of the day. The whips have marked their sides, and you will often see oxen that have an eye, or both of them, taken away by the long cutting whip-lashes. The wagon-oxen of many Indian and white contractors worked every day, all their lives through, and did not know of the Sabbath.

It is a strange thing that we have done to the oxen. The bull is in a constant state of fury, rolling his eyes, shovelling up the earth, upset by everything that gets within his range of vision – still he has got a life of his own, fire comes from his nostrils, and new life from his loins; his days are filled with his vital cravings and satisfactions. All of that we have taken away from the oxen, and in reward we have claimed their existence for ourselves. The oxen walk along within our own daily life, pulling hard all the time, creatures without a life, things made for our use. They have moist, limpid, violet eyes, soft muzzles, silky ears, they are patient and dull in all their ways; sometimes they look as if they were thinking about things.

There was in my time a law against bringing a wagon or cart on the roads without a brake, and the wagon-drivers were supposed to put on the brakes down all the long hills of the country. But the law was not kept; half the wagons and carts on the roads had no brakes to them, and on the others the brakes were but rarely put on. This made downhill work terribly hard on the oxen. They had to hold the loaded wagons up with their bodies, they laid their heads back under the labour until their horns touched the hump on their back; their sides went like a pair of bellows. I have many times seen the carts of the firewood merchants which came along the Ngong Road, going into Nairobi the one after the other, like a long caterpillar, gain speed down the hill in the Forest Reserve, the oxen violently zig-zagging down in front of them. I have also seen the oxen stumble and fall under the weight of the cart, at the bottom of the hill.

The oxen thought: 'Such is life, and the conditions of the world. They are hard, hard. It has all to be borne – there is nothing for it. It is a terribly difficult thing to get the carts down the hill, it is a matter of life and death. It cannot be helped.'

If the fat Indians of Nairobi, who owned the carts, could have brought themselves to pay two rupees and have the brakes put in order, or if the slow young Native driver on the top of the loaded cart had had it in him to get off and put on the brake, if it was there, then it could have been helped, and the oxen could have walked quietly down the hill. But the oxen did not know, and went on, day after day, in their heroic and desperate struggle with the conditions of life.

Of the Two Races

The relation between the white and black races in Africa in many ways resembles the relation between the two sexes.

If the one of the two sexes were told that they did not play any greater part in the life of the other sex than this other sex plays within their own existence, they would be shocked and hurt. If the lover or the husband were told that he did not play any greater part in the life of his wife or his mistress than she played in his own existence, he would be puzzled and indignant. If a wife or a mistress were told that she did not play any greater part in the life of her husband or her lover than he played in her life, she would be exasperated.

The real old-time men's story that was never meant to get to the ears of women goes to prove this theory; and the talk of the women, when they sit amongst themselves and know that no man can hear them, goes to prove it.

The tales that white people tell you of their Native servants are conceived in the same spirit. If they had been told that they played no more important part in the lives of the Natives than the Natives played in their own lives, they would have been highly indignant and ill at ease.

If you had told the Natives that they played no greater part in the life of the white people than the white people played in their lives, they would never have believed you, but would have laughed at you. Probably in Native circles, stories are passing about, and being repeated, which prove the all-absorbing interest of the white people in the Kikuyu or Kavirondo, and their complete dependence upon them.

A War-time Safari

When the war broke out, my husband and the two Swedish assistants on the farm volunteered and went down to the German border, where a provisional intelligence service was being organized by Lord Delamere. I was then alone on the farm. But shortly afterwards there began to be talk of a concentration camp for the white women of the country; they were believed to be exposed to danger from the Natives. I was thoroughly frightened then, and thought: If I am to go into a ladies' concentration camp in this country for months – and who knows how long the war is going to last? – I shall die. A few days later I got the chance to go, with a young Swedish farmer, a neighbour of ours, to Kijabe, a station higher up the railway line, and there to be in charge of a camp to which the runners from the border brought in their news, which had then to be telegraphed on to headquarters in Nairobi.

At Kijabe I had my tent near the station, amongst stacks of firewood for the railway engines. As the runners came in at all hours of the day or night, I came to work much together with the Goan stationmaster. He was a small, mild man, with a burning thirst for knowledge, unaffected by the war around him. He asked me many questions of my country, and made me teach him a little Danish, which he thought would at some time come in highly useful to him. He had a small boy of ten, named Victor; one day as I walked up to the station, through the trellis-work of the verandah, I heard him going on teaching Victor his grammar: 'Victor, what is a pronoun? – What is a pronoun, Victor? – You do not know? – Five hundred times have I told you!'

The people down by the border kept on demanding provisions and ammunition to be sent to them; my husband wrote and instructed me to load up four ox-wagons and to send them down as soon as possible. But I must not, he wrote, let them go without a white man in charge of them, for nobody knew where the Germans were, and the Masai were in a state of high excitement at the idea of war, and on the move all over the Reserve. In those days the Germans were supposed to be everywhere, and we kept sentinels by the great railway bridge of Kijabe to prevent them blowing it up.

I engaged a young South African by the name of Klapprott, to go with the wagons, but when they were all loaded up, on the evening before the expedition was to start off, he was arrested as a German. He was not a German, and could prove it, so that only a short time afterwards he got out of the arrest and changed his name. But at that hour I saw in his arrestation the finger of God, for now there was nobody but me to take the wagons through the country. And in the early morning, while the old constellations of the stars were still out, we set off down the long endless Kijabe Hill, with the great plains of the Masai Reserve – iron-grey in the faint light of the dawn – spread at our feet, with lamps tied under the wagons, swinging, and with much shouting and cracking of whips. I had four wagons, with a full team of sixteen oxen to each, and five spare oxen, and with me twenty-one young Kikuyus and three Somalis: Farah, Ismail, the gun-bearer, and an old cook also named Ismail, a very noble old man. My dog Dusk walked by my side.

It was a pity that the police, when arresting Klapprott, had at the same time arrested his mule. I had not been able to recover it in all Kijabe so that for the first few days I had to walk in the dust beside the wagons. But late I bought a mule and saddle from a man whom I met in the Reserve, and again some time after a mule for Farah.

I was out then for three months. When we came down to our place of destination, we were sent off again to collect the stores of a big American shooting safari that had been camping near the border, and had left in a hurry at the news of the war. From there the wagons had to go to new places. I learned to know the fords and water-holes of the Masai Reserve, and to speak a little Masai. The roads everywhere were unbelievably bad, deep with dust, and barred with blocks of stone taller than the wagons; later we travelled mostly across the plains. The air of the African highlands went to my head like wine: I was all the time slightly drunk with it, and the joy of these months was indescribable. I had been out on a shooting safari before, but I had not till now been out alone with Africans.

The Somali and I, who felt responsible for the government's property, lived in constant fear of losing the oxen from lions. The lions were on the road, following after the big transports of supplies of sheep and provisions, which now continually were travelling along it to the border. In the early mornings, as we drove on, we could see, for a long way, the fresh spoor of the lions in the dust, upon the wagon-tracks of the road. At night, when the oxen were outspanned, there was always a risk of lions round the camp frightening them, and making them stampede and spread all over the country, where we would never find them again. So we built tall circular fences of thorn-trees round our outspanning and camping-places, and sat up with rifles by the camp-fires.

Here both Farah and Ismail, and old Ismail himself, felt at such a safe distance from civilization that their tongues were loosened, and they would narrate strange happenings of Somaliland, or tales out of the Koran and the *Arabian Nights*. Both Farah and Ismail had been to sea, for the Somali are a seafaring nation, and were, I believe, in old days, great pirates of the Red Sea. They explained to me how every live creature on the earth has got its replica at the bottom of the sea: horses, lions, women, and giraffes, all live down there, and from time to time have been observed by sailors. They also recounted tales of horses which live at the bottom of the rivers of Somaliland, and at full-moon nights come up to the grassland to copulate with the Somali mares grazing there, and breed foals of wonderful beauty and swiftness. The vault of the nocturnal sky swung back over our heads as we sat on, new constellations of stars came up from the east. The smoke from the fire in the cold air carried long sparks with it, the fresh firewood smelt sour. From time to time the oxen suddenly all at once stirred, stamped and squeezed together, sniffing up in the air, so that old Ismail would climb on to the top of the loaded wagon, and there swing his lamp, to observe and to frighten off anything that might be about outside the fence.

We had many great adventures with lions: 'Beware of Siawa,' said the Native leader of a transport going north, whom we met on the road. 'Do not camp here. There are two hundred lions at Siawa.' So we tried to get past Siawa before nightfall, and hurried on, and as haste makes waste on a safari more than anything else, about sunset a wheel of the last wagon stuck on a big stone, and it could go no further. While I was now holding the lamp for the people working to lift it off, a lion took one of our spare oxen not three yards from me. By shouting and cracking the whips, for my rifles were with the safari, we managed to frighten off the lion, and the ox, that had run away with the lion on his back, came back to us, but it had been badly mauled, and died a couple of days later.

Many other strange things happened to us. At one time an ox drank up all our supply of paraffin, died on us, and left us without light of any kind until we got to an Indian dhuka in the Reserve, deserted by the owner, where strangely some of the goods were still untouched.

We were for a week camped close to a big camp of the Masai Morani, and the young warriors, in war-paint, with spears and long shields, and head-dresses of lion-skin, were round my tent day and night, to get news of the war and of the Germans. My own people of the safari liked this camp, because here they bought milk from the Morani's herd of cattle that trekked about with them and was herded by the young Masai boys, the Laioni, who as yet are too young to become warriors. The juvenile Masai soldier-girls, very lively and pretty, came into my tent to call on me. They would always ask for the loan of my hand-mirror, and, when they held it up to one another, they bared their two rows of shining teeth to the mirror, like angry young carnivora.

All news of the movements of the enemy had to pass through Lord Delamere's camp. But Lord Delamere was moving all over the Reserve in such incredibly swift marches, that nobody ever knew where his camp was to be found. I had nothing to do with intelligence work, but I wondered how the system worked for the people employed in it. Once my way took me within a couple of miles of Lord Delamere's camp, and I rode over with Farah and had tea with him. The place, although he was to break camp next day, was like a city, swarming with Masai. For he was always very friendly with them, and in his camp they were so well regaled that it had become like the lion's den of the fable: all footsteps turning in and none out. A Masai runner, sent with a letter to Lord Delamere's camp, would never show himself again with an answer. Lord Delamere, in the centre of the stir, small, and exceedingly polite and courteous as ever, his white hair down on his shoulders, seemed eminently at ease here, told me everything about the war, and offered me tea with smoked milk in it, after the Masai fashion.

My people showed great forbearance with my ignorance of oxen, harness, and safari ways; they were indeed as keen to cover it up as I was myself. They worked well for me all through the safari, and never grumbled, although in my inexperience I asked more of everyone, both men and oxen, than could really be expected of them. They carried bath-water for me on their heads a long way across the plain, and when we outspanned at noon, they constructed a canopy against the sun, made out of spears and blankets, for me to rest under. They were a little scared of the wild Masai, and much disturbed by the idea of the Germans, of whom strange rumours went about. Under the circumstances I was to the expedition, I believe, a kind of guardian angel, or mascot.

Six months before the outbreak of the war, I had first come out to Africa, on the same boat as General von Lettow Vorbeck, who was now the highest in command of the German forces in East Africa. I did not know then that he was going to be a hero, and we had made friends on the journey. When we dined together in Mombasa, before he went farther on to Tanganyika and I went up-country, he gave me a photograph of himself in uniform and on horseback, and wrote on it:

> 'Das Paradies auf Erde
> Ist auf dem Rücken der Pferde'
> Und die Gesundheit des Leibes
> Am Busen des Weibes.'

Farah, who had come to meet me in Aden, and who had seen the general and been aware that he was my friend, had taken the photograph with him on the safari and kept it with the money and the keys of the expedition to show to the German soldiers if we were made prisoners, and he attached great value to it.

How beautiful were the evenings of the Masai Reserve when after sunset we arrived at the river or the water-hole where we were to outspan, travelling in a long file. The plains with the thorn-trees on them were already quite dark, but the air was filled with clarity – and over our heads, to the west, a single star which was to grow big and radiant in the course of the night was now just visible, like a silver point in the sky of citrine topaz. The air was cold to the lungs, the long grass dripping wet, and the herbs on it gave out their spiced astringent scent. In a little while on all sides the cicadas would begin to sing. The grass was me, and the air, the distant invisible mountains were me, the tired oxen were me. I breathed with the slight night-wind in the thorn-trees.

After three months I was suddenly ordered home. As things began to be systematically organized and regular troops came out from Europe, my expedition, I believe, was found to be somewhat irregular. We went back, passing our old camping-places with heavy hearts.

This safari lived for a long time in the memory of the farm. Later on I had many other safaris, but for some reason – either because we had at the time been in the service of the Government, a sort of official ourselves, or because of the war-like atmosphere about it – this particular expedition was dear to the hearts of the people who had been on it. Those who had been with me then came to look upon themselves as a safari-aristocracy.

Many years afterwards they would come up to the house and talk about the safari, just to freshen up their memory of it, and to go through one or another of our adventures then.

The Swaheli Numeral System

At the time when I was new in Africa, a shy young Swedish dairyman was to teach me the numbers in Swaheli. As the Swaheli word for nine, to Swedish ears, has a dubious ring, he did not like to tell it to me, and when he had counted: 'seven, eight,' he stopped, looked away, and said: 'They have not got nine in Swaheli.'

'You mean,' I said, 'that they can only count as far as eight?'

'Oh, no,' he said quickly. 'They have got ten, eleven, twelve, and so on. But they have not got nine.'

'Does that work?' I asked, wondering. 'What do they do when they come to nineteen?'

'They have not got nineteen either,' he said, blushing, but very firm, 'nor ninety, nor nine hundred,' – for these words in Swaheli are constructed out of the number nine – 'But apart from that they have got all our numbers.'

The idea of this system for a long time gave me much to think of, and for some reason a great pleasure. Here, I thought, was a people who have got originality of mind, and courage to break with the pedantry of the numeral series.

One, two, three are the only three sequential prime numbers, I thought, so may eight and ten be the only sequential even numbers. People might try to prove the existence of the number nine by arguing that it should be possible to multiply the number three with itself. But why should it be so? If the number two has got no square root, the number three may just as well be without a square number. If you work out the sum of digits of a number until you reduce it to a single figure, it makes no difference to the results if you have got the number nine, or any multiple of nine, in it from the beginning, so that here nine may really be said to be non-existent, and that, I thought, spoke for the Swaheli system.

It happened that I had at that time a houseboy, Zacharia, who has lost the fourth finger of his left hand. Perhaps, I thought, that is a common thing with Natives, and is done to facilitate their arithmetic to them, when they are counting upon their fingers.

When I began to develop my ideas to other people, I was stopped, and enlightened. Yet I have still got the feeling that there exists a native system of numeral characters without the number nine in it, which to them works well and by which you can find out many things.

I have, in this connection, remembered an old Danish clergyman who declared to me that he did not believe that God had created the eighteenth century.

'I will not let Thee go except Thou bless me'

When in Africa in March the long rains began after four months of hot, dry weather, the richness of growth and the freshness and fragrance everywhere are overwhelming.

But the farmer holds back his heart and dares not trust to the generosity of nature: he listens, dreading to hear a decrease in the roar of the falling rain. The water that the earth is now drinking in must bring the farm, with all the vegetable, animal, and human life on it, through four rainless months to come.

It is a lovely sight when the roads of the farm have all been turned into streams of running water, and the farmer wades through the mud with a singing heart, out to the flowering and dripping coffee-fields. But it happens in the middle of the rainy season that in the evening the stars show themselves through the thinning clouds; then he stands outside his house and stares up, as if hanging himself on to the sky to milk down more rain. He cries to the sky: 'Give me enough and more than enough. My heart is bared to thee now, and I will not let Thee go except Thou bless me. Drown me if you like, but kill me not with caprices. No *coitus interruptus*, heaven, heaven!'

Sometimes a cool, colourless day in the months after the rainy season calls back the time of the *marka mbaya*, the bad year, the time of the drought. In those days the Kikuyu used to graze their cows round my house, and a boy amongst them who had a flute from time to time played a short tune on it. When I have heard this tune again, it has recalled in one single moment all our anguish and despair of the past. It has got the salt taste of tears in it. But at the same time I found in the tune, unexpectedly, surprisingly, a vigour, a curious sweetness, a song. Had those hard times really had all these in them? There was youth in us then, a wild hope. It was during those long days that we were all of us merged into a unity, so that on another planet we shall recognize one another, and the things cry to each other, the cuckoo clock and my books to the lean-fleshed cows on the lawn and the sorrowful old Kikuyus: 'You also were there. You also were part of the Ngong farm.' That bad time blessed us and went away.

The friends of the farm came to the house, and went away again. They were not the kind of people who stay for a long time in the same place. They were not the kind of people either who grow old; they died and never came back. But they had sat contented by the fire, and when the house, closing round them, said: 'I will not let you go except you bless me,' they laughed and blessed it, and it let them go.

An old lady sat in a party and talked of her life. She declared that she would like to live it all over again, and held this fact to prove that she had lived wisely. I thought: Yes, her life has been the sort of life that should really be taken twice before you can say that you have had it. An arietta you can take *da capo*, but not a whole piece of music – not a symphony and not a five-act tragedy either. If it is taken over again it is because it has not gone as it ought to have gone.

My life, I will not let you go except you bless me, but then I will let you go.

The Eclipse of the Moon

One year we had an eclipse of the moon. A short time before it was to take place I had the following letter from the young Indian stationmaster of Kikuyu station:

'HONOURED MADAM – I have been kindly instructed that the light of the sun is going to be put out for seven days running. Leave alone the railway trains, I beg you kindly inform me, as I believe that nobody else will kindly inform me, whether during this period I shall leave my cows to graze in the surroundings, or shall I collect them into the stable? – I have the honour to be, Madam, Your obedient servant.

PATEL.'

Natives and Verse

The Natives, who have a strong sense of rhythm, know nothing of verse, or at least did not know anything before the times of the schools, where they were taught hymns. One evening out in the maize-field, where we had been harvesting maize, breaking off the cobs and throwing them on to the ox-carts, to amuse myself, I spoke to the field labourers, who were mostly quite young, in Swaheli verse. There was no sense in the verses, they were made for the sake of the rhyme – 'Ngumbe na-penda chumbe, Malaya mbaya. Wakamba na-kula mamba.' The oxen like salt – whores are bad – the Wakamba eat snakes. It caught the interest of the boys, they formed a ring round me. They were quick to understand that meaning in poetry is of no consequence, and they did not question the thesis of the verse, but waited eagerly for the rhyme, and laughed at it when it came. I tried to make them themselves find the rhyme and finish the poem when I had begun it, but they could not, or would not, do that, and turned away their heads. As they had become used to the idea of poetry, they begged: 'Speak again. Speak like rain.' Why they should feel verse to be like rain I do not know. It must have been, however, an expression of applause, since in Africa rain is always longed for and welcomed.

Of the Millennium

At the time when the near return of Christ to the earth had become a certainty, a committee was formed to decide upon the arrangements for his reception. After some discussion, it sent out a circular which prohibited all waving and throwing about of palm-branches as well as all cries of 'Hosanna'.

When the Millennium had been going on for some time, and joy was

universal, Christ one evening said to Peter that he wanted, when everything was quiet, to go out for a short walk with him alone.

'Where do you want to go, Lord?' Peter asked.

'I should like,' answered the Lord, 'just to take a walk from the
Praetorium, along that long road, up to the Hill of Calvary.'

Kitosch's Story

Kitosch's story has been in the papers. A case rose from it, and a jury was
set to go through it from beginning to end, searching for enlightenment;
some of the enlightenment will still be found in the old documents.

Kitosch was a young Native in the service of a young white settler of
Molo. One Wednesday in June, the settler lent his brown mare to a friend,
to ride to the station on. He sent Kitosch there to bring back the mare,
and told him not to ride her, but to lead her. But Kitosch jumped on to
the mare, and rode her back, and on Saturday the settler, his master, was
told of the offence by a man who had seen it. In punishment the settler,
on Sunday afternoon, had Kitosch flogged, and afterwards tied up in his
store, and here late on Sunday night Kitosch died.

Upon the matter the High Court was set in Nakuru, in the Railway
Institute, on the 1st of August.

The Natives who gathered and sat round the Railway Institute will
have been wondering what it was all about. To their mind the case was
plain, for Kitosch had died, of that there was no doubt, and, according
to Native ideas, a compensation for his death should now be made to his
people.

But the idea of justice of Europe varies from that of Africa, and, to the
jury of white men, the problem of guilt and innocence at once presented
itself. The verdict in the case might be one of murder, or manslaughter,
or of grievous hurt. The judge reminded the jury that the degree of an
offence rests upon the intentions of the person concerned, and not upon
the results. What, then, had been the intentions, and the attitude of mind,
of the persons concerned in the Kitosch case?

To decide upon the intention and attitude of mind of the settler, the
court had him cross-examined for many hours a day. They were trying to
make up a picture of what had happened, and brought in all the details
that they could lay hands on. It is in this way written down that when the

settler called Kitosch, he came, and stood three yards away. This insignificant detail in the report is of great effect. Here they are at the opening of the drama, the white and the black man, at three yards' distance.

But from now on, as the story advances, the balance of the picture is broken, and the figure of the settler is blurred and grows smaller. It cannot be helped. It becomes only an accessory figure in a great landscape, a pale puny face, it loses its weight, and looks like a figure cut out in paper, and it is blown about, as by a draught, by the unknown freedom to do what it likes.

The settler stated that he began by asking Kitosch who had given him permission to ride the brown mare, and that he repeated this question forty to fifty times; he admitted at the same time that nobody could possibly have given Kitosch any such permission. Here his perdition begins. In England he would not have been able to ask a question forty to fifty times, he would have been stopped, in one way or the other, long before the fortieth time. Here in Africa were people to whom he could shriek the same question fifty times over. In the end Kitosch answered that he was not a thief, and the settler stated that it was as a result of the insolence of the answer that he had the boy flogged.

At this point the report has got a second irrelevant, and effective, detail. It says that during the flogging, two Europeans, who are designated friends of the settler, came over to see him. They looked on for ten minutes, or a quarter of an hour, and walked away.

After the flogging the settler could not let Kitosch go.

Late in the evening, he tied Kitosch with a rein, and locked him into his store. When the jury asked him why he did so, he gave an answer that had no sense, he said that he wanted to keep such a boy from running about on the farm. After supper, he went back to the store, and found Kitosch lying unconscious a little way from where he had tied him up, with the reins, loosened. He called in his Baganda cook, and with his assistance tied up the boy tighter than before, with his hands fastened to a post at his back, and with his right leg tied to a post in front. He left the store, locking the door, but half an hour later went back there, got hold of his cook and the kitchen-Toto, and let them into the store. Then he went to bed, and the next thing he remembered, he said, was that the Toto came from the store, and told him that Kitosch had died.

The jury kept in mind the words that the degree of an offence rests upon the intention, and looked for an intention. They went into a number of detailed questions about the flogging of Kitosch, and about what happened after, and as you read the papers you seem to see them shake their heads.

But what now had been the intention and the attitude of mind of Kitosch? This, when gone into, was found to be a different thing. Kitosch had had an intention, and in the end it came to weigh in the scales of the case. It can be said that by his intention, and his attitude of mind, the African, in his grave, saved the European.

Kitosch had not much opportunity for expressing his intention. He was locked up in the store, his message, therefore, comes very simply, and in a single gesture. The night-watch states that he cried all night. But it was not so, for at one o'clock he talked with the Toto, who was in the store with him. He indicated to the child that he must shout to him, because the flogging had made him deaf. But at one o'clock he asked the Toto to loosen his feet, and explained that in any case he could not run away. When the Toto had done as he asked him, Kitosch said to him that he wanted to die. At four, the child said, he again said that he wanted to die. A little while after, he rocked himself from side to side, cried: 'I am dead!' and died.

Three doctors gave evidence in the case.

The district surgeon, who had done the post mortem examination, pronounced death to be due to the injuries and wounds that he had found on the body. He did not believe that any immediate medical attention could have saved Kitosch's life.

The two doctors from Nairobi, called in for the defence, were, however, of a different mind.

The flogging in itself, they held, was not sufficient to have caused death. An important factor came into the matter, not to be ignored: that was the will to die. On this point, the first doctor stated, he could speak with authority, for he had been in the country twenty-five years, and knew the Native mind. Many medical men could support him that the wish to die, in a Native, had actually caused death. In the present case the matter was particularly clear, for Kitosch had himself said that he wanted to die. The second doctor bore him up in this point of view.

It was very likely, the doctor now went on, that if Kitosch had not taken this attitude, he would not have died. If, for instance, he had eaten something, he might not have lost courage, for starvation is known to reduce courage. He added that the wound on the lip might not be due to a kick, but might be just a bite by the boy himself, in severe pain.

The doctor, furthermore, did not believe that Kitosch would have made up his mind to die till after nine o'clock, as by that time he seemed to have tried to escape. Neither had he died till after nine o'clock. When he had been caught in the attempt to escape, and had been tied up again, the fact of being a prisoner, the doctor said, might have weighed on his mind.

The two doctors from Nairobi summed up their view of the case. The death of Kitosch, they held, was due to the flogging, to starvation, and to the wish to die, the latter being the subject of special emphasis. The wish to die might, they considered, have been caused by the effects of the flogging.

After the doctors' evidence, the case turned upon what was called in court 'The wish-to-die theory'. The district surgeon, who was the only one who had seen Kitosch's body, rejected the theory, and gave examples of cancer patients of his practice who had wished to die but all the same had not died. These people, however, were found to have been Europeans.

The jury in the end gave a verdict of Guilty of grievous hurt. The same verdict was applied to the Natives accused, but it was considered that as they had acted under the orders of their master, a European, it would be an injustice to imprison them. The Judge imposed a sentence of two years R.I. on the settler, and of one day on each of the Natives.

It seems to you, as you read the case through, a strange, a humiliating fact that the Europeans should not, in Africa, have power to throw the African out of existence. The country is his native land, and whatever you do to him, when he goes he goes by his own free will, and because he does not want to stay. Who is to take the responsibility for what happens in a house? The man who owns it, who has inherited it.

By this strong sense in him of what is right and decorous, the figure of Kitosch, with his firm will to die, although now removed from us by many years, stands out with a beauty of its own. In it is embodied the fugitive-ness of the wild things who are, in the hour of need, conscious of a refuge somewhere in existence; who go when they like; of whom we can never get hold.

Some African Birds

Just at the beginning of the long rains, in the last week of March, or the first week of April, I have heard the nightingale in the woods of Africa. Not the full song: a few notes only – the opening bars of the concerto, a rehearsal, suddenly stopped and again begun. It was as if, in the solitude of the dripping woods, someone was, in a tree, tuning a small cello. It was, however, the same melody, and the same abundance and sweetness, as were soon to fill the forests of Europe, from Sicily to Elsinore.

We had the black and white storks in Africa, the birds that build their nests upon the thatched village roofs of northern Europe. They look less imposing in Africa than they do there, for here they had such tall and ponderous birds as the marabout and the secretary bird to be compared to. The storks have got other habits in Africa than in Europe, where they live as married couples and are symbols of domestic happiness. Here they are seen together in big flights, as in clubs. They are called locust-birds in Africa, and follow along when the locusts come upon the land, living high on them. They fly over the plains, too, where there is a grass-fire on, circling just in front of the advancing line of small leaping flames, high up in the scintillating rainbow-coloured air, and the grey smoke, on watch for the mice and snakes that run from the fire. The storks have a gay time in Africa. But their real life is not here, and when the winds of spring bring back thoughts of mating and nesting, their hearts are turned towards the north, they remember old times and places and fly off, two and two, and are shortly after wading in the cold bogs of their birthplaces.

Out of the plains, in the beginning of the rains, where the vast stretches of burnt grass begin to show fresh green sprouting, there are many hundred plovers. The plains always have a maritime air, the open horizon recalls the sea and the long sea-sands, the wandering wind is the same, the charred grass has a saline smell, and when the grass is long it runs in waves all over the land. When the white carnation flowers on the plains you remember the chopping white-specked waves all round you as you are tacking up the Sund. Out on the plains the plovers likewise take on the appearance of sea-birds, and behave like sea-birds, on a beach, legging it, on the close grass, as fast as they can for a short time, and then rising before your horse with high shrill shrieks, so that the light sky is all alive with wings and birds' voices.

The crested cranes, which come on to the newly rolled and planted maize-land, to steal the maize out of the ground, make up for the robbery by being birds of good omen, announcing the rain; and also by dancing to us. When the tall birds are together in large numbers, it is a fine sight to see them spread their wings and dance. There is much style in the dance, and a little affectation, for why, when they can fly, do they jump up and down as if they were held on to the earth by magnetism? The whole ballet has a sacred look, like some ritual dance; perhaps the cranes are making an attempt to join heaven and earth like the winged angels walking up and down Jacob's Ladder. With their delicate pale grey colouring, the little black velvet skull-cap and the fan-shaped crown, the cranes have all the air of light, spirited frescoes. When, after the dance, they lift and go away, to keep up the sacred tone of the show they give out, by the wings or the voice, a clear ringing note, as if a group of church bells had taken wing and were sailing off. You can hear them a long way away, even after the birds themselves have become invisible in the sky: a chime from the clouds.

The greater hornbill was another visitor to the farm, and came there to eat the fruits of the Cape-Chestnut tree. They are very strange birds. It is an adventure or an experience to meet them, not altogether pleasant, for they look exceedingly knowing. One morning before sunrise I was woken up by a loud jabbering outside the house, and when I walked out on the terrace I saw forty-one hornbills sitting in the trees on the lawn. There they looked less like birds than like some fantastic articles of finery set on the trees here and there by a child. Black they all were, with the sweet, noble black of Africa, deep darkness absorbed through an age, like old soot, that makes you feel that for elegance, vigour, and vivacity no colour rivals black. All the hornbills were talking together in the merriest mood, but with choice deportment, like a party of heirs after a funeral. The morning air was as clear as crystal, the sombre party was bathing in freshness and purity, and, behind the trees and the birds, the sun came up, a dull red ball. You wonder what sort of a day you are to get after such an early morning.

The flamingos are the most delicately coloured of all the African birds, pink and red like a flying twig of an oleander bush. They have incredibly long legs and bizarre and recherché curves of their necks and bodies, as if from some exquisite traditional prudery they were making all attitudes and movements in life as difficult as possible.

I once travelled from Port Said to Marseilles in a French boat that had on board a consignment of a hundred and fifty flamingos which were going to the *Jardin d'Acclimatation* in Marseilles. They were kept in large dirty cases with canvas sides, ten in each, standing up close to one another. The keeper, who was taking the birds over, told me that he was counting on losing twenty per cent of them on the trip. They were not made for that sort of life; in rough weather they lost their balance, their legs broke, and the other birds in the cage trampled on them. At night when the wind was high in the Mediterranean and the ship came down in the waves with a thump, at each wave I heard, in the dark, the flamingos shriek. Every morning, I saw the keeper taking out one or two dead birds, and throwing them overboard. The noble wader of the Nile, the sister of the lotus, which floats over the landscape like a stray cloud of sunset, had become a slack cluster of pink and red feathers with a pair of long, thin sticks attached to it. The dead birds floated on the water for a short time, knocking up and down in the wake of the ship before they sank.

Pania

The deerhounds, from having lived for innumerable generations with man, have acquired a human sense of humour, and can laugh. Their idea of a joke is that of the Natives, who are amused by things going wrong. Perhaps you cannot get above this class of humour until you also get an art, and an established Church.

Pania was Dusk's son. I walked with him one day near the pond, where there was a row of tall, thin blue-gum trees, when he ran away from me up to one of the trees and came back again half-way, to make me come with him. I went up to the tree, and saw a serval-cat sitting high up in it. The serval-cats take your chickens, so that I shouted to a Toto walking by, and sent him up to the house for my gun, and when I had it brought, I shot the serval-cat. She came down from her great height with a thump, and Pania was upon her in a second, shaking her and pulling her about, very pleased with the performance.

Some time after I again came by the same road, past the pond; I had been out to shoot partridge, but had got none, and both Pania and I were downcast. All at once Pania flew up to the farthest tree of the row, barking round it in a state of the highest excitement, then rushed back to me, and again back to the tree. I was pleased that I had got my gun with me, and at the prospect of a second serval-cat, for they have got pretty, spotted skins. I ran up to the tree. But, when I looked up, there was a black domestic cat sitting, very angry, as high up as possible in the swaying top of the tree I lowered my gun. 'Pania,' I said, 'you fool! It's a cat.'

As I turned round to Pania, he stood at a little distance, looking at me and splitting his sides with laughter. When his eyes met mine he rushed up to me, danced, wagged his tail, whined, put his feet on my shoulders, and his nose to my face, then jumped back again to give free course to his laughter.

He expressed by pantomime: 'I know. I know. It was a tame cat. I knew all the time. Indeed, you must excuse me. But if you only knew the figure you cut, rushing up to a tame cat with a gun!'

All that day, from time to time, he went through the same agitation of mind, and the same behaviour, expressing the most overwhelmingly friendly feelings towards me, and then withdrawing a little to have an unhindered laugh.

An insinuating note came into his friendliness. 'You know,' he said, 'that in this house it is only you and Farah that I ever laugh at.'

Even in the evening when he was asleep, in front of the fire, I heard him in his sleep groaning and whimpering a little with laughter. I believe that he remembered the event a long time after, when we passed the pond and the trees.

Esa's Death

Esa, who was taken away from me during the war, after the armistice came back and lived on the farm peacefully. He had a wife by the name of Mariammo, a thin, black, hard-working woman, who carried firewood to the house. Esa was the gentlest servant I ever had, and quarrelled with nobody.

But something had happened to Esa in his exile, and he had come back changed. Sometimes I was afraid that he might imperceptibly die on me, like a plant that has had its roots cut through.

Esa was my cook, but he did not like to cook, he wanted to be a gardener. Plants were the only things for which he had preserved a real live interest. But while I had another gardener I had no other cook, and so held back Esa in the kitchen. I had promised him that he should go back to his garden-work, but I kept him off from month to month. Esa on his own had dammed in a bit of ground by the river, and planted it as a surprise to me. But as he had been alone at it, and was not a strong man, the dam was not solid enough, and in the long rains it went away altogether.

The first disturbance of his quiet non-existence came upon Esa when his brother died in the Kikuyu Reserve and left him a black cow. By then it became evident how much Esa had been sucked out by life, he could no longer stand up to any strong manifestation of it. In particular, I believe, he could not quite stand happiness. He asked me for three days' leave to go and fetch the cow and, on his return, I saw that he had been stirred and harassed, like the hands and feet of people who have been benumbed by cold, and brought into a warm room.

All Natives are gamblers, and under the illusion, created by the black cow, that from now fortune was going to smile on him, Esa began to develop a terrible confidence in things; he had great dreams. He felt that life was before him still; he decided to take a new wife. When he told me of his plan, he was already negotiating with his future father-in-law, who lived on the Nairobi road, and had a Swaheli wife. I tried to make him change his mind. 'You have got a very good wife,' I said to him, 'and your head is already grey, you cannot be needing another. Stay with us now and live in peace.' Esa took no offence at my arguments, the little gentle Kikuyu stood up erect before me, and in his vague way stuck to his decision. Shortly after he brought his new wife, Fatoma, to the farm.

That Esa should ever hope for any good to come from his new marriage showed that he had lost his judgement. The bride was very young, hard, and sulky, dressed in the Swaheli fashion, with the lasciviousness of her mother's nation, but with no gracefulness or gaiety in her. But Esa's face was radiant with triumph, and great plans; he was behaving, in his innocence, like a man on the verge of general paralysis. Mariammo, the patient slave, kept in the background, and seemed unconcerned.

It is possible that Esa had now a short time of greatness and rejoicing, but it did not last, and his peaceful existence on the farm went to pieces through his new wife. A month after the wedding she ran away from him, to live with the Native soldiers in the barracks of Nairobi. For a long time Esa used to ask for a day's leave to go into town and fetch her back, and in the evening returned with the dark, reluctant girl. The first time he went confidently and very decided; he would get her – what about it, was she not his lawful wife? Later he walked off in a bewildered, sad re-search of his dreams and the smile of fortune.

'What do you want her back for, Esa?' I said to him. 'Let her go. She does not want to come back to you, and no good will come from this.'

But Esa had not got it in him to let her go. Towards the end he came down in his expectations of life, and it was simply the monetary value of his woman that he sought to retain. The other boys laughed at him, when he trudged off, and told me that the soldiers laughed at him, too. But Esa had never paid much attention to what other people thought of him, and in any case he was past it now. He went in persistently and faithfully to recover his lost property, as a man will go in search of a runaway cow.

One morning Fatoma informed my houseboys that Esa was sick, and could not cook that day, but he would be up next day, she said. But late in the afternoon the boys came in and told me that Fatoma had disappeared, and that Esa had been poisoned and was dying. When I came out, they had carried him, on his bed, out in the square between the boys' huts.

It was obvious that he had not got long to live. He had been given some sort of Native poison, similar to strychnine, and must have suffered terribly in his hut, under the eyes of the murderous young wife, until she felt that she had safely finished him, and had made off. He still had a few spasms that contracted his body, but he was all rigid and cold, like a dead man. His face was much changed, and froth, mixed with blood, ran out from the corners of his pale-blue mouth. Farah had gone to Nairobi in the car, so that I could not get Esa into the hospital, but I do not think that I should have done that in any case; there was no help for him.

Before he died Esa looked at me for a long time, but I do not know if he recognized me. With the consciousness in his dark, animal-like eyes now went the remembrance of the country such as I had always wished to have known it, when it had been like a Noah's Ark, with the game all round the little Native boy herding his father's goats on the plain. I held his hand, a human hand, a strong ingenious tool, which had held weapons, planted vegetables and flowers, caressed; which I had taught to make omelettes. Would Esa himself hold his life to have been a success or a failure? It would have been difficult to tell. He had gone along his own little, slow, twined paths and had been through many things, always a peaceful man.

When Farah came home he took much trouble to have Esa buried with the full orthodox ceremonial, for he had been a pious Mohammedan. The priest, whom we called out from Nairobi, could not come till next evening, so that Esa's funeral took place at night, with the Milky Way on the sky, and lamps in the funeral procession. His grave was walled up, in the Mohammedan way, under a big tree in the forest. Mariammo now came forward and took her place amongst the mourners, and bewailed Esa loudly in the night air.

Farah and I held a council as to what we ought to do about Fatoma, and we decided to do nothing. It evidently went against Farah to take steps to have a woman punished by the law. I gathered from him that the Mohammedan law does not hold a woman to account. Her husband is responsible for what she does, and must pay the fine for what misfortunes she causes, as he must pay the fine for what damage his horse may do. But if the horse throws the owner and kills him? Well yes, Farah agrees, that is a sad accident. After all, Fatoma herself had had reason to complain about her fate, now she would be left to fulfil it as she chose to, in the barracks of Nairobi.

Of Natives and History

The people who expect the Natives to jump joyfully from the stone age to the age of motor-cars forget the toil and labour which our own fathers have had, to bring us all through history up to where we are.

We can make motor-cars and aeroplanes, and teach the Natives to use them. But the true love of motor-cars cannot be made, in human hearts, in the turn of a hand. It takes centuries to produce it, and it is likely that Socrates, the Crusades, and the French Revolution, have been needed in the making. We of the present day, who love our machines, cannot quite imagine how people in the old days could live without them. But we could not make the Athanasian Creed, or the technique of the Mass, or of a five-act tragedy, and perhaps not even of a sonnet. And if we had not found them there ready for our use, we should have had to do without them. Still we must imagine, since they have been made at all, that there was a time when the hearts of humanity cried out for these things, and when a deeply felt want was relieved when they were made.

Father Bernard came over on his motor bicycle one day, his bearded face all beaming with bliss and triumph, to lunch with me, and to bring me tidings of great joy. The day before, he told me, nine young Kikuyu, from the Church of Scotland Mission, had come and asked to be received into the Roman Catholic Church, because they had, upon meditation and discussion, come to hold with the doctrine of Transubstantiation of that Church.

All the people whom I told of this happening laughed at Father Bernard, and explained that the young Kikuyus had seen a chance of higher wages, of lighter work, or of getting a bicycle to ride on, at the French Mission, and had therefore invented their conversion in regard to Transubstantiation. For we ourselves, they said, cannot understand it, and we do not even like to think about it, so that to the Kikuyu it must be altogether inadmissible. But it is not quite sure that it is so; Father Bernard knew the Kikuyus well. The minds of the young Kikuyu may now be walking on the shadowy paths of our own ancestors, whom we should not disown in their eyes, who held their ideas about Transubstantiation very dear. Those people of five hundred years ago were in their day offered higher wages, and promotion, and easier terms of life, even sometimes their very lives, and to everything they preferred their conviction about Transubstantiation. They were not offered a bicycle, but Father Bernard himself, who had got a motor bicycle, attached less value to it than to the conversion of the nine Kikuyus.

The modern white people in Africa believe in evolution and not in any sudden creative act. They might then run the Natives through a short practical lesson of history to bring them up to where we are. We took these nations over not quite forty years ago; if we compare that moment to the moment of the birth of the Lord, and allow them to catch up with us, three years to our hundred, it will now be time to send them out Saint Francis of Assisi, and in a few years Rabelais. They would love and appreciate both better than we do, of our century. They liked Aristophanes when some years ago I tried to translate to them the dialogue between the farmer and his son, out of 'The Clouds'. In twenty years they might be ready for the Encyclopaedists, and then they would come, in another ten years, to Kipling. We should let them have dreamers, philosophers, and poets out, to prepare the ground for Mr Ford.

Where shall they find us then? Shall we in the meantime have caught them by the tail and be hanging on to it, in our pursuit of some shade, some darkness, practising upon a tomtom? Will they be able to have our motor-cars at cost price then, as they can now have the doctrine of Transubstantiation?

The Earthquake

One year, about Christmas, we had an earthquake; it was strong enough to turn over a number of Native huts, it was probably of the power of an angry elephant. It came in three shocks, each of them lasted a few seconds, and there was a pause of a few seconds in between them. These intervals gave people time to form their ideas of the happening.

Denys Finch-Hatton, who was at the time camped in the Masai Reserve, and was sleeping in his lorry, told me when he came back that as he was woken up by the shock he thought, 'A rhino had got underneath the lorry.' I myself was in my bedroom going to bed when the earthquake came. At the first tug I thought, 'A leopard has got up on the roof.' When the second shock came, I thought, 'I am going to die, this is how it feels to die.' But in the short stillness between the second and third shock, I realized what it was, it was an earthquake, and I had never thought that I should live to see that. For a moment now I believed that the earthquake was over. But when the third and last shock of it came, it brought with it such an overwhelming feeling of joy that I do not remember ever in my life to have been more suddenly and thoroughly transported.

The heavenly bodies, in their courses, have it in their power to move human minds to unknown heights of delight. We are not generally conscious of them; when their idea is suddenly brought back, and actualized to us, it opens up a tremendous perspective. Kepler writes of what he felt when, after many years' work, he at last found the laws of the movement of the planets:

'I give myself over to my rapture. The die is cast. Nothing I have ever felt before is like this. I tremble, my blood leaps. God has waited six thousand years for a looker-on to his work. His wisdom is infinite, that of which we are ignorant is contained in him, as well as the little that we know.'

Indeed it was exactly the same transport which took hold of me and shook me all through, at the time of the earthquake.

The feeling of colossal pleasure lies chiefly in the consciousness that something which you have reckoned to be immovable has got it in it to move on its own. That is probably one of the strongest sensations of joy and hope in the world. The dull globe, the dead mass, the earth itself, rose and stretched under me. It sent me out a message, the slightest touch, but of unbounded significance. It laughed so that the Native huts fell down and cried: *E pur si muove.*

Early next morning, Juma brought me my tea and said: 'The King of England is dead.'

I asked him how he knew.

'Did you not, Memsahib,' he said, 'feel the earth toss and shake last night? That means that the King of England is dead.'

But luckily the King of England lived for many years after the earthquake.

George

On a cargo-boat to Africa I once made friends with a little boy named George, who was travelling out with his mother and his young aunt. One day, on the deck, he detached himself from his women and, followed by their eyes, walked up to me. He announced that it was his birthday next day, he would be six years old, and his mother was going to ask the English passengers for tea, would I come? he said.

'But I am not English, George,' said I.

'What are you?' he asked, in great surprise.

'I am a Hottentot,' I said.

He stood up straight, and looked at me very gravely.

'Never mind,' he said, 'I hope you will come.'

He walked back to his mother and aunt and announced to them in a nonchalant way, but with so much firmness that it cut short any objection: 'She is a Hottentot. But I want her.'

Kejiko

I once had a fat riding-mule that I had named Molly. The mule-sice gave her another name, he called her *Kejiko*, which means 'the spoon', and when I asked him why he called her the spoon, he answered: 'Because she looks like a spoon.' I walked all round her to find out what he had in his mind, but to me she did not look, from any side, the least like a spoon.

Some time after I happened to be driving Kejiko, with three other mules, in a cart. When I got up in the driver's high seat, I had a kind of bird's eye view of the mules. Then I saw that the sice had been right. Kejiko was unusually narrow across the shoulder and had broad plump hindquarters, she looked very much like a spoon with the rounded side up.

If Kamau the sice and I myself had each been painting a portrait of Kejiko, the pictures would have been as different as possible. But God and the angels would have seen her as Kamau saw her. He that cometh from above is above all, and what he hath seen that he testifieth.

The Giraffes Go to Hamburg

I was staying in Mombasa in the house of Sheik Ali bin Salim, the Lewali of the coast, a hospitable, chivalrous old Arab gentleman.

Mombasa has all the look of a picture of paradise, painted by a small child. The deep sea-arm round the island forms an ideal harbour; the land is made out of whitish coral-cliff grown with broad green mango trees and fantastic bald grey baobab trees. The sea at Mombasa is as blue as a cornflower, and, outside the inlet to the harbour, the long breakers of the Indian Ocean draw a thin crooked white line and give out a low thunder even in the calmest weather. The narrow-streeted town of Mombasa is all built from coral-rock, in pretty shades of buff, rose, and ochre, and above the town rises the massive old fortress, with walls and embrasure, where three hundred years ago the Portuguese and the Arabs held out against one another; it displays stronger colours than the town, as if it had, in the course of the ages, from its high site drunk in more than one stormy sunset.

The flamboyant red acacia flowers in the gardens of Mombasa, unbelievably intense of colour and delicate of leaf. The sun burns and scorches Mombasa; the air is salt here, the breeze brings in every day fresh supplies of brine from the East, and the soil itself is salted so that very little grass grows, and the ground is bare like a dancing-floor. But the ancient mango trees have a dense dark-green foliage and give benignant shade; they create a circular pool of black coolness underneath them. More than any other tree that I know of, they suggest a place to meet in, a centre for human intercourse; they are as sociable as the village-wells. Big markets are held under the mango trees, and the ground round their trunks is covered with hen-coops, and piled up water-melons.

Ali bin Salim had a pleasant white house on the mainland, at the curve of the sea-arm, with a long row of stone steps down to the sea. There were guests' houses alongside it, and in the big room of the principal building, behind the verandah there were collected many fine Arab and English things: old ivory and brass, china from Lamu, velvet armchairs, photographs, and a large gramophone. Amongst these, inside a satin-lined casket, were the remnants of a full tea-set in dainty English china of the forties, which had been the wedding-present of the young Queen of England and her Consort, when the Sultan of Zanzibar's son married the Shah of Persia's daughter. The Queen and the Prince had wished the married couple such happiness as they were themselves enjoying.

'And were they as happy?' I asked Sheik Ali when he took out the little cups, one by one, and placed them on the table to show them to me.

'Alas no,' said he, 'the bride would not give up riding. She had brought her horses with her, on the dhow that carried her trousseau. But the people of Zanzibar did not approve of ladies riding. There was much trouble about it, and, as the Princess would sooner give up her husband than her horses, in the end the marriage was dissolved and the Shah's daughter went back to Persia.'

In the harbour of Mombasa lay a rusty German cargo-steamer, homeward bound. I passed her in Ali bin Salim's rowing boat with his Swaheli rowers, on my way to the island and back. Upon the deck there stood a tall wooden case, and above the edge of the case rose the heads of two giraffes. They were, Farah, who had been on board the boat, told me, coming from Portuguese East Africa, and were going to Hamburg, to a travelling menagerie.

The giraffes turned their delicate heads from the one side to the other, as if they were surprised, which they might well be. They had not seen the sea before. They could only just have room to stand in the narrow case. The world had suddenly shrunk, changed and closed round them.

They could not know or imagine the degradation to which they were sailing. For they were proud and innocent creatures, gentle amblers of the great plains; they had not the least knowledge of captivity, cold, stench, smoke, and mange, nor of the terrible boredom in a world in which nothing is ever happening.

Crowds, in dark smelly clothes, will be coming in from the wind and sleet of the streets to gaze on the giraffes, and to realize man's superiority over the dumb world. They will point and laugh at the long slim necks when the graceful, patient, smoky-eyed heads are raised over the railings of the menagerie; they look much too long in there. The children will be frightened at the sight and cry, or they will fall in love with the giraffes, and hand them bread. Then the fathers and mothers will think the giraffes nice beasts, and believe that they are giving them a good time.

In the long years before them, will the giraffes sometimes dream of their lost country? Where are they now, where have they gone to, the grass and the thorn-trees, the rivers and waterholes and the blue mountains? The high sweet air over the plains has lifted and withdrawn. Where have the other giraffes gone to, that were side by side with them when they set going, and cantered over the undulating land? They have left them, they have all gone, and it seems that they are never coming back.

In the night where is the full moon?

The giraffes stir, and wake up in the caravan of the menagerie, in their narrow box that smells of rotten straw and beer.

Good-bye, good-bye, I wish for you that you may die on the journey, both of you, so that not one of the little noble heads, that are now raised, surprised, over the edge of the case, against the blue sky of Mombasa, shall be left to turn from one side to the other, all alone, in Hamburg, where no one knows of Africa.

As to us, we shall have to find someone badly transgressing against us, before we can in decency ask the giraffes to forgive us our transgressions against them.

In the Menagerie

About a hundred years ago, a Danish traveller to Hamburg, Count Schimmelmann, happened to come upon a small itinerant menagerie, and to take a fancy to it. While he was in Hamburg, he every day set his way round the place, although he would have found it difficult to explain what was to him the real attraction of the dirty and dilapidated caravans. The truth was that the menagerie responded to something within his own mind. It was winter and bitterly cold outside. In the sheds the keeper had been heating the old stove until it was a clear pink in the brown darkness of the corridor, alongside the animals' cages, but still the draught and the raw air pierced people to the bone.

Count Schimmelmann was sunk in contemplation of the hyena, when the proprietor of the menagerie came and addressed him. The proprietor was a small pale man with a fallen-in nose, who had in his days been a student of theology, but who had had to leave the faculty after a scandal, and had since step by step come down in the world.

'Your Excellency does well to look at the hyena,' said he. 'It is a great thing to have got a hyena to Hamburg, where there has never been one till now. All hyenas, you will know, are hermaphrodites, and in Africa, where they come from, on a full-moon night they will meet and join in a ring of copulation wherein each individual takes the double part of male and female. Did you know that?'

'No,' said Count Schimmelmann with a slight movement of disgust.

'Do you consider now, your Excellency,' said the showman, 'that it should be, on account of this fact, harder to a hyena than to other animals to be shut up by itself in a cage? Would he feel a double want, or is he, because he unites in himself the complementary qualities of creation, satisfied in himself, and in harmony? In other words, since we are all prisoners in life, are we happier, or more miserable, the more talents we possess?'

'It is a curious thing,' said Count Schimmelmann, who had been following his own thoughts and had not paid attention to the showman, 'to realize that so many hundreds, indeed thousands of hyenas should have lived and died, in order that we should, in the end, get this one specimen here, so that people in Hamburg shall be able to know what a hyena is like, and the naturalists to study from them.'

They moved on to look at the giraffes in the neighbouring cage.

'The wild animals,' continued the Count, 'which run in a wild landscape, do not really exist. This one, now, exists, we have got a name for it, we know what it is like. The others might as well not have been, still they are the large majority. Nature is extravagant.'

The showman pushed back his worn fur cap; underneath it he himself had not got a hair on his head. 'They see one another,' he said.

'Even that may be disputed,' said Count Schimmelmann after a short pause. 'These giraffes, for instance, have got square markings on the skin. The giraffes, looking at one another, will not know a square and will consequently not see a square. Can they be said to have seen one another at all?'

The showman looked at the giraffe for some time and then said: 'God sees them.'

Count Schimmelmann smiled. 'The giraffes?' he asked.

'Oh yes, your Excellency,' said the showman, 'God sees the giraffes. While they have been running about and have played in Africa, God has been watching them and has taken a pleasure in their demeanour. He has made them to please him. It is in the Bible, your Excellency,' said the showman. 'God so loved the giraffe that he created them. God has himself invented the square as well as the circle, surely your Excellency cannot deny that he has seen the squares on their skin and everything else about them. The wild animals, your Excellency, are perhaps a proof of the existence of God. But when they go to Hamburg,' he concluded, putting on his cap, 'the argument becomes problematic.'

Count Schimmelmann, who had arranged his life according to the ideas of other people, walked on in silence to look at the snakes, close to the stove. The showman, to amuse him, opened the case in which he kept them, and tried to make the snake within it wake up; in the end, the reptile slowly and sleepily wound itself round his arm. Count Schimmelmann looked at the group.

'Indeed, my good Kannegieter,' he said with a little surly laugh, 'if you were in my service, or if I were king, and you my minister, you would now have your dismissal.'

The showman looked up at him nervously. 'Indeed, Sir, should I?' he said, and slipped down the snake into the case. 'And why, Sir? If I may ask,' he added after a moment.

'Ah, Kannegieter, you are not so simple as you make out,' said the Count. 'Why? Because, my friend, the aversion to snakes is a sound human instinct, the people who have got it have kept alive. The snake is the deadliest of all the enemies of men, but what, except our own instinct of good and evil, is there to tell us so? The claws of the lion, the size and the tusks of the elephant the horns of the buffalo, all jump to the eye. But the snakes are beautiful animals. The snakes are round and smooth, like the things we cherish in life, of exquisite soft colouring, gentle in all their movements. Only to the godly man this beauty and gracefulness are in themselves loathsome, they smell from perdition, and remind him of the fall of man. Something within him makes him run away from the snake as from the devil, and that is what is called the voice of conscience. The man who can caress a snake can do anything.' Count Schimmelmann laughed a little at his own course of thoughts, buttoned his rich fur coat, and turned to leave the shed.

The showman had stood for a little while in deep thoughts. 'Your Excellency,' he said at last, 'you must needs love snakes. There is no way round it. Out of my own experience in life, I can tell you so, and indeed it is the best advice that I can give you: You should love the snakes. Keep in your mind, your Excellency, how often – keep in mind, your Excellency, that nearly every time that we ask the Lord for a fish, he will give us a serpent.'

Fellow-Travellers

At the table on the boat to Africa I sat between a Belgian going to the Congo, and an Englishman who had been eleven times to Mexico to shoot a particular kind of wild mountain-sheep, and who was now going out to shoot bongo. In making conversation on both sides, I got mixed up in the languages, and when I meant to ask the Belgian if he had travelled much in his life, I asked him: *Avez-vous beaucoup travaillé dans votre vie?* He took no offence, but, drawing out his tooth-pick, he answered gravely: *Enormément, Madame.* From this time he made it his object to tell me of all the labours of his life. In everything that he discussed, a certain expression came back: *Notre mission. Notre grand mission dans le Congo.*

One evening, as we were going to play cards, the English traveller told us about Mexico and of how a very old Spanish lady, who lived on a lonely farm in the mountains, when she heard of the arrival of a stranger, had sent for him and ordered him to give her the news of the world. 'Well, men fly now, Madame,' he said to her.

'Yes, I have heard of that,' said she, 'and I have had many arguments with my priest about it. Now you can enlighten us, sir. Do men fly with their legs drawn up under them, like the sparrows, or stretched out behind them, like the storks?'

He also, in the course of our talk, made a remark about the ignorance of the Natives of Mexico, and of the schools there. The Belgian, who was dealing, paused with the last card in his hand, looked piercingly at the Englishman, and said: *Il faut enseigner aux nègres à être honnêtes à travailler. Rien de plus.* Laying down the card with a bang on the table, he repeated with great determination: *Rien de plus. Rien. Rien. Rien.*

The Naturalist and the Monkeys

A Swedish Professor of Natural History came out to the farm to ask me to intervene for him with the Game Department. He had come to Africa, he told me, to find out at what phase of the embryo state the foot of the monkeys, that has got a thumb to it, begins to diverge from the human foot. For this purpose he meant to go and shoot Colobus monkeys on Mount Elgon.

'You will never find out from the Colobus monkeys,' I said to him. 'They live in the tops of the cedar trees, and are shy and difficult to shoot. It would be the greatest luck should you get the embryo you want.'

The Professor was hopeful, he was going to stay out till he had got his foot, he said, even if it was to be for years. He had applied to the Game Department for permission to shoot the monkeys he wanted. The permission he was, in view of the high scientific object of his expedition, certain to get, but so far he had had no reply.

'How many monkeys have you asked to be allowed to shoot?' I asked him.

He told me that he had, to begin with, asked for permission to shoot fifteen hundred monkeys.

Now I knew the people at the Game Department, and I assisted him to send in a second letter, asking for a reply by return of post, since the Professor was keen to get off on his research. The answer from the Game Department did, for once, come by return of post. The Game Department, they wrote, were pleased to inform Professor Landgren that, in view of the scientific object of his expedition, they had seen their way to make an exception from their rules, and to raise the number of monkeys on his licence from four to six.

I had to read the letter over twice to the Professor. When the contents at last were clear to him, he became so downcast, so deadly shocked and hurt, that he did not say a single word. To my expressions of condolence he made no reply, but walked out of the house, got into his car and drove away sadly.

When things did not go so much against him, the Professor was an entertaining talker, and a humorist. In the course of our debates about the monkeys he enlightened me upon various facts and developed many of his ideas to me. One day he said: 'I will tell you of a highly interesting experience of mine. Up at Mount Elgon, I found it possible to believe for a moment in the existence of God. What do you think of that?'

I said that it was interesting, but I thought: There is another interesting question, which is – Has it been possible for God, at Mount Elgon, to believe for a moment in the existence of Professor Landgren?

Karomenya

There was on the farm a little boy of nine named Karomenya who was deaf and dumb. He could give out a sound, a sort of short, raw roar, but it was very rare and he did not like it himself, but always stopped it at once, panting a few times. The other children were afraid of him and complained that he beat them. I first made Karomenya's acquaintance when his play-fellows had knocked him on the head with the branch of a tree, so that his right cheek was thick, and festering with splinters that had to be dug out with a needle. This was not such a martyrdom to Karomenya as one would have thought; if it did hurt him, it also brought him into contact with people.

Karomenya was very dark, with fine moist black eyes and thick eye-lashes; he had an earnest grave expression and hardly ever a smile on his face, and altogether much of the look of a small black Native bull-calf. He was an active, positive creature, and as he was cut off from com-municating with the world by speech, fighting to him had become the manifestation of his being. He was also very good at throwing stones, and could place them where he wanted with great accuracy. At one time Karomenya had a bow and arrow, but it did not work well with him, as if an ear for the ring of the bow-string were, by necessity, part of the archer's craft. Karomenya was sturdily built and very strong for his age. He would probably not have exchanged these advantages over the other boys for their faculty of speech and hearing, for which, I felt, he had no particular admiration.

Karomenya, in spite of his fighting spirit, was no unfriendly person. If he realized that you were addressing him, his face at once lighted up, not in a smile but in a prompt resolute alacrity. Karomenya was a thief, and took sugar and cigarettes when he saw his chance, but he immediately gave away the stolen goods to the other children. I once came upon him as he was dealing out sugar to a circle of boys, himself in the centre; he did not see me, and that is the only time when I have seen him come near to laughing.

I tried, for a time, to give Karomenya a job in the kitchen or the house, but he failed in the offices, and was himself, after a while, bored with the work. What he liked was to move heavy things about, and to drag them from one place to another. I had a row of white-washed stones along my drive, and, with his assistance, I one day moved one of them and rolled it all the way up to the house, to make the drive symmetrical. The next day, while I was out, Karomenya had taken up all the stones and had rolled them up to the house in a great heap, and I could never have believed that a person of his size would have been capable of that. It must have cost him a terrible effort. It was as if Karomenya knew his place in the world and stuck to it. He was deaf and dumb, but he was very strong.

Karomenya, most of all things in the world, wanted a knife, but I dared not give him one, for I thought that he might easily, in his striving for contact with other people, have killed one or more of the other children on the farm with it. He will have got one, though, later in life; his desire was so vehement, and God knows what use he has made of it.

The deepest impression I made on Karomenya was when I gave him a whistle. I had myself used it for some time to call in the dogs. When I showed it to him he took very little interest in it; then, as on my instruction he put it to his mouth and blew it, and the dogs, from both sides, came rushing at him, it gave him a great shock, his face darkened with surprise. He tried it once more, found the effect to be the same, and looked at me, a severe bright glance. When he got more used to the whistle, he wanted to know how it worked. He did not, for this purpose, look at the whistle itself, but when he had whistled for the dogs and they came, he scrutinized them with knit brows as if to find out where they had been hit. After this time Karomenya took a great liking to the dogs, and often, so to say, had the loan of them, taking them out for a walk. I used, when he walked off with them on a lead, to point to the place in the western sky where the sun should be standing but the time that he must be back, and he pointed to the same place, and was always very punctual.

One day, as I was out riding, I saw Karomenya and the dogs a long way away from my house, in the Masai Reserve. He did not see me, but thought that he was all on his own and unobserved. Here he let the dogs have a run, and then whistled them in, and he repeated the performance three or four times, while I watched him from my horse. Out on the plain, where he thought that nobody knew, he gave himself up to a new idea and aspect of life.

He carried his whistle on a string round his neck, but one day he had not got it. I asked him by pantomime what had become of it, and he answered by pantomime that it was gone – lost. He never asked me for another whistle. Either he thought that a second whistle was not to be had, or else he meant, now, to keep away altogether from something in life that was not really his affair. I am not even sure that he had not thrown away the whistle himself, unable to reconcile it with his other ideas of existence.

In five or six years, Karomenya is either to go through much suffering, or he will suddenly be lifted into heaven.

Pooran Singh

Pooran Singh's little blacksmith's shop down by the mill was a miniature Hell on the farm, with all the orthodox attributes of that place. It was built of corrugated iron, and when the sun shone down upon the roof of it, and the flames of the furnace rose inside it, the air itself, in and around the hut, was white hot. All day long, the place resounded with the deafening noise of the forge – iron on iron, on iron once more – and the hut was filled with axes, and broken wheels, that made it look like some ancient gruesome picture of a place of execution.

All the same the blacksmith's shop had a great power of attraction, and when I went down to watch Pooran Singh at work I always found people in it and round it. Pooran Singh worked at a superhuman pace, as if his life depended upon getting the particular job of work finished within the next five minutes, he jumped straight up in the air over the forge, he shrieked out his orders to his two young Kikuyu assistants in a high bird's voice and behaved altogether like a man who is himself being burnt at the stake, or like some chafed over-devil at work. But Pooran Singh was no devil, but a person of the meekest disposition; out of working hours he had a little maidenly affectation of manner. He was our Fundeed of the farm, which means an artisan of all work, carpenter, saddler, and cabinet-maker, as well as blacksmith; he constructed and built more than one wagon for the farm, all on his own. But he liked the work of the forge best, and it was a very fine, proud sight, to watch him tyring a wheel.

Pooran Singh, in his appearance, was something of a fraud. When fully dressed, in his coat and large folded white turban, he managed, with his big black beard, to look a portly, ponderous man. But by the forge, bared to the waist, he was incredibly slight and nimble, with the Indian hour-glass torso.

I liked Pooran Singh's forge, and it was popular with the Kikuyu, for two reasons.

First, because of the iron itself, which is the most fascinating of all raw materials, and sets people's imagination travelling on long tracks. The plough, the sword and cannon and the wheel – the civilization of man – man's conquest of Nature in a nutshell – plain enough to be understood or guessed by the primitive people – and Pooran Singh hammered the iron.

Secondly, the Native world was drawn to the forge by its song. The treble, sprightly, monotonous, and surprising rhythm of the blacksmith's work has a mythical force. It is so virile that it appals and melts the women's hearts, it is straight and unaffected and tells the truth and nothing but the truth. Sometimes it is very outspoken. It has an excess of strength and is gay as well as strong, it is obliging to you and does great things for you, willingly, as in play. The Natives, who love rhythm, col-lected by Pooran Singh's hut and felt at their ease. According to an ancient Nordic law a man was not held responsible for what he had said in a forge. The tongues were loosened in Africa as well in the blacksmith's shop, and the talk flowed freely; audacious fancies were set forth to the inspiring hammer-song.

Pooran Singh was with me for many years and was a well-paid func-tionary of the farm. There was no proportion between his wages and his needs, for he was an ascetic of the first water. He did not eat meat, he did not drink, or smoke, or gamble, his old clothes were worn to the thread. He sent his money over to India for the education of his children. A small silent son of his, Delip Singh, once came over from Bombay on a visit to his father. He had lost touch with the iron, the only metal that I saw about him was a fountain pen in his pocket. The mythical qualities were not carried on in the second generation.

But Pooran Singh himself, raging above the forge, kept his halo as long as he was on the farm, and I hope as long as he lived. He was the servant of the gods, heated through, white-hot, an elemental spirit. In Pooran Singh's blacksmith's shop the hammer sang to you what you wanted to hear, as if it was giving voice to your own heart. To me myself the hammer was singing an ancient Greek verse, which a friend had translated:

Eros struck out, like a smith with his hammer,
So that the sparks flew from my defiance.
He cooled my heart in tears and lamentations.
Like red-hot iron in a stream.

A Strange Happening

When I was down in the Masai Reserve, doing transport for the Government, I one day saw a strange thing, such as no one I know has ever seen. It took place in the middle of the day, while we were trekking over grass-country.

The air in Africa is more significant in the landscape than in Europe, it is filled with loomings and mirages, and is in a way the real stage of activities. In the heat of midday the air oscillates and vibrates like the string of a violin, lifts up long layers of grass-land with thorn-trees and hills on it and creates vast silvery expanses of water in the dry grass.

We were walking along in this burning live air, and I was, against my habit, a long way in front of the wagons, with Farah, my dog Dusk and the Toto who looked after Dusk. We were silent, for it was too hot to talk. All at once the plain at the horizon began to move and gallop with more than the atmosphere; a big herd of game was bearing down upon us from the right, diagonally across the stage.

I said to Farah: 'Look at all these wildebeests.' But a little after, I was not sure that they were wildebeests; I took up my field-glasses and looked at them, but that too is difficult in the middle of the day. 'Are they wildebeests, Farah, do you think?' I asked him.

I now saw that Dusk had all his attention upon the animals, his ears up in the air, his far-seeing eyes following their advance. I often used to let him have a run after the gazelles and antelopes on the plains, but to-day I thought that it would be too hot, and told the Toto to fasten his lead to his collar. At the same moment, Dusk gave a short wild yell and jumped forward so that the Toto was thrown over, and I snatched the lead myself and had to hold him with all my might. I looked at the game. 'What are they?' I asked Farah.

It is very difficult to judge distances on the plains. The quivering air and the monotony of the scenery make it so, also the character of the scattered thorn-trees, which have the exact shape of mighty old forest trees, but are in reality only twelve feet high, so that the giraffes raise their heads and necks above them. You are continually deceived as to the size of the game that you see at a distance and may, in the middle of the day, mistake a jackal for an eland, and an ostrich for a buffalo. A minute later Farah said: 'Memsahib, these are wild dogs.'

The wild dogs are generally seen three or four at a time, but it happens that you meet a dozen of them together. The Natives are afraid of them, and will tell you that they are very murderous. Once as I was riding in the Reserve close to the farm I came upon four wild dogs which followed me at a distance of fifteen yards. The two small terriers that I had with me then kept as close to me as possible, actually under the belly of the pony, until we came across the river and on to the farm. The wild dogs are not as big as a hyena. They are about the size of a big alsatian dog. They are black, with a white tuft at the tip of the tail and of the pointed ears. The skin is no good, it has rough uneven hair and smells badly.

Here there must have been five hundred wild dogs. They came along in a slow canter, in the strangest way, looking neither right nor left, as if they had been frightened by something, or as if they were travelling fast with a fixed purpose on a track. They just swerved a bit as they came nearer to us; all the same they hardly seemed to see us, and went on at the same pace. When they were closest to us, they were fifty yards away. They were running in a long file, two or three or four side by side, it took time before the whole procession had passed us. In the middle of it, Farah said: 'These dogs are very tired, they have run a long way.'

When they had all gone by, and were disappearing again, we looked round for the safari. It was still some way behind us, and exhausted by our agitation of mind we sat down where we stood in the grass, until it came up to us. Dusk was terribly upset, jerking his lead to run after the wild dogs. I took him round the neck. If I had not tied him up in time, I thought, he would by now have been eaten up.

The drivers of the wagons detached themselves from the safari and came running up to us, to ask what it had all been. I could not explain to them, or to myself, what had made the wild dogs come along in so great a number in such a way. The Natives all took it as a very bad omen – an omen of the war, for the wild dogs are carrion-eaters. They did not afterwards discuss the happening much among themselves, as they used to discuss all the other events of the safari.

I have told this tale to many people and not one of them has believed it. All the same it is true, and my boys can bear me witness.

The Parrot

An old Danish shipowner sat and thought of his young days and of how he had, when he was sixteen years old, spent a night in a brothel in Singapore. He had come in there with the sailors of his father's ship, and had sat and talked with an old Chinese woman. When she heard that he was a native of a distant country she brought out an old parrot, that belonged to her. Long, long ago, she told him, the parrot had been given her by a high-born English lover of her youth. The boy thought that the bird must then be a hundred years old. It could say various sentences in the languages of all the world, picked up in the cosmopolitan atmosphere of the house. But one phrase the old Chinawoman's lover had taught it before he sent it to her, and that she did not understand neither had any visitor ever been able to tell her what it meant. So now for many years she had given up asking. But if the boy came from far away perhaps it was his language, and he could interpret the phrase to her.

The boy had been deeply, strangely moved at the suggestion. When he looked at the parrot, and thought that he might hear Danish from that terrible beak, he very nearly ran out of the house. He stayed on only to do the old Chinese woman a service. But when she made the parrot speak its sentence, it turned out to be classic Greek. The bird spoke its words very slowly, and the boy knew enough Greek to recognize it; it was a verse from Sappho:

> 'The moon has sunk and the Pleiads
> And midnight is gone,
> And the hours are passing, passing,
> And I lie alone.'

The old woman, when he translated the lines to her, smacked her lips and rolled her small slanting eyes. She asked him to say it again, and nodded her head.

5
FAREWELL
TO THE
FARM

'Gods and men, we are all deluded thus!'

Hard Times

My farm was a little too high up for growing coffee. It happened in the cold months that we would get frost on the lower land and in the morning the shoots of the coffee-trees, and the young coffee-berries on them, would be all brown and withered. The wind blew in from the plains, and even in good years we never got the same yield of coffee to the acre as the people in the lower districts of Thika and Kiambu, at four thousand feet.

We were short of rain, as well, in the Ngong country, and three times we had a year of real drought, which brought us very low down. In a year in which we had fifty inches of rain, we picked eighty tons of coffee, and in a year of fifty-five inches, nearly ninety tons; but there were two bad years in which we had only twenty-five and twenty inches of rain, and picked only sixteen and fifteen tons of coffee, and those years were disastrous to the farm.

At the same time coffee prices fell: where we had got a hundred pounds a ton we now got sixty or seventy. Times grew hard on the farm. We could not pay our debts, and we had no money for the running of the plantation. My people at home, who had shares in the farm, wrote out to me and told me that I would have to sell.

I thought out many devices for the salvation of the farm. One year I tried to grow flax on our spare land. Flax-growing is a lovely job, but it needs much skill and experience. I had a Belgian refugee to give me advice on it, and when he asked me how much land I meant to plant, and I told him three hundred acres, he immediately exclaimed: *Ça, Madame, c'est impossible.* I might grow five acres or even ten with success, he said, but no more. But ten acres would take us nowhere, and I put in a hundred and fifty acres. A sky-blue flowering flax-field is a marvellously pretty sight – like a piece of heaven on earth, and there can be no more gratifying kind of goods to be turning out than the flax fibre, tough and glossy, and slightly greasy to the touch. You follow it in your thoughts as it is sent away, and imagine it made into sheets and nightgowns. But the Kikuyu could not, in the turn of a hand and without constant supervision, be taught to be accurate enough in the pulling and retting and scutching of it; and so my flax-growing was no success.

Most of the farmers in the country were, in those years, trying their hand at some such scheme, and to a few of them in the end an inspiration came. Things turned out well for Ingrid Lindstrom of Njoro: at the time when I had left the country, and after she had slaved for twelve years at her market gardening, pigs, turkeys, castor-oil bushes, and soya beans, had seen them all fail, and wept over them, she saved her farm for her family and herself by planting pyrethrum, which is sent to London and is there used in making insecticides. But I myself had no luck with my experiments, and when the dry weather and the wind from the Athi plains set in, the coffee-trees drooped and the leaves turned yellow; on parts of the farm we got bad coffee diseases like thrips and antestia.

To bring the coffee on we tried to manure the fields. It had always, as I had been brought up with European ideas on farming, gone against me to take the crops out of the land, without manuring. When the squatters of the farm heard of the project they came forward to help me, and brought out, from their cattle and goat bomas, the manure of decades. It was delicate peaty stuff that was easy to handle. We ploughed up a furrow between the rows of coffee-trees, with the small new ploughs with a single ox to them that we had bought in Nairobi, and, since we could not get a cart into the fields, the women of the farm carried the manure in sacks on their backs, and spread it in the furrow, a sack to the tree, so that we could lead back the oxen and ploughs, and cover it up. It was pleasant work to watch, and I expected great things from it, but as it came to happen, no one ever saw the effects of the manuring.

Our real trouble was that we were short of capital, for it had all been spent in the old days before I took over the running of the farm. We could not carry through any radical improvements, but had to live from hand to mouth – and this, in the last years, became our normal mode of living on the farm.

If I had had the capital, I thought, I would have given up coffee, have cut down the coffee-trees, and have planted forest trees on my land. Trees grow up so quickly in Africa, in ten years' time you walk comfortably under tall blue-gum trees, and wattle trees, which you have yourself, in the rain, carried in boxes from the nurseries, twelve trees in a box. I would have had then, I reflected, a good market for both timber and firewood in Nairobi. It is a noble occupation to plant trees, you think of it many years after with content. There had been big stretches of native forest on the farm in the old days, but it had been sold to the Indians for cutting down, before I took over the farm; it was a sad thing. I myself in the hard years had had to cut down the wood on my land round the factory for the steam-engine, and this forest, with the tall stems and the live green shadows in it, had haunted me. I have not felt more sorry for anything I have done in my life, than for cutting it down. From time to time, when I could afford it, I planted up bits of land with eucalyptus trees, but it did not come to much. It would be, in this way, fifty years before I had got the many hundred acres planted up, and had changed the farm into a singing wood, scientifically run, with a sawmill by the river. The squatters of the farm, though, whose ideas of time were different from those of the white people, kept on looking forward hopefully to the time when everybody would have abundance of firewood – such as the people had had in the old days – from the forest that I was now soon going to plant.

I had also plans for keeping cattle and running a dairy on the farm. We were situated in an unclean area, which means that you have got East Coast fever on the land, and that if you will keep grade stock you have got to dip your cattle. It makes it harder to compete with the cattle people up-country in the clean areas, but then I had Nairobi so close that I could send in milk there by car in the morning. We once owned a herd of grade cows, and then we built a fine cattle dip on the plain. But we had to sell out, and the cattle dip, overgrown with grass, afterwards stood like a sunk and overturned ruin of a castle in the air. Later on, when in the evening, at milking time, I walked down to Mauge's or Kaninu's boma, and smelled the sweet scent of the cows, I felt again a pang of longing for cow-stables and a dairy of my own. When I rode on the plain, in my mind I saw it dotted, as with flowers, with brindled cows.

But these plans grew very distant in the course of the years, and in the end they could hardly be distinguished. I did not mind either, if I could only make the coffee pay, and keep the farm going.

It is a heavy burden to carry a farm on you. My Natives, and my white people even, left me to dread and worry on their behalf, and it sometimes seemed to me that the farm oxen and the coffee-trees themselves were doing the same. It appeared to be agreed upon, then, by the speaking creatures and the dumb, that it was my fault that the rains were late and the nights so cold. And in the evening it did not seem right that I should sit down quietly to read; I was driven out of my house by the fear of losing it. Farah knew of all my sorrows, and he did not approve of my walks at night. He talked about the leopards that had been seen close to the house when the sun was down: and he used to stand on the verandah, a white-robed figure just visible in the dark, until I came in again. But I was too sad to get any idea of leopards into my mind. I knew that I did no good whatever by going round on the roads of the farm in the night, and still I went, like a ghost that is just said to walk, without any definition as to why or where to.

Two years before I left Africa I was in Europe on a visit. I travelled back in the coffee-picking season, so that I could not get news of the harvest before I came to Mombasa. All the time on the boat I was weighing the problem in my mind: when I was well and life was looking friendly, I reckoned that we would have got seventy-five tons, but when I was unwell or nervous I thought: We are bound to get sixty tons in any case.

Farah came to meet me in Mombasa, and I dared not ask him about the coffee crop straight away; for some time we talked of other news of the farm. But in the evening as I was going to bed, I could not put it off any longer and I asked him how many tons of coffee they had picked on the farm in all. The Somalis are generally pleased to announce a disaster. But here Farah was not happy, he was extremely grave himself, standing up by the door, and he half closed his eyes and laid back his head, swallowing his sorrow, when he said: 'Forty tons, Memsahib.' At that I knew that we could not carry on. All colour and life faded out of the world round me; the bleak and stifling Mombasa hotel room, with the cemented floor, old iron bedstead and worn mosquito-net, took on a tremendous significance as the symbol of the world, without any single ornament or article of embellishment of human life in it. I did not say anything more to Farah, and he did not speak again, but went away, the last friendly object in the world.

Still the human mind has great powers of self-renewal, and in the middle of the night I thought, with Old Knudsen, that forty tons was something, but that pessimism – pessimism was a fatal vice. And in any case I was going home now, I would be turning up the drive once more. My people were there, and my friends would come out to visit me. In ten hours I was to see, from the railway, to the south-west, the blue silhouette against the sky of the Ngong Hills.

The same year the grasshoppers came on the land. It was said that they came from Abyssinia; after two years of drought up there, they travelled south and ate up all vegetation on their way. Before we ever saw them, there were strange tales circulating in the country of the devastation that they had left behind them – up north, maize and wheat and fruit farms were all one vast desert where they had passed. The settlers sent runners to their neighbours to the south to announce the coming of the grass-hoppers. Still you could not do much against them even if you were warned. On all the farms people had tall piles of firewood and maize-stalks ready and set fire to them when the grasshoppers came, and they sent out all the farm labourers with empty tins and cans, and told them to shout and yell and beat the tins to frighten them from landing. But it was a short respite only, for however much the farmers would frighten them the grasshoppers could not keep up in the air for ever; the only thing that each farmer could hope for was to drive them off to the next farm to the south, and the more farms they were scared away from, the hungrier and more desperate were they, when in the end they settled. I myself had the great plains of the Masai Reserve to the south, so that I might hope to keep the grasshoppers on the wing and send them over the river to the Masai.

I had three or four runners announcing the arrival of the grasshoppers, from neighbourly settlers of the district, already, but nothing more had happened, and I began to believe that it was all a false alarm. One afternoon I rode over to our dhuka, a farm shop of all goods, kept for the farm labourers and the squatters by Farah's small brother Abdullai. It was on the highroad, and an Indian in a mule-trap outside the dhuka rose in his trap and beckoned to me as I passed, since he could not drive up to me on the plain.

'The grasshoppers are coming, madam, please, on to your land,' said he when I rode up to him.

'I have been told that many times,' I said, 'but I have seen nothing of them. Perhaps it is not so bad as people tell.'

'Turn round kindly, madam,' said the Indian.

I turned round and saw, along the northern horizon, a shadow on the sky, like a long stretch of smoke, a town burning, 'a million-peopled city vomiting smoke in the bright air,' I thought, or like a thin cloud rising.

'What is that?' I asked.

'Grasshoppers,' said the Indian.

I saw a few grasshoppers, perhaps twenty in all, on the path across the plain as I rode back. I passed my manager's house and instructed him to have everything ready for receiving the grasshoppers. As together we looked north the black smoke on the sky had grown up a little higher. From time to time while we were watching it, a grasshopper swished past us in the air, or dropped on the ground and crawled on.

The next morning as I opened my door and looked out, the whole landscape outside was the colour of pale dull terra-cotta. The trees, the lawn, the drive, all that I could see, was covered with the dye, as if in the night a thick layer of terra-cotta-coloured snow had fallen on the land. The grasshoppers were sitting there. While I stood and looked at it all, the scenery began to quiver and break, the grasshoppers moved and lifted, after a few minutes the atmosphere fluttered with wings, they were going off.

That time they did not do much damage to the farm, they had been staying with us over the night only. We had seen what they were like, about an inch and a half long, brownish grey and pink, sticky to touch. They had broken a couple of big trees in my drive simply by sitting on them, and when you looked at the trees and remembered that each of the grasshoppers could only weigh a tenth of an ounce, you began to conceive the number of them.

The grasshoppers came again; for two or three months we had continued attacks of them on the farm. We soon gave up trying to frighten them off, it was a hopeless and tragi-comical undertaking. At times a small swarm would come along, a free corps which had detached itself from the main force, and would just pass in a rush. But at other times the grasshoppers came in big flights, which took days to pass over the farm, twelve hours' incessant hurling advance in the air. When the flight was at its highest it was like a blizzard at home, whistling and shrieking like a strong wind, little hard furious wings to all sides of you and over your head, shining like thin blades of steel in the sun, but themselves darkening the sun. The grasshoppers keep in a belt, from the ground up to the top of the trees, beyond that the air is clear. They whir against your face, they get into your collar and your sleeves and shoes. The rush round you makes you giddy and fills you with a particular sickening rage and despair, the horror of the mass. The individual amongst it does not count, kill it and it makes no difference to anybody. After the grasshoppers have passed and have gone towards the horizon like a long streak of thinning smoke, the feeling of disgust at your own face and hands, which have been crawled upon by grasshoppers, stays with you for a long time.

A great flight of birds followed the advance of the grasshoppers, circled above them and came down and walked in the fields when they settled, living high on the horde: storks and cranes – pompous profiteers.

At times the grasshoppers settled on the farm. They did not do much harm to the coffee-plantation; the leaves of the coffee-trees, similar to laurel leaves, are too hard for them to chew. They could only break a tree here and there in the field.

But the maize-fields were a sad sight when they had been on them and had left, there was nothing there now but a few laps of dry leaves hanging from the broken stalks. My garden by the river, that had been irrigated and kept green, was now like a dust-heap – flowers, vegetables, and herbs had all gone. The shambas of the squatters were like stretches of cleared and burnt land, rolled even by the crawling insects, with a dead grasshopper in the dust here and there as the sole fruit of the soil. The squatters stood and looked at them. The old women who had dug and planted the shambas, standing on their heads, shook their fists at the last faint black disappearing shadow in the sky.

A lot of dead grasshoppers were left behind the army everywhere. On the highroad, where they had sat, and where the wagons and carts had passed, and had driven over them, now, after the swarm had gone, the wheel-tracks were marked, like rails of a railway, as long as you could see them, with little bodies of dead grasshoppers.

The grasshoppers had laid their eggs in the soil. Next year, after the long rains, the little black-brown hoppers appeared – grasshoppers in the first stage of life, that cannot fly, but which crawl along and eat up everything upon their march.

When I had no more money, and could not make things pay, I had to sell the farm. A big company in Nairobi bought it. They thought that the place was too high up for coffee, and they were not going in for farming. But they meant to take up all the coffee-trees, to divide up the land and lay out roads, and in time, when Nairobi should be growing out to the west, they meant to sell the land for building-plots. That was towards the end of the year.

Even as it was then, I do not think that I should have found it in me to give up the farm if it had not been for one thing. The coffee crop that was still unripe upon the trees belonged to the old owners of the farm, or to the Bank which was holding a first mortgage in it. This coffee would not be picked, handled in the factory and sent off, till May or later. For such a period I was to remain on the farm, in charge of it, and things were to go on, unaltered to the view. And during this time, I thought, something would happen to change it all back, since the world, after all, was not a regular or calculable place.

In this way began for me a strange era in my existence on the farm. The truth that was underlying everything was that it was no longer mine, but such as it was, this truth could be ignored by the people incapable of realizing it, and it made no difference to things from day to day. It was then, from hour to hour, a lesson in the art of living in the moment, or, it might be said, in eternity, wherein the actual happenings of the moment make but little difference.

It was a curious thing that I myself did not, during this time, ever believe that I would have to give up the farm or to leave Africa. I was told that I must do so by the people round me, all of them reasonable men; I had letters from home by each mail to prove it, and all the facts of my daily life pointed to it. All the same nothing was farther from my thoughts, and I kept on believing that I should come to lay my bones in Africa. For this firm faith I had no other foundation, or no other reason, than my complete incompetence to imagine anything else.

During these months, I formed in my own mind a programme, or system of strategy, against destiny, and against the people in my surroundings who were her confederates. I shall give in, I thought, from this time forward, in all minor matters, to save myself unnecessary trouble. I shall let my adversaries have their way from day to day in these affairs, in talk and writing. For in the end I shall still come out triumphant and shall keep my farm and the people on it. Lose them, I thought, I cannot: it cannot be imagined, how then can it happen?

In this way I was the last person to realize that I was going. When I look back upon my last months in Africa, it seems to me that the lifeless things were aware of my departure a long time before I was so myself. The hills, the forests, plains and rivers, the wind, all knew that we were to part. When I first began to make terms with fate, and the negotiations about the sale of the farm were taken up, the attitude of the landscape towards me changed. Till then I had been part of it, and the drought had been to me like a fever, and the flowering of the plain like a new frock. Now the country disengaged itself from me, and stood back a little, in order that I should see it clearly and as a whole.

The hills can do the same thing in the week before the rains. On an evening as you look at them, they suddenly make a great movement and uncover, they become as manifest, as distinct and vivid in form and colour, as if they meant to yield themselves to you, with all that they contain, as if you could walk from where you sit, on to the green slope. You think: if a bushbuck now walked out in the open, I might see its eyes as it turned its head, its ears moving; if a little bird settled on a twig of a bush, I should hear it sing. In the hills, in March, this gesture of abandon means that the rains are near, but here, to me, it meant parting.

I have before seen other countries, in the same manner, give themselves to you when you are about to leave them, but I had forgotten what it meant. I only thought that I had never seen the country so lively, as if the contemplation of it would in itself be enough to make you happy all your life. Light and shade shared the landscape between them; rainbows stood in the sky.

When I was with other white people, lawyers and businessmen of Nairobi, or with my friends who gave me advice about my journey, my isolation from them felt very strange, and sometimes like a physical thing – a kind of suffocation. I looked upon myself as the one reasonable person amongst them all; but once or twice it happened to me to reflect that if I had been mad, amongst sane people, I should have felt just the same.

The Natives of the farm, in the stark realism of their souls, were conscious of the situation and of my state of mind, as fully as if I had been lecturing to them upon it, or had written it down for them in a book. All the same, they looked to me for help and support, and did not, in a single case, attempt to arrange their future for themselves. They tried their very best to make me stay on, and for this purpose invented many schemes which they confided to me. At the time when the sale of the farm was through, they came and sat round my house from the early morning till night, not so much in order to talk with me as just to follow all my movements. There is a paradoxical moment in the relation between the leader and the followers: that they should see every weakness and failing in him so clearly, and be capable of judging him with such unbiased accuracy, and yet should still inevitably turn to him, as if in life there were, physically, no way round him. A flock of sheep may be feeling the same towards the herdboy, they will have infinitely better knowledge of the country and the weather than he, and still will be walking after him, if needs be, straight into the abyss. The Kikuyu took the situation better than I did, on account of their superior inside knowledge of God and the Devil, but they sat round my house and waited for my orders; very likely all the time between themselves expatiating freely upon my ignorance and my unique incapacity.

You would have thought that their constant presence by my house, when I knew that I could not help them, and when their fate weighed heavily on my mind, would have been hard to bear. But it was not so. We felt, I believe, up to the very last, a strange comfort and relief in each other's company. The understanding between us lay deeper than all reason. I thought in these months much of Napoleon on the retreat from Moscow. It is generally thought that he went through agonies in seeing his grand army suffering and dying round him, but it is also possible that he would have dropped down dead on the spot if he had not had them. In the night, I counted the hours till the time when the Kikuyus should turn up again by the house.

Death of Kinanjui

In that same year the Chief Kinanjui died. One of his sons came to my house late in the evening and asked me to go back with him to his father's village, for he was dying: *Na-taka kufa* – he wants to die – the Natives have it.

Kinanjui was now an old man. A great thing had lately happened in his life: the quarantine regulations of the Masai Reserve had been suspended. The old Kikuyu chief, as soon as he heard of it, set forth in person, with a few retainers, deep down south in the Reserve, to wind up his multifarious accounts with the Masai, and bring back with him the cows that belonged to him, together with the calves that they had produced in their exile. While he was down there he had fallen ill; as far as I could understand he had been butted in the thigh by a cow, which seemed a becoming cause of death to a Kikuyu chief, and the wound had gone gangrenous. Kinanjui had been staying too long with the Masai, or had been too ill to undertake the long journey, when at last he turned his face homewards. Probably he had so set his heart on getting all his stock with him, that he had not had it in him to leave until they were all collected, and it is also possible that he had let himself be nursed by one of his married daughters there, until a slight misgiving had risen in him as to her goodwill to bring him through his illness. In the end he started, and it seemed that his attendants had done their best for him and had taken great trouble to get him home, carrying the deadly sick old man for long distances on a stretcher. Now he lay dying in his hut, and had sent for me.

Kinanjui's son had come to my house after dinner, and it was dark when Farah and I and he drove over to his village, but the moon was up and in her first quarter. On the way Farah opened up the subject of who was to succeed Kinanjui as chief of the Kikuyu. The old Chief had many sons; it appeared that there were various influences at work in the Kikuyu world. Two of his sons, Farah told me, were Christians, but one was a Roman Catholic, and the other a convert to the Church of Scotland, and each of the two missions was sure to take pains to get their pretender proclaimed. The Kikuyus themselves, it seemed, wanted a third, younger, heathen son.

The road for the last mile was nothing more than a cattle-track over the sward. The grass was grey with dew. Just before we got to the village we had to cross a river-bed with a little winding silvery stream in the middle; here we drove through a white mist. Kinanjui's big manyatta, when we got up to it, was all quiet under the moon, a wide compound of huts, small peaked store-huts and cattle-bomas. As we were turning into it, in the light of our lamps I caught sight, under a thatched roof, of the car which Kinanjui had bought from the American Consul at the time when he came over to the farm to give judgement in the case of Wanyangerri. She looked completely forlorn, all rusty and dilapidated, and surely now Kinanjui would be giving her no thought, but would have turned back to the ways of his fathers, and demanded to see cows and women round him.

The village that looked so dark was not asleep, the people were up and came and surrounded us when they heard the car. But it was changed from what it used to be. Kinanjui's manyatta was always a lively and noisy place, like a well spouting from the ground and running over on all sides; plans and projects were crossing one another in all directions, and all under the eye of the pompous, benevolent, central figure of Kinanjui. Now the wing of death lay over the manyatta, and, like a strong magnet, it had altered the patterns below, forming new constellations and groups. The welfare of each member of the family and tribe was at stake, and such scenes and intrigues as are always played round a royal death-bed were, you felt, alive here, in the strong smell of cows, and in the dim moonlight. As we got out of the car, a boy with a lamp came along and took us up to Kinanjui's hut, and a crowd of people went with us and stood outside it.

I had never before been inside Kinanjui's house. This royal mansion was a good deal bigger than the ordinary Kikuyu hut, but when I entered it I found it to be no more luxuriously furnished. There was a bedstead made out of sticks and reins in it, and a few wooden stools to sit on. Two or three fires burned on the stamped clay floor, the heat in the hut was suffocating, and the smoke was so dense that at first I could not see who was in there, although they had a hurricane-lamp standing on the floor. When I had got a little more used to the atmosphere I saw that there were three old bald men in the room with me, uncles or councillors of Kinanjui, a very old woman who hung on a stick and remained close to the bed, a young pretty girl, and a boy of thirteen – and what new constellation, worked by the magnet, was this, in the Chief's death-chamber?

Kinanjui lay flat on his bed. He was dying, he was already half-way into death and dissolution, and the stench about him was so sifling that at first I dared not open my mouth to speak for fear that I should be sick. The old man was all naked, he was lying upon a tartan rug that I had once given him, but probably he could not stand any weight at all on his poisoned leg. The leg was terrible to look at, so swollen that you could not distinguish the place of the knee, and in the lamplight I could see that it was streaked all the way from the hip to the foot with black and yellow streaks. Underneath the leg, the rug was dark and wet as if water was all the time running from it.

Kinanjui's son, who had come to the farm to fetch me, brought in an old European chair, with one leg shorter than the others, and placed it very close to the bed, for me to sit on.

Kinanjui's head and trunk were so emaciated that all the structure of his big skeleton stood forth. He looked like a huge dark wooden figure roughly cut with a knife. His teeth and his tongue showed between his lips. His eyes were half dimmed, milky in his dark face. But he could still see, and when I came up to the bed he turned his eyes on me and kept them on my face all the time that I was in the hut.

Very very slowly he dragged his right hand across his body to touch my hand. He was in terrible pain, but he was still himself and was still carrying great weight, naked upon his bed. From the look of him, I thought that he had come back from his journey triumphant, and had got all his cattle back with him, in spite of his Masai sons-in-law. I remembered, while I sat and looked at him, that he had had one weakness: he had been afraid of thunder, and when a thunderstorm broke, while he was in my house, he adopted a rodent manner and looked round for a burrow. But here now he feared no more the lightning flash, nor the all-dreaded thunder-stone: he had plainly, I thought, done his worldly task, gone home, and taken his wages in every sense. If he were clear enough in his mind to look back at his life, he would find very few instances in which he had not got the better of it. A great vitality and power of enjoyment, a manifold activity were at their end here, where Kinanjui lay still. 'Quiet consummation have, Kinanjui' – I thought.

The old men in the hut stood by, as if they had lost the faculty of speech. It was the boy who had been in there when I came, and whom I took to be a late-born son of Kinanjui's, who now came up close to his father's bed and talked to me, in accordance, I thought, with what had been agreed upon before I arrived.

The doctor from the mission, he explained, had heard of Kinanjui's illness and had been to see him. He had told the Kikuyus that he would come back again to fetch the dying chief into the mission hospital, and they were expecting the lorry from the mission which was to bring him there, that same night. But Kinanjui did not want to go into hospital. That was why he had sent for me. He wanted me to take him with me to my own house, and he meant me to take him now, before the people from the mission should return. While the boy spoke, Kinanjui looked at me.

I sat and listened with a heavy heart.

If Kinanjui had lain dying at any time in the past, a year ago or even three months ago, I would have taken him with me to my house on his asking for it. But today it was a different thing. Things had gone badly with me lately and had made me fear that they would go on worse. I had been spending days in the offices of Nairobi, listening to businessmen and lawyers, and at meetings with the creditors of the farm. The house, to which Kinanjui asked me to take him, was no longer my own house.

Kinanjui, I thought, as I sat and looked at him, was going to die, he could not be saved. He would die in my car on the way home, or at the arrival to the house. The mission people would come and blame me for his death; everybody who heard of it would agree with them.

All this, from my seat on the broken chair in the hut, looked to me as a weight too heavy to take on. I had not got it in me any longer to stand up against the authorities of the world. I did not have it in me now to brave them all, not all of them.

I tried two or three times to make up my mind to take Kinanjui and my courage failed me every time. I thought then that I should have to leave him.

Farah had stood by the door, and had followed the boy's speech. When he saw me sitting on silent, he came up to me and in a low eager voice began an explanation of how we were best to lift Kinanjui into the car. I got up and went with him to the background of the hut, somewhat away from the eyes and the stench of the old man on the bed. I told Farah then that I was not going to take Kinanjui back with me. Farah was completely unprepared for this turn of things; his eyes and whole face darkened with surprise.

I should have liked to have stayed a little with Kinanjui, but I did not want to see the people from the mission arrive and take him away.

I went up to Kinanjui's bed and told him that I could not take him with me back to my house. There was no need to give reasons, so we left it at that. The old men in the hut, when they understood that I declined, gathered round me and stirred uneasily, the boy stepped back a little and stood immovable, he had no more to do. Kinanjui himself did not stir or change in any way, he kept his eyes on me as he had done all the time.

He looked as if something like this had happened to him before, which very likely it had.

'Kwaheri, Kinanjui,' I said – Good-bye.

His burning fingers moved a little against my palm. Already before I had got to the door of the hut, when I turned and looked back, the dimness and smoke of the room had swallowed up the big outstretched figure of my Kikuyu Chief. As I came out again from the hut it was very cold. The moon was now low down at the horizon, it must have been past midnight. Just then in the manyatta one of Kinanjui's cocks crew twice.

Kinanjui died that same night, in the mission hospital. Two of his sons came over to my house next afternoon to tell me. At the same time they asked me to the funeral, which was to take place on the following day, near his village, at Dagoretti.

The Kikuyu, when left to themselves, do not bury their dead, but leave them above ground for the hyenas and vultures to deal with. The custom had always appealed to me, I thought that it would be a pleasant thing to be laid out to the sun and the stars, and to be so promptly, neatly, and openly picked and cleansed; to be made one with Nature and become a common component of a landscape. At the time when we had the Spanish flu on the farm, I heard the hyenas round the shambas all night, and often, after those days, I would find a brown smooth skull in the long grass of the forest, like a nut dropped down under a tree, or on the plain. But the practice does not go with the conditions of civilized life. The Government had taken much trouble to make the Kikuyu change their ways, and to teach them to lay their dead in the ground, but they still did not like the idea at all.

Kinanjui, they now told me, was to be buried, and I thought that the Kikuyu would have agreed to make an exception from their habit because the dead had been a chief. Perhaps they would like to make a great Native show and gathering of the occasion. I drove over to Dagoretti, on the following afternoon, expecting to find all the old minor chiefs of the country, and to see a big Kikuyu festivity.

But Kinanjui's funeral was altogether a European and clerical affair. There were a few government representatives present, the district commissioner and two officials from Nairobi. But the day and the place belonged to the clergy; and the plain, in the afternoon sun, was black with them. Both the French Mission and the Missions of the Church of England and Scotland were richly represented. If they wished to impress the Kikuyu with the feeling that here they had laid their hand on the dead chief, and that he now belonged to them, they succeeded. They were so obviously in power that one felt it to be out of the question for Kinanjui to get away from them. This is an old trick of the Church's. Here I saw for the first time, in any number to speak of, the mission-boys, the converted Natives, half sacerdotally attired, whatever office they might be filling, fat young Kikuyus with spectacles and folded hands, who looked like ungenial eunuchs. Probably Kinanjui's two Christian sons were there, laying down their religious disagreements for the day, but I did not know them. Some of the old chiefs were attending the funeral. Keoy was there, and I talked with him for some time of Kinanjui. But they kept themselves much in the background of the show.

Kinanjui's grave had been dug under a couple of tall eucalyptus trees on the plain, and a rope was extended round it. I had come early and therefore stood close to the grave, by the rope, from where I could watch the assemblage grow and settle, like flies, round it.

They brought Kinanjui from the mission on a lorry, and lifted him down near the grave. I do not think that I have ever in my life been more taken aback and appalled than I was then, at the sight of him. He had been a big man, and I remembered him as I had seen him when he came walking over to the farm amongst his senators, even as he had looked lying on his bed, two nights ago. But the coffin in which they now brought him was a nearly square box, surely no more than five feet long. I did not take it to be a coffin when I first set eyes on it; it must be, I thought, some box of appliances for the funeral. But it was Kinanjui's coffin. I have never known why it was chosen; perhaps it was a thing that they had had at the Scotch Mission. But how had they got Kinanjui down there and how was he now lying in it? They placed the coffin on the ground, close to where I stood.

The coffin had a large silver plate on it with an inscription, which told, I was afterwards informed, that it had been given by the mission to the Chief Kinanjui, and with a scriptural text on it.

There was a long funeral service. One after another, the missionaries stood forth and spoke, and I suppose that they got in much profession and admonition. But I did not hear any of it, I was holding on to the rope round Kinanjui's grave. Some of the Christian Natives followed them up, and brayed out over the green plain.

In the end Kinanjui was lowered into the ground of his own country, and covered with it.

I had taken my houseboys with me to Dagoretti so that they should see the funeral, and they were staying to talk with their friends and relations there, and coming back on foot, so that Farah and I drove home by ourselves. Farah was as silent as the grave we had left. It had been hard for Farah to swallow the fact that I would not take Kinanjui back to my house with me; for two days he had been like a lost soul, and in the clutch of great doubts and depressions.

Now as we drove up before the door he said: 'Never mind, Memsahib.'

The Grave in the Hills

Denys Finch-Hatton had come in from one of his safaris, and he had stayed for a little while on the farm, but, when I began to break up my house and to pack, and he could stay there no longer, he went away and lived in Hugh Martin's house in Nairobi. From there he drove out to the farm every day and dined with me, sitting – towards the end, when I was selling my furniture – on one packing-case and dining from another. We sat there late into the night.

A few times, Denys and I spoke as if I was really going to leave the country. He himself looked upon Africa as his home, and he understood me very well and grieved with me then, even if he laughed at my distress at parting with my people.

'Do you feel,' he said, 'that you cannot live without Sirunga?'

'Yes,' I said.

But most of the time when we were together, we talked and acted as if the future did not exist; it had never been his way to worry about it, for it was as if he knew that he could draw upon forces unknown to us if he wanted to. He fell in naturally with my scheme of leaving things to themselves, and other people to think and say what they liked. When he was there, it seemed to be a normal thing, and in accordance with our own taste, that we should sit upon packing-cases within an empty house. He quoted a poem to me:

> 'You must turn your mournful ditty
> To a merry measure,
> I will never come for pity,
> I will come for pleasure.'

During those weeks, we used to go up for short flights out over the Ngong Hills or down over the Game Reserve. One morning, Denys came out to the farm to fetch me quite early, just as the sun was up, and then we saw a lion on the plain south of the hills.

He talked of packing up his books, that had been in my house for many years, but he never got any further with the job.

'You keep them,' he said, 'now I have no place to put them.'

He could not make up his mind at all where to go when my house should be closed. Once, upon the persistent advice of a friend, he went so far as to drive in to Nairobi, and to take a look at the bungalows to be let there, but he came back so repelled with what he had seen that he did not even like to talk about it, and at dinner, when he began to give me a description of the houses and the furniture, he stopped himself and sat silent over it, with a dislike and sadness in his face that was unusual to him. He had been in contact with a kind of existence the idea of which was unbearable to him.

It was, however, a completely objective and impersonal disapprobation, he had forgotten that he himself had meant to be a party to this existence, and when I spoke of it, he interrupted me. 'Oh, as to me,' he said, 'I shall be perfectly happy in a tent in the Masai Reserve, or I shall take a house in the Somali village.'

But on this occasion he, for once, spoke of my future in Europe. I might be happier there than on the farm, he thought, and well out of the sort of civilization that we were going to get in Africa. 'You know,' he went on, 'this Continent of Africa has a terribly strong sense of sarcasm.'

Denys owned a piece of land down at the coast, thirty miles north of Mombasa on the Creek of Takaunga. Here were the ruins of an old Arab settlement, with a very modest minaret and a well – a weathered growth of grey stone on the salted soil, and in the midst of it a few old mango trees. He had built a small house on his land and I had stayed there. The scenery was of a divine, clean, barren marine greatness, with the blue Indian Ocean before you, the deep Creek of Takaunga to the south, and the long steep unbroken coastline of pale grey and yellow coral-rock as far as the eye reached.

When the tide was out, you could walk miles away seawards from the house, as on a tremendous, somewhat unevenly paved Piazza, picking up strange long peaked shells and starfish. The Swaheli fishermen came wandering along here, in a loin-cloth and red or blue turbans, like Sindbad the sailor come to life, to offer for sale multi-coloured spiked fish, some of which were very good to eat. The coast below the house had a row of scooped-out deep caves and grottoes, where you sat in shade and watched the distant glittering blue water. When the tide came in, it filled up the caves to the level of the ground on which the house was built, and in the porous coral-rock the sea sang and sighed in the strangest way, as if the ground below your feet were alive; the long waves came running up Takaunga Creek like a storming army.

It was full moon while I was down at Takaunga, and the beauty of the radiant, still nights was so perfect that the heart bent under it. You slept with the door open to the silver sea; the playing warm breeze in a low whisper swept in a little loose sand, on to the stone floor. One night a row of Arab dhows came along, close to the coast, running noiselessly before the monsoon, a file of brown shadow-sails under the moon.

Denys sometimes talked of making Takaunga his home in Africa, and of starting his safaris from there. When I began to talk of having to leave the farm, he offered me his house down there, as he had had mine in the highlands. But white people cannot live for a long time at the coast unless they are able to have many comforts, and Takaunga was too low and too hot for me.

In the month of May of the year when I left Africa, Denys went down to Takaunga for a week. He was planning to build a larger house and to plant mango trees on his land. He went away in his aeroplane and was intending to make his way home around by Voi, to see if there were any elephants there for his safaris. The Natives had been talking much of a herd of elephants which had come on to the land round Voi from the west, and in particular of one big bull, twice the size of any other elephant, that was wandering in the bush there, all by himself.

Denys, who held himself to be an exceptionally rational person, was subject to special kinds of moods and forebodings, and under their influence at times he became silent for days or for a week, though he did not know of it himself and was surprised when I asked him what was the matter with him. The last days before he started on this journey to the coast, he was in this manner absent-minded, as if sunk in contemplation, but when I spoke of it he laughed at me.

I asked him to let me come with him, for I thought what a lovely thing it would be to see the sea. First he said yes, and then he changed his mind and said no. He could not take me; the journey round Voi, he told me, was going to be very rough, he might have to land, and to sleep in the bush, so that it would be necessary for him to take a Native boy with him. I reminded him that he had said that he had taken out the aeroplane to fly me over Africa. Yes, he said, so he had; and if there were elephants at Voi, he would fly me down there to have a look at them, when he knew the landing places and camping grounds. This was the only time that I asked Denys to take me with him on his aeroplane that he would not do it.

He went off on Friday the eighth. 'Look out for me on Thursday,' he said when he went, 'I shall be back in time to have luncheon with you.'

When he had started in his car for the aerodrome in Nairobi, and had turned down the drive, he came back to look for a volume of poems that he had given to me, and that he now wanted with him on his journey. He stood with one foot on the running-board of the car, and a finger in the book, reading out to me a poem that we had been discussing.

'Here are your grey geese,' he said.

> 'I saw grey geese flying over the flatlands
> Wild geese vibrant in the high air –
> Unswerving from horizon to horizon
> With their soul stiffened out in their throats –
> And the grey whiteness of them ribboning the enormous skies
> And the spokes of the sun over the crumpled hills.'

Then he drove away for good, waving his arm to me.

While Denys was down in Mombasa, in landing he broke a propeller. He wired back to Nairobi to get the spare parts that he wanted, and the East Africa Company sent a boy to Mombasa with them. When the aeroplane was fixed, and Denys was again going up in it, he told the Airways boy to come up with him. But the boy would not come. This boy was used to flying, and had been up with many people, and with Denys himself, before now, and Denys was a fine pilot and had a great name with the Natives in this capacity as in all others. But this time the boy would not go up with him.

A long time after, when he met Farah in Nairobi and they were talking things over, he said to Farah: 'Not for a hundred rupees would I, then, have gone up with Bwana Bedâr.' The shadow of destiny, which Denys himself had felt the last days at Ngong, was seen more strongly now, by the Native.

So Denys took Kamau with him to Voi, his own boy. Poor Kamau was terrified of flying. He had told me, at the farm, that when he got up and away from the ground, he fixed his eyes at his feet and kept them there till he got down to earth again, so frightened did he feel if ever he cast a glance over the side of the aeroplane, and saw the landscape from its great height.

I looked out for Denys on Thursday, and reckoned that he would fly from Voi at sunrise and be two hours on the way to Ngong. But when he did not come, and I found that I had got things to do in Nairobi, I drove in to town.

Whenever I was ill in Africa, or much worried, I suffered from a special kind of compulsive idea. It seemed to me then that all my surroundings were in danger or distress, and that in the midst of this disaster I myself was somehow on the wrong side, and therefore was regarded with distrust and fear by everybody.

This nightmare was in reality a reminiscence of the time of the war. For then for a couple of years people in the Colony had believed me to be a pro-German at heart, and had looked at me with mistrust. Their suspiciousness rose from the fact that I had, in the innocence of my heart, a short time before the outbreak of war, been up at Naivasha buying horses for General von Lettow down in German East Africa. He had asked me, when we travelled out to Africa together six months before, to buy him ten Abyssinian breeding-mares, but during my first time in the country I had had other things to think of, and had forgotten about it, so that it was only later, when he kept on writing of the mares to me, that in the end I went up to Naivasha to buy them for him. The war broke out so shortly after, that the mares never got out of the country. Still I could not get away from the fact that I had, at the outbreak of the war, been buying up horses for the German army. The suspicion against me did not, however, last till the end of the war, it passed away when my brother, who had been volunteering with the English, got the V.C. in the Amiens push, north of Roye. That event was even announced in the *East African Standard* under the headline of: *An East-African V.C.*

At the time I had taken my isolation lightly, for I was not in the least pro-German, and I thought that I should be able to clear things up if it became necessary. But it must have gone deeper with me than I knew of, and for many years after, when I was very tired or when I had a high temperature, the feeling of it would come back. During my last months in Africa, when everything was going wrong with me, it sometimes suddenly fell upon me like a darkness, and in a way I was frightened of it, as of a sort of derangement.

On this Thursday in Nairobi the nightmare unexpectedly stole upon me, and grew so strong that I wondered if I were beginning to go mad. There was, somehow, a deep sadness over the town, and over the people I met, and in the midst of it everybody was turning away from me. There was nobody who would stop and talk to me: my friends, when they saw me, got into their cars and drove off. Even old Mr Duncan, the Scotch grocer, from whom I had bought groceries for many years, and with whom I had danced at a big ball at Government House, when I came in looked at me with a kind of fright and left his shop. I began to feel as lonely in Nairobi as on a desert island.

I had left Farah on the farm to receive Denys, so that I had nobody to talk with. The Kikuyus are no good in such a case, for their ideas of reality, and their reality itself, are different from ours. But I was to lunch with Lady McMillan at Chiromo, and I thought that there I should find white people to talk to, and get back my balance of mind.

I drove up to the lovely old Nairobi house of Chiromo, at the end of the long bamboo avenue, and found a luncheon-party there. But it was the same thing at Chiromo as in the streets of Nairobi. Everybody seemed mortally sad, and as I came in the talk stopped. I sat beside my old friend Mr Bulpett, and he looked down and said only a few words. I tried to throw off the shadow that was by now lying heavily upon me, and to talk to him of his mountain-climbings in Mexico, but he seemed to remember nothing about them.

I thought: These people are no good to me, I will go back to the farm. Denys will be there by now. We will talk and behave sensibly, and I shall be sane again and know and understand everything.

But when we had finished luncheon, Lady McMillan asked me to come with her into her small sitting-room, and there told me that there had been an accident at Voi. Denys had capsized with his machine, and had been killed in the fall.

It was then as I had thought: at the sound of Denys's name even, truth was revealed, and I knew and understood everything.

Later on, the District Commissioner at Voi wrote to me and gave me the particulars of the accident. Denys had been staying with him over night, and had left from that aerodrome in the morning, his boy in the aeroplane with him, for my farm. After he had left he turned and came back quickly, flying low, at two hundred feet. Suddenly the aeroplane swayed, got into a spin, and came down like a bird swooping. As it hit the ground it caught fire; the people who ran to it were stopped by the heat. When they got branches and earth, and had thrown them on the fire, and got it out, they found that the aeroplane had been all smashed up, and the two people in it had been killed in the fall.

For many years after this day the Colony felt Denys's death as a loss which could not be recovered. Something fine then came out in the average colonist's attitude towards him, a reverence for values outside their understanding. When they spoke of him it was most often as an athlete; they would discuss his exploits as a cricketer and a golfer, and of these things I had never heard myself, so that it was only now that I learned of his great fame in all games. Then when the people had been paying tribute to him as a sportsman, they would add that, of course, he had been very brilliant. What they really remembered in him was his absolute lack of self-consciousness, or self-interest, and unconditional truthfulness which outside of him I have only met in idiots. In a colony, these qualities are not generally held up for imitation, but after a man's death they may be, perhaps, more truly admired than in other places.

The Natives had known Denys better than the white people; to them his death was a bereavement.

When, in Nairobi, I was told of Denys's death I tried to get down to Voi. The Airway Company was sending down Tom Black to report on the accident, and I drove to the aerodrome to ask him to take me with him, but as I got into the aerodrome, his aeroplane lifted and sailed off, towards Voi.

It might still be possible to get through by car, but the long rains were on, and I had to find out what the roads were like. While I sat and waited for the report on the roads, I remembered how Denys had told me that he wished to be buried in the Ngong Hills. It was a strange thing that I had not recollected it before, but it had been so far from my thoughts that they should mean to bury him at all. Now it was as if a picture had been shown to me.

There was a place in the hills, on the first ridge in the Game Reserve, that I myself, at the time when I thought that I was to live and die in Africa, had pointed out to Denys as my future burial-place. In the evening, while we sat and looked at the hills from my house, he remarked that then he would like to be buried there himself as well. Since then, sometimes when we drove out in the hills, Denys had said: 'Let us drive as far as our graves.' Once when we were camped in the hills to look for buffalo, we had in the afternoon walked over to the slope to have a closer look at it. There was an infinitely great view from there; in the light of the sunset we saw both Mount Kenya and Kilimanjaro. Denys had been eating an orange, lying in the grass, and had said that he would like to stay there. My own burial-place was a little higher up. From both places we could see my house in the forest far away to the east. We were going back there the next day, for ever, I thought, in spite of the widespread theory that all must die.

Gustav Mohr had come from his farm to my house, when he heard of Denys's death, and when he did not find me there he looked me up in Nairobi. A little while after, Hugh Martin came and sat down with us. I told them of Denys's wish, and of the burial-place in the hills, and they wired to the people at Voi. Before I went back to the farm they informed me that they would bring Denys's body up by train next morning, so that the funeral could take place in the hills at noon. I must have his grave ready there by then.

Gustav Mohr went with me to the farm, to sleep there, and help me in the morning. We would have to be out in the hills just before sunrise to decide on the place, and to have the grave dug in time.

It rained all night, and there was a fine drizzling rain in the morning when we went away. The wagon-tracks on the road were full of water. Driving up in the hills was like driving into clouds. We could not see the plains below to our left, nor the slopes or peaks of the hills to our right; the boys who came with us in a lorry disappeared behind us at a distance of ten yards, and the mist grew thicker as the road mounted. By the signboard on the road, we found where we got into the Game Reserve, so we drove on a few hundred yards and then got out of the car. We left the lorry, and the boys, on the highroad until we should have found the place we wanted. The morning air was so cold that it bit the fingers.

The place of the grave must not be too far away from the road nor where the ground was too steep to bring up a lorry. We walked together for a little while, talking of the mist, then we parted and went along by different paths, and after a few seconds we could no longer see one another.

The great country of the hills opened up reluctantly round me, and closed again, the day was like a rainy day in a northern country. Farah was walking with me with a wet rifle; he thought that we might walk into a herd of buffalo. The things close by, that suddenly appeared just before us, looked fantastically big. The leaves of the grey wild-olive bush, and the long grass, higher than ourselves, were dripping wet and smelled strongly – I had on a mackintosh and rubber boots, but after a while I was drenched, as if I had been wading up a stream. It was very still here in the hills; only at times when the rain came down stronger, there was a whisper to all sides. Once the mist parted, and I saw a stretch of indigo blue land before me and beyond me, like a slate – it must have been one of the tall peaks far away – a moment after it was again covered by the drifting grey rain and mist. I walked and walked, and in the end I stood quite still. There was nothing to do here until the weather cleared up.

Gustav Mohr shouted to me three or four times to find out where I was, and came up to me, the rain on his face and hands. He told me that we had been going about in the mist for an hour, and that if we did not settle the place for the grave now, we would not have it ready in time.

'But I cannot see where we are,' I said, 'and we cannot lay him where the ridges close up the view. Let us wait a little longer.'

We stood in silence in the long grass, and I smoked a cigarette. Just as I was throwing it away, the mist spread a little, and a pale cold clarity began to fill the world. In ten minutes we could see where we were. The plains lay below us, and I could follow the road by which we had come, as it wound in and out along the slopes, climbed towards us, and, winding, went on. To the south far away below the changing clouds, lay the broken, dark blue foothills of Kilimanjaro. As we turned to the north the light increased; pale rays for a moment slanted in the sky and a streak of shining silver drew up the shoulder of Mount Kenya. Suddenly, much closer, to the east below us, was a little red spot in the grey and green, the only red there was, the tiled roof of my house on its cleared place in the forest. We did not have to go any farther, we were in the right place. A little while after, the rain started again.

About twenty yards higher up than where we stood, there was a narrow natural terrace in the hillside. Here we marked out the place for the grave, by the compass, laying it east to west. We called up the boys, and set them to cut the grass with pangas, and to dig the wet soil. Mohr took some of them with him to make a road for the lorry, from the high road to the grave; they levelled out the ground, cut off branches from the bush and heaped them on the path, for the ground was slippery. We could not bring the road all the way up to the grave, near it the ground was too steep. It had been silent up here till now, but when the boys began to work, I heard that there was an echo in the hills. It answered to the strokes of the spades, like a little dog barking.

Some cars came out from Nairobi, and we sent down a boy to show them the way, for in the great country they would not notice the small group of people by the grave in the bush. The Somalis of Nairobi came out, they left their mule-traps on the highroad, and walked slowly up, three or four together, mourning in the Somali way, as if wrapping up their heads and withdrawing from life. Some of Denys's friends from up-country, who had had news of his death, came driving from Naivasha, Gil-Gil, and Elmenteita, their cars all covered with mud from the long fast drive. Now the day grew clearer, and the four tall peaks of the hills showed above us against the sky.

Here in the early afternoon they brought out Denys from Nairobi, following his old safari-track to Tanganyika, and driving slowly on the wet road. When they came to the last steep slope, they lifted out and carried the narrow coffin, that was covered with the flag. As it was placed in the grave, the country changed and became the setting for it, as still as itself; the hills stood up gravely, they knew and understood what we were doing in them; after a little while they themselves took charge of the ceremony, it was an action between them and him, and the people present became a party of very small lookers-on in the landscape.

Denys had watched and followed all the ways of the African highlands, and better than any other white man he had known their soil and seasons, the vegetation and the wild animals, the winds and smells. He had observed the changes of weather in them, their people, clouds, the stars at night. Here in the hills, I had seen him only a short time ago, standing bareheaded in the afternoon sun, gazing out over the land, and lifting his field-glasses to find out everything about it. He had taken in the country, and in his eyes and his mind it had been changed, marked by his own individuality, and made part of him. Now Africa received him, and would change him, and make him one with herself.

The Bishop of Nairobi, I was told, had not wanted to come out, because there had not been time to have the burial ground consecrated, but there was another clergyman present, who read out the funeral service, which I had never heard before, and in the great space his voice sounded small and clear, like the voice of a bird in the hills. I thought that Denys would like the whole thing best when it was over. The priest read out a Psalm: 'I will lift up mine eyes unto the hills.'

Gustav Mohr and I sat on for a little while, after the other white people had left. The Mohammedans waited till we had gone and then went and prayed by the grave.

In the days after Denys's death, his safari servants came in, and gathered on the farm. They did not say why they came, and did not ask for anything, but sat down with their backs to the wall of the house, and the backs of their hands resting upon the pavement, most of the time in silence, contrary to the habits of Natives. Malimu and Sar Sita came there, Denys's bold, shrewd, fearless gun-bearers and trackers, who had been with him on all his safaris. They had been out with the Prince of Wales, and many years after, the Prince remembered their names, and said that the two of them together had been hard to beat. Here the great trackers had lost the track, and sat immovable. Kanuthia, his motor-driver, came in, who had driven over many thousand miles of rough country, a slim young Kikuyu with the watchful eyes of a monkey; now he sat by the house like a sad and chilly monkey in a cage.

Bilea Isa, Denys's Somali servant, came down from Naivasha to the farm. Bilea had been to England twice with Denys, had been to school there, and spoke English like a gentleman. Some years ago, Denys and I had attended Bilea's wedding in Nairobi; it was a magnificent feast that lasted for seven days. On that occasion, the great traveller and scholar had gone back to the ways of his ancestors; he had been dressed in a golden robe, and had bowed down to the ground when he welcomed us, and he danced the sword-dance, all wild with the desperado spirit of the desert. Bilea came down to see his master's grave, and sit on it; he came back from it and spoke very little, after a little while, he sat with the others with his back to the wall, and the backs of his hands resting on the pavement.

Farah went out and stood and talked with the mourners. He himself was very grave. 'It would not have been so bad,' he said to me, 'that you were going away from the country, if only Bedâr had still been here.'

Denys's boys stayed for about a week, then one after the other they left again.

I often drove out to Denys's grave. In a bee-line, it was not more than five miles from my house, but round by the road it was fifteen. The grave was a thousand feet higher up than my house, the air was different here, as clear as a glass of water; light sweet winds lifted your hair when you took off your hat; over the peaks of the hills, the clouds came wandering from the east, drew their live shadow over the wide undulating land, and were dissolved and disappeared over the Rift Valley.

I bought at the duca a yard of the white cloth which the Natives call *Americani*, and Farah and I raised three tall poles in the ground behind the grave, and nailed the cloth on to them, then from my house I could distinguish the exact spot of the grave, like a little white point in the green hill.

The long rains had been heavy, and I was afraid that the grass would grow up and cover the grave so that its place would be lost. Therefore one day we took up all the whitewashed stones along my drive, the same that Karomenya had had trouble in pulling up and carrying to the front door; we loaded them into my box-body car and drove them up into the hills. We cut down the grass round the grave, and set the stones in a square to mark it; now the place could always be found.

As I went so often to the grave, and took the children of my household with me, it became a familiar place to them; they could show the way out there to the people who came to see it. They built a small bower in the bush of the hill near it. In the course of the summer, Ali bin Salim, whose friend Denys had been, came from Mombasa to go out and lie on the grave and weep, in the Arab way.

One day I found Hugh Martin by the grave, and we sat in the grass and talked for a long time. Hugh Martin had taken Denys's death much to heart. If any human being at all had held a place in his queer seclusive existence, it would have been Denys. An ideal is a strange thing; you would never have given Hugh credit for harbouring the idea of one, neither would you have thought that the loss of it would have affected him, like, somehow, the loss of a vital organ. But since Denys's death he had aged and changed much, his face was blotched and drawn. All the same he preserved his placid, smiling likeness to a Chinese Idol, as if he knew of something exceedingly satisfactory, that was hidden to the general. He told me now that he had, in the night, suddenly struck upon the right epitaph for Denys. I think that he had got it from an ancient

Greek author, he quoted it to me in Greek, then translated it in order that I should understand it. It went: 'Though in death fire be mixed with my dust yet care I not. For with me now all is well.'

Later on, Denys's brother, Lord Winchilsea, had an obelisk set on his grave, with an inscription out of 'The Ancient Mariner', which was a poem that Denys had much admired. I myself had never heard it until Denys quoted it to me – the first time was, I remember, as we were going to Bilea's wedding. I have not seen the obelisk; it was put up after I had left Africa.

In England there is also a monument to Denys. His old school-fellows, in memory of him, built a stone bridge over a small stream between two fields at Eton. On one of the balustrades is inscribed his name, and the dates of his stay at Eton, and on the other the words: 'Famous in these fields and by his many friends much beloved.'

Between the river in the mellow English landscape and the African mountain ridge ran the path of his life; it is an optical illusion that it seemed to wind and swerve – the surroundings swerved. The bowstring was released on the bridge at Eton, the arrow described its orbit, and hit the obelisk in the Ngong Hills.

After I had left Africa, Gustav Mohr wrote to me of a strange thing that had happened by Denys's grave, the like of which I have never heard. 'The Masai,' he wrote, 'have reported to the District Commissioner at Ngong, that many times, at sunrise and sunset, they have seen lions on Finch-Hatton's grave in the Hills. A lion and a lioness have come there, and stood, or lain, on the grave for a long time. Some of the Indians who have passed the place in their lorries on the way to Kajado have also seen them. After you went away, the ground round the grave was levelled out, into a sort of big terrace. I suppose that the level place makes a good site for the lions, from there they can have a view over the plain, and the cattle and game on it.'

It was fit and decorous that the lions should come to Denys's grave and make him an African monument. 'And renowned be thy grave.' Lord Nelson himself, I have reflected, in Trafalgar Square, has his lions made only out of stone.

Farah and I Sell Out

Now I was alone on the farm. It was no longer mine, but the people who had bought it had offered me to stay in the house as long as I liked, and for legal reasons were leasing it to me for a shilling a day.

I was selling my furniture, which gave Farah and me a good deal to do. We had to have all the china and table-glass on view upon the dinner table: later on, when the table had been sold, we arranged it in long rows on the floor. The cuckoo of the clock sang out the hours arrogantly over the rows, then it was itself sold, and flew off. One day I sold my table-glass, and then in the night thought better of it, so that in the morning I drove to Nairobi and asked the lady who had bought it to call off the deal. I had no place to put the glass, but the fingers and lips of many friends had touched it, they had given me excellent wine to drink out of it; it was keeping an echo of old table-talk, and I did not want to part with it. After all, I thought, it would be an easy thing to break.

I had an old wooden screen with painted figures of Chinamen, Sultans and Negroes, with dogs on leads, which had had its place by the fire. There in the evenings, when the fire burned clear, the figures would come out, and serve as illustrations to the tales that I told Denys. After I had looked at it for a long time, I folded it up and packed it in a case, wherein the figures might all have a rest for the time being.

Lady McMillan was at this time finishing the McMillan Memorial of Nairobi, that she had built to her husband, Sir Northrup McMillan. It was a fine building, with a library and reading rooms. She now drove out to the farm, sat and talked sadly of old days, and bought most of my old Danish furniture, that I had taken out from home with me, for the library. I was pleased to know that the cheerful, wise and hospitable chests and cabinets were to remain together, in a milieu of books and scholars, like a small circle of ladies who, in times of revolution, find an asylum in a University.

My own books I packed up in cases and sat on them, or dined on them. Books in a colony play a different part in your existence from what they do in Europe; there is a whole side of your life which there they alone take charge of; and on this account, according to their quality, you feel more grateful to them, or more indignant with them, than you will ever do in civilized countries.

The fictitious characters in the books run beside your horse on the farm, and walk about in the maize-fields. On their own, like intelligent soldiers, they find at once the quarters that suit them. On the morning after I had been reading *Chrome Yellow* at night – and I had never heard of the author's name, but had picked up the book in a Nairobi bookshop, and was as pleased as if I had discovered a new green island in the sea – as I was riding through a valley of the Game Reserve, a little duiker jumped up, and at once turned himself into a stag for Sir Hercules with his wife and his pack of thirty black and fawn-coloured pugs. All Walter Scott's characters were at home in the country and might be met anywhere; so were Odysseus and his men, and strangely enough many figures from Racine. Peter Schlemihl had walked over the hills in seven-league boots, Clown Agheb the honey-bee lived in my garden by the river.

Other things were sold out of the house, packed and sent off, so that the house, in the course of these months, became *das Ding an sich*, noble like a skull, a cool and roomy place to dwell in, with an echo to it, and the grass of the lawn growing long up to the doorstep. In the end there were no things in the rooms at all, and to my mind at the time they seemed, in this state, more fit to live in than they had been before.

I said to Farah, 'This is how we ought to have had it all the time.'

Farah understood me very well, for all Somali have something of the ascetic in them. Farah during this time was set and concentrated upon assisting me in everything; but he was growing to look more and more like a true Somali, such as he had looked in Aden, where he had been sent to meet me, when I first came to Africa. He was much concerned about my old shoes, and confided to me that he was going to pray to God every day that they might last until I got to Paris.

During these months, Farah wore his best clothes every day. He had a lot of fine clothes: gold-embroidered Arab waistcoats that I had given him, and a very elegant scarlet gold-laced uniform waistcoat that Berkeley Cole had given him, and silk turbans in beautiful colours. Generally he kept them all in chests, and wore them only on special occasions. But now he put on the best he had. He walked one step behind me in the streets of Nairobi, or waited on the dirty stairs in the government buildings and the lawyer's offices, dressed like Solomon in all his glory. It took a Somali to do that.

I had now also got to deal with the fate of my horses and my dogs. I had all the time meant to shoot them, but many of my friends wrote to

me and asked me to let them have them. After that, whenever I rode out
and had the dogs with me, it did not seem fair on them to shoot them –
they had much life in them still. It took me a long time to decide the
matter, I do not think that I have ever changed my mind so often over
any other question. In the end I decided to give them to my friends.

I rode into Nairobi on my favourite horse, Rouge, going very slowly
and looking round to the north and the south. It was a very strange thing
to Rouge, I thought, to be going in by the Nairobi road, and not to be
coming back. I installed him, with some trouble, in the horse-van of the
Naivasha train. I stood in the van and felt, for the last time, his silky
muzzle against my hands and my face. I will not let thee go, Rouge, except
thou bless me. We had found together the riding-path down to the river
amongst the Native shambas and huts, on the steep slippery descent he
had walked as nimbly as a mule, and in the brown running river-water
I has seen my own head and his close together. May you now, in a valley
of clouds, eat carnations to the right and stock to the left.

The two young deerhounds that I had then, David and Dinah, Pania's
offspring, I gave to a friend on a farm near Gil-Gil, where they would get
good hunting. They were very strong and playful, and when they were
fetched in a car and drove off from the farm in great style, they panted,
their heads close together over the side of the car, their tongues hanging
out, as if they were on the track of a new splendid kind of game. The quick
eyes and feet, and the live hearts, went away from the house and the plains,
to breathe and sniff, and run happily on new grounds.

Some of my people now left the farm. As there was to be no coffee and
no coffee-mill there any longer, Pooran Singh found himself out of work.
He did not want to take on another job in Africa, and in the end he made
up his mind to go back to India.

Pooran Singh, who mastered the minerals, outside of his workshop was
like a child. He could not in the least realize that the end of the farm had
come; he grieved over it, wept clear tears that ran down in his black beard,
and for a long time worried me with his attempts to make me remain on
the farm, and with his plans for keeping it going. He had taken much pride
in our machinery, such as it was, and was now for a while as if nailed to
the steam-engine and the coffee-dryer in the factory, his soft dark eyes
consuming every nut in them. Then, when in the end he had been convinced of the hopelessness of the situation, he gave it all up in one
movement, he was still very sad, but quite passive, and sometimes when
I saw him he talked much to me of his travelling plans. When he went
away, he carried no luggage with him but a small box of tools and a
soldering outfit, as if he had already sent his heart and life over the ocean,

and there was now only his thin, unassuming, brown person and the soldering pan to follow it.

I wanted to give Pooran Singh a present before he left, and I had hoped that I might have something in my possession which he would like, but when I spoke to him of it he at once with great joy declared that he wanted a ring. I had no ring and no money to buy him one. This had happened already some months ago, at the time when Denys was coming out to dine at the farm, and so at dinner I told him of the position. Denys had once given me an Abyssinian ring of soft gold, to be screwed on so that it would fit any finger. He now thought that I was looking at it with the intention of giving it to Pooran Singh, for he used to complain that whenever he gave me anything I would at once give it away to my coloured people. To prevent such a thing happening, he took it from my hand and put it on his own and said that he would keep it until Pooran Singh had gone. It was a few days before he went to Mombasa, and in this way the ring was buried with him. Before Pooran Singh left I had, however, raised enough money by the sale of my furniture to buy him the ring he wanted in Nairobi. It was of heavy gold with a big red stone, that looked like glass. Pooran Singh was so happy about it that he shed a few tears again, and I believe that the ring helped him over his final parting with the farm and with his machinery. For his last week, he wore it every day, and whenever he came to the house, he held up his hand, and showed it to me with a radiant, gentle smile. At Nairobi station, the last thing that I saw of him was the slim dark hand, that had worked on the forge with such furious speed. It was stretched out through the window of the crowded and overheated Native railway carriage, in which Pooran Singh had placed himself upon his tool-box, and the red stone in it shone like a little star while it went up and down, waving good-bye.

Pooran Singh went to the Punjab to his family. He had not seen them for many years, but they had kept in touch with him by sending him photographs of themselves, which he preserved down in his little corrugated iron house by the factory, and showed to me with great tenderness and pride. I had several letters from Pooran Singh already from the boat to India. They all began in the same way: 'Dear Madam. Good-bye,' and then went on to give me his news and to report on his adventures of the journey.

A week after Denys's death one morning a strange thing happened to me.

I lay in bed and thought of the events of the last months. I tried to understand what it really was that had happened. It seemed to me that

I must have, in some way, got out of the normal course of human existence, into a maelstrom where I ought never to have been. Wherever I walked, the ground fell away under me, and the stars fell from the sky. I thought of the poem about Ragnarok, in which this fall of the stars is described, and of the verses about the dwarfs who sigh deeply in their caves in the mountains, and die from fear. All this could not be, I thought, just a coincidence of circumstances, what people call a run of bad luck, but there must be some central principle within it. If I could find it, it would save me. If I looked in the right place, I reflected, the coherence of things might become clear to me. I must, I thought, get up and look for a sign.

Many people think it an unreasonable thing, to be looking for a sign. This is because of the fact that it takes a particular state of mind to be able to do so, and not many people have ever found themselves in such a state. If in this mood, you ask for a sign, the answer cannot fail you; it follows as the natural consequence of the demand. In that same way an inspired card-player collects thirteen chance cards on the table, and takes up what is called a hand of cards – a unity. Where others see no call at all, he sees a grand slam staring him in the face. Is there a grand slam in the cards? Yes, to the right player.

I came out of the house looking for a sign, and wandered at haphazard towards the boys' huts. They had just let out their chickens, which were running here and there amongst the houses. I stood for a little while and looked at them.

Fathima's big white cock came strutting up before me. Suddenly he stopped, laid his head first on one side and then on the other, and raised his comb. From the other side of the path, out of the grass, came a little grey chameleon that was, like the cock himself, out on his morning reconnoitring. The cock walked straight upon it – for the chickens eat these things – and gave out a few clucks of satisfaction. The chameleon stopped dead at the sight of the cock. He was frightened, but he was at the same time very brave, he planted his feet on the ground, opened his mouth as wide as he possibly could, and, to scare his enemy, in a flash he shot out his club-shaped tongue at the cock. The cock stood for a second as if taken aback, then swiftly and determinately he struck down his beak like a hammer and plucked out the chameleon's tongue.

The whole meeting between the two had taken ten seconds. Now I chased off Fathima's cock, took up a big stone and killed the chameleon, for he could not live without his tongue; the chameleons catch the insects that they feed on with their tongue.

I was so frightened by what I had seen – for it had been a gruesome and formidable thing in a miniature format – that I went away and sat down on the stone seat by the house. I sat there for a long time, and Farah brought me out my tea, and put it on the table. I looked down on the stones and dared not look up, such a dangerous place did the world seem to me.

Very slowly only, in the course of the next few days, it came upon me that I had had the most spiritual answer possible to my call. I had even been in a strange manner honoured and distinguished. The powers to which I had cried had stood on my dignity more than I had done myself, and what other answer could they then give? This was clearly not the hour for coddling, and they had chosen to connive at my invocation of it. Great powers had laughed to me, with an echo from the hills to follow the laughter, they had said among the trumpets, among the cocks and chameleons, Ha ha!

I was so pleased that I had been out this morning in time to save the chameleon from a slow, painful death.

It was about this time – although it was before I had sent away my horses – that Ingrid Lindstrom came down from her farm at Njoro to stay with me for a little while. This was a friendly act of Ingrid's, for it was difficult for her to get away from her own farm. Her husband, to make money to pay off their Njoro land, had taken a job with a big Sisal company in Tanganyika, and was at the same time sweating down there at an altitude of two thousand feet, just as if Ingrid had been leasing him out in the quality of a slave, for the sake of the farm. She was therefore, in the meantime, running it on her own; she had extended her poultry yards, and her market garden, and had got pigs, and broods of young turkeys up there, which she could ill afford to leave, even for a few days. All the same, for my sake she gave it all in charge of Kemosa, and rushed down to me as she would run to the assistance of a friend whose house was on fire, and she came without Kemosa this time, which was probably, under the circumstances, a good thing for Farah. Ingrid understood and realized to the bottom of her heart, with great strength, with something of the strength of the elements themselves, what it is really like, when a woman farmer has to give up her farm, and leave it.

While Ingrid was staying with me, we did not discuss either the past or the future, and did not mention the name of a single friend or acquaintance; we closed our two minds round the disaster of the hour. We walked together from the one thing on the farm to the other, naming them as we passed them, one by one, as if we were taking mental stock of my loss, or as if Ingrid were, on my behalf, collecting material for a book of complaints to be laid before destiny. Ingrid knew well enough from her own experience that there is no such book, but all the same the idea of it forms part of the livelihood of women.

We went down to the oxen's boma, and sat on the fence, counting the oxen as they came in. Without words I pointed them out to Ingrid: 'These oxen,' and without words she responded: 'Yes, these oxen,' and recorded them in her book. We went round to the stables to feed the horses with sugar, and when they had finished, I stretched out my sticky and beslab-bered palms, presenting them to Ingrid and crying, 'These horses.' Ingrid sighed back laboriously, 'Yes, these horses,' and noted them down. In my garden by the river she could not reconcile herself to the idea that I must leave the plants that I had brought from Europe; she wrung her hands over the mint, sage and lavender, and talked of them again later on, as if she were pondering on some scheme by which I might arrange to take them with me.

We spent the afternoon in contemplation of my small herd of Native cows which grazed on the lawn. I went through their age, characteristics, and yielding of milk, and Ingrid groaned and shrieked over the figures as if she had been bodily hurt. She scrutinized them carefully one by one, not with any view to trade, for my cows were going to my houseboys, but so as to value and weigh up my loss. She clung to the soft sweet-smelling calves; she had herself after long struggles got a few cows with calves on her farm, and against all reason, and against her own will, her deep furious glances blamed me for deserting my calves.

A man who was walking beside a bereaved friend and who was all the time in his own mind repeating the words: 'Thank God it is not me,' would, I believe, feel badly about it, and would try to suppress the feeling. It is a different thing in two women who are friends, and of whom the one is manifesting her deep sympathy in the distress of the other. There it goes without saying that the more fortunate friend will all the while in her heart repeat the same thing: 'Thank God it is not me.' It causes no bad feeling between the two, but on the contrary brings them closer together, and gives to the ceremony a personal element. Men, I think, cannot easily or harmoniously envy or triumph over one another. But it goes without saying that the bride triumphs over the bridesmaids, and that the lying-in-visitors envy the mother of the child; and none of the parties feel the worse on that account. A woman who had lost a child might show its clothes to a friend, aware that the friend was repeating in her heart: 'Thank God it is not me,' – and it would be to both of them a natural and befitting thing. It was so with Ingrid and me. As we walked over the farm, I knew that she was thinking of her own farm, praising her luck that it was still hers, and holding on to it with all her might, and we got on very well on that. In spite of our old khaki coats and trousers, we were in reality a pair of mythical women, shrouded respectively in white and black, a unity, the Genii of the farmer's life in Africa.

After a few days Ingrid said good-bye to me, and went up by the railway to Njoro.

I could no longer ride out, and my walks without the dogs had become very silent and sedate, but I still had my car, and I was glad to have her, for in these months I had much to do.

The fate of my squatters weighed on my mind. As the people who had bought the farm were planning to take up the coffee-trees, and to have the land cut up and sold as building-plots, they had no use for the squatters, and as soon as the deal was through, they had given them all six months' notice to get off the farm. This to the squatters was an unforeseen and bewildering determination, for they had lived in the illusion that the land was theirs. Many of them had been born on the farm, and others had come there as small children with their fathers.

The squatters knew that in order to stay on the land they had got to work for me one hundred and eighty days out of each year, for which they were paid twelve shillings for every thirty days; these accounts were kept at the office of the farm. They also knew that they must pay the hut-tax to the Government, of twelve shillings to a hut, a heavy burden on a man, who with very little else in the world would own two or three grass-huts – according to the number of his wives, for a Kikuyu husband must give each of his wives her own hut. My squatters had, from time to time, been threatened to be turned off the farm for an offence, so that they must in some way have felt that their position was not entirely unassailable. The hut-tax they much disliked, and when I collected it on the farm for the Government, they gave me a great deal to do, and much talk to listen to. But they had still looked upon these things as common vicissitudes of life, and had never given up the hope of somehow getting round them. They had not imagined that there might be, to them all, an underlying universal principle, which would at its own hour manifest itself in a fatal, crushing manner. For some time they chose to regard the decision of the new owners of the farm as a bugbear, which they could courageously ignore.

In some respects, although not in all, the white men fill in the mind of the Natives the place that is, in the mind of the white men, filled by the idea of God. I once had a contract drawn up with an Indian timber-merchant, it contained the words: an act of God. I was not familiar with the expression, and the lawyer who was drawing up the contract tried to explain it to me.

'No, no, madam,' he said, 'you have not quite caught the meaning of the term. What is completely unforeseeable, and not consonant with rule or reason, that is an act of God.'

In the end, the certainty of their notice to quit brought the squatters in dark groups to my house. They felt the denunciation as a consequence of my departure from the farm – my own bad luck was growing, and was spreading over them as well. They did not blame me for it, for that was talked out between us; they asked me where they were to go.

I found it, in more than one way, difficult to answer them. The Natives cannot, according to the law, themselves buy any land, and there was not another farm that I knew of big enough to take them on as squatters. I told them that I had myself been told when I had made inquiries in the matter, that they must go into the Kikuyu Reserve and find land there. On that they again gravely asked me if they should find enough unoccupied land in the Reserve to bring all their cattle with them? And, they went on, would they be sure all to find land in the same place, so that the people from the farm should remain together, for they did not want to be separated?

I was surprised that they should be so determined to stay together, for on the farm they had found it difficult to keep peace, and had never had much good to say of one another. Still, here they all came, the big swaggering cattle-owners like Kathegu, Kaninu, and Mauge, hand in hand, so to say, with the humble unportioned workers of the soil like Waweru and Chotha, who did not own so much as one goat; and they were all filled with the same spirit, and as intent upon keeping one another as on keeping their cows. I felt that they were not only asking me for a place to live on, but that they were demanding their existence of me.

It is more than their land that you take away from the people, whose native land you take. It is their past as well, their roots and their identity. If you take away the things that they have been used to see, and will be expecting to see, you may, in a way, as well take their eyes. This applies in a higher degree to the primitive people than to the civilized, and animals again will wander back a long way, and go through danger and sufferings, to recover their lost identity, in the surroundings that they know.

The Masai when they were moved from their old country, north of the railway line, to the present Masai Reserve, took with them the names of their hills, plains, and rivers; and gave them to the hills, plains, and rivers in the new country. It is a bewildering thing to the traveller. The Masai were carrying their cut roots with them as a medicine, and were trying, in exile, to keep their past by a formula.

Now, my squatters were clinging to one another from the same instinct of self-preservation. If they were to go away from their land, they must have people round them who had known it, and so could testify to their identity. Then they could still, for some years, talk of the geography and the history of the farm, and what one had forgotten the other would remember. As it was, they were feeling the shame of extinction falling on them.

'Go, Msabu,' they said to me, 'go for us to the Selikali, and obtain from them that we may take all our cattle with us to the new place and that we shall all remain together where we are going.'

With this began for me a long pilgrimage, or beggar's journey which took up my last months in Africa.

On the Kikuyus' errand I first went to the District Commissioners of Nairobi and Kiambu, then to the Native Department and the Land Office, and in the end to the Governor, Sir Joseph Byrne, whom I had not met till then, for he was only just out from England. In the end I forgot what I went for. I was washed in and out as by the tide. Sometimes I had to stay for a whole day in Nairobi, or to go in two or three times in a day. There were always a number of squatters stationed by my house, when I came back, but they never asked me for my news; they kept watch there in order to communicate to me, by some Native magic, stamina on the course.

The government officials were patient and obliging people. The difficulties in the matter were not of their making; it was really a problem to find, in the Kikuyu Reserve, an unoccupied stretch of land big enough to take in the full number of the people and their cattle.

Most of the officials had been in the country for a long time, and knew the Natives well. They would only vaguely suggest the resource of making the Kikuyu sell out some of their stock. For they knew that under no circumstances would they do so, and by bringing their herds on to a place that was too small for them, they would cause, in years to come, endless trouble with their neighbours in the Reserve, for other District Commissioners up there to go into, and settle.

But when we came to the second request of the squatters, that they should remain together, the people in authority said that there was no real need for that.

'Oh reason not the need,' I thought, 'our basest beggars are in the poorest things superfluous' – and so on. All my life I have held that you can class people according to how they may be imagined behaving to King

Lear. You could not reason with King Lear, any more than with an old Kikuyu, and from the first he demanded too much of everybody; but he was a king. It is true that the African Native has not handed over his country to the white man in a magnificent gesture, so that the case is in some ways different from that of the old king and his daughters; the white men took over the country as a Protectorate. But I bore in mind that not very long ago, at a time that could still be remembered, the Natives of the country had held their land undisputed, and had never heard of the white men and their laws. Within the general insecurity of their existence the land to them was still steadfast. Some of them were carried off by the slave-traders and were sold at slave-markets, but some of them always remained. Those who were taken away, in their exile and thraldom all over the eastern world, would long back to the highlands, for that was their own land. The old dark clear-eyed Native of Africa, and the old dark clear-eyed elephant – they are alike; you see them standing on the ground, weighty with such impressions of the world around them as have been slowly gathered and heaped up in their dim minds; they are themselves features of the land. Either one of the two might find himself quite perplexed by the sight of the great changes that are going on all around him, and might ask you where he was, and you would have to answer him in the words of Kent: 'In your own kingdom, Sir.'

In the end, just as I was beginning to feel that I must drive in to Nairobi and back, and talk on in government offices all my life, I was suddenly informed that my application had been granted. The government had agreed to give out a piece of the Dagoretti Forest Reserve to the squatters of my farm. Here they could form a settlement of their own, not far from their old place, and after the disappearance of the farm they could still preserve their faces and their names, as a community.

The news of this decision was received on the farm with deep silent emotion. It was impossible to tell from the faces of the Kikuyu whether they had all the time had faith in this issue of the case, or whether they had despaired of it. As soon as it was settled, they immediately entered on a course of multifarious complicated requests and propositions that I refused to deal with. They still stayed on by my house, watching me in a novel way. Natives have such feeling for, and faith in, fortune, that now, after our one success, they may have begun to trust that all was going to be well, and that I was to stay on the farm.

As for me myself, the settlement of the squatters' fate was a great appeasement to me. I have not often felt so contented.

Then, after two or three days, the feeling came upon me that my work in the country had been brought to an end, and that now I might go. The coffee harvest on the farm was finished, and the mill standing still, the house was empty, the squatters had got their land. The rains were over, and the new grass was already long on the plains and in the hills.

The plan which I had formed in the beginning, to give in in all minor matters, so as to keep what was of vital importance to me, had turned out to be a failure. I had consented to give away my possessions one by one, as a kind of ransom for my own life, but by the time that I had nothing left, I myself was the lightest thing of all, for fate to get rid of.

There was a full moon in those days, it shone into the bare room and laid the pattern of the windows on the floor. I thought that the moon might be looking in and wondering how long I meant to stay on, in a place from which everything else had gone. 'Oh no,' said the moon, 'time means very little to me.'

I would have liked to stay on until I could have seen the squatters installed in their new place. But the surveying of the land took time, and it was uncertain when they would be able to move on to it.

Farewell

At that time, it came to pass that the old men of the neighbourhood resolved to hold a Ngoma for me.

These Ngomas of the Ancients had been great functions in the past, but now they were rarely danced, and during all my time in Africa I have never seen one of them. I should have liked to do so, for the Kikuyu themselves thought highly of them. It was considered an honour to the farm that the old men's dance was to be performed there; my people talked of it a long time before it was to take place.

Even Farah, who generally looked down on the Native Ngomas, was this time impressed by the resolution of the old men. 'These people are very old, Memsahib,' he said, 'very very old.'

It was curious to hear the young Kikuyu lions speak with reverence and awe of the coming performance of the old dancers.

There was one thing about these Ngomas of which I did not know – namely that they had been prohibited by the Government. The reason for the prohibition I do not know. The Kikuyu must have been aware of the interdiction, but they chose to overlook it; either they reasoned that in these great troubled times, things might be done that in ordinary times could not be done, or else they really forgot about it in the midst of the strong emotions set going by the dance. They did not even have it in them to keep silent about the Ngoma.

The old dancers when they arrived were a rare, sublime sight. There were about a hundred of them, and they all arrived at the same time, and must have collected somewhere at a distance from the house. The old Native men are chilly people, and generally wrap and muffle themselves up well in furs and blankets, but here they were naked, as if solemnly stating the formidable truth. Their finery and war-paint were discreetly put on, but a few of them wore, on their old bald skulls, the big head-dresses of black eagle's feathers that you see on the heads of the young dancers. They did not need any ornaments either, they were impressive in themselves. They did not, like the old beauties of the European ball-room, strive to obtain a youthful appearance; the whole point and weight of the dance, to them themselves, and to the onlookers, lay in the old age of the performers. They had a queer sort of marking on them, the like of which I have never seen, chalked stripes running along their crooked limbs as if they were, in their stark truthfulness, emphasizing the stiff and brittle bones underneath the skin. Their movements, as they advanced in a slow prelusive march, were so strange that I wondered what sort of dance I was now to be shown.

As I stood and looked at them a fancy came back to me that had taken hold of me before: It was not I who was going away. I did not have it in my power to leave Africa, but it was the country that was slowly and gravely withdrawing from me, like the sea in ebb-tide. The procession that was passing here – it was in reality my strong pulpy young dancers of yesterday and the day before yesterday, who were withering before my eyes, who were passing away for ever. They were going in their own style, gently, in a dance, the people were with me, and I with the people, well content.

The old men did not speak, not even to one another, they were saving their strength for the coming efforts.

Just as the dancers had ranged themselves for the dance, an Askari from Nairobi arrived at the house with a letter for me, that the Ngoma must not take place.

I did not understand it, for it was to me a quite unlooked-for thing, and I had to read the paper through twice or three times. The Askari who had brought it was himself so impressed with the importance of the show he had upset, that he did not open his mouth to the old people or to my houseboys, nor strut or swagger in the usual manner of Askaris, who are pleased to show off their plenitude of power to other Natives.

During all my life in Africa I have not lived through another moment of such bitterness. I had not before known my heart to heave up in such a storm against the things happening to me. It did not even occur to me to speak; the nothingness of speech by now was manifest to me.

The old Kikuyu themselves stood like a herd of old sheep, all their eyes under the wrinkled lids fixed upon my face. They could not, in a second, give up the thing on which their hearts had been set. Some of them made little convulsive movements with their legs; they had come to dance and dance they must. In the end I told them that our Ngoma was off.

The piece of news, I knew, would in their minds take on a different aspect, but what I could not tell. Perhaps they realized at once how completely the Ngoma was off, for the reason that there was no longer anybody to dance to, since I no longer existed. Perhaps they thought that it had, in reality, already been held, a matchless Ngoma, of such force that it made naught of everything else, and that, when it was over, everything was over.

A small Native dog on the lawn profited by the stillness to yap out loudly, and the echo ran through my mind:

> '... The little dogs and all,
> Tray, Blanch, and Sweetheart, see, they bark at me.'

Kamante, who had been put in charge of the tobacco that was to have been dealt out to the Ancients after the dance, in his habitual silent resourcefulness here thought the moment convenient for bringing it, and stepped forward with a big calabash filled with snuff. Farah waved him back, but Kamante was a Kikuyu, in understanding with the old dancers, and he had his way. The snuff was a reality. We now distributed it amongst the old men. After a little while they all walked away.

The people of the farm who grieved most at my departure were I think the old women. The old Kikuyu women have had a hard life, and have themselves become flint-hard under it, like old mules which will bite you if they can come to it. They were more difficult for any disease to kill off than their men, as I learned in my practice as a doctor, and they were wilder than the men, and, even more thoroughly than they, devoid of the faculty of admiration. They had borne a number of children and had seen many of them die; they were afraid of nothing. They carried loads of firewood – with a rein round their foreheads to steady them – of three hundred pounds, tottering below them, but unsubdued; they worked in the hard ground of their shambas, standing on their heads from the early morning till late in the evening. 'From thence she seeketh the prey, and her eyes behold afar off. Her heart is as firm as a stone, yea as hard as a piece of the nether millstone. She mocketh at fear. What time she lifteth up herself on high, she scorneth the horse and his rider. Will she make many supplications unto thee? Will she speak soft words unto thee?' And they had a stock of energy in them still; they radiated vitality. The old women took a keen interest in everything that was going on on the farm, and would walk ten miles to look at a Ngoma of the young people; a joke, or a cup of tembu, would make their wrinkled toothless faces dissolve in laughter. This strength, and love of life in them, to me seemed not only highly respectable, but glorious and bewitching.

The old women of the farm and I had always been friends. They were the people who called me Jerie, the men and the children – except the very young – never used the name for me. Jerie is a Kikuyu female name, but it has some special quality – whenever a girl is born to a Kikuyu family a long time after her brothers and sisters, she is named Jerie, and I suppose that the name had a note of affection in it.

Now the old women were sorry that I was leaving them. From this last time, I keep the picture of a Kikuyu woman, nameless to me, for I did not know her well; she belonged, I think, to Kathego's village, and was the wife or widow of one of his many sons. She came towards me on a path on the plain, carrying on her back a load of the long thin poles which the Kikuyu use for constructing the roofs of their huts – with them this is women's work. These poles may be fifteen feet long; when the women carry them they tie them together at the ends, and the tall conical burdens give to the people underneath them, as you see them travelling over the land, the silhouette of a prehistoric animal, or a giraffe. The sticks which this woman was carrying were all black and charred, sooted by the smoke of the hut during many years; that meant that she had been pulling down her house and was trailing her building materials, such as they were, to new grounds. When we met she stood dead still, barring the path to me, staring at me in the exact manner of a giraffe in a herd, that you will meet on the open plain, and which lives and feels and thinks in a manner unknowable to us. After a moment she broke out weeping, tears streaming over her face, like a cow that makes water on the plain before you. Not a word did she or I myself speak, and, after a few minutes, she ceded the way to me, and we parted, and walked on in opposite directions. I thought that after all she had some materials with which to begin her new house, and I imagined how she would set to work, and tie her sticks together, and make herself a roof.

The little herdboys on the farm, who had never in their lives known of a time when I had not been living in the house, on the other hand had a great deal of excitement and tension of suspense out of the idea that I was going away. It may have been to them difficult, and daring, to imagine the world without me in it, as if providence had been known to be abdicating. They rose to the surface of the long grass when I was passing and cried out to me: 'When are you going away, Msabu? Msabu, in how many days are you going away?'

When in the end, the day came on which I was going away, I learned the strange learning that things can happen which we ourselves cannot possibly imagine, either beforehand, or at the time when they are taking place, or afterwards when we look back on them. Circumstances can have a motive force by which they bring about events without aid of human imagination or apprehension. On such occasions you yourself keep in touch with what is going on by attentively following it from moment to moment, like a blind person who is being led, and who places one foot in front of the other cautiously but unwittingly. Things are happening to you, and you feel them happening, but except for this one fact, you have no connection with them, and no key to the cause or meaning of them. The performing wild animals in a circus go through their programme, I believe, in that same way. Those who have been through such events can, in a way, say that they have been through death – a passage outside the range of imagination, but within the range of experience.

Gustav Mohr came out in his car in the early morning to go in to the railway station with me. It was a cool morning with but little colour in the air or the landscape. He himself looked pale, and blinked, and I remembered what an old Norwegian captain of a whaler down in Durban had explained to me, that the Norwegians are undismayed in any storm, but their nervous system cannot stand a calm. We had tea together on the millstone table, as we had had many times before. Here, to the west, the hills before us, with a little floating grey mist in the creeks, lived gravely through another moment of their many thousand years. I was very cold as if I had been up there.

My houseboys were still in the empty house, but they had, so to say, already moved their existence to other quarters, their families and their belongings had been sent off. Farah's women, and Saufe, had gone to the Somali village of Nairobi in a lorry the day before. Farah himself was going with me as far as Mombasa, and so was Juma's young son Tumbo, because he wanted to do so more than anything else in the world, and where, as a parting gift, he had been given the choice between a cow and the journey to Mombasa, he had chosen the journey.

I said good-bye to each of my houseboys, and, as I went out, they, who had been carefully instructed to close the doors, left the door wide open behind me. This was a typical Native gesture, as if they meant that I was to come back again, or else they did so to emphasize that there was now nothing more to close the doors of the house on, and they might as well be open to all the winds. Farah was driving me, slowly, at the pace of a riding-camel I suppose, round by the drive and out of sight of the house.

As we came to the pond, I asked Mohr if we would not have time to stop for a moment, and we got out, and smoked a cigarette by the bank. We saw some fish in the water, which were now to be caught and eaten by people who had not known old Knudsen, and were not aware of the importance of the fish themselves. Here Sirunga, my squatter Kaninu's small grandson, who was an epileptic, appeared to say a last good-bye to me, for he had been round by the house to do so, incessantly, for the last days. When we got into the cars again and went off, he started to run after the cars as fast as he could, as if whirled on in the dust by the wind, for he was so small – like the final little spark from my fire. He ran all the way to where the farm-road joined the highroad, and I was afraid that he might come with us on to the highroad as well; it would have been then as if now all the farm were scattered and blown about in husks. But he stopped up at the corner; after all he did still belong to the farm. He stood there and stared after us, as long as I could see the turning of the farm-road.

On the way in to Nairobi, we saw a number of grasshoppers in the grass and on the road itself. A few whirred into the car, it looked as if they were coming back upon the country once more.

Many of my friends had come down to the station to see me off. Hugh Martin was there, heavy and nonchalant, and as he came and said good-bye to me, I saw my Doctor Pangloss of the farm as a very lonely figure, a heroic figure, who had bought his loneliness with everything he had, and somehow an African symbol. We took a friendly leave: we had had much fun together, and many wise talks. Lord Delamere was a little older, a little whiter, and with his hair cut shorter than when I had had tea with him in the Masai Reserve, when I came down there with my ox-transport, at the beginning of the war, but as exceedingly and concernedly courteous and polite now as then. Most of the Somalis of Nairobi were on the platform. The old cattle-trader Abdallah came up and gave me a silver ring with a turquoise in it, to bring me luck. Bilea, Denys's servant, gravely asked me to give his respects to his master's brother in England, in whose house he had stayed in the old days. The Somali women, Farah told me on the way down in the train, had been at the station in rickshas,

but when they had seen so many Somali men collected there, they had lost
heart and had just driven back.

Gustav Mohr and I shook hands when I was already in the train. Now
that the train was going to move, was already moving, he had got back
his balance of mind. He wished so strongly to impart courage to me that
he blushed deeply; his face was flaming and his light eyes shining at me.

At the Samburu station on the line, I got out of the train while the
engine was taking in water, and walked with Farah on the platform.

From there, to the south-west, I saw the Ngong Hills. The noble wave
of the mountain rose above the surrounding flat land, all air-blue. But it
was so far away that the four peaks looked trifling, hardly distinguishable,
and different from the way they looked from the farm. The outline of the
mountain was slowly smoothed and levelled out by the hand of distance.

SHADOWS ON
THE GRASS

CONTENTS

ILLUSTRATIONS

FARAH

As here, after twenty-five years, I again take up episodes of my life in Africa, one figure, straight, candid, and very fine to look at, stands as doorkeeper to all of them: my Somali servant Farah Aden. Were any reader to object that I might choose a character of greater importance, I should answer him that that would not be possible.

Farah came to meet me in Aden in 1913, before the First World War. For almost eighteen years he ran my house, my stables and safaris. I talked to him about my worries as about my successes, and he knew of all that I did or thought. Farah, by the time I had had to give up the farm and was leaving Africa, saw me off in Mombasa. And as I watched his dark immovable figure on the quay growing smaller and at last disappear, I felt it as if I were losing a part of myself, as if I were having my right hand set off, and from now on would never again ride a horse or shoot with a rifle, nor be able to write otherwise than with my left hand. Neither have I since then ridden or shot.

In order to form and make up a Unity, in particular a creative Unity, the individual components must needs be of different nature, they should even be in a sense contrasts. Two homogeneous units will never be capable of forming a whole, or their whole at its best will remain barren. Man and woman become one, a physically and spiritually creative Unity, by virtue of their dissimilarity. A hook and an eye are a Unity, a fastening; but with two hooks you can do nothing. A right-hand glove with its contrast the left-hand glove makes up a whole, a pair of gloves; but two right-hand gloves you throw away. A number of perfectly similar objects do not make up a whole – a couple of cigarettes may quite well be three or nine. A quartet is a Unity because it is made up of dissimilar instruments. An orchestra is a Unity, and may be perfect as such, but twenty double-basses striking up the same tune are Chaos.

A community of but one sex would be a blind world. When in 1940 I was in Berlin, engaged by three Scandinavian papers to write about Nazi Germany, woman – and the whole world of woman – was so emphatically subdued that I might indeed have been walking about in such a one-sexed community. I felt a relief then, as I watched the young soldiers marching west, to the frontier, for in a fight the adversaries become one, and the two duellists make up a Unity.

The introduction into my life of another race, essentially different from mine, in Africa became to me a mysterious expansion of my world. My own voice and song in life there had a second set to it, and grew fuller and richer in the duet.

Within the literature of the ages one particular Unity, made up of essentially different parts, makes its appearance, disappears and again comes back: that of Master and Servant. We have met the two in rhyme, blank verse and prose, and in the varying costumes of the centuries. Here wanders the Prophet Elisha with his servant Gehazi – between whom one would have supposed the partnership to have come to an end after the affair with Naaman, but whom we meet in a later chapter apparently in the best of understanding. Here walk Terence's Davus and Simo, and Plautus' Calidorus and Pseudolus. Here Don Quixote rides forth, with Sancho Panza on his mule by the croup of Rosinante. Here the Fool follows King Lear across the heath in the storm and the black night, here Leporello waits in the street while inside the palazzo Don Giovanni 'reaps his sweet reward'. Phileas Fogg struts on to the stage with one single idea in his head and versatile Passepartout at his heels. In our own streets of old Copenhagen Jeronimus and Magdelone promenade arm in arm, while behind their broad and dignified backs Henrik and Pernille make signs to one another.

The servant may be the more fascinating of the two, still it holds true of him as of his master that his play of colours would fade and his timbre abate, were he to stand alone. He needs a master in order to be himself. Leporello, after having witnessed his scapegrace master's lurid end, will still, I believe, from time to time in a circle of friends have produced his list of Don Giovanni's victims and have read out triumphantly: 'In Spain are a thousand and three!' The Fool, who is killed by the endless night on the moor, would not have become immortal without the mad old King, to whose lion's roar he joins his doleful, bitter and tender mockery. Henrik and Pernille, if left by Holberg in their own native milieu of Copenhagen valets and ladies' maids, would not have twinkled and sparkled as they do against the background of the sedateness of Jeronimus and Magdelone and the pale romance of Leander and Leonore.

I had in Africa many servants, whom I shall always remember as part of my existence there. There was Ismael, my gun-bearer, a mighty hunts-man brought up and trained exclusively in the hunter's world, a great tracker and weather prophet, expressing himself in hunter's terminology and speaking of my 'big' and my 'young' rifle. It was Ismael who after his return to Somaliland addressed his letter to me 'Lioness Blixen' and began it: 'Honourable Lioness'. There was old Ismael, my cook and faithful companion on safaris, who was a kind of Mohammedan saint. And there was Kamante, a small figure to look at but great, even formidable, in his total isolation. But Farah was my servant by the grace of God.

Farah and I had all the dissimilarities required to make up a Unity: difference of race, sex, religion, milieu and experience. In one thing only were we equal: we had agreed that we were the same age. We were not able to settle the matter exactly, since the Mohammedans reckon with lunar years.

We wander through a long portrait gallery of historical interest: portraits of kings and princes, of great statesmen, poets, and sailors. Amongst all these one face strikes us, an anonymous character, resting in himself, confident of his own nature and dependent on no one. The catalogue that you take up and into which you look tells you: 'Portrait of a Gentleman'. I shall name my chapter on Farah in an unpretentious way: 'Portrait of a Gentleman'.

In our day the word 'gentleman' is taken less seriously than before, or seems to us to have once taken itself a bit too seriously. But so did Farah take himself seriously.

If the word may be taken to describe or define the person who has got the code of honour of his period and milieu in his own blood, as an instinct – such as the rules of the game will be in the blood of the true cricket or football player, to whom it would not be possible in any situation to throw the ball at the head of his adversary – Farah was the greatest gentleman I have ever met. Only it was, to begin with, difficult to decide what would be the code of honour to a high-born Mohammedan in the house of a European pioneer.

Farah was a Somali, which means that he was no Native of Kenya but an immigrant to the country from Somaliland further north. In my day there were a large number of Somali in Kenya. They were greatly superior to the Native population in intelligence and culture. They were of Arab blood and looked upon themselves as pure-blood Arabs, in some cases even as descendants of the Prophet. On the whole they thought very highly of themselves. They were all fanatical Mohammedans.

The Natives of the land, the Kikuyu, Wakamba, Kawirondo and Masai, have got their own old mysterious and simple cultural traditions, which seem to lose themselves in the darkness of very ancient days. We ourselves have carried European lights to the country quite lately, but we have had the means to spread and establish it quickly. In between, an oriental civilization, violent, cruel and very picturesque, gained a foothold in the Highlands through the slave and ivory trade.

The finest ivory in the world comes from East Africa, and the old slave traffic, a long time before the discovery of America, was carried on along these coasts. From here slaves were freighted eastward to Arabia, Persia, India and China, also northward to the Levant; you will see little black Negro pages in old Venetian pictures. From here came the forty black slaves who, together with forty white, carried Aladdin's jewels to the Sultan on their heads. Zanzibar was the great centre of the trade. The Sultan of Zanzibar, I was told when I was there in 1916, was still paid an appanage of £5,000 as compensation for his loss of income from the slave trade. I have seen, at Zanzibar, the market-place and the platform where slaves were put up for sale.

The old commercial intercourse has left its traces in the language of the country. Each tribe of East Africa has got its own language, but all over the Highlands a primitive, ungrammatical lingua franca is spoken: Swahili, the tongue of the coastal tribes. Small children even, herding goats and sheep on the plains, would understand and answer as we asked our way, or questioned them about water or game, in Swahili. I spoke Swahili to my Native servants and labourers on the farm, but as the farm lay in the Kikuyu district, our particular local jargon contained many Kikuyu words and turns of phrase.

The trade also brought the Somali to the country. Most likely Farah's ancestors had been enterprising buyers-up, very likely also hunters and robbers in the Highlands, and possibly pirates on the Red Sea.

The Somali are very handsome people, slim and erect as all East African tribes, with sombre, haughty eyes, straight legs and teeth like wolves. They are vain and have knowledge of fine clothes. When not dressed as Europeans – for many of them would wear discarded suits of their masters' from the first London tailors and would look very well in them – they had on long robes of raw silk, with sleeveless black waistcoats elaborately embroidered in gold. They always wore the turbans of the orthodox Mohammedans in exquisite many-coloured cashmeres; those who had made the pilgrimage to Mecca might wear a green turban.

The dark nations of Africa, strikingly precocious as young children, seemed to come to a standstill in their mental growth at different ages. The Kikuyu, Kawirondo and Wakamba, the people who worked for me on the farm, in early childhood were far ahead of white children of the same age, but they stopped quite suddenly at a stage corresponding to that of a European child of nine. The Somali had got further and had all the mentality of boys of our own race at the age of thirteen to seventeen. In such young Europeans, too, the code of honour, the deadly devotion to the grand phrase and the grand gesture is the passion urging them on to heroic deeds and heroic self-sacrifice, and also at times sinking them into a dark melancholy and resentment unintelligible to grown-up people. The Somali woman seemed to have stolen a small march upon her male, and from the time when she can first walk until venerable high age presents the picture of the classic *jeune fille* of Europe: coquettish, wily, covetous beyond belief, and sweetly merciful at the core.

I had read the old Nordic Sagas as a child, and now in my intercourse with the Somali I was struck by their likeness to the ancient Icelanders. I was therefore pleased to find Professor Östrup, who is an authority on both nations, making use of a common term to characterize Arabs and Icelanders: he calls them 'attitudinizers'. The same ravenous ambition to distinguish themselves before all others, and at any cost to immortalize themselves through a word or gesture, lies deep in the hearts of the sons of the desert as it did in the hearts of the untamed, salt young seafarers of the Northern Seas.

On the African plains the picture of Ejnar Tambeskälve, the unrivalled young archer, the friend of King Olav Tryggveson, who was with him in the naval battle of Svoldr in the year 1002, was brought back to me. As Ejnar's bowstring burst with a loud boom and the King through the din of the battle cried out: 'What burst there so loudly?' he screeched back: 'The Kingdom of Norway off thy hand, King Olav!' The wild-eyed warrior boy, standing up straight in the stern of the ship, may have felt with satisfaction that now what was to be achieved had been achieved. And we who today read about him may agree with him, since by now few people will remember who won or lost the battle of Svoldr, or what were the consequences of it, while Ejnar Tambeskälve's *grand mot* has been remembered through a thousand years.

In my dealings with Farah and his tribe I felt that whatever else I might risk from their hand, I did not run the risk of being pitied – no more than I would do in my dealings with a young boy at home.

Personally I have always had a predilection for boys, and have at times reflected that the strong sex reaches its highest point of loveableness at the age of twelve to seventeen – to get it back, in a second flowering, at the age of seventy to ninety. So were the Somali from the first day irresistible to me. With the later European settlers, however, they were not popular.

I myself came out to the Protectorate of British East Africa before the First World War, while the Highlands were still in very truth the happy hunting grounds, and while the white pioneers lived in guileless harmony with the children of the land. Most of the immigrants had come to Africa, and had stayed on there, because they liked their African existence better than their existence at home, would rather ride a horse than go in a car and rather make up their own campfire than turn on the central heating. Like me they wished to lay their bones in African soil. They were almost all themselves country-bred and open-air people; many of them were younger sons of old English families, schooled early in life by elderly, dignified keepers and stablemen and were accustomed to proud servants. Themselves untamed, with fresh hearts, they were capable of forming a Hawkeye-Chingachgook fellowship with a dark, untamed nomad or hunter; they accepted and trusted the Somali, as the Somali accepted and trusted them.

During the war, and the first years after it, no new settlers landed. But in the following years an energetic advertising of the Colony of Kenya as a country of unique economic possibilities was started in England, and 'Closer Settlement' was made the catchword. It brought out a new class of settlers, people who had grown up and lived in one town or one community in England, and who were strangely provincial compared to the African Natives, who were at any time prepared for anything. Plots of land were also given out as rewards to British non-commissioned officers, most of whom were city people, who in the loneliness of the great landscapes felt that they had been promised more than they were given.

To me it was a sad programme. From the point of view of emigration, I reflected, Kenya, with an altitude and a climate in which white people could not take on manual labour, and with a vast Native population, would never be an area of great moment. When I first came to the country there were about five thousand white people there; she might, I thought, possibly take in ten times as many. But then, I was told, Australia and New Zealand and Canada could at the same time take in up to fifty or a hundred millions. And from the point of view of the country itself, the 'true home of my heart', a closer white settlement was a dubious benefit, and it was the quality, not the quantity, of white settlers which we should have at heart. I laugh, and I suppose I ought to blush, when I call to mind that at this time I wrote to a very superior political personage in England and developed my views to him. I am indeed touched when I remember that he did really send an answer to my letter, in a courteous, if non-committal, note.

To these later arrivals to the country the Somali, her earliest immigrants, seemed haughty and unmanageable and were, I believe, on the whole as intolerable as to me and my friends they were indispensable. So it came that our particular clan of early settlers – arrogantly looking upon ourselves as Mayflower people – might be characterized as those Europeans who kept Somali servants and to whom a house without a Somali would be like a house without a lamp. Here were Lord Delamere and Hassan, Berkeley Cole and Jama, Denys Finch-Hatton and Bilea, and I myself and Farah. We were the people who, wherever we went, were followed, at a distance of five feet, by those noble, vigilant and mysterious shadows.

Berkeley Cole and I, in a private jargon of ours, distinguished between respectability and decency, and divided up our acquaintances, human and animal, in accordance with the doctrine. We put down domestic animals as respectable and wild animals as decent, and held that, while the existence and prestige of the first were decided by their relation to the community, the others stood in direct contact with God. Pigs and poultry, we agreed, were worthy of our respect, inasmuch as they loyally returned what was invested in them, and in their most intimate private life behaved as was expected of them. We watched them in their sties and yards, perseveringly working at the return of investments made, pleasantly feeding, grunting and quacking. And leaving them there, to their own homely, cosy atmosphere, we turned our eyes to the unrespectable, destructive wild boar on his lonely wanderings, or to those unrespectable, shameless cornthieves, the wild geese and duck, in their purposeful line of flight across the sky, and we felt their course to have been drawn up by the finger of God.

We registered ourselves with the wild animals, sadly admitting the inadequacy of our return to the community – and to our mortgages – but realizing that we could not possibly, not even in order to obtain the highest approval of our surroundings, give up that direct contact with God which we shared with the hippo and the flamingo. Nine thousand feet up we felt safe, and we laughed at the ambition of the new arrivals, of the Missions, the business people and the Government itself, to make the continent of Africa respectable. A time came when we began to feel uneasy about the matter. The Protestant Missions gave much time, energy and money to make the Natives put on trousers – in which they looked like giraffes in harness. The French Fathers were in better understanding with the children of the land, but they did not have – as they ought to have had – Saint Francis of Assisi at their Mission station; they were themselves but frail souls, and at home had been loaded with a heavy, mixed cultural cargo, which they dared not throw off. The businessmen, under the motto of 'Teach the Native to Want', encouraged the African to evaluate himself by his possessions and to keep up respectably with his neighbours. The Government, turning the great wild plains into game Reserves, seemed to succeed in making the lions themselves take on the look of kindly patresfamilias – times might come when our old feline friends would have their regular meals served them from Game Department canteens. It was doubtful whether sans them the graminivora would preserve their innocence of the period before the Fall, whether then the kongoni would still keep their lonely watcher silhouetted on top of a hill, the eland their silky skin swaying in the dewlap as they trotted along, and their moist eyes, the impala their flying leap. Must there then, even in Africa, be no live creature standing in direct contact with God?

Ay, but there will be, I consoled myself, as long as I have got Farah with me. For Farah, although gravely posing as a highly respectable major-domo, Malvolio himself, was a wild animal, and nothing in the world would ever stand between him and God. Unfailingly loyal, he was still at heart a wild animal, a cheetah noiselessly following me about at a distance of five feet, or a falcon holding on to my finger with strong talons and turning his head right and left. The qualities with which he served me were cheetah or falcon qualities.

When Farah first took service in my house, or first took my house into possession – for from that day he spoke of 'our house', 'our horses', 'our guests' – it was no common contract which was set up, but a covenant established between him and me *ad majorem domus gloriam*, to the ever greater glory of the house. My well-being was not his concern, and was hardly of real importance to him, but for my good name and prestige he did, I believe, hold himself responsible before God.

Farah was a highly picturesque figure in my house as he stepped forth on its threshold. In his relations with my Native servants he was unwaveringly fair and impartial, and he had a deeper knowledge of them and their course of thought than I could well account for, for I hardly ever saw him converse with them. Farah spoke English correctly, and French as well, for he had in his young days been cabin-boy on a French man-of-war, but he had a few expressions of his own which I ought to have set him right about, but which instead in our talks together I took to using myself. He said 'exactly' for 'except': 'All the cows have come home exactly the grey cow,' and I still at times find myself making use of the word in the same way.

Farah had the typical Somali voice, recognizable among all voices of the world, low, guttural, with a two-fold ring to it, for it was friendly but lent itself excellently well to a particular contempt or scorn. At times Farah like most Somali annoyed me by having so little *Gemütlichkeit* in his mental make-up. I accounted for it by the tribes' abstinence from wine or spirits through a thousand years, and reflected that the sight of an old uncle dead drunk would have been a wholesome remedy against the desert dryness of the Somali mind.

He once told me that he did not like the Jews because they 'ate antruss', and for a while I wondered which would be the food that shocked him in the Jews, since the pork forbidden to Mohammedans is forbidden to the children of Israel as well. In the end, however, I gathered from him that what roused his indignation was the Jewish practice of charging interest on money lent, a proceeding forbidden to and despised by the Mohammedans. He said of an ambitious English friend of the house: 'He never get Sir,' meaning that he would never obtain the honour of being knighted. At the time when the locusts came upon us the Natives roasted and ate them; I had a mind to try them myself, but still somehow doubtful asked Farah what they tasted like. 'I know not, Memsahib,' he answered, 'I eat not such small birds.' He had a partiality for the demonstrative adjective: 'This Arab horse dealer offers you this horse at this price,' and rarely spoke about his fellow-men but in the same way: 'this Kamante', 'this Prince of Wales'. Thomas Mann in his book *Joseph in Egypt* tells us that the ancient Egyptians had the same usage, and that Joseph taught himself to speak according to their taste: 'As we came to this fortress this good old man said to this officer.' It may be a particular African inclination.

Farah strictly saw to it that our Native servants groomed the horses and polished the silver of the house till they shone. He drove my old Ford car as if it had been a Rothschild's Rolls-Royce. And he expected from me a corresponding loyalty to the paragraphs of our covenant. As a consequence of this attitude he was a highly expensive functionary in the house, not only because his salary was disproportionately larger than that of my other servants, but because he did without mercy demand my house to be run in grand style.

Farah was my cashier, he had charge of all money I took home from the bank and of my keys. He never drew up any accounts for me and would hardly have been able to do so, nor would it ever have occurred to me to demand it from him. I never doubted but that he did to the best of his ability spend my money in the interest of my house. Only there always remained to me a strong exciting element of suspense as to his views of the interests of the house.

I once asked him: 'Farah, can you give me five rupees?' And he asked me in return: 'What do you want them for, Memsahib?' 'I want to buy a new pair of slacks,' I said. Farah shook his head. 'We cannot afford that this month, Memsahib,' he said. He told me: 'I pray to God that your old riding-boots may last till your new ones arrive out from London.' Farah had good knowledge of riding-boots and felt it to be below my dignity to walk about in boots made by the Indians of Nairobi.

To make up for it he was liberal in other matters. He decreed: 'We must have champagne for dinner tonight, Memsahib.' My English friends, who in between their long safaris stayed in my house, kept it in wine at a very high standard, but it happened when they were away for a long time that I ran short of wine. 'We have got so little champagne left, Farah,' I said. 'We must have champagne,' Farah said again. 'Have you forgotten, Memsahib, that there is a Memsahib coming for dinner?' My guests as a rule were men.

When Prince Wilhelm of Sweden was coming for tea to the farm, in his honour I wanted to make a kind of Swedish cake called *Klejner*, for which you need a little bit, what the cookery-books call a pinch, of cardamom. As Farah was going to Nairobi I added the cardamom to his shopping list. 'I do not know,' I said, 'whether the white grocers will have it. But if you cannot get it with them you must go to the Indians.' The great Indian tradesmen, Suleiman Virjee and Allidina Visram, were personal friends of Farah's and owned more than half of the native trade-quarter, which was called the Bazaar.

Farah came back late in the evening and reported: 'This precious spice, Memsahib, which other Europeans do not know, but which we must have, was very difficult to get. First I went to these white grocers, but they had not got it. Then I went to Suleiman Virjee, and he had it. And then I bought for five hundred rupees.' A rupee was two shillings. 'You are crazy, Farah,' I said. 'I meant you to buy for ten cents.' 'You did not tell me so,' said Farah. 'No, I did not tell you so,' I said. 'I thought you had human intelligence. But in any case I have no use for five hundred rupees' worth of cardamom, and you will have to give it back to Suleiman Virjee where you got it.' I at once realized that it would be impossible to make Farah carry out my order. It was not the inconvenience that he feared, for no kind of inconvenience means anything to a Somali. But he would not allow Suleiman Virjee to believe that a house like ours could do with less than five hundred rupees' worth of cardamom.

He thought the matter over and said: 'No. No, that would not be good, Memsahib. But I will tell you what we will do. I shall take over this lot.' So we left it at that, and the Somali are such furious tradespeople that Farah at once got the hitherto unknown article introduced on the farm, so that soon every self-esteeming Kikuyu went about chewing cardamom and dashingly spitting out the capsules. I tried it myself and it was not bad. I feel that Farah will have made a handsome profit on the transaction.

Farah's knowledge of Native mentality came in useful to me.

Once, at the end of a month, when I had been paying out their wages to my people on the farm, in going through my accounts I found that a hundred-rupee note was missing and must have been stolen. I passed on the sad news to Farah, and he at once very calmly declared that he would get me my money back. 'But how?' I asked him. 'There have been more than a thousand people up here, and we have no idea at all as to who may be the thief.' 'Nay, but I will get you your money back,' said Farah.

He walked away, and towards evening returned carrying with him a human skull. This may sound highly dramatic, but was in itself nothing out of the normal. For centuries the Natives had not buried their dead but had laid them out on the plains where jackals and vultures would take care of them. One might at any time, riding or walking there, in the long grass knock against an amber-coloured thigh-bone or a honey-brown skull.

Farah rammed down a pole outside my door and nailed the skull to the top of it. I stood by and watched him without enthusiasm. 'What is the good of that, Farah?' I asked him. 'The thief will already be far away. And must I now have that skull of yours set up just outside my door?' Farah did not answer, he took a step back to survey his work and laughed. But next morning, by the foot of the pole a stone was lying, and underneath it a hundred-rupee note. By what dark, crooked paths it had got there I was not told, and now shall never know.

Farah, as already told, was a strict Mohammedan, burning in the spirit.

In speaking about Mohammedans and Mohammedanism, I am well aware that I got to know in Africa only a primitive, unsophisticated Mohammedanism. Of Mohammedan philosophy or theology I know nothing; from my own experience I can but tell how Islam manifests itself in the course of thought and conduct of the unlearned Orthodox. All the same I feel that you cannot live for a long time among Mohammedans without your own view of life being in some way influenced by theirs.

I have been told that the word 'Islam' in itself means submission: the Creed may be defined as the religion which ordains acceptance. And the Prophet does not accept with reluctance or with regret but with rapture. There is in his preaching, as I know it from his unlearned disciples, a tremendous erotic element.

'Sweet scents, incense and perfumes are dear to my heart,' says the Prophet. 'But the glory of women is dearer. The glory of women is dear to my heart. But the glory of prayer is dearer.'

In contrast to many modern Christian ideologies, Islam does not occupy itself with justifying the ways of God to man; its Yes is universal and unconditional. For the lover does not measure the worth of his mistress by a moral or social rod. But the mistress, by absorbing into her own being the dark and dangerous phenomena of life, mysteriously transluminates and sanctifies them, and imbues them with sweetness. An old Danish love poem has it: 'There is witchcraft on your lips, an abyss within your gaze.' What the wooer desires is freedom to adore, what he craves and thirsts for is the assurance of being loved back. Kadidja's caravaneer, with his eyes on the new moon, in the words of a later author, even though in a somewhat altered sense, is 'God's own mad lover, dying on a kiss'.

I sometimes wondered whether the tribes of the desert had become what they were by having been in the hand of the Prophet for twelve hundred years, or whether his Creed has taken such deep roots in them because from the very beginning they were of one blood with him. I imagined that just as the erotic aloofness of the founder of Christianity has left his disciples in a kind of void, or of chronic uneasiness and remorse, within this province of life, so has the formidable, indomitable potency of the Prophet pervaded his followers and made mighty latent forces in them fetch headway. Eroticism runs through the entire existence of the great wanderers. Horses and camels are desirable and exquisite possessions in a man's life, and well worth that he should risk it for their sake. But they cannot compete or compare with women. To the hearts of the ascetic, hardened, ruthless tribes it is the number and the quality of the wives which decides a man's success and happiness in life, and his own worth.

When, on the farm, I was called upon to give judgement in matters between my Mohammedan people, I looked up rules and regulations in the manual of Mohammedan law, *Minhaj et Talibin*. It is a thick and heavy, highly imposing book to have carried about with you, a surprising work as well to a North European mind in its taboos and recommendations, enlightening as to the Mohammedan view of life, infinitely detailed in its regulations on legal purity, prayer, fasting and distribution of alms and particularly upon woman and her position in the community of the Orthodox. 'The law,' the classic states, 'forbids a man to clothe himself in silk. But a woman may wear clothes of silk and should do so whenever this be in all decency possible to her.' The Somali whom I knew did, however, wear silk, but Farah explained to me that they would do so only when outside their own country and in the service of other people – and surely my old valued friend Ali bin Salim of Mombasa, or the old Indian high priest who came to see me on the farm, wore but the finest and most delicate wools. The book also lays down as law that a husband shall supply his wife not only with the necessary nourishment, lodgings and clothes, but that he shall also give her such and such luxuries within his means, which are truly worthy of her and will make her truly value her husband. 'In the case, however,' it adds, 'of a woman of remarkable beauty, jurists may find themselves not entirely in accordance and will have to weigh the matter between them.' The very grave and somewhat pedantic book thus registers woman's beauty as an indisputable, juridical asset in existence.

Kikuyu Ndito from the Ngong farm

They rush forth, these warriors of the great fantasias, to meet the will of God – his adorable will – as the Jews rush forth to meet the Sabbath: 'Get thee up, brethren, to welcome the bride!' Or David, King of Israel, in his Psalm 119: 'O how love I thy law!' They are a communion of yes-sayers, they are in love with danger, with death and with God.

As Job's laments are not silenced by expositions of the justice and mercy of God, but it is before the revelation of God's greatness that the complainer surrenders and consents, the Prophet surrenders and consents:

'God is great.' In the same way did Farah consent, when after three weeks' hard tracking we came up close to a herd of elephants and I shot and missed, and the elephants marched away so that we never saw them again. In the same way did he consent when in a year of drought, news was brought him from Somaliland that half his camels had perished, and when I told him of Denys Finch-Hatton's death: 'God is great.'

It is a general notion among Christians that Mohammedanism is more intolerant than Christianity, but such is not my own experience. There were three great prophets – *Nebbes* – Farah told me, Mohammed, Jesus and Moses. He would not recognize Christ as the Son of God, for God could have no son in the flesh, but he would agree that he had no human father. He named him Isa ben Mariammo. About Mariammo he spoke much, praising her beauty and virginity – she had, he said, been walking in her mother's garden when an angel had brushed her shoulder with his wing; through this she had conceived. He smacked his own small son Saufe because he repeated some words of abuse about the Virgin which naughty Kikuyu totos from the Scotch Mission had taught him.

When in the thirties I was staying in the south of England with Denys's brother, the Earl of Winchilsea, the painter John Philpot came down to paint the portrait of my hostess, who was very lovely. He had travelled much in North Africa, and on an afternoon when we were walking together in the park he recounted to me an experience of his from there.

In the First World War, he said, he had had a shell-shock or a nervous breakdown; he would never feel sure that he was doing what he ought to do.

'When I was painting a picture,' he explained, 'I felt that I ought to make up my bank account. When I was making up my bank account, I felt that I ought to go for a walk. And when, in a long walk, I had got five miles away from home, I realized that I ought to be, at this very moment, in front of my easel. I was constantly in flight, an exile everywhere.

'It happened by then that I and my African servant in our travels in Morocco came to a small town or village. I cannot really describe the place to you, it looked like any other North African village. It stood in a flat plain, and in itself it was nothing but a number of mud-built huts with an old, broad mud-built wall round it. The only particular thing that I remember about it is its great multitude of storks, a stork's nest on almost every house. But at the moment when I had come through the gate in the wall I felt that this was a place of refuge. There came upon me a strange, blissful calm, a happiness like what you feel when a high fever leaves you. "Here," I thought, "one can remain."

'And as now I had stayed in the village for a fortnight, all the time in that same sweet peace of soul and giving no thought to the past or to the future, on a day when I was once more painting a picture, an old man, a priest, came up and spoke to me. "I hear from your servant," he said, "that you have finished your wanderings and will stay with us, since here you have found rest." I answered him that it was as he said, but that I could not explain to myself why it should be so.

'"Master," said the old man, "I shall explain it to you. There is something special about our village, things have happened here that have happened nowhere else. It came about, not when I was a boy myself but when my father was a boy of twelve, and he has related it to me as it happened. Turn your eyes to the gate in the wall behind us. Above it you will see a ledge, where two men can sit, for in old days watchmen were here looking out for foes that might approach across the plain. To this very ledge above the gate came the Prophet himself and your Prophet Jesus Christ. They met here to talk together of man's lot on earth and of the means by which the people of the earth might be helped. Those standing down below could not hear what they said to one another. But they could see the Prophet, as he explained his thoughts, striking his hand against his knee, and thereupon Jesus Christ lifting his hand and answering him. They sat there, deep in talk, till night fell and the people could no longer see them. And it is from that time, Master, that our village has got peace of heart to give away."

'I wonder,' said Mr Philpot, 'whether a clergyman of the Church of England would have told that tale.'

Like all Mohammedans Farah was without fear. Europeans call the Islamitic view of life fatalism. I myself do not think that the Prophet's followers see the happenings of life as predestined and therefore inescapable. They are fearless because confident that what happens is the best thing.

Farah, in one of my first years in Africa, stood beside me when a wounded lion charged – 'charged home' as hunters say, meaning that now only death will stop him. Farah had no rifle with him, and at that time, I believe, but slight faith in my marksmanship. But he did not move, I do not think that he winced. Good luck had it that in my second shot I hit the lion so that he rolled over like a hare, then Farah very quietly walked up to him and inspected him.

At a later time, though, to my surprise I heard Farah speak in deep admiration of my skill with a rifle. During one of our long safaris, when in the morning after a night's shooting I was still in bed in my tent, a young Englishman who had his camp some miles south of ours, and who had heard about us from the Natives, came over to inquire about water and game and to have company. He and Farah were talking together outside the tent, and I could follow their conversation through the canvas. 'What kind of Bwana are you out with?' the Englishman asked. 'Is he a good shot, and are you getting anything?' 'I am with no Bwana,' Farah answered, 'but with a Memsahib from a distant country. And she never misses a thing.'

On this occasion Farah seemed to enjoy talking about me. Generally the Somali will not discuss women and you cannot make them tell you of their wives and daughters. Only in regard to their mothers do they make an exception, and the Koran, Farah said, orders that each time you name your father with reverence you should name your mother with reverence twenty-five times. In this point as in others the Somali are like the old Icelanders. Tormod Kolbrunnaskjald was exiled from Iceland because he had sung of the girl he loved, naming her 'Kolbrunna'.

It is a strange thing that I should have this taboo in me still. At times, when people speak or write about me, I feel that I am breaking my covenant with Farah.

When the Prince of Wales, the present Duke of Windsor, in 1928 came on his first visit to Kenya, I had been invited by my friend Joanie Grigg, the Governor's wife, to stay for a week at Government House. I felt that this was an opportunity of bringing the cause of the Natives, in the matter of their taxation, before the Prince, and was happy about this chance of getting the ear of the future King of England. 'Only,' I said to myself, 'it will have to be done in a pleasant manner. For if it does not amuse him he will do nothing about it.'

As I sat beside the Prince at dinner I cautiously tried to turn his interest the way I wanted, and he did indeed on the next day come out to the farm to have tea with me. He walked with me into the huts of the squatters and made inquiries as to what they possessed in the way of cattle and goats, what they might earn by working on the farm and what they paid in taxes, writing down the figures. It was to me later on, when I was back in Denmark, a heart-breaking thing that my Prince of Wales should be King of England for only eleven months.

In the course of another evening I had been describing to the Prince the big Ngomas on the farm, and as he said good night to me he added: 'I should like to dine with you on Friday and to see such an Ngoma.' This was Tuesday night, and for the next two days the Prince would be up at Nanyuky for the races.

When I came up to my rooms in Government House I found Farah there waiting for orders for the morrow, for you always bring your own servant with you when staying in the houses of friends. I said to him: 'Something terrible has happened to us, Farah. The Prince is coming out on Friday to dine and to see our people dance. And you know that they will not dance at this time of year.' For these Ngomas were ritual dances connected with the harvest, and all settlers knew well enough that in this matter the Natives would rather die than break with a sacred law of a thousand years.

Farah was as deeply shaken by the news as I myself. For a few minutes he was struck dumb and turned into stone. In the end he spoke. 'If it be indeed so, Memsahib,' he said, 'to my mind there is only one thing for us to do. I shall take the car and go round to the big Chiefs. I shall speak to them and tell them that now they must come to help you. I shall remind them that three months ago you helped them.' I had had the luck to be able to assist the Natives in a matter between them and the Government concerning salt-rocks to which they had formerly brought their cattle to lick salt. 'But then,' Farah added with some misgiving, 'I can do nothing about this dinner. You will have to look after that, with Kamante, Memsahib.' There was some distance and hardly any roads between the manyattas of the great Chiefs, and the old men would seize this opportunity to talk. I answered: 'Nay, give no thought to that. I and Kamante will be able to look after it. For I think that you are right and that this is the best thing we can do.'

I returned to the farm to make preparations for Friday with a somewhat heavy heart, and Farah drove out from it, an ambassador on a tricky mission. When on the morning of Friday he was not back, the entire household, preparing the lobster up from Mombasa, the spurfowl brought in by Masai Morani, and Kamante's Cumberland sauce for the ham, was dead silent. It would be a dark, eternal shame to our house and to all of us, were the prince to come out to see an Ngoma, and we to have no Ngoma to show him.

But already at eight or nine o'clock our own young men and girls of the farm began to hang round the house, in the mysterious way of the Natives aware that great things were about to happen. During the next few hours dance-loving young people from farms further away followed, coming up the long avenue in small groups. Kamante, for once taking an optimistic view of a situation, remarked to me that this was like the time when the locusts came: one by one, then a number together, then in the end more than we would be able to count. At eleven o'clock we heard the car coming up the drive asthmatically. She was all plastered in mud and dust, and Farah himself as he stepped out of her seemed to have faded, in the way of dark people when thoroughly exhausted. I felt that all through these two nights he must have sat up in unceasing palaver with the old Chiefs. Yet at the very first glance we all knew him to have come back victorious.

'Memsahib,' he said in a voice almost as hoarse as that of the car, 'they are coming. They are coming all of them, and they are bringing with them their young men and their virgins.'

They did indeed follow close on the track of the car, swarming, as Kamante had predicted it, locust-like, a stream of supple, fiery young people of both sexes, set on dancing, should it cost them their life. The small groups of an old Chief and his aged counsellors, in rich, heavy monkey-skin cloaks, advanced in state, isolated from the common crowd by ten feet of empty space before and after them.

That night there were between two and three thousand dancers at the dancing-place by my house. The moon was full, and there was no breath of wind, the circle of small fires blazed and glowed a long way into the woods and sent up thin columns of smoke towards the sky. It was a fine Ngoma, I have seen no finer anywhere.

The Prince made the tour of the forest ballroom, stopping to speak to the old Chiefs one after the other. He spoke to them in Swahili, and they, hanging on to their sticks, gave him their answers keenly from smiling, toothless mouths, after which, for obvious reasons, the conversation ceased. He made an impression on the Ancients; afterwards they liked to speak about him. Africans laugh for reasons different from those of Europeans, most often from sheer spite but often also from mere content – for a long time they laughed when they spoke of the Prince, as if we had been discussing a very precious baby. I believe that the Prince himself was pleased with his Ngoma.

A fortnight later I again sent for the Kikuyu Chiefs. I had, I said to them, on the day of the Ngoma found myself in a difficult position, I had asked them to help me and they had helped me, now I wanted to thank them. I handed over a present to each of them, but by now I do not remember whether of a particularly fine rug or a goat.

A very old man, after they had had a few minutes to let my message sink into them, came up and spoke to me. 'Now you have told us, Msabu,' he said, 'that on the day of the great Ngoma you found yourself in a difficult position, and you asked us to help you and we helped you. Now you wanted to thank us, so you have given each of us a present. May we now say something to you?' This is a common address with Natives; you cannot well refuse the request, but after it you will have to be prepared for anything. I told the old man that he was free to say to me what he liked. 'Msabu,' he said with much weight and satisfaction. 'I shall, then, like to tell you something of which among ourselves we have talked much, and about which we are happy. We think that on the night when the Toto a Soldani came here to see our young men and virgins dance, among the Msabus present you had on the nicest frock. It pleased our hearts, Msabu, it still pleases our hearts when we think about it. For we all think that here, every day on the farm, you are terribly badly dressed.'

I did not contradict him. Generally on the farm I wore old khaki slacks stained with oil, mud and fouling. I felt that my people had dreaded, that upon a historical occasion on the farm and at a moment when I had called upon them to do their utmost, to see me let them down.

For the sake of my female readers I shall here insert that at the time of the Prince's visit I had not been to Europe for four years and could have no real idea as to what fashions there were like. So I asked the house in Paris, which had got my measures and was to make my frock, to follow their own notions about what would be truly chic. *'Nous sommes convaincus, Madame,'* they wrote back, *'que vous serez la plus belle.'* They had had the good sense to make me, in the heyday of the chemise frock – which was nothing but two vertical lines starting below the armpits and cut off above the knee – a so-called *robe de style* not likely to go out of fashion, with a hooped skirt of great fullness, in silver brocade. I think that it pleased the hearts of my people to see me, among the lank women of the dinner party, suddenly swell out to an unexpected voluminousness.

As now the old Chiefs and I in our talk together had got on to that very pleasant theme of my frock, I wanted to hear more of what they thought about it. But at this moment Farah stepped on to the stage, followed by Kamante carrying a wooden bowl that contained tombacco – snuff – for my guests. He looked approving but stern. He was not insensitive to popularity, but he was resolved on keeping the Kikuyu in their place, and me in mine.

'Wait a little, Farah,' I said. 'I am talking with the old people, they are talking with me.'

'No, Memsahib,' said Farah. 'No. Now these Kikuyus have said enough about this frock. Now it is time that they have this tombacco.'

Then came the hard times on the farm, and my certainty that I could not keep it. And then began my ever-repeated travels to Nairobi with such sorry aims as keeping my creditors quiet, obtaining a better price for the farm and, at the very end, after I had in reality lost the farm and become, so to say, a tenant in my own house, securing for my squatters the piece of land in the Reserve where according to their wish they could remain together. It took a long time before I could make the Government consent to my scheme. On these expeditions Farah was always with me.

And now it happened that he unlocked and opened chests of which till then I had not known, and displayed a truly royal splendour. He brought out silk robes, gold-embroidered waistcoats, and turbans in glowing and burning reds and blues, or all white – which is a rare thing to see and must be the real gala head-dress of the Somali – heavy gold rings and knives in silver- and ivory-mounted sheaths, with a riding whip of giraffe hide inlaid with gold, and in these things he looked like the Caliph Harun-al-Rashid's own bodyguard. He followed me, very erect, at a distance of five feet, where I walked, in my old slacks and patched shoes, up and down Nairobi streets. There he and I became a true Unity, as picturesque, I believe, as that of Don Quixote and Sancho Panza. There he lifted up me and himself to a classic plane, such as that of which the Norwegian poet Wergeland speaks:

> Death follows the happy man like a stern master,
> The unfortunate like a servant,
> Who is ever ready to receive his master's cloak and mask.

When I had sold all the contents of my house, my panelled rooms became sounding-boards. If I sat down on one of the packing-cases containing things to be sent off, which were now my only furniture, voices and tunes of old rang through the nobly bare room intensified, clear. When during these months a visitor came to the farm, Farah stood forth, holding open the door to the empty rooms as if he had been doorkeeper to an imperial palace.

No friend, brother or lover, no nabob suddenly presenting me with the amount of money needed to keep the farm, could have done for me what my servant Farah then did. Even if I had got nothing else for which to be grateful to him – but that I have got, and more than I can set down here – I should still for the sake of these months, now, thirty years after, and as long as I live, be in debt to him.

BARUA
A SOLDANI

Readers of my book *Out of Africa* may remember how, on a New Year's morning, before sunrise – while the stars, on the point of withdrawing and vanishing into the dome of the sky, were still hanging on it like big luminous drops, and the air still had in it the strange limpidity and depth, like well water, of African dawn – together with Denys Finch-Hatton and his Kikuyu chauffeur, Kanuthia, I was driving along a very bad road in the Masai Reserve, and there shot a lion upon a dead giraffe.

Later on Denys and I were accused of having shot the giraffe, a thing not allowed by the game laws. The Game Department in your shooting licence gave you the right to hunt, shoot or capture so and so many head of such and such game – I sometimes wondered by what right the Game Department dealt out such rights – and the giraffe was not included. Lions, however, you might shoot at any time, within the distance of thirty miles to a farm. But Kanuthia could bear us up in our statement that the giraffe had been dead a day or two before we came upon it.

I do not know whether the lion had actually killed the giraffe. Lions kill by breaking the necks of their victims, and in view of the height of a giraffe's shoulders and neck the thing seems unlikely. On the other hand the strength and energy of a lion are indeed incredible things, and hunters have solemnly assured me that they have seen giraffes being killed by lions.

The squatters on my farm during the past three months had been up to the house begging me to shoot a lion *'mbaya sana'* – very bad – which was following and worrying their herds. The lion that I met this morning and which, even on our close approach, remained on the back of his prey, absorbed in his meal and one with it, and only slightly stirring in the dim air, might well be the very same killer, the cause of so much woe over precious cows and bullocks. We were about twenty miles from the border of the farm, but a distance of twenty miles means nothing to a lion. If it were he, ought I not to shoot him when he himself gave me the chance? Denys, as Kanuthia slowed down the car, whispered to me: 'You shoot this time.' I had not got my own rifle with me, so he handed me his. I was

never keen to shoot with his rifle, it was too heavy and in particular too
long for me. But my old friend, Uncle Charles Bulpett, had told me: 'The
person who can take delight in a sweet tune without wanting to learn it,
in a beautiful woman without wanting to possess her, or in a magnificent
head of game without wanting to shoot it, has not got a human heart.'
So that the shot, here before daybreak, was in reality a declaration of love
– and ought not then the weapon to be of the very first quality?

Or it may be said that hunting is ever a love-affair. The hunter is in love
with the game, real hunters are true animal lovers. But during the hours
of the hunt itself he is more than that, he is infatuated with the head of
game which he follows and means to make his own; nothing much besides
it exists to him in the world. Only, in general, the infatuation will be
somewhat one-sided. The gazelles and antelopes and the zebra, which on
safari you shoot to get meat for your porters, are timid and will make
themselves scarce and in their own strange way disappear before your
eyes; the hunter must take wind and terrain into account and sneak close
to them slowly and silently without their realizing the danger. It is a fine
and fascinating art, in the spirit of that masterpiece of my countryman
Sören Kierkegaard, *The Seducer's Diary*, and it may, in the same way,
provide the hunter with moments of great drama and with opportunity
for skill and cunning, and for self-gratulations. Yet to me this pursuit was
never the real thing. And even the big game, in the hunting of which there
is danger, the buffalo or the rhino, very rarely attack without being
attacked, or believing that they are being attacked.

Elephant-hunting is a sport of its own. For the elephant, which through
centuries has been the one head of game hunted for profit, in the course
of time has adopted man into his scheme of things, with deep distrust. Our
nearness to him is a challenge which he will never disregard; he comes
towards us, straightly and quickly, on his own, a towering, overwhelming
structure, massive as cast iron and lithe as running water. 'What time he
lifteth up himself on high, the mighty are afraid.' Out go his ears like a
dragon's wings, giving him a grotesque likeness to the small lap-dog called
a papillon; his formidable trunk, crumpled up accordion-like, rises above
us like a lifted scourge. There is passion in our meeting, positiveness on
both sides; but on his side there is no pleasure in the adventure, he is driven
on by just wrath, and is settling an ancient family feud.

In very old days the elephant, upon the roof of the earth, led an
existence deeply satisfying to himself and fit to be set up as an example
to the rest of creation: that of a being mighty and powerful beyond
anyone's attack, attacking no one. The grandiose and idyllic modus
vivendi lasted till an old Chinese painter had his eyes opened to the

sublimity of ivory as a background to his paintings, or a young dancer
of Zanzibar hers to the beauty of an ivory anklet. Then they began to
appear to all sides of him, small alarming figures in the landscape drawing
closer: the Wanderobo with his poisoned arrows, the Arab ivory-hunter
with his long silver-mounted muzzle-loader, and the white professional
elephant-killer with his heavy rifle. The manifestation of the glory of God
was turned into an object of exploitation. Is it to be wondered at that he
cannot forgive us?

Yet there is always something magnanimous about elephants. To
follow a rhino in his own country is hard work; the space that he clears
in the thorn-thicket is just a few inches too low for the hunter, and he will
have to keep his head bent a little all the time. The elephant on his march
through dense forest calmly tramples out a green fragrant tunnel, lofty
like the nave of a cathedral. I once followed a herd of elephants for over
a fortnight, walking in shade all the time. (In the end, unexpectedly, on
the top of a very steep hill and in perfect security myself, I came upon the
whole troop pacing in Indian file below me. I did not kill any of them and
never saw them again.) There is a morally edifying quality as well in the
very aspect of an elephant – on seeing four elephants walking together on
the plain, I at once felt that I had been shown black stone sculptures of
the four major Prophets. On the chessboard the elephant takes his course,
irresistible, in a straight line. And the highest decoration of Denmark is
the Order of the Elephant.

But a lion-hunt each single time is an affair of perfect harmony, of deep,
burning, mutual desire and reverence between two truthful and un-
daunted creatures, on the same wavelength. A lion on the plain bears a
greater likeness to ancient monumental stone lions than to the lion which
today you see in a zoo; the sight of him goes straight to the heart. Dante
cannot have been more deeply amazed and moved at the first sight of
Beatrice in a street of Florence. Gazing back into the past I do, I believe,
remember each individual lion I have seen – his coming into the picture,
his slow raising or rapid turning of the head, the strange, snakelike
swaying of his tail. 'Praise be to thee, Lord, for Brother Lion, the which
is very calm, with mighty paws, and flows through the flowing grass, red-
mouthed, silent, with the roar of the thunder ready in his chest.' And he
himself, catching sight of me, may have been struck, somewhere under his
royal mane, by the ring of a similar Te Deum: 'Praise be to thee, Lord,
for my sister of Europe, who is young, and has come out to me on the
plain in the night.'

In old days the lion was likely to come out of the matter triumphant.
Later we have got such effective weapons that the test of strength can

hardly be called fair – still I have had more than one friend killed by lions. Nowadays great sportsmen hunt with cameras. The practice started while I was still in Africa; Denys as a white hunter took out millionaires from many countries, and they brought back magnificent pictures, the which however to my mind (because I do not see eye to eye with the camera) bore less real likeness to their object than the chalk portraits drawn up on the kitchen door by our Native porters. It is a more refined sport than shooting, and provided you can make the lion join into the spirit of it you may here, at the end of a pleasant, platonic affair, without bloodshed on either side, blow one another a kiss and part like civilized beings. I have no real knowledge of the art; I was a fairly good shot with a rifle, but I cannot photograph.

When I first came out to Africa I could not live without getting a fine specimen of each single kind of African game. In my last ten years out there I did not fire a shot except in order to get meat for my Natives. It became to me an unreasonable thing, indeed in itself ugly or vulgar, for the sake of a few hours' excitement to put out a life that belonged in the great landscape and had grown up in it for ten or twenty, or – as in the case of buffaloes and elephants – for fifty or a hundred years. But lion-hunting was irresistible to me; I shot my last lion a short time before I left Africa.

As now on this New Year's morning as noiselessly as possible I got down from the car and, through the long wet grass that washed my hands, the rifle, and my face, slowly walked closer to the lion, he stirred, rose and stood up immovable, his shoulder towards me, as fine a target for a shot as in the course of a lifetime you would get anywhere in the world. The sun by now was just below the horizon, the morning sky behind the dark silhouette was clear like liquid gold. I was struck by a thought: 'I have seen you before, I know you well. But from where?' The answer came at once: 'It is a lion out of the royal coat of arms of Denmark, one of our three dark-blue lions on gold ground. *Lion posant or* it is called in the heraldic language – he knows it himself.' As I sat down on the ground, got Denys's rifle into position on my knee and took aim, I made a resolution: 'If I get this lion, the King of Denmark is to have the skin.'

As the shot fell, booming loudly in the still morning landscape and echoing from the hills, it looked to me as if the lion was carried a couple of feet straight upwards into the air before he came down and collapsed. He had been hit in the heart, it was as it should be.

I have told in my book of how I sat and watched Denys and Kanuthia flaying the lion. Going back to that morning after so many years it seems all alive and clear round me, hard to leave once more. I knew then,

The author and her Scotch deerhound, Dusk,
in the garden at Ngong, 1919

without reflecting, that I was up at great height, upon the roof of the
world, a small figure in the tremendous retort of earth and air, yet one
with it; I did not know that I was at the height and upon the roof of my

own life. The grass on the slope where I sat was short as a mowed lawn, the Masai having burned it off in patches in order to get fresh grazing for their herds, the Highland air was intoxicating, like wine, the shadows of the vultures ran across my feet. From where I sat I could gaze far away: at a very long distance, by the line of the tall acacia trees somewhat below me, three giraffes came into sight, stood still for a few minutes and walked off. 'Praise be to thee, Lord, for Sister Giraffe, the which is an ambler, full of grace, exceedingly demure and absent-minded, and carries her small head high above the grass, with long lashes to her veiled eyes, and which is so much a lady that one refrains from thinking of her legs, but remembers her as floating over the plain in long garbs, draperies of morning mist or mirage.'

Now it fell out that this lion was an exceptionally fine specimen, what out in his own country they call a black-maned lion, with his thick dark mane growing all back over his shoulder-blades. Denys's gun-bearer, who had seen many hundred lion-skins, declared this one to be the finest he had ever come across. And as in that same spring I was going on a visit to Denmark after four years in Africa, I took the skin with me and on my way, in London, gave it to the firm of Rowland Ward to be cured and set up.

When in Denmark I told my friends that I meant to give King Christian X the lion-skin, they laughed at me.

'It is the worst piece of snobbery that we have ever heard of,' they said.

'Nay, but you do not understand,' I answered them. 'You have not lived for a long time outside your own country.'

'But what in the world is the King to do with the skin?' they asked. 'He does not mean to appear at New Year's levee as Hercules! He will be in despair about it.'

'Well,' I said, 'if the King will be in despair, he will have to be in despair. But I do not think it need come to that, for he will have some attic at Christiansborg or Amalienborg where he can put it away.'

It so happened that Rowland Ward did not manage to have the skin ready by autumn when I was going back to Africa, so that I could not myself present it to the King, but had to leave this privilege to an old uncle of mine who was a chamberlain to the Court. If the King was really in despair about it he hid it very nobly. Some time after my return to the farm I had a kind letter from him, in which he thanked me for his lion-skin.

A letter from home always means a lot to people living for a long time out of their country. They will carry it about in their pocket for several days, to take it out from time to time and read it again. A letter from a

king will mean more than other letters. I got the King's letter about
Christmas-time, and I pictured to myself how the King had sat at his
writing-table at Amalienborg, gazing out over a white Amalienborg
Square with the snow-clad equestrian statue of his great-great-great
grandfather, King Frederic V, in a wig and classic armour, in the midst
of it. A short time ago I myself had been part of the Copenhagen world.
I stuck the letter into the pocket of my old khaki slacks and rode out on
the farm.

The farm work that I was going to inspect was the clearing of a square
piece of woodland where we were to plant coffee, a couple of miles from
my house. I rode through the forest, which was still fresh after the short
rains. Now once more I was part of the world of Africa.

Half an hour before I came out to the wood-fellers a sad accident had
taken place amongst them. A young Kikuyu, whose name was Kitau, had
not managed to get away quick enough when a big tree fell, and had had
one leg crushed beneath it. I heard his long moanings while still at a
distance. I speeded up Rouge upon the forest path. When I came to the
place of disaster Kitau's fellow-workers had dragged him out from
beneath the fallen tree and laid him on the grass; they were thronging
round him there, separating when I came up but standing close by to
watch the effect of the catastrophe on me and to hear what I would say
about it.

Kitau was lying in a pool of blood, his leg had been smashed above the
knee and was sticking out from his body at a grotesque and cruel angle.

I made the wood-fellers hold my horse and sent off a runner to the
house to have Farah bring out the car, so that I might drive Kitau to the
hospital in Nairobi. But my small Ford box-body car was getting on in
years; she rarely consented to run on more than two cylinders and indeed
it went against her to be started at all. With a sinking heart I realized that
it would be some time before she came up.

While waiting for her I sat with Kitau. The other wood-fellers had
withdrawn some distance. Kitau was in great pain, weeping all the time.

I always had morphia at hand in my house for injured people of the
farm carried up there, but here I had neither the medicine nor the syringe.
Kitau, when he realized that I was with him, groaned out dolefully:
'Saidea mimi' – help me – 'Msabu.' And again: 'Saidea mimi. Give me
some of the medicine that helps people,' the while groping over my arm
and knee. When out riding on the farm I usually had bits of sugar in my
pockets to give to the totos herding their goats and sheep on the plain and
at the sight of my crying out for sugar. I brought out such bits and fed
Kitau with them – he would or could not move his badly bruised hands,

and let me place the sugar on his tongue. It was as if this medicine did somehow relieve his pain; his moans, while he had it in his mouth, changed into low whimperings. But my stock of sugar came to an end, and then once more he began to wail and writhe, long spasms ran through his body. It is a sad experience to sit by somebody suffering so direly without being able to help; you long to get up and run away or, as with a badly injured animal, to put an end to the anguish – for a moment I believe I looked round for some kind of weapon for the purpose. Then again came the repeated clock-regular moaning of Kitau: 'Have you got no more, Msabu? Have you got nothing more to give me?'

In my distress I once more put my hand into my pocket and felt the King's letter. 'Yes, Kitau,' I said, 'I have got something more. I have got something *mzuri sana*' – very excellent indeed. 'I have got a *Barua a Soldani*' – a letter from a king. 'And that is a thing which all people know, that a letter from a king, *mokone yake*' – in his own hand – 'will do away with all pain, however bad.' At that I laid the King's letter on his chest and my hand upon it. I endeavoured, I believe – out there in the forest, where Kitau and I were as if all alone – to lay the whole of my strength into it.

It was a very strange thing that almost at once the words and the gesture seemed to send an effect through him. His terribly distorted face smoothed out, he closed his eyes. After a while he again looked up at me. His eyes were so much like those of a small child that cannot yet speak that I was almost surprised when he spoke to me. 'Yes,' he said. 'It is *mzuri*,' and again, 'yes, it is *mzuri sana*. Keep it there.'

When at last the car arrived and we got Kitau lifted on to it, I meant to take my seat at the steering-wheel, but at that he immediately worked himself into a state of the greatest alarm. 'No, Msabu,' he said, 'Farah can drive the car, you must tell him to do so. You will sit beside me and hold the Barua a Soldani to my stomach as before, or otherwise the bad pain will come back at once.' So I sat on the boards beside him, and all the way into Nairobi held the King's letter in position. When we arrived at the hospital Kitau once more closed his eyes and kept them closed, as if refusing to take in any more impressions. But with his left hand on my clothes he kept sure that I was beside him while I parleyed with the doctor and the matron. They did indeed allow me to keep close beside him while he was laid on the stretcher, carried into the building and placed on the operating table; and as long as I saw him he was quiet.

I may in this place tell that they did really in hospital manage to set his broken leg. When he got out he could walk, even if he always limped a little.

I may also here tell that later on, in Denmark, I learned from the King himself that my lion-skin had obtained a highly honourable place in the state-room of Christiansborg Castle, with the skin of a polar bear to the other side of the throne.

But now the rumour spread amongst the squatters of my farm that I had got this Barua a Soldani, with its miracle-working power. They began to come up to my house one by one, warily, to find out more about it – the old women first, mincing about like old hens turning their heads affectedly to find a grain for their young ones. Soon they took to carrying up those of their sick who were in bad pain, so that they might have the letter laid on them and for a while be relieved. Later they wanted more. They demanded to borrow the King's letter, for the day or for the day and night, to take with them to the hut for the relief of an old dying grandmother or a small ailing child.

The Barua a Soldani amongst my stock of medicine from the very first was accurately and strictly placed in a category of its own. This decision was taken by the Natives themselves without my giving any thought to the matter. It would do away with pain, in this capacity it was infallible, and no ache or pang could hold out against it. But it must be made use of solely in uttermost need.

It did happen from time to time that a patient with a very bad tooth-ache in his misery cried out to me to let him have Barua a Soldani. But his appeal would be met by his surroundings with grave disapprovement and indignation or with haughty, scornful laughter. 'You!' they cried back to him, 'there is nothing the matter with you but that you have got a bad tooth! You can go down to old Juma Bemu and have him pull it out for you. How could you have the King's letter? Nay, but here is old Kathegu very ill in his hut with long, hard pains in his stomach, and going to die tonight. His small grandson is up here to have Barua a Soldani for him until tomorrow from Msabu. To him she will give it.' By this time I had had a leather bag with a string to it made for the King's letter. So the small toto, standing up straight on the terrace, would take the remedy carefully from my hands, hang it round his neck and walk away, with his own hands upon it. He would stand up straight on the terrace again next morning. Ay, his grandfather had died at sunrise, but Barua a Soldani had helped him well all night.

I have seen this particular attitude, or this particular mentality, in the dark people in other matters as well. They stood in a particular relation to the ways and conditions of life. There are things which can be done and others which cannot be done, and they fell in with the law, accepting what came with a kind of aloof humility – or pride.

When Fathima, Farah's wife, was to give birth to her first child, she was very ill; for an hour or two her surroundings, and her mother herself, had given up hope about her. Her mother, an imposing figure in my establishment, had arranged for about a dozen Somali ladies of the first families of Nairobi to be present. They arrived in Aly Khan's mule-traps, looking very lovely and lively, like old Persian pictures, in their long ample skirts and veils, and filled with sympathy and zeal. The waves of woman's world closed over Farah's house, at some distance from the huts of my house-boys. Farah himself, grave and more subdued than I had ever seen him, together with all other male creatures of my household, had been shooed a hundred yards away. The women then set to heating up the room in which the birth was taking place, to an almost unbearable heat, with charcoal in basins, and to make the air thick with childbed-incense. I sat out there for a while, half unconscious, not because I imagined that I could be of any use whatever, but because I felt it to be the correct thing and expected of me.

Fathima was a very lovely creature, with big dark eyes like a doe's, so slim that one wondered where she could possibly be storing her baby, supple in all her movements and in daily life of a risible temper. I felt sorry for her now. The gentle midwives were busy, bending and again straightening up the girl and from time to time knocking her in the small of the back with their fists as if to knock out the child. For the time that I was there I saw them dealing out only one kind of medicine: a matron amongst them brought along an earthenware dish, on the inner side of which a holy man of the town had drawn up, in charcoal, a text from the Koran; the lettering was washed off carefully with water, and the water poured into the mouth of the labouring young woman.

This great event on the farm took place at the time when the Prince of Wales – the present Duke of Windsor – was on his first visit to the country. Among the celebrations in his honour was a *concours hippique* in Nairobi, and I had entered my Irish pony Poor-box for the jumping competition – he was at the moment in training at Limoru. In the midst of the bustle round me and in a moment of things looking very dark, I suddenly called to mind that I had promised to bring over a bag of oats for him there, so I would have to leave for a couple of hours. I drove away sadly, taking Kamante with me in the car.

On the way back from Limoru I came past the French Mission and remembered that the Fathers for some time had been promising me seed of a particular kind of lettuce from France. As I pulled up the car, Kamante, who during our drive had not said a word, spoke to me. Fathima was a favourite with Kamante, she was the only human being for whose intelligence I had ever heard him express any kind of respect. 'Are you,' he asked me, 'going into the church to beg the lady in there, who is your friend, to help Fathima?' The lady in the church, who was my friend, was the Virgin Mary, whose statue Kamante had seen when on Christmas night he had accompanied me to midnight mass. I could not very well say no, so I answered yes, and went into the church before going to the refectory. It was cool in the church, and in the face of the highly vulgar papier mâché statue of the Virgin, with a lily in her hand, there was something soothing and hopeful.

When I came back to my house, Fathima's baby was born, and she herself was doing well. I congratulated her mother and Farah in his forest exile. The small boy brought into the world that day was Ahamed, called Saufe, who later became a great figure on the farm. Kamante said to me: 'You see, Msabu, it was good that I reminded you to ask the lady who is your friend to help Fathima.'

Now, one would have imagined that with knowledge of my intimacy with a person of such power, Kamante upon some other occasion would have come back to have me make use of it. But this never happened. There are things which can be done, and other things which cannot be done. And we who know the laws must fall in with them.

In the course of time, however, my squatters tried to find out more about that King of my own country who had written the letter. They asked me if he was tall, and were here, I believe, still under the impression of the personality of the Prince of Wales, who had dined on the farm, and who had made them wonder at the fact that a person of such great might should be so slim and slight. I was pleased to be able to reply truthfully that there was not a taller man in his kingdom. They then wanted to know whether the horse on which he rode was more *kali* – fierce – than my own horse, Rouge; then again, if he laughed. This last must have been a matter of importance to the Natives in their relations with us. 'Your *kabilla*' – tribe – they said to me, 'is different to those of the other white people. You do not get angry with us as they do. You laugh at us.'

I have still got the King's letter. But it is now undecipherable, brown and stiff with blood and matter of long ago.

In a showcase at the Museum of Rosenborg, in Copenhagen, the tourist can see a piece of yellow texture covered with tawny spots. It is the handkerchief of King Christian IV, which the King held to his eye socket when, in the naval battle of Kolberger Heide three hundred years ago, his eye was smashed by a Swedish shot. A Danish poet of the last century has written an enthusiastic ode about these proud, edifying marks.

The blood on my sheet of paper is not proud or edifying. It is the blood

SHADOWS ON THE GRASS

of a dumb nation. But then the handwriting on it is that of a king, *mokone yake*. No ode will be written about my letter; still, today it is, I believe, history as much as the relic of Rosenborg. Within it, in paper and blood, a covenant has been signed between the Europeans and the Africans – no similar document of this same relationship is likely to be drawn up again.

THE
GREAT
GESTURE

I was a fairly famous doctor to the squatters of the farm, and it happened that patients came down from Limoru or Kijabe to consult me. I had been, in the beginning of my career, miraculously lucky in a few cures, which had made my name echo in the manyattas. Later I had made some very grave mistakes, of which I still cannot think without dismay, but they did not seem to affect my prestige; at times I felt that the people liked me better for not being infallible. This trait in the Africans comes out in other of their relations with the Europeans.

My consultation hour was vaguely from nine to ten, my consultation room the stone-paved terrace east of my house.

On most days my activity was limited to driving in the sick people to the hospital in Nairobi or up to that of the Scotch Mission at Kikuyu, both of which were good hospitals. There would almost always be plague about somewhere in the district; with this you were bound to take the sufferers to Nairobi plague hospital, or your farm would be put in quarantine. I was not afraid of plague, since I had been told that one would either die from the disease or rise from it as fit as ever, and since, besides, I felt that it would be a noble thing to die from an illness to which popes and queens had succumbed. There would likewise almost always be smallpox about, and gazing at old and young faces round me, stamped for life like thimbles, I was afraid of smallpox, but Government regulations strictly kept us to frequent inoculations against the illness. As to other diseases like meningitis or typhoid fever, whether I drove the patients into Nairobi or tried to cure them myself out on the farm, I was always convinced that I should not catch the sickness – my faith may have been due to an instinct, or may have been in itself a kind of protection. The first *sais* that I had on the farm, Malindi – who was a dwarf, but a great man with horses – died from meningitis actually in my arms.

Most of my own practice was thus concerned with the lighter accidents of the place – broken limbs, cuts, bruises and burns – or with coughs, children's diseases and eye diseases. At the start I knew but little above what one is taught at a first-aid course. My later skill was mostly obtained through experiments on my patients, for a doctor's calling is demoralizing. I arrived at setting a broken arm or ankle with a splint, advised all through the operation by the sufferer himself, who very likely might have performed it on his own, but who took pleasure in setting me to work. Ambition a few times made me try my hand at undertakings which later I had to drop again. I much wanted to give my patients Salvarsan – which in those days was a fairly new medicine and was given in big doses – but although my hand was steady with a rifle I was nervous about it with a syringe for intravenous injections. Dysentery I could generally keep in check with small, often-repeated doses of Epsom salt, and malaria with quinine. Yet it was in connection with a case of malaria that I was nearest to becoming a murderer.

On a day in the beginning of the long rains Berkeley Cole came round the farm from up-country, on his way to Nairobi. A little while after, Juma appeared to report that an old Masai Chief with his followers was outside, asking for medicine for a son of his who had been taken ill, evidently – from the symptoms reported – with malaria.

The Masai were my neighbours; if I rode across the river which formed the border of my farm I was in their Reserve. But the Masai themselves were not always there. They trekked with their big herds of cattle from one part of the grass-land – which was about the size of Ireland – to another, according to the rains and the condition of the grazing. When again they came round my way and set to patch up their huts of cow-hide for a sojourn of some time, they would send over to notify me, and I would ride over to call on them.

If I had been alone this afternoon, I should have gone outside to talk the case over with the old Chief, to hand him the quinine and altogether to get Masai news. But Berkeley, dried after his drive and revived by a glass or two, was in one of his sweet, dazzling moods and entertaining me on old Ireland memories of his, so that I sat on with him. I just handed over the keys of the medicine chest to Kamante, who was the skilled and deep amanuensis to my doctor and had dealt out quinine to our patients a hundred times, telling him to count up the tablets to the father of the sick boy and to instruct him to give his son two of them in the evening and six in the course of the next day. But after dinner, while Berkeley and I by the fireside were listening to my records of Petrouchka just out from Europe, Juma once more stood in the door, an ominous spectre in his long white *kansu*, to inform me that the old Masai was back with a small lot of his people. For his son, after having taken my medicine, had got very ill indeed, with terrible pains in his stomach. I called in the Masai Chief, and found that he was an old acquaintance of mine. I knew his son well

too, his name was Sandoa; like the big Masai Chief, he was a Moran of
two years ago, and it was he who had taught me to shoot with a bow and
arrow. Calling to mind that the most inexplicable fits of idiocy might
occur even in the most intelligent Natives, I had Kamante woken up and
ordered him to show me the box from which he had taken the quinine.
And it was Lysol.

Berkeley said: 'We had better go out there at once.' But it was raining
heavily; the road round Mbagathi Bridge was impassable, so that it would
be useless to think of starting a car, and we should have to take the shorter
cut across the river on foot. I collected the bicarbonate and oil which I
used against accidents with corrosives, and we took two boys with hurricane lamps with us. The Masai also had brought lamps. The descent to
the river, in the tall wet bush and long wet grass, was steep and stony, but
the Masai knew of a better way than my riding-path, and when we came
to the river itself, which had swelled high with the rain, they carried me
across.

On the way none of us had spoken. As now, to the other side of the
river, we were ascending the long slope of the Masai Reserve, I said to
Berkeley: 'If Sandoa is dead by the time we get there, I shall not go back
to the farm. I shall stay on with the Masai. If they will have me.' I had
no answer from Berkeley, only, the next moment, a sudden, wild,
extremely rude curse straight in my face. For he had in that second put
his foot into the long marching column of an army of Siafu. The Siafu
are the universally dreaded, man-eating ants of Africa, the which, left to
themselves, will eat you up alive. My dogs in their hut at night when they
had got the Siafu on them would yell out miserably in their agony, until
you rushed out to save them. My friend Ingrid Lindström of Njoro at one
time had her whole flock of turkeys devoured by the killers. They are
about mostly at night, and in the rainy season. If you happen to get the
Siafu on you, there is nothing for you but to tear off your clothes and have
the person nearest at hand pluck them out of your flesh. Now, turning
round to see what was happening to Berkeley, I saw him, in the midst of
the infinite black African night and of the Masai plain, his trousers at his
heels, changing feet as if he were treading water, with one toto holding
up a hurricane lamp and another picking out the burning, ferocious
creatures from his strangely white legs.

When we came to the Masai manyatta we found Sandoa still alive. By
a stroke of luck, or by some kind of intuition, he had taken but one tablet
of Kamante's medicine – possibly also the intestines of Masai Morani are
hardier than those of other human beings. I administered the bicarbonate
and oil to him, feeling that I ought to be on my knees with gratitude, and

I saw him well on his way to recovery before, in the grey light of dawn, Berkeley and I returned to my house.

Snake-bites were frequent, but although I lost oxen and dogs from snake-bite I never lost a human patient from them. The spitting cobra caused pain and distress; I still have before me the picture of an old squatter woman staggering up to the house wailing and blind after having her face spat in while cutting wood in the forest – she must have been chopping with her mouth wide open, for her tongue and gums were swollen to suffocation and had turned a deadly pale blue. But the effect of the poison could be relieved with bicarbonate and oil and would pass after a while.

Fashion – the ambition to be *comme il faut* – made itself felt in the ailments on the farm, as in other departments of Native life. At one time the truly chic thing was to come to the house for worm-medicine. I did not myself taste the mixture, which looked very nasty in its bottle, like green slime, but the people, old and young, drank it down with pride. After a while I warned my patients that I had no faith in their need of worm-medicine, and that if they wanted to go on taking it as an apéritif they would in the future have to pay for it themselves – and I thereby put an end to that particular kind of dandyism. A very old squatter a couple of years later presented himself at the house and begged to have the 'green medicine'. His wife, he informed me, had got a *nyoka* – which word really means a snake – in her stomach, and at night it would roar so loudly that neither he nor she could sleep. On my doorstep he looked *démodé*, the last adherent to a fashion of the past.

My patients and I thus worked together in good understanding. Only one shadow lay over the terrace: that of the hospital. During my early days in Africa, till the end of the First World War, the shadow was light like that of trees in spring; later on it grew and darkened.

For some of my years on the farm I had been holding the office of *fermier général* there – that is, in order to save the Government trouble I collected the taxes from my squatters locally and sent in the sum total to Nairobi. In this capacity I had many times had to listen to the Kikuyu complaining that they were made to pay up their money for things which they would rather have done without: roads, railways, street lighting, police – and hospitals.

I wished to understand them and to know how deep was their reluctance against the hospital, and to what it was really due, but it was not easy, for they would not let me know; they closed up when I questioned them, they died before my eyes, as Africans will. One must wait and be

Aweru, an old Kikuyu squatter of the farm

patient in order to find the right moment for putting salt on the tail of the timid, dark birds.

It fell to Sirunga, in one of his little quicksilver movements, to give me a kind of information.

Sirunga was one of the many grandchildren of my big squatter Kaninu, but his father was a Masai. His mother had been among those pretty young girls whom Kaninu had sold across the river, but she had come back again to her father's land with her baby son. He was a small, slightly built child with a sudden, wild, flying gracefulness in all his movements and a corresponding, incalculable, crazy imagination of a kind which I have not met in any other Native child, and which maybe will have been due to the mixture of blood. The other boys kept back from Sirunga, they called him 'Sheitani' – the Devil – and at first I laughed at it – for even with a good deal of mischief in him Sirunga could be nothing but a very small devil – but later on I realized that in the boys' eyes he was possessed by the Devil, and his smallness then made the fact the more tragic. Sirunga suffered from epilepsy.

I did not know of it until I happened to see him under an attack. I was lying on the lawn in front of the house talking with him and some other totos when all at once he rose up straight and announced: 'Na taka kufa' – I am dying, or literally, I want to die, as they say in Swahili. His face grew very still, the mouth so patient. The boys round him at once spread to all sides. The attack, when it came upon him, was indeed terrible to watch, he stiffened in cramp and foamed from the mouth. I sat with my arms round him; I had never till then seen an epileptic attack and did not know what to do about it. Sirunga's amazement as he woke up in my arms was very deep, he was used to seeing everybody run away when he was seized with a fit, and his dark gaze at my face was almost hostile. All the same after this he kept close to me – I have before written about him that he held the office of an inventive fool or jester and followed me everywhere like a small, fidgety, black shadow. His mighty uncontrolled fantasies and whims were totally confused and highly confusing to listen to. Sirunga, at a time when we had an epidemic on the farm, explained to me that once – long long long ago – all people had been very ill. It was, Msabu, when the sun was pregnant with the moon – walked with the moon in the stomach – but as the moon jumped out and was born, they grew well again. I did not connect his fantasy with hospitals, from which no such universal cure could rightly be expected; it was the words 'long long long ago' which gave me my perspective.

At the time when the Natives of the Highlands were free to die as they liked, they would follow the ways of their fathers and mothers. When a

Kikuyu fell ill, his people carried him out of his hut on his bedstead of sticks and hides, since a hut in which a person had died must not again be lived in but had to be burned down. Out here under the tall fringed trees his family sat round him and kept him company, squatter friends came up to give the news and gossip of the farm, at night small charcoal fires were made up on the ground round the bed. If the sick man got well he was carried back into the hut. If he died he was brought across the river out on the plain, and was left there to the quick and neat cleaning and polishing of jackals and vultures, and of the lions coming down from the hills.

I myself was in sympathy with the tradition of the Natives, and I instructed Farah – who showed himself deeply averse to the idea, for the Mohammedans wall up the graves of their dead and perform solemn rites by the side of them – if I died on the farm to let me travel in the track of my old squatters across the river. There were so many of the true qualities of the Highland country in the *castrum doloris* out there under the big firmament, with its wild, free, gluttonous undertakers: silent drama, a kind of silent fun – at which after a day or two the main character himself would be smiling – and silent nobility. The silent, all-embracing genius of consent.

The Government prohibited and put an end to the funeral custom of old days, and the Natives gave it up unwillingly. The Government and the Missions then undertook to build hospitals, and, seeing the reluctance of the people of the land to go into them, were surprised and indignant, and blamed them for being ungrateful and superstitious, or for being cowards.

The Africans, though, feared pain or death less than we ourselves did, and life having taught them the uncertainty of all things, they were at any time ready to take a risk. An old man with a headache once asked me if I might not be able to cut off his head, take out the evil from it, and set it back in its right place, and if I had consented I think that he would have let me make the experiment. It was other things in us which at times set their nerves on edge.

For they had had our civilization presented to them piecemeal, like incoherent parts of a mechanism which they had never seen functioning, and the functioning of which they could not on their own imagine. We had been transforming, to them, Rite into Routine. What by now most of all they feared from our hands was boredom, and on being taken into hospital they may well have felt that they were in good earnest being taken in to die from boredom.

They had deep roots to their nature as well, down in the soil and back in the past, the which, like all roots, demanded darkness. When, in his small confused Kikuyu-Masai mind, Sirunga had given me a small contorted key, the reference to a past – 'long long long ago' – an African past of a thousand years, I took it into my course of thought. We white people, I reflected, were wrong when in our intercourse with the people of the ancient continent we forgot or ignored their past or did indeed decline to acknowledge that they had ever existed before their meeting with us. We had deliberately deprived our picture of them of a dimension, thus allowing it to become distorted to our eyes and blurred in its Native harmony and dignity, and our error of vision had caused deep and sad misunderstandings between us and them. The view to me later on was confirmed as I observed the fact that white people to whom the past was still a reality – in whose minds the past of their country, their name and blood or their home was naturally alive – would get on easier with the Africans and would come closer to them than others, to whom the world was created yesterday, or upon the day when they got their new car.

The dark people, then, as the clever doctor from Volaia approached, may well have gone through the kind of agony which one will imagine a tree to be suffering at the approach of a zealous forester intending to pull up her roots for inspection. Their hearts in an instinctive deadly nausea turned from the medical examinations of the hospitals, such as they did from the *kipanda*, the passport giving the name and data of its bearer, which some years later the Government made compulsory to each individual Native of the Highlands.

We Nations of Europe, I thought, who do not fear to floodlight our own inmost mechanisms, are here turning the blazing lights of our civilization into dark eyes, fitly set like the eyes of doves by the rivers of waters (Song of Solomon 5:12), essentially different to ours. If for a long enough time we continue in this way to dazzle and blind the Africans, we may in the end bring upon them a longing for darkness, which will drive them into the gorges of their own, unknown mountains and their own, unknown minds.

We may, if we choose to, I thought further, look forward to the day when we shall have convinced them that it be a meritorious and happy undertaking to floodlight a whole continent. But for that they will have to get other eyes. The intelligent, efficient and base Swahili of the coast have got such eyes.

The outcome of these various circumstances was this: that I would from time to time find myself unemployed as a doctor, and my consulting room empty.

It would most often happen after I had been taking a patient into hospital. But it might be brought about, suddenly, by reasons unknown to me and probably unknowable, like the sudden pause which may occur amongst labourers in the field. They would then, after a week, bring me up a patient or two with a high fever or a broken limb, too far gone for treatment. I would feel that I was being made a fool of, and lose patience with my people, I would speak to them without mercy:

'Why,' I asked them, 'must you wait to come to me with your broken arms and legs until they are gangrenous, and the stench, as I am driving you to Nairobi, makes me myself sick? – or with a festering eye until the ball of it has shrunk and withered so that the cleverest doctor of Volaia will not be able to cure it? The old fat Msabu matron in the Nairobi hospital will be angry with me once more and will tell me that I do not mind whether my people on the farm live or die – and in the future she shall be right. You are more obstinate than your own goats and sheep, and I am tired of working for you, and from now on I shall bandage and dose your goats and sheep and leave you yourself to be one-legged and one-eyed, such as you choose to be.'

Upon this they would stand for some time without a word, and then, very sullenly, let me know that they would in the future bring me up their injuries in good time, if on my side I would promise not to take them into hospital.

During the last few months that I was still on the farm, at the time when very slowly it was being made clear to me that my fight of many years was lost, and that I should have to leave my life in Africa and go home to Europe, I had as a patient a small boy of six or seven named Wawerru, who had got bad burns on both legs. Burns are an ailment which you would often get to treat in the Kikuyu, for they built up piles of charcoal in their huts and slept round them, and it happened that in the course of the night the coals slid down on top of the sleepers.

In the midst of a strangely non-real existence, unconnected with past or future, the moments that I spent in doctoring Wawerru were sweet to me, like a breeze on a parched plain. The French Fathers had presented me with a new kind of ointment for burns, just out from France. Wawerru was a slight, slant-eyed child, late-born in his family and spoilt, in so far as he believed that nobody would do him anything but good. He or his elder brothers who carried him up to the house had managed to grasp the idea of a treatment every third day, and his sores were yielding to my cure. Kamante as my amanuensis was aware of the happiness that the task gave me, his lynx eyes every third day would seek out the small group amongst the patients on the terrace, and one time, when they had missed a day, he gave himself the trouble to walk down to Wawerru's manyatta and to admonish his family about their duties. Then suddenly Wawerru did not appear, he vanished out of my existence. I questioned another toto about him; *'Sejui'* – I know not – he answered. A few days later I rode down to the manyatta, my dogs running with me.

The manyatta lay at the foot of a long, green grass-slope. It contained a large number of huts, for Wawerru's father had got several wives, with a hut to each of them and – in the way of most wealthy Kikuyu – a central hut of his own, into which he could retire from the world of femininity to meditate in peace, and there was also an irregular suburb of bigger and smaller granaries to the settlement.

As I rode down the slope, I saw Wawerru himself sitting on the grass, playing with a couple of other totos. One of his playfellows caught sight of me and notified him, and he at once, without so much as a glance in my direction, set off into the maze of the huts and disappeared to my eyes. His legs were still too weak to carry him, he scuttled along with wondrous quickness on all fours like a mouse. I quite suddenly was thrown into a state of flaming anger at the sight of such ingratitude. I set Rouge into a canter to catch up with him, and at the moment when, in the exact way of a mouse with its hole, he slipped into a hut, I jumped from the saddle and followed him. Rouge was a wise horse; if I left him, the reins loose round his neck, he would stand still and wait for me till I came back. I had my riding whip in my hand.

The hut to my eyes, as I came into it from the sunlight of the plain, was almost dark; there were a few dim figures in it, old men or women. Wawerru, when he realized that he had been run to earth, without a sound rolled over on his face. Then I saw that the long bandages, with which I had taken so much trouble, had been unwound, and that from heel to hip his legs were smeared with a thick coat of cow-dung. Now cow-dung is not actually a bad remedy for burns, since it coagulates quickly and will keep the air out. But at the moment the sight and smell of it to me were nauseating, as if deadly – in a kind of self-preservation I tightened my grip on the whip.

I had not, till now, in my mind associated my success or failure in curing Wawerru's legs with my own fate, or with the fate of the farm. Standing here in the hut, adjusting my eyes to the twilight of it, I saw the two as one, and the world round me grew infinitely cheerless, a place of no hope. I had ventured to believe that efforts of mine might defeat destiny. It was brought home to me now how deeply I had been mistaken; the balance-sheet was laid before me, and proved that whatever I took on was destined to end up in failure. Cow-dung was to be my harvest. I bethought myself of the old Jacobite song:

Now all is done that could be done.
And all is done in vain.

I spoke no word, I do not think that I gave out any sound at all. But the tears all at once welled out from behind my eyelids, and I could not stop them. In a few moments I felt my face bathed in tears. I kept standing like that for what seemed to me a long time, and the silence of the hut to me was deep. Then, as the situation had to end somehow, I turned and went out, and my tears still flowed abundantly, so that twice I missed the door. Outside the hut I found Rouge waiting; I got into the saddle and rode away slowly.

When I had ridden ten yards, I turned round to look for my dogs. I then saw that a number of people had come out from the huts and were gazing after me. Riding on another ten or twenty yards, I was struck by the thought that this in my squatters was an unusual behaviour. In general, unless they wanted something from me and would shout for it – as the totos, popping from the long grass, screeched out for sugar – or wanted just to send off a friendly greeting; 'Jambu, Msabu!' they let me pass fairly unnoticed. I turned round again to have another look at them. This second time there were still more people standing on the grass, immovable, following me with their eyes. Indeed the whole population of the manyatta would have got on their legs to watch Rouge and me slowly disappearing across the plain. I thought: 'They have never till now seen me cry. Maybe they have not believed that a white person ever did cry. I ought not to have done it.'

The dogs, having finished their investigation of the various scents of the manyatta and their chasing of its hens, were coming with me. We went home together.

Early next morning, before Juma had come in to draw the curtains of my windows, I sensed, by the intensity of the silence round me, that a crowd was gathered at short distance. I had had the same experience before and have written about it. The Africans have got this to them – they will make their presence known by other means than eyesight, hearing or smell, so that you do not tell yourself: 'I see them,' 'I hear them,' or 'I smell them,' but: 'They are here.' Wild animals have got the same quality, but our domestic animals have lost it.

'They have come up here, then,' I reflected. 'What are they bringing me?' I got up and went out.

There were indeed a great many people on the terrace. As I kept standing silent, looking at them, they, silent too, formed a circle round me; they obviously would not have let me go away had I wanted to. There were old men and women here, mothers with babies on their back, impudent Morani, coy Nditos – maidens – and lively, bright-eyed totos. Gazing from one face to another I realized what in our daily life together I never thought of: that they were dark, so much darker than I. Slowly they thronged closer to me.

Confronted with this kind of dumb, deadly determination in the African, a European in his mind will grope for words in which to formulate and fix it – in the same way as that in which, in the fairy-tale, the man pitting his strength against the troll must find out the name of his adversary and pin him down to a word, or be in a dark, trollish manner, lost. For a second my mind, running wildly, responded to the situation in a wild question: 'Do they mean to kill me?' The moment after I struck on the right formula. My people of the farm had come up to tell me: 'The time has come.' 'It has, I see,' in my mind I assented. 'But the time for what?'

An old woman was the first to open her mouth to me.

The old women of the farm were all good friends of mine. I saw less of them than of the small restless totos, who were ever about my house, but they had agreed to assume the existence of a particular understanding and intimacy between them and me, as if they had all been aunties of mine. Kikuyu women with age shrink and grow darker; seen beside the cinnamon-coloured Nditos, sap-filled, sleek lianas of the forest, they look like sticks of charcoal, weightless, desiccated all through, with a kind of grim jocosity at the core of them, noble, high-class achievements of the skilled charcoal-burner of existence.

This old woman of the terrace now, in the grip of her left hand, held forth her right hand to me, as if she were making me a present of it. Across the wrist ran a scarlet burn. 'Msabu,' she whimpered into my face. 'I have got a sick hand, sick. It needs medicine.' The burn was but superficial.

An old man with a cut in the leg from his woodchopper's axe came up next, then a couple of mothers with feverish babies, then a Moran with a split lip and another with a sprained ankle, and an Ndito with a bruise in one round breast. None of the injuries were serious. I was even pressed upon to examine a collection of splinters in the palm of a hand, from a climb for honey in a tree.

Slowly I took in the situation. My people of the farm, I realized, today, in a common great resolution had agreed to bring me what, against all reason and against the inclination of their own hearts, I had wanted from them. They must have been grappling with, imparting to one another and discussing between them the fact: 'We have been trying her too hard. She clearly is unable to bear any more. The time has come to indulge her.'

It could not be explained away that I was being made a fool of. But I was being made so with much generosity.

After a minute or two I could not help laughing. And as, scrutinizing my face, they caught the change in it, they joined me. One after another all faces round me lightened up and broke in laughter. In the faces of toothless old women a hundred delicate wrinkles screwed up cheeks and chin into a baroque, beaming mask – and they were no longer scars left by the warfare of life, but the traces of many laughters.

The merriment ran along the terrace and spread to the edge of it like ripples on water. There are few things in life as sweet as this suddenly rising, clear tide of African laughter surrounding one.

> Legend has it that a Gaul
> seeing wild, fierce Gallic courage
> mowed down round him by the rigid
> discipline of Roman legions,
>
> heavenwards shot his last arrow
> at the God whom he had worshipped,
> at the God who had betrayed him.
> And then fell with cloven forehead.
>
> From the bones of fallen Gauls
> peasants of the land built fences
> round their fair and fruitful vineyards.
> No one had a nobler burial.

ECHOES
FROM THE
HILLS

I have the great good luck in life that when I sleep I dream, and my dreams are always beautiful. The nightmare, with its squint-eyed combination of claustrophobia and *horror vacui*, I know from other people's accounts only, and mostly, for the last twenty years, from books and theatre. This gift of dreaming runs in my family, it is highly valued by all of us and makes us feel that we have been favoured above other human beings. An old aunt of mine asked to have written on her tombstone: 'She saw many a hard day. But her nights were sweet.'

But our beautiful dreams are not confined to the spheres of the idyll or the child's play, or to any such sphere as in the life of day-time is considered safe or pleasant. Horrible events take place in them, monsters appear, abysses open, wild turbulent flights and pursuits are familiar features of theirs. Only, on entering their world, horror changes hue. Monstrosity and monsters, Hell itself – they turn to favour and to pretti-ness.

I have read or been told that in a book of etiquette of the seventeenth century the very first rule forbids you to tell your dreams to other people, since they cannot possibly be of interest to them. I do not want to sin against seventeenth-century good manners and am not, here, going to report to my readers any particular dream of mine. But since dreams in general to me are a matter of interest, I shall set down a few general remarks about them. Should these remarks turn out somewhat vague and hazy, as if shimmering to the eyes, the reader will have to forbear with me. It is in the nature of things. Dreams, like smells, decline to yield up their inmost being to words.

The first characteristic of my dreams is this: I move in a world deeply and sweetly familiar to me, a world which belongs to me and to which I myself belong more intensely than is ever the case in my waking exist-ence. Yet I do not in the dream meet anybody or anything which, outside of it, I know or have ever known. It has happened to me, as a child, to dream of a particularly dear dog – then I at once realized that Natty Bumppo had gone from the world of the living – but otherwise those cherished places within, or towards, which I travel, those friends, infinitely dear to my heart, whom I am rushing forward to meet and from whom I cannot bear to part, I have never seen.

Only during one time of my life, and only in connection with one kind of place and people, have phenomena of an outer world found their way into my dreams. It was in itself to me a strange and stirring experience.

The second characteristic of my dreams is their vastness, their quality of infinite space. I move in mighty landscapes, among tremendous heights, depths and expanses and with unlimited views to all sides. The loftiness and airiness of the dream come out again in its colour scheme of rare, luminous blues and violets, and mystically transparent browns – all of which I promise myself to remember in the day-time, yet there can never recall. Dream trees are very much taller than day-time trees; I vow to myself to keep in mind that such be the real height of trees, yet when I wake up I fail to do so. Long perspectives stretch before me, distance is the password of the scenery, at times I feel that the fourth dimension is within reach. I fly, in dream, to any altitude, I dive into bottomless, clear, bottle-green waters. It is a weightless world. Its very atmosphere is joy, its crowning happiness, unreasonably or against reason, is that of triumph.

For we have in the dream forsaken our allegiance to the organizing, controlling and rectifying forces of the world, the Universal Conscience. We have sworn fealty to the wild, incalculable, creative forces, the Imagination of the Universe.

To the Conscience of the world we may address ourselves in prayer, it will faithfully reward its faithful servants according to their desert, and its highest award is peace of mind.

To the imagination of the world we do not pray. We call to mind how, when last we did so, we were asked back, quick as lightning, where we had been when the morning stars sang together, or whether we could bind the sweet influences of Pleiades. Without our having asked them for freedom, these free forces have set us free as mountain winds, have liberated us from initiative and determination, as from responsibility. They deal out no wages, each of their boons to us is a gift, baksheesh, and their highest gift is inspiration. A gift may be named after both the giver and the receiver, and in this way my inspiration is my own, more even than anything else I possess, and is still the gift of God.

The ship has given up tacking and has allied herself to the wind and the current; now her sails fill and she runs on, proudly, upon obliging waves. Is her speed her own achievement and merit or the work and merit of outside powers? We cannot tell. The dancer in the waltz gives herself into the hands of her skilled partner; is the flight and wonder of the dance, now, her own achievement or his? Neither the ship nor the dancer, nor the dreamer, will be able to answer or will care to answer. But they will, all three, have experienced the supreme triumph of Unconditional Surrender.

One last word about dreams:

Some people tell me that the capacity of dreaming belongs to childhood and early youth, and that as your faculties of seeing and hearing ebb away your talent for dreaming will go with them. My own experience tells me that it is the other way. I dream today more than I ever did as a child or a young girl, and in my present dreams things stand out more clearly than ever, and more to be wondered at.

At times I believe that my feet have been set upon a road which I shall go on following, and that slowly the centre of gravity of my being will shift over from the world of day, from the domain of organizing and regulating universal powers, into the world of Imagination. Already now I feel, as when at the age of twenty I was going to a ball in the evening, that day is a space of time without meaning, and that it is with the coming of dusk, with the lighting of the first star and the first candle, that things will become what they really are, and will come forth to meet me.

The unruly river, which has bounced along wildly, sung out loudly and raged against her banks, will widen and calm down, will in the end fall silently into the ocean of dreams, and silently experience the supreme triumph of Unconditional Surrender.

During my first months after my return to Denmark from Africa, I had great trouble in seeing anything at all as reality.

My African existence had sunk below the horizon, the Southern Cross for a short while stood out after it, like a luminous track in the sky, then faded and disappeared. The landscapes, the beasts and the human beings of that existence could not possibly mean more to my surroundings in Denmark than did the landscapes, beasts and human beings of my dreams at night. Their names here were just words, the name of Ngong was an address. It was no good, it might even be bad manners, to talk about them.

Fate had willed it that my visitors to the farm by that time had already gone, or were just about to go. They were none of them people to stay for a long time in the same place. Sir Northrup MacMillan, Galbraith and Berkeley Cole and Denys Finch-Hatton had set out before myself; shortly after my departure Lord Delamere, Lord Francis Scott and Hugh Martin followed them. The Swede, Eric von Otter, who had distinguished himself in the war in Africa, died in his faraway post up north, my gallant young friend and helpmate, Gustav Mohr, was drowned ferrying his safari across a river. There they were, all of them, nine thousand feet up, safe in the mould of Africa, slowly being turned into African mould themselves. And here was I, walking in the fair woods of Denmark, listening to the waves of Öresund. To the south-east, a long way off, the plains of the farm, where in years of drought we had fought the wild, gluttonous grass-fires, and the squatters' plots, with the pigeons cooing high about the chattering and the sounds of cooking below, were being cut up into residential plots for Nairobi business people, and the lawns, across which I had seen the zebras galloping, were laid out into tennis courts. These things were what are called facts, but were difficult to retain.

What business had I had ever to set my heart on Africa? The old continent had done well before my giving it a thought; might it not have gone on doing so? As I myself could not find the answer, a great master supplied it. He said: 'What is Africa to you or you to Africa ...?' And again, laughing:

> If it do come to pass
> That any man turn ass,
>   Leaving his wealth and ease,
>   A stubborn will to please,
> Ducdame ...
>   Here shall he see
>   Gross fools as he,
> An if he will come to me.

Dear Master, you have never failed me, your word has been a lamp unto my feet and a light unto my path. Now I shall tell you, and prove to you, how right you have been in speaking about the stubborn will.

For a while, after I had published my book *Seven Gothic Tales*, I considered the possibility of running a children's hospital in the Masai Reserve. There was much disease among the Masai, mostly such as we had brought upon them; on my safaris I had seen many blind children. But the Masai refused to take their sick to hospital.

The Masai did not like us and had no reason to do so. For we had put an end to their bird-of-prey raids on the agricultural tribes, we had taken their spears and their big almond-shaped shields from them, and had splashed a bucket of water upon the halo of a warrior nation, hardened through a thousand years into a personification of that ideal of Nietzsche: 'Man for war, and woman for the warrior's delight, all else is foolishness.'

Once when I was on safari deep in the Reserve, a very old Masai came up and seated himself by my campfire; after a while he began to speak, and it was like hearing a boulder speak. I myself spoke sufficient Masai to inquire about game and water, and no more. For it is to my mind a language impossible to learn, maybe because the course of thought of the tribe speaking it is alien to our own. When on a path in the Reserve you meet a Masai you greet him: 'Saubaa.' If you meet a Masai woman you salute her: 'Tarquenya.' I have never succeeded in learning what was the meaning of the difference. But on my safaris I has an interpreter with me. 'Nowadays,' according to him, the Moran – warrior – of sixty years ago told us, 'it is no pleasure to live. But in the old days it was good fun. When then the Kikuyu or the Wakamba had got a fat piece of land, and fat herds of cattle, goats and sheep on it, we Morani came to them. First we killed all men and male children with steel' – the Masai warriors had long, fine spears and short, strong swords – 'and we were allowed to stay on in the village until we had eaten up the sheep and goats there. Then before going away again, we killed off the women with wood' – for the Masai also in their belts carried wooden clubs, surprisingly light and effective. I do not know if our old guest was actually calling up a past, or if in his long nocturnal monologue he was picturing to himself an ideal state of things, and was slowly getting drunk on his vision of it. He walked away at last and disappeared into the night, a bald, skinny bird of prey of a dying species.

Neither did the white settlers in general like the Masai, who refused to work for them and kept up a sullen and arrogant manner in their dealings with them. But I myself had always been on friendly terms with my neighbours of the Masai Reserve, and they might, I felt, consent to bring their sick children to a nursing home of mine. I travelled to London to see Dr Albert Schweitzer on one of his visits to England and to learn about conditions from him. He kindly gave me the information I wanted. But I soon realized that the expenses of the undertaking would by a long way exceed my means – you do not make as much money on writing books as is generally believed. The images of an existence nine thousand feet up, under the long hill of Bardamat, among Masai children, dissolved like to other mirages above the grass.

The letters from my old servants in Africa would come in, unpredictably making their appearance in my Danish existence, strange, moving documents, although not much to look at. I wondered what would have made my correspondents feel just at that moment the necessity of walking in fifteen or twenty miles to Nairobi in order to send off these messages to me. At times they were dirges or elegies, at other times factual reports or even *chroniques scandaleuses*.

Two or three such epistles might follow quickly upon one another, then there might be many months in which the old continent was dumb.

But once a year at least I would be certain to get news of all my people.

From the time when I left Africa until the outbreak of the Second World War, every year before Christmas I sent out a small amount of money to my old firm of solicitors, Messrs. W. C. Hunter and Company, of Nairobi. They would always be able to get Farah's address, for he had his home and family in the Somali village of the town, even when he himself was away trading horses from Abyssinia or following some great white hunter on his safaris, and Farah would look up and collect his old staff. Thus in the whitewashed Nairobi office my household was gathered together once more, each member of it was handed my Christmas present and was told to deliver in return, for my information, a short report on how he was and on what had happened to him in the course of the year. The bulletin, probably very slowly drawn from him, was put down by the clerk of the office in sober English and was easy to read, but had no voice to it.

But my people, inspired by what to them might seem an actual, renewed meeting with me – for the African has a capacity for disregarding distances of space and time – on leaving the solicitor's quarters laid their way round by the post office, looked up the Indian professional letter-writer in his stall there and had this learned man set down for them a second message to me. In such way the letter, first translated in the mind of the sender from his native Kikuyu tongue into the lingua franca of Swahili, had later passed through the dark Indian mind of the scribe, before it was finally set down, as I read it, in his unorthodox English. Yet in this shape it bore a truer likeness to its author than the official, conventional note, so that as I contemplated the slanting lines on the thin yellow paper, I for a moment was brought face to face with him.

Juma wrote: 'Some fire came into my house and ended one excellent goat.' He also acquainted me with the negotiations around his daughter Mahô's marriage, speaking with scorn of the purchase price offered by her Kikuyu suitor. The moving passage about my predilection for little Mahô and the trouble I had taken to teach her to read obviously called for a reply from me, which might prove useful in the bargaining.

Ali Hassan, who had been personal boy to my mother when she had come out to visit me on the farm, during the Italian-Abyssinian war had accompanied General Llewellyn to Addis Ababa, and wrote: 'Things was not very good here. If the old Memsahib was been in this place, this people would not behaved such as they do.' Ali had Swahili blood in him, and the swift, incalculable manner of the Swahili. At first I had found him somewhat incongruous in my house. But he was steadier than he looked, a good worker, observant and with an unexpected mildness of mind.

Kamante wrote: 'I got newly female infant from my wife, who is somewhat good sort.'

Farah did not lay his way by the post office. He will have dictated his letters in English himself. They were much like him, gravely and gracefully standing on his own dignity and mine, avoiding any manifestation of pity for any of us. He wrote about a parrot which he had purchased from an Indian friend as a present for me, and which could speak. When, he wrote, he had taught it a few more phrases and names of old mutual friends and acquaintances, if I was not coming back to Africa he would try to get it sent to Denmark. As in the end it proved to be impossible to realize this scheme, Farah gave the parrot to his mother-in-law, who all the time had much admired it, and sent me a few feathers plucked off it to show me what colour it had been. His personal feelings towards me, and the remembrance of our long acquaintance, came out in these letters, suddenly, and as in a new key, in the prayers to God for me preceding his signature.

Through these years I also kept up a correspondence with Abdullahi, my Somali servant, who by now was back in his own country. I have mentioned Abdullahi only very briefly before. Still he had for some years been a picturesque figure on the farm, with his own colours to him. I feel that he ought by now to be brought into the picture.

Abdullahi was Farah's small brother. He will have been ten years old by the time when Farah decided that the house needed a page more consistent with its dignity than the Kikuyu totos who till now had held the office, and had him sent down from Somaliland. Farah at first had asked for another boy, his sister's son, but the grandmother of the child, Farah's mother, had refused to part with him, for he was, she sent us word, of too high value to the tribe on account of his talent for tracking down camels which had strayed away at night. His mother's decisions to Farah were always unappealable, so it was Abdullahi Ahamed who one day appeared on my doorstep, and who for some years became one with the house.

In order to show his impartiality, Farah treated his little brother with sternness; a couple of times in the beginning of our acquaintance I felt called upon to take the side of the child. But in this, as in much of Farah's attitude and activity as major-domo, there was a good deal of pose, for the bond of blood to all Somali is supreme and sacred, and when at the time of the Spanish flu Abdullahi lay ill, Farah worried over him like a cat with her kitten. The two together made me think of Joseph and Benjamin, the Viceregent of Egypt laying his hand on the shoulder of the little Bedouin and speaking: 'God be gracious to thee, my son.'

Abdullahi had a round, chubby face, an unusual thing in a Somali, and a self-effacing manner, behind which one guessed weighty latent reserves. He was a loyal servant to the house, particularly pleasant to me because he was personally so clean and neat, and because I found in him a rare talent for gratitude. His individuality first manifested itself in an unexpected skill as a chess player. He stood by, quiet as a mouse, while Denys and Berkeley, who both considered themselves superior players, sat by the board. When questioned he told them that he knew the game of chess, and when, experimentally, they took him on as an opponent, he played in unbroken silence and almost invariably won his game. Later on I found him to be a talented arithmetician as well. Denys had left an Oxford book of mathematics in the house. If I read out to Abdullahi one of its problems: 'Divide up a number in four parts, so that the one part plus 4, the second part divided by 4, the third multiplied by 4, and the fourth part minus 4 will produce the same result,' he sank into a kind of dumb ecstasy, and the next day would bring me the solution without being able to explain how he had arrived at it.

When Abdullahi had been at Ngong for a year he confided to me his passionate ambition to go to school. I felt it to be in a way legitimate, but since there was no Mohammedan school in the Highlands, I should have to send him to the Islamic school in Mombasa, and at the time I could ill afford to do so. When I told him: 'I have not got the money, Abdullahi,' he took in the fact resignedly, but from time to time, on an evening when Farah was not in the house, he came up to ask me: 'Have you got more money now, Memsahib?'

Abdullahi's period of service in the house was marked by one dramatic event. I had been ordered by the doctor to take six drops of arsenic in a glass of water with my meals. When one day at lunch I had forgotten to do so and sat reading in the library, I asked Abdullahi to prepare and bring the dose, took the glass from him without looking up from my book, and at the moment when I drank down its contents realized that it must have been filled with pure arsenic. I asked Abdullahi about it, and he told me, stiffening, that it was so. I did not feel ill at the time, only strangely stunned, as if I had received a blow. 'Then I think that I shall die, Abdullahi,' I said, 'and you must send Farah in to me.' Later on, Farah told me that his little brother had come rushing in to his house, had cried out: 'I have killed Memsahib! Go in to her, you! And goodbye to you all, for I am going away and am never coming back,' and with these words had vanished. By the time when Farah came, I myself had really begun to believe that I was going to die. I made him carry me on to my bed, and my agony there grew worse and lasted for more than twelve hours. I had no knowledge of arsenic poisoning and no instructions in my books of how to treat it. But after a while I bethought myself of Alexandre Dumas' novel *La Reine Margot*, which I had got in the house. This book tells of how treacherous enemies of King Charles IX smear the pages of a book on stag-hunting with arsenic, so that the King, continuously wetting his finger to turn them, is slowly poisoned, and it also mentions the remedy by which the physician-in-ordinary tries to save the King's life.

Abdullahi

I had Farah find *Queen Margot* on my bookshelf, managed to look up the cure of milk and white-of-egg used, and started upon it, Farah lifting up my head so that I might swallow the medicine. In the midst of the treatment I remembered having been told that great quantities of arsenic will turn the patient a livid blue. In case it was really so, I reasoned, it was hardly worth struggling for life, so I sent for Kamante and had him stand by the bed, from time to time holding up my mirror to me. About midnight I began to think that I might after all remain alive, and about dawn to wonder about how we were to get Abdullahi back. Only after three days did the Masai scouts set on his track bring him in, the picture of a run-down, stunned scapegoat pardoned back from the desert.

When Abdullahi had been with me for three or four years, an event, small in itself, changed his fate.

In those days it was difficult to get a book to read in Nairobi. My bookseller would tell me that he had just got a beautiful consignment of books out from home, and then place before me a pile of such poor printed matter as seemed a shame to have good, seaworthy ships bring out. All the same it has twice there happened to me to pick up a book by an entirely unknown author, and the day after to write home telling my people to note down the author's name. The first of the two was Aldous Huxley's *Crome Yellow*, the second Ernest Hemingway's *The Sun Also Rises*. Now Huxley's *Little Mexican* was published. Among the tales of this book is the story 'Young Archimedes', telling of a little boy with a genius for mathematics, by a vain and silly adoptive mother prevented from studying it and driven into such despair that in the end he throws himself from a balcony and dies. The night after I had read it I woke up almost as terrified as when I had left the baby bushbuck Lulu to her fate in the hands of Kikuyu totos. Within the following week I managed to scrape money together, and had Abdullahi sent off to the high school of Mombasa. He was very happy there, and his teachers wrote me that he was progressing steadily and beautifully.

Abdullahi travelled up from Mombasa a couple of times to visit us on the farm. He wore the clothes in which he had left us, and which by now had become somewhat scanty in length and short at the sleeves; he was evidently saving up his modest pocket-money for more books. These holiday visits after a year were rendered difficult by the fact that Farah had married, so that it had become illegal for Abdullahi to stay beneath his roof. In Somaliland, as in Jewry, when a man dies his younger brother marries his widow in order to raise up his seed, and I gathered that the close connection between a youthful brother and sister-in-law is considered dangerous as a possible incentive to fratricide. In a nation of such strict loyalty in family affairs the rule betrays a strange belief in the fatality of passion. I was sorry about the taboo, for I felt that Abdullahi and Fathima, of the same age and both clear-eyed and easy-going, would have got on very well together *en tout bien tout honneur*.

When I left the country, Abdullahi did not care to stay there any longer either, but went back to Somaliland. From there he wrote to me, and I wrote back. He had not got Kamante's gift of letter-writing; his epistles to Denmark, beyond the fact that he was alive, gave little but a firm determination to hold on to me.

In the summer of 1936 I told him: 'I am now writing a book about the farm. You are in it, and Farah, and Pooran Singh, and Bwana Finch-Hatton, and the dogs and Rouge. If I have good luck with this book, maybe I shall come back to Africa. So now you must pray to God for me.' Abdullahi wrote back: 'You need not tell me to pray to God for you, for that I do every day. But since in your letter you tell me that you are now writing a book about the farm, and that I am in it, and Farah and Pooran Singh, and Bwana Finch-Hatton, and the dogs, and Rouge, and that if you have good luck with this book maybe you will come back to Africa, I have set three very holy men on to pray for you every day. Then when these prayers are helpful to you, will you give me a typewriter?' What the three holy men were to get out of the arrangement I knew not, but felt that this must remain a matter between them and Abdullahi. My book *Out of Africa* was published in 1937 and had sufficient good luck, I decided, to bring me under an obligation towards Abdullahi, so I ordered a model typewriter for him in London, with his name on it. When the firm informed me that they could not guarantee its delivery, since from the last place to which they could forward it by post it must still travel for nine days on camel-back, I wrote to Abdullahi that he would have to arrange about the camel himself. He must have done so, for three months later I had a very neatly typed letter from him.

In the spring of 1939 I received a travelling grant, and began making up plans for travelling, in the month of Ramadan, with the pilgrims to Mecca, together with Farah and Farah's mother. On the farm Farah and I had many times discussed how, when we grew rich, we would go on such a pilgrimage, and had pictured to ourselves how we were to purchase excellent Arab horses, to obtain as escort from Ibn Saud and to journey happily through fair Arabia. Now I got as far as establishing contact with the Arabian Embassy in London.

Then with the Second World War, and with the German occupation of Denmark in April 1940, I was quite suddenly cut off from both Arabia and Africa, as from humanity altogether.

The next two or three years stand out by nothing but their nothingness; they look, today, like the Coalsack in the firmament of time. The King in his proclamation had enjoined us to maintain an attitude of calm and dignity, a prize was set on lying dead, a penalty on being alive.

All the same, impressions and reminiscences would drift into the Coalsack. A cultural gospel forced upon one, the status and name of protectorate imposed upon one's country. A new recognition of the importance of ancient traditions, of a three-thousand-year-old truth: 'Honour thy father and thy mother: that thy days may be long upon the land which the Lord thy God giveth thee.' In the Coalsack I unexpectedly encountered an old acquaintance, the *kipanda*, in the shape of that identification-card which each inhabitant of the country had to carry wherever he or she went. Through it I came to know for certain – what till then I had only guessed – that to be thus turned perfectly flat, two-dimensional, is extremely boring and may well make you feel the risk of being bored to death.

For my own part, in order to save my reason, I had recourse to the remedy which, for that same purpose, I had used in Africa in times of drought: I wrote a novel. I advised my friends to do the same, for it took one's mind off German soldiers drilling in gas-masks round one's house and setting up their barracks on one's land. When I started on the first page of the book, I had no idea whatever what was going to happen in it, it ran on upon its own and – as was probably inevitable under the circumstances – developed into a tale of darkness. But when in the summer of 1943 the German persecution of Danish Jews set in, and most homes along the coast of the Sound were housing Jewish fugitives of Copenhagen waiting to be got across to Sweden, I slackened in my work; it began to look crude and vulgar to me to compete with the surrounding world in creating horrors. Also, as in the following months the Danish resistance movement fetched headway, we all began to rise from our sham graves, drawing the air more freely and ceasing to gasp for breath. My lifesaving book on its own put on a happy ending and – since I looked upon it as a highly illegitimate child – it was published under the pseudonym of Pierre Andrézel.

I gave much thought, all during those dark years, to my African servants. I held on to them to have them prove to me that they were still there. They would be moving about and talking; I tried to follow their movements and to hear what they were talking about. On their new Dagoretti farms, would they be discussing old days and asking one another, gravely, in the manner of the priest in church: 'Do you believe in the communion of the past? Do you believe in life gone by?'

It was then that my old companions began to put in an appearance in my dreams at night, and by such behaviour managed to deeply upset and trouble me. For till then no living people had ever found their way into those dreams. They came in disguise, it is true, and as in a mirror darkly, so that I would at times meet Kamante in the shape of a dwarf-elephant or a bat, Farah as a watchful leopard snarling lowly round the house, and

Sirunga as a small jackal, yapping – such as the Natives tell you that jackals will do in times of disaster – with one forepaw behind his ear. But the disguise did not deceive me, I recognized each of them each time, and in the mornings I knew that we had been together, for a short meeting on a forest path or for a journey. So I could no longer feel sure that they did still actually exist, or indeed that they had ever actually existed, outside of my dreams.

People work much in order to secure the future; I gave my mind much work and trouble, trying to secure the past.

And then, in the end, the Liberation came.

As now the dark, slimy waters began to decrease, Noah from his Ararat gazed round towards the four corners of the earth for a sprig of green.

The first live leaf was brought me all across the Atlantic. I had finished my *Winter's Tales* in 1942, when it had been out of the question to get the manuscript off to England or America from Denmark. By rare good luck, and with the aid of mighty friends, I managed to get it with me to Stockholm and to make the British Embassy there forward it by their daily plane. I wrote to my publishers in London and New York: 'I can sign no contract and I can read no proofs. I leave the fate of my book in your hands.' For three years I lived in the ignorance of that irresponsible person who shot an arrow into the air and left it to fall to earth he knew not where. Now, in the fair month of May 1945, by one of the very first overseas mails, I received my book in the Armed Services Edition and shortly after, through the Red Cross, a number of moving and cheering letters from American officers and soldiers who had happened to read *Winter's Tales* just before or after some attack in Italy or the Philippines. I gave one of my two copies to the King, who was pleased to know that from his dumb country one voice at least had been heard in far places.

I sent a dove off south: I wrote to Messrs. Hunter and Company for information about my servants. They wrote back to inform me that Farah had died, and that without him they were unable to get on to any of the others.

The news of Farah's death to me was hard to take into my mind and very hard to keep there. How could it be that he had gone away? He had always been the first to answer a call. Then after a while I recognized the situation: more than once before now I had sent him ahead to some unknown place, to pitch camp for me there.

As to the others of my staff, now that I should no longer have Farah to look them up, it would, I reflected, be for them to find me. At the same time I could not be sure whether they would indeed set to do so or not. For they might not have grasped the fact that my long silence had been involuntary, but might quite well have taken it as a sign of my displeasure with them. 'I shall have to sit still and wait for them,' I thought, 'as I waited at sunset for the bushbuck to step out into the glades of my grounds.'

A few months later I had a letter from Government House in Nairobi, with the very coat of arms of Great Britain on it. Sir Philip Mitchell, the then Governor, told me that he was writing upon the repeated request of his boy Ali Hassan. Ali, he said, was the best servant he had ever had, but from the beginning he had made it clear to his master that he looked upon himself as still being in my service, and that if ever I came back to Africa he would feel free to leave Government House without notice.

Here Ali at least had come forth, then, in great state, accompanied by the Lion and the Unicorn. He would order the others back as well, and we would all be gathered together once more. I started on a correspondence with Ali. From the style of his letters I gathered that for these years he had – in contrast to earlier days – been living in a household with no financial worries. But he was faithful to the past, naming the horses and the dogs and bringing back things that I myself had forgotten. 'Do you remember,' he wrote, 'how the people give you name and call you: She who first of all see the New Moon?' In his repeated 'things have changed' there was a gentle melancholy, which I recognized from the recollections of other Africans, who will dwell with preference on sad things. There was in his letter the sound of a lonely horn in the woods, a long way off.

He generously forgave me my own *faux pas*. 'Do you remember, Memsahib,' he wrote, 'the time when you dismissed us all because of this bitch?' I remembered it very well. I had brought out a Scotch deerhound bitch for my dog Pania, travelling, for her sake, in the midst of winter from Antwerp on a cargo boat. The first time she was in heat I had had to go into Nairobi, so had instructed all my servants, whatever they did, not to let her out of her hut. I came back tired and went to bed, and I there received a note from my manager regretting the fact that Heather had been let out, and that now most likely his Airedale terrier King would be the sire of her puppies. I at once flew into such anger that I walked straight from my bed on to the pergola, in which my entire household, sitting peacefully together, were having a sunset chat. But when I opened my mouth to tell them what I thought of them, I had no voice, I had to go back into the house to find it, and even to repeat the manoeuvre. As soon as I could speak, I dismissed all my people at one time, for I felt that I could not bear to see any of their faces again. None of them went, or –

I believe – for a moment thought of going, and no catastrophe followed. Whatever had happened in my absence, Heather's puppies turned out pure-bred, and very lovely.

Juma, Ali wrote, was now a very old man, with grandchildren and great-grandchildren. He lived upon the plot in the Masai Reserve that I had obtained for him. His son Tumbo was a lorry-driver in Nairobi.

Saufe, Farah's son, was doing well as a horse-trader. He was soon going to marry, and as he was only seventeen years old by then, the fact was a sign of his prosperity.

The news of Kamante, Ali wrote, was good, then bad, then a little better, then again somewhat sad. He had been clever all these years, 'same as he been in the house', and on his land near Dagoretti he had a fine herd of cattle, sheep and goats. But he had gone blind. This, according to a clever doctor of Nairobi, might be bettered by an operation. But an operation would cost much money.

I found, as I laid down Ali's letter, that I was not surprised to learn that Kamante had gone blind. His watchful eyes, so keenly observant that he had at times made me think of that 'loyal servant' of Grimm's fairy-tale who had to wear a cloth round his eyes in order not to destroy what he gazed at, at the same time in an eerie way had in them the introspective-ness which you will find in the eyes of a blind man. I remembered, from our very first meeting, when I had knocked against the dying child on the plain, those glassy, patient eyes turned towards me, and I felt that I must have them light up once more, even although I myself was never again to meet their unbiased, stock-taking glance.

I have had news from my old servants later on, through other people, and at last from themselves.

Sir Philip Mitchell in the beginning of the fifties looked me up in Denmark. 'I dare not come home from Europe to Ali,' he said, 'without having seen you.' While we dined together we had a sad little talk about the changes in the world. I realized to what extent my own book about Africa had become history, a document of the past. It was, I thought, as I listened to Sir Philip describing present-day conditions in Kenya, as much out of date as a papyrus from a pyramid.

My old friend Negley Farson in his book of 1950, *Last Chance in Africa*, speaks of Ali as Sir Philip's major-domo and reports how, at his and Sir Philip's fishing camp on the Thika, Ali repeats his statement that he is Memsahib Blixen's boy. 'I rose,' Mr Farson tells, 'high in Ali's esteem when I told him that I had lunched in Denmark with his Memsahib. After that I could do no wrong.'

The Danish author John Buchholzer in 1955 travelled in Somaliland to collect Somali folklore and poetry, and published a book, *Africa's Horn*, on his journey. One chapter of the book turns upon the new national and religious movement against the Europeans and relates how, in the market-place of the small town of Hargeisa, the author is being stoned by an angry crowd and is saved from their hands through the intervention of a passing young Somali official. The young man next day looks him up in his quarters and asks him if really, as has been said, he is a Dane. He presents himself as Abdullahi Ahamed, for many years in the past the servant of a Danish lady known to all tribes of Somali. Abdullahi here, in the book, goes through the long list of my benefactions towards him, including the typewriter.

It was pleasant to come across this passage of the book. It was more pleasant still to receive a letter from Abdullahi himself, inspired by his meeting with Mr Buchholzer. For ten years, Abdullahi states, he has been deeply grieving not to hear from me; it now gives him much satisfaction that I have sent out such a nice gentleman to re-establish contact between us. He has actually married Farah's young widow and has a small son by her. The whole family, however, he informs me, is at the moment sunk in deep sadness over the death of Fathima's mother, the child's grand-mother – so that old women appear to play as great a part in the life of the tribes as in my day. In his letter to me, too, Abdullahi remembers the typewriter. It gave him, he says, a decisive advantage over competitors in the career, and he owes to it that he has now for three years been holding the office of judge in Hargeisa.

'I am,' he concludes his letter, 'carrying my official duties successfully, with dignity and popularity.'

There lives in Copenhagen a talented young journalist, Mr Helge Christensen, who from boyhood has been keen on ornithology and many years ago got my mother's permission to study bird life in the woods of Rungstedlund. Mr Christensen in an international competition won a flying trip to Nairobi and came to Rungstedlund to ask me whether I wanted him to take out greetings to friends of mine in Kenya. I asked him, if possible, to look up Juma and Kamante. But Ali Hassan being away at the time, I felt that it might be a difficult task to pick out by their names only two Kikuyu among two millions. Mr Christensen, though, held on to his promise and was successful.

Juma he tracked down by going out to the residential district of Karen, named after me, and making inquiries at its central club-house, formerly my own house. He was here told that an old man by the name of Juma from time to time would come up and ask permission to walk in the grounds, 'to think, there, of the time that had once been', for an afternoon would walk on the paths beneath the tall trees and then again would disappear. A kitchen toto from the club believed that he knew from where the old man came, and was taken into the car to point out the rough grass-track winding into the Masai Reserve – a long way, the traveller thought, for an old man to walk in order to meditate on the past. Juma's manyatta here, below the blue hills of Ngong, surely is one of the loveliest spots in the world. It had, Mr Christensen told me, grown into a big place and was swarming with young people and children, who thronged round the car. Juma himself was called forth from his hut, a patriarch, full of days, somewhat long in the teeth, a little vague about the present but brightening up as he got on to days gone by, and in the end explaining to his wives and his offspring that his Memsahib had sent out this good Bwana with gifts, thanksgivings for his excellent service in her house. Two eagles, Mr Christensen told me, circling high above the heads of host and visitor, were pointed out as old friends of the Memsahib's, eager to have news of her. Juma once had heard them cry, 'God bless her.' The scream of an eagle, as I myself heard it on a day when I was flying with Denys Finch-Hatton, is like anything but a blessing.

Kamante was found further away from Nairobi, in the midst of the maze of shambas with hemp, corn and sweet potatoes, and of grass-land. I was told that he received his visitor as if he had been expecting him this very afternoon, which may well have been the case, for Kamante was resourceful. Kamante had never shown any faith whatever in my intelligence, yet he now enlarged upon my wisdom and competence, pointing out to my countryman the wide area of land which, against all resistance and intrigue, I had forced the Government of Kenya to yield up to him. Like Abdullahi and Juma he took it that his guest had been sent out as a personal ambassador of mine to get his news and inquire into his wants. He was anxious to send back by him such news and information as I should be interested in, weighing his words and from time to time making a pause to collect his thoughts. The operation on his eyes had been successful, inasmuch as he could now see his cows. He could not count them, he said, which was a sad thing, but when in the evening they had been brought back into their boma he could make them out dimly, like a multitude of sweet potatoes within a pot of furiously boiling water, thronging and rolling about and jumping upon one another, which was pleasant.

Mr Christensen has published a small book, *Juma and Kamante*, on his visit to my two old servants. It contains two woodcut portraits of the title-characters; the one of Juma is very good.

Quite recently, and quite by chance, I have in another Danish paper come upon a later interview with Kamante, whom the journalist has succeeded in tracing and running to earth. Kamante is well, and would like to come to Denmark to take service with me once more, at the same time he fears that he is too old, and that it might be better to send me one of his sons. Somewhat uneasy at giving the information – as I am uneasy at passing it on here – Kamante tells the Danish journalist that he has been a year in prison for taking the Mau-Mau oath. I did not know of the circumstance; it has given me matter for thought. Has the deep, unconquerable sceptic here at last met with something in which it was possible to him to have faith? Has the eternal hermit, the 'rogue' head of game, by his own choice totally isolated from the herd, here at last through a dark inhuman formula experienced some kind of human fellowship? In order to make up for the awkwardness of the situation, Kamante brings out from his pocket a letter from me to him and shows it to my countryman. 'Look,' he says, 'Msabu writes to me: "My good and faithful servant Kamante."' As again he folds up the letter and sticks it into his pocket, he adds: 'And so I am.'

I have had news of another former resident of the farm, the blind Dane, Old Knudsen, who for some time lived in a small house on it, all salted and embittered through the experiences of a tragic life, but with great flaming inner visions to make up for his loss of sight, a grey and bent indomitable optimist.

Last March I had a letter from an American lady of the University of Maryland. A fortnight before, she had been dining with a Danish economist just back from a recent mission to East Africa; they had been talking about me and my book *Out of Africa*, and he had told her that at the Danish Consulate to Tanganyika he had been given information which he wanted to bring to my attention. When a few days later he had died in his hotel in Washington, Mrs Stevenson passed on this information to me. 'What he had learned from the Danish Consul,' she wrote, 'and what I feel that he would want you to know, was that Old Knudsen's scheme for extracting phosphate from the bottom of Lake Naivasha was *not* wild. Some discovery has been made which verifies his theory. I did not get the details, but I feel that you should know.'

Thus, with deep satisfaction, I now see before me Old Knudsen righted, for a while laying down his harp in order to grip old fishermen's and mariners' tools, laughing out in triumph over Old Knudsen's enemies.

I hear, these days, with intervals of one month, or half a year, from my old servants in Africa.

So there they are, out from their coverts in the woods, in the rays of sunset, treading cautiously still, but looking round them more confidently than when they first came into sight, lifting and turning their heads. It is content to watch you so, friends and comrades, I wish you may wander and gaze there, so high up in the air, in the strange freedom of your hearts, for a long time still. You have kept me company through many years; I shall not again frivolously doubt your actuality, I shall, from now, leave to you the rich world of reality. And you may hand me over to those dreams of mine which will take charge of me.

Juma has died. But I have recent news of Ali and Kamante.

Ali writes good English now. He has seen my photograph in the paper. 'Really and truthfully it makes my heart very much pleased to see your photo. Really and truthfully it fills all my heart with joy when I hear your name spoken. Or when I speak your name.'

As I admire his handwriting and grammar, I sometimes seem to see Berkeley's little wry smile as in his mind he followed a line of wild duck on the glass-clear sky. And I wonder whether one more of them, fascinated by the decoys below, will here be slowing its flight to drop, in the end, like an arrow-head let off backwards by some heavenly archer, into the water of the pond, in order to become respectable.

But Kamante, all through a triple layer of idiom, in a many-times-folded note, manages to preserve his originality. His last letter, of a month ago, ends up:

'I certainly convinced when I pray for you to almighty God that this prayer he will bestow without fault. So I pray that God will be kind to you now and then.'